Cheevey

GERALD DIPEGO

SCEPTRE

British Library Cataloguing in Publication Data

DiPego, Gerald
   Cheevey
   1.American fiction – 20th century
   I.Title
   813.5'4[F]

ISBN 0 340 66632 3

Typeset by Palimpsest Book Production Limited,
Polmont, Stirlingshire
Printed and bound in Great Britain by
Cox and Wyman Ltd, Reading, Berkshire

Hodder and Stoughton
A division of Hodder Headline PLC
338 Euston Road
London NW1 3BH

Gerald DiPego

Gerald DiPego is a successful screen writer whose credits include *Sharkey's Machine* and *Phenomenon*, starring John Travolta. He was born on Chicago's south side and grew up working in the family grocery store, later attending Northern Illinois University and the University of Missouri, where he majored in journalism. He worked as a reporter and a teacher before turning to writing and now lives in Los Angeles.

SCEPTRE

For Chris,
And to my sons, Justin and Zack,
And to the boy who was me.

Prologue

Yesterday, at about noon, a heavy mirror fell off the wall and smashed on the floor. There was no earthquake, not even a truck going by. The nail and the hook are still on the wall. I found that a metal screw in the back of the mirror had given way. For twelve years that screw had held the wire that supported the mirror. Then, on a particular second of a particular day, it let go. I've been thinking about all those years when that screw was on its way to letting go, as if, buried inside of it, was some invisible clock.

I think these clocks are hiding inside all the objects around us, all the things we count on to stay in place.

I know there was such a clock inside the workings of my family. I may have noticed my family straining and loosening over time, but as I ran through my days and slept through my nights, I expected that we would all stay in place – my mother and my father and Phil and Mari and Bob and Ballyhoo and me, Cheevey.

We were all part of a machine, counterweights in a clock, but I never heard it ticking, and there was no earthquake, not even a truck going by the day the supports gave way, and we fell. It was a falling that took place over a month of a particular summer that I will never think of as a milestone in my life, but more of an explosion.

The broken mirror is a memory. I picked up the large

pieces, carefully, and the smaller ones I swept away. Only the hook on the wall is still there to remind me of the moment, the screw, the invisible clocks. But the fall and crash of the Cheever family unleashed more than glass and dust. There were truths in the rubble, some shameful and some exalting, and all of them still too sharp and clear to be called memory and to be removed from sight. We are the pieces, and we cannot be swept away.

∫

William Cheever 1948

William Cheever stands on State Street in Chicago on a bone cold night in February of 1948, and, for the first time in his life, he worships. He is outside a department store, looking in the large window, standing in the front rank of a scarved and coated crowd of silent watchers which includes his mother and his father. William is thirteen years old and staring at the phenomenon called television. He has never seen it before.

Here is an electronic moving picture inside a box, a box that can be moved into a home. One can own this moving, changing, speaking, living picture. One can carry it home and have it, plug it in and snap it on. Anytime.

William stares at the three small screens, his mouth slightly open, his eyes fixed, and in this moment his life changes profoundly and forever. While the others in the blue-grey crowd on this winter night see progress and entertainment, William discovers his religion. While the others watch a puppet show, a silent singer and *Drums Along the Mohawk*, William watches not what is on the screen, but the screens themselves, the changing electronic dots, the living pictures. As the others bunch their hands deep in their coat pockets and hunch their shoulders to keep the cold from their necks and smile and shake their heads with amusement and appreciation and even wonder, William feels worship as keen as a sword.

The boy smiles also, but it is the small, deep smile of the convert at the moment of conversion, a smile that nearly weeps. Here is a thin, serious, neglected boy whom no one asks to know. In school his teachers ask him questions of fact, and in stores clerks ask what he wants to buy. The barber asks him how to cut his hair. His mother asks him what he would like to eat, and his father asks him if he has enough money in his pocket. His friend asks him if he will play touch football again next Saturday, but no one in the world asks to know him or wonders what he feels.

William is not conscious of this neglect or its effect on him. It does not cause him pain. It causes him nothing. That is, it causes a nothingness to grow inside of him, a kind of well in his soul. It is abstract and fundamental loneliness, and he cannot name it. He does not know why he is a sad and quiet boy. He does not know why others seem animated and happy and passionate. He cannot define his basic feeling as emptiness, but yet on this ice-sharp night outside the glass of the store window, as he smiles a small, deep smile, as his lips remain parted and his eyes fixed, he begins to feel something enter him, as though the moving electronic dots are pouring into the well in his soul, and these living bits of picture are filling that dark and tender untouched void for the first time in all his thirteen years.

$\int$

Claude Cheever 1992

Maybe this is all a tangent. The real story, the important one, might be taking place now in the window of my father's television store. Almost every day a ragged man with a big putty face settles down for a few hours on the sidewalk in front of Westland Video. He comes with dirty blankets and with paper bags wrinkled from a hundred openings and closings. His once-blue trousers and three sweaters and shoes and hands and moony face have all been dyed to match by the grit of the streets. A police officer told me that the man's name is Jack, and since then I've called him Jack-o-lantern because of his big, nearly toothless mouth and his round eyes.

He sits on the sidewalk and watches his reflection in the window glass, studies it, really, and sometimes speaks to it. I'm assuming it's his reflection. To Jack-o-lantern it's another being. I've often tried to overhear him, but when I come near, even when I'm washing the window and acting very absorbed in the job, Jack becomes very guarded and lowers his voice even more, and sometimes they wink at each other, Jack and the man in the glass, as if to say, 'We can't talk now, but ... more later.'

Maybe something very important is going on between Jack-o-lantern and the glass man. Maybe the secrets of the universe are being traded there while the cars go by and customers come in and out and I stand here washing the window. Maybe my whole life adds up to less than one of Jack's whispered words or one gesture from the big putty face of the man in the glass. My mind is open to that.

I'm turning twenty in two weeks. It's a difficult maneuver. It has a leap in it, a jump across a chasm. It makes my heart-rate increase when I think about it. It's not that if I fall, I'll remain nineteen forever. It's just that so much more is expected of a twenty year old. People will ask about my job and my salary. They will inquire about my plans.

I attend Santa Monica college, and my plans are vague. I don't spend time planning. That would make me very nervous. It would be like trying to dream. So I'm counting on someday looking around and finding myself inside a plan. This will happen to me while I'm running or shooting pool or washing this store window.

Westland Video is on Wilshire Boulevard in Santa Monica, California, only twelve blocks and then a cliff and then a highway from the Pacific Ocean, but the weather is hot and stubborn this summer and a lot more humid than it's supposed to be. I'm tempted to ask Jack and the glass man why that is, but instead I just dip the long-handled mop once more into the soapy water and smear another section of glass.

I wash this window every Saturday, and I'm always surprised at how dirty it is. All week I think I'm looking through clear glass, but I'm really looking through dirt, and the dirtier it gets, the more my eyes adjust, and it's only in the weekly cleaning of it, only in the slow, downward stroke of the squeegee, that I see how nearly blind I was. Soon I'm not looking at the newly cleaned glass at all, but through it into the store.

For a moment it feels as though I have an opportunity for a fresh, clear look into the store and into the man standing in front of a row of seven television sets, every screen showing the same baseball game. The man is William Cheever, my father, and as my squeegee wipes away the dirt, I feel myself growing still and staring hard as he is revealed so clearly, the tall frame, rumpled white shirt, thinning but still-brown hair and the profile, cocked a bit, the face etching gradually around the eyes as a slight smile establishes itself and holds, and I look at the screen wondering what he could be smiling at, since there is no sound on the sets, and the picture shows only a batter wiping his hands – and then I realize for the five thousandth time that he's not smiling at anything in particular. He is just happy to be looking at television, peacefully happy. My father likes me, I suppose, but I can't remember ever being able to cause that particular peaceful grin to appear. I remember trying. I still try. His smiles for me are quick, nervous smiles-in-passing. I try not to take offense at this. He never really focuses on anyone for any length of time, but I admit to a small sting somewhere in my chest every time his eyes slide off me without sticking.

More than the rest of the world, more than any customer or creditor, shouldn't I be granted a special audience? I'm one of his children. Shouldn't his eyes hook me like an arm and pull me close inside some privileged circle where he grins at me in deep appreciation of my existence – the way he is grinning now at the seven screens and the seven pitchers who are winding up and then glaring a warning at the seven first-base runners?

I realize I don't understand my father any better today than I did before. My stare is just bounching off, not penetrating, in spite of the clean glass.

'Cheevey!'

Before I check the glass for the reflection, I know what I'm going to see. I can hear Danny Benko's Volkswagen hammering and whining on the boulevard, and I know he's standing up through the sun roof, his hat brim back, eyes squinting at me in his fleshy face. Maybe Chin is with him, slouching on the passenger side.

I check the glass, and the scene is very close. Chin is slouched in back and Ben Carpenter is hulking in the passenger seat and Benko is squinting and shouting over his engine: 'Wanna meet us at Johnny Rockets?'

'Which one?' I don't know why I'm asking that question, because I can't meet them. When I finish the windows, I need to go to my sister's and babysit. I suppose I'm only curious, and if later I want to picture them in the restaurant without me, I'll know which one.

'The one on the promenade,' Benko says.

'No, I can't. I'm babysitting for Mari.'

Benko keeps squinting at me and then he says, 'Then why'd you ask which Johnny Rockets?' That's why I like Danny Benko. Except for Mari and Ballyhoo, he's my closest friend.

I jog from the store to Mari's home in less than fifteen minutes. She lives in a second-floor apartment with a steep outside staircase, and I take these steps two at a time. My run from the store to the park and through the park to Pico Boulevard and down Pico to Third Street started two years ago when Mari moved in. Two years ago I had to stop running and walk, panting, up this same staircase. These stairs measure my strength and endurance and show me the changes, presenting a small victory. I don't have any particular goal in mind. I don't run races. I don't care to compete, except with these stairs.

The cement and steel staircase vibrates with my steps and

shakes the building and brings Ballyhoo to the apartment's screen door before I reach it. Seeing someone through a screen softens and blurs them, like a grainy photograph, and Ballyhoo looks even more beautiful than usual, looking out at me. What I witness on his face is expectation evolving into joy. He knew his uncle was coming, and here I am. He becomes very excited when he knows I'm coming, though not in a wild way. Mari talks about how *pleased* he is when he knows I'm going to babysit or take him somewhere. I know what she means. He's a pretty calm boy for three and a half, and the look spreading on his face right now is of deep pleasure. He's the deepest person I know.

I'm wearing a big grin, too, watching him try to open the screen door to greet me. He can't quite reach the lock so he quits and just stares, and both of us are a little embarrassed by just how glad we are to see each other.

'Ballyhoo!'

He laughs, just three climbing notes on a flute, and then Mari is appearing out of the grey gloom beyond the screen and unlocking the door. I enter and pick up the boy and feel his little arms encircle my neck, and he tightens his grip for a second, giving me a miniature hug.

'Sorry, I'm all sweaty, guy.'

'What's new?' Mari says, meaning I'm *always* arriving sweaty. 'Hurry and shower, will you? We've gotta go.' I keep T-shirts and underwear at Mari's because I always shower after a run.

'Hi, Cheevey.' Mari's girlfriend, Dash, says this into a magazine, then takes a beat and looks up and smiles at me. I can't decide if she's affected or actually theatrical. She's a person of big gestures, long pauses, lingering stares, seductive smiles. I'm not sure if these are practiced or natural. For instance, now she's yawning and stretching there on the couch, her arms straight out, even her legs straightening and coming off the floor, eyes closed, mouth gaping. I'm setting Ballyhoo down on his feet and glancing at her and trying not to. She's wearing a thin, short, little-girl kind of dress, showing a lot of tanned thigh and her breasts push against the fabric as she stretches, and I catch all this in an uncomfortable sweep of my eyes.

I can be comfortable around very pretty girls, but never with Dash. I've known her for three years, but she always seems to draw my eyes to her, even when I know I'm an idiot to stare because it's going to make me feel like a voyeur and because I might get caught, but I always chance it. Her yawn ends in a groan that ends in a sentence.

'It's sooo hot. God, it makes me hotter looking at you.'

I stand there trying for some little bit of smoothness, but the sweat is dripping off my nose and burning my eyes. 'I better shower,' I mumble, and I walk away with Ballyhoo who is holding on to three of my fingers.

Before I go into the bathroom, I squat eye-level with the boy and dip into the well of his stare. We smile slightly, but the greeting is now over and this is business.

'Video game?'

He shakes his head.

'The fort?'

He pauses, considering.

'Walk to frozen yogurt?'

His bottomless eyes slowly fill with a vision. 'With the wagon,' he says.

I nod agreement and then make a fist and give him a mock punch in the belly. He gives me a mock punch on the chin. It's our way of kissing, I suppose.

Mari's son is my only nephew. I have no niece. Mari is twenty-six. Our brother Phil is thirty, but is unmarried with no children. My mother named us all with French or French-sounding names. On my brother's birth certificate, he is named Phillipe, though no one dares call him that, not even my mother. 'Mari' was an inspiration, French-like, with that jaunty dot floating over the name, but it's just 'Marie' after all, when you say it. My mother calls me Claude, and pronounces it in the French way, though she is only one-eighth French from several generations ago. My friends have always called me Cheevey, being more comfortable with my last name, and soon even the family picked it up, at least Phil and Mari did. They were rebelling against my mother, I think. Dad calls me Claudy.

My father's name is William, so Mari wanted to name her son William. Her husband Bob wanted to call him Hugh, after his own father, so they settled on William Hugh Horton or Billy Hugh – and that's where Ballyhoo comes from. Only Mari and I use 'Ballyhoo' and Ballyhoo himself. His father, Bob, hates to hear it and blames me for its invention and doesn't like me very much anyway.

While I'm in the shower, somebody comes into the bathroom all in a rush. Mari would only do this in an emergency, so as I'm trying to glance through the fogged glass of the shower, thinking there's something wrong, I hear Dash say, 'I'm not looking, Cheevey, I swear to God,' and I quickly turn back again, away from the foggy blur of her as I hear, over the shower, 'I just *have* to pee, but I swear my eyes are closed.'

So my bare ass is pointing at this very pretty friend of my sister's, and I'm tempted to crane around and glance, but I don't, because I'm feeling embarrassed, and I don't especially want to see her sitting on a toilet anyway, and then the toilet is flushing and the shower is going cold, making me gasp, and I hear her say, 'Byeee,' and the door is closed again. Through the door I can hear Mari's voice, scaled upward in surprise and disapproval. 'Da-ash?! Did you go *in* there?'

I'm walking to the frozen yogurt store, pulling Ballyhoo in a high-sided, four-wheel wagon. He is standing up, holding on to the wooden slats, staring ahead, and his face is serious as he absorbs the city and alters it, shaping some fantasy. I know he's fantasizing because I can hear him talking in a low voice now and then, giving commands, I think. When I glance back, he seems to be some tiny Roman general or emperor, standing in his chariot, and I am four white horses.

'Make the way,' Ballyhoo is saying in a low voice.

'Make the way.' He is only mildly embarrassed because I'm watching and listening. This does not bring him out of his fantasy. 'Make the way for Jaka.' I don't want to break in and ask who Jaka is. For all I know this is *not* a fantasy. Maybe children under four are constantly stepping in and out of a parallel universe. After four we begin to forget how it's done.

'Make the way,' I say aloud. 'For Jaka.' Ballyhoo smiles just a little without losing his commanding manner, and we both continue down Pico Boulevard this way, the emperor and his guard. I appreciate his sharing of the fantasy. Walking down Pico alone, I'd never say a word.

Ballyhoo has brown-blond curls and fine little arms and hands. I've already mentioned the depth of his brown eyes, but his mouth is the most unique part of him, slanting just a bit to give him a slightly uneven grin that looks knowing, worldly, wry. He calls me 'Cheeva.' I know I'd charge a locomotive for him and knock it off the tracks if he was in danger, even though I'm not a fighter.

Before we reach the yogurt store, I'm conscious of a car rolling along beside us on the boulevard. I look over and see Bob, Ballyhoo's father, driving his Honda at about three miles an hour, staring at us. He looks like he's trying to figure us out, and his look is dark. I seldom see Bob looking happy, but maybe he's happier when I'm not around. I hope so for Mari's sake and for Ballyhoo. Bob is also blond, good-looking if he would ever smile. He's nearly as tall as I am and wider. He runs, too, but on a track. He's one year younger than Mari, and he finished law school two years ago, but he failed the bar exam. That's the one thing I like about Bob.

Bob hits the horn, and I stop, and now Ballyhoo looks over. Bob flicks his eyebrows at his son and sort of smiles, but his darkness has returned by the time he turns back to me.

'Where are you *going*?!'

'Get some yogurt.'

'Now?! Where's Mari?'

'She . . .'

We're interrupted by car horns because Bob is blocking a lane. He turns around and glares death at the impatient drivers, but I don't think Bob is a fighter, either. He throws them the finger and then drives ahead and parks at a red curb, and I move on, pulling Ballyhoo toward the parked car. Bob gets out and meets us halfway, but he walks directly toward me and starts talking to me when I think he should go to Ballyhoo and give and get a hug hello. He'd be a happier man if he did that. I know Bob is jealous of me and Ballyhoo. He has accused me of spoiling the boy, but he probably knows better. There is no real play in the man. I've never seen him down on the floor with Ballyhoo unless he's got a screwdriver in his hand, and he's trying to fix a broken toy which he is cursing. He never pretends to be anything but Bob, and he never gets goofy. At least he doesn't do these things when I'm around. I'm hoping that in his private moments with his son he's more tender and silly, but I doubt it. Mari says it's because his parents treated him like he was a little adult – and because Bob's under a lot of pressure, working at an insurance job which he hates while taking classes for an MBA while studying again for the bar exam. All his siblings are lawyers, Mari told me, his mother and father, too. Even their neighbors are lawyers, she said, and even the family dog. I try to like Bob. Every time.

'Don't give him yogurt now. It's almost dinnertime. Where is she?'

'I don't know. She and Dash went out.'

'Jesus. Did she say anything about dinner?'

'No . . .'

'Jesus.'

I hadn't thought about dinnertime. Bob is absolutely right about spoiling the boy's appetite – except it's so hot today, *still* hot and humid at five forty-five.

'Well, it's so hot,' I say, 'why don't we all get yogurt and fruit – nuts, too? I mean, that's sort of healthy. So . . .'

'You buying?' Bob says that in a mean way, as if I'm some sort of sponger, which I'm not. I'm still trying hard to like him today, so I let it go.

'Sure. I'll treat. We could all . . .'

'No, I was just . . .' Bob sighs and looks off, his way of almost apologizing.

'Daddy. Can I have a twirl?'

Bob finally focuses on Ballyhoo. 'A what?'

'That's three flavors of yogurt swirled together,' I say before I realize I should just shut up and let him converse with his son.

Bob stares at me as if he's trying to figure it out, to picture the yogurt swirling together, or maybe he's trying to figure *me* out. I give him one of those kind, mild smiles by tightening my lips, and I raise my eyebrows to ask silently about the yogurt again.

'I'll take him home,' Bob says, already moving toward Ballyhoo. 'Why don't you bring the wagon?' He lifts the boy out of the wagon and starts toward his car.

'Da-ad!'

'It's too late for yogurt.'

'*Da-ad*!'

'C'mon, Billy. It's too close to dinnertime.'

Bob is speaking gently enough to his son, but I'm afraid if Ballyhoo goes for one more try, Bob's temper will break out. I've seen him shake the boy; not too hard, but hard enough to break my heart. Ballyhoo just looks at me sadly, over his father's shoulder, about to cry. I watch them nearing the car, and I wish, I even sort of pray, that Bob will hold Ballyhoo closer, tighter, when the weeping begins. Slowly the little face disassembles and the crying starts on the intake, then the first loud wail comes, mourning the end of the yogurt adventure and the end of Jaka, the emperor. Ballyhoo's forehead rests on his father's shoulder as the next, louder wail comes out, almost a scream, and in that moment Bob does cradle the boy against him and pats his back with at least a distracted kind of sympathy, and I'm grateful.

The wagon is too big to fit in the car, so I walk it back and leave it in the garage, then I go up to the apartment to say goodbye to Ballyhoo, but Bob asks me to stay. He says he might go shopping for food. Then he showers and changes clothes while I sit on the floor near Ballyhoo. The boy's face is still tear-streaked and his breath shudders inside his little chest from time to time, but he's already showing me one of his wide, flat storybooks and pointing to pictures. We take turns naming the animals, giving them first and middle names, too. John Francis Tiger. Herman Albert Weasel. 'Herman German Parrot,' Ballyhoo says, and I laugh, and he smiles that wry grin, and the weeping and the yogurt seem forgotten.

Bob shops for food and then arrives home with Mari. Maybe they just converged at the same time outside, or he saw her and picked her up. I don't know. But we hear their voices commingled on the staircase, and Ballyhoo rushes over there to open the screen. It's always kept locked so he doesn't tumble down the steep stairs, so I have to go unlatch it, and I wish I didn't have to. I wish I could stay on the floor seemingly absorbed in the storybook because Bob and Mari are arguing.

'What about a note?!' he's saying. 'Your brother doesn't tell me a goddamn' thing.'

'I forgot to tell him what to tell you.'

There is the sound of apology in Mari's voice. That's what I hate the most. He doesn't have to be so mad over this. Through the screen I see him rake her with his eyes. 'Jesus,' he says, and the word is hot and sharp. She turns away and looks at me and mumbles, 'Hi, Cheeve,' as I unsnap the lock – but Bob just carries on like I'm not there, except he must know this is more painful to her because I *am* there.

'So I'm supposed to just sit around like a jerk and wait?'

'I told you, I forgot. Hi, Bally.'

'Would you not call him that?'

Mari kisses the top of the boy's head, and he speaks to her shoes, saying, 'I wanted a twirl.'

'Yeah, your brother wants to give him ice cream for dinner.'

'Yogurt with fruit and nuts,' I say. I've stopped trying to like Bob today. He throws me his hot, sharp look, but Mari is picking up the boy.

'I'll give you a twirl,' she says, and she dances a few circles in the room, dodging toys.

'You know I've got a class tonight.' Bob storms on into the kitchen. Mari stops dancing and gives me a look over the head of her son. It's kind of a funny-tired look, but there is still that ounce of apology there that I hate.

'Want to stay and eat?' She looks hopeful, even a little needy when she says this, but it's very hard for me to be around them, especially when Bob is pissed, and he usually is.

'Better take off.'

'Wait. Your money.'

'I'll get it next time.'

'No. Wait. Bob. Pay Cheevey, will you?' I watch her dance her son into the kitchen. I wave, and I see one of those fine miniature arms and hands rise up over Mari's shoulder and wave back. I catch a one-eyed look as his mother turns him, and he presses against her. That deep, brown, bottomless look seems to say: 'I know. I understand all that is happening here. My father is selfish and difficult. My mother is intimidated and self-doubting, and you can't help me, Cheevey. I know this.'

Then Mari turns him and backs into the kitchen, pushing through the swinging door and giving me a goodbye smile. She may not be as flashy-looking as Dash. Mari is small and squarish rather than curvy. Her features may not be as fine, but when they gather into a smile, they seem to tap some well inside of her, and a real glow surfaces, of warmth and joy. Dash doesn't have that. Nobody else in my family does, either. It's a fragile thing, though, evaporating even as I see it form, and it's gone before she turns into the kitchen.

Bob passes her, coming out through the swinging door and moving toward me, but calling back into the kitchen: 'Just put the pizza in before you do anything else.' Then he turns to me and says, 'How much?'

'Four, I guess.'

'Well, *is* it four?'

I just stare at him. There's so much I want to say to the man, not just about his attitude, either. I have a lot to say about buying a frozen pizza and heating up your kitchen on a day as warm as this when a large frozen yogurt with real strawberries, bananas and walnuts is a lot more healthful and appropriate, but I just turn and leave and walk down the staircase, leaving him sputtering with those four goddamn' dollars still in his hand.

'What? What? Oh, so now . . . Oh, what, I hurt your feelings? Oh, great. Jesus. Christ. You people. Jesus!'

I hear him slam the inner door, and part of me hopes he caught a finger in it, but that's a pretty evil thought, so I just push it away as my feet hit the sidewalk, and without thinking about it, I'm jogging again.

I take another shower when I get home, feeling my usual percentage of guilt for tapping the water table and wondering if my skin will flake and my hair dry out, but mostly I'm remembering Mari's bathroom, and Dash walking in, and I'm thinking of what I *could've* said, replaying the moment in my mind and extending it. This time, when she says, 'I swear to God I'm not looking,' I say, 'Oh, yes, you are.' She says, 'No, I just have to pee.' I say, 'Mind if I just go on soaping myself? I was getting to the good part.' That evokes one of her loud, brazen laughs and sets the right tone. She says, 'Need any help?' I say, 'Oops. Dropped the soap. Will you get it?' Her laughter is even more throaty and mixed with sounds of delight. She says, 'Careful, Cheevey, I just might,' daring me, and I say, 'It would be awfully tight with two in here,' and I get another deep, delighted laugh, and I hear her lock the bathroom door. Then she's opening the shower door, and I just keep soaping myself, and she approaches my back and touches me, and I turn, and she's giggling until I kiss her smile away and take her breath, and then, as we keep the kiss, never coming apart, I begin to help her take off her clothes, peeling her dress down slowly because it's wet and sticking to her body, and then brushing the wet, thin underwear off her breasts and hips and ass . . .

While I'm imagining this, my penis is thickening and rising slowly like some blind primordial animal following its DNA program. No thought. Pure instinct. I admire that. I don't want to masturbate now, so I just watch it retreat and return to its primordial sleep as the shower beats on it like a hard tropical rain.

*   *   *

My mother makes salads for dinner during the summer. They're big salads, and they taste good, but I usually have to go out for a burger around nine o'clock. I could skip the salads and eat a bigger meal on my own, but then I'd never have a chance to speak with my parents, and they would probably never speak to each other. There is less talking in my house every year, and especially this summer. The silence is expanding, becoming more confident, ranging through the house like some dark animal, but I try to beat it back.

When Mari and my brother Phil lived at home, the silence was cowed in some corner somewhere, kept at bay by Phil ordering us around or by the long talks between Mari and me. We still talk for hours sometimes.

I wasn't so aware of it then, but my parents had already made friends with the silence. After dinner, my father would go into the small den and watch television, and he didn't like being interrupted unless there was a very good reason. He wasn't crabby about it. 'This is my time alone,' he'd say. The television does not beat back the silence. The two exist together and feed off each other. My father still goes into the den after dinner. He doesn't need to explain it any more.

My mother would clean the kitchen with our help – not Phil's help; he ate and ran – but Mari and I didn't mind the drying and cleaning and straightening. I'm still very neat. But once the kitchen was clean, my mother would go into the master bedroom. She has a kind of office in there, a long table with a computer on it and many books and papers. She does accounting at home for our store and a few other stores, though she's not an official CPA, but at night she studies in there. She studies the French language and French cooking and travel books about France. She says she fell in love with France in college and always dreamed of going there. My family has been to French

Canada many times, but France is something my mother is saving for, saving her money and saving her appetite, I think. She doesn't want to spoil her feast by going to France on some brief tour – which is all she could afford. What she wants is, 'A long while in France,' she used to say. 'With no schedule.' Meanwhile, she still goes to French Canada now and then or New Orleans, but it is with one of her 'French groups.' They are Francophile clubs, and her only social life exists within them.

So after dinner, my father goes to the television, and my mother goes, as Mari says, to France – which is what Mari came to call the master bedroom. The house quiets. The television drones, and the computer clacks now and then (she's compiling a French cookbook for one of her clubs), but there is no sound from anything alive. Our family dog died ten years ago. The cat outlived him for only eight months. Even a fly buzzing in the house sounds strange to me now. I expect the silence, which has grown large and powerful, to trap the fly and eat it.

During dinner I attack the silence on three fronts.

'Mom, I've been reading more about the French Foreign Legion.'

'I hope you don't read that instead of your homework.'

No matter how well I do in school, my mother always feels she has to nudge me now and then. Even though it is fairly automatic by now, I still appreciate it.

'Guess where their most famous battle was fought?'

She looks at me now, a cluster of salad on her fork. She resembles Mari, but smaller and more twisted. Her back pain has been getting worse over the years. She sits on and against pillows, and holds her body in what seem to be awkward positions that give her some relief. She is thinking, her small-featured, dark-eyed face tightening a bit around the question.

'Oh, I'd say Morocco, I suppose.'

My mother says she loves French 'history,' but what she really means is she loves the vestiges of it, the cobble stones and cathedrals. She's not very strong on what happened there before Coco Chanel, so this is a very good guess for her.

'No, but very good guess. Perfect guess. It *is* a country that starts with "M", though.'

'Oh, Claude, just tell me.'

'Nope. What's a major country that begins with "M"?'

She keeps staring, her fork still holding the salad. My dad is looking up, vaguely smiling, and the silence is withering in the tension of the moment, knowing that more words are sure to come.

'Minnesota, Montana . . .' My dad begins a list.

'No, Dad, *countries*.' His vague smile widens. The silence trembles.

'Mongolia,' my mother says. She *does* know her Atlas. 'Uhhhhh, Manchuria . . . Oh, Claude.'

'You are almost there, Mom.'

'Marshall Islands?'

'No, Dad, but *great* try! Very good thinking. Obscure. Unique.'

The silence is slinking away. I'm gloating.

'Mexico?'

'Right, Mom. *Brava. Ole.* Little town called Camerone – just a hacienda, really. But it was one of those fight-to-the-last-man things where they got their famous slogan. You know?'

I wait again, baiting the silence, but it has slunk away.

'*Beau Geste*,' my father says, now with an absent chuckle. My mother is eating her salad and shaking her head, drifting already. I can see it, and it makes me desperate.

'"The Legion dies," I say, '"it never surrenders."'

But they're both gone, jumping back inside themselves. It happens that fast. The silence takes tentative steps forward.

'Dad, did you sell the big Zenith? Those people seemed . . .'

He's already shaking his head, his mouth turning down. The slow economy is keeping the store on the red-black border, and this is not a safe subject, but I'm risking it. He'll usually do several minutes on the store if he's pushed.

'Just a little portable. Kitchen counter portable . . . And rented a set with a VCR. Rented.' His head-shaking continues, and he's pushing his plate back, making a disgusted face. I'm losing *him*, too.

As he slides his plate away, it clinks hard against the serving bowl that holds the asparagus. It's a sharp, painful sound that brings everybody's eyes to the point of contact. We all see that the plate has chipped and that the dime-size chip lies now on the tablecloth. There is no apology in his look, instead a dark challenge as his eyes jump to my mother, and I follow the motion. She meets his stab with her own. Crossed swords. It is only a second, and then they each look away, but I am not used to seeing naked blades between them. I can feel my chest constricting. My voice is more urgent.

'Should've seen Ballyhoo today.' I'm forcing a smile into my plate, stabbing the last of the asparagus. 'He was . . .'

'Why do you call him that?' My mother tends to whine each question. 'You know Bob hates it.'

'Anyway, you should've seen him.' I'm chuckling now, but when I look up, I see that neither of my parents is hooked by this. Even their grandson can't keep them outside. They're moving in and closing doors behind them. Only the silence is answering my chuckle now – its turn to gloat. My words are rushed.

'He was standing up in his wagon as I pulled him down the street, and as he rolled along . . . Dad, I'm telling you.'

'What?' My father had pushed back from the table, and he is rising now.

'I have *café au lait*,' my mother says automatically as she eats.

'I'll get it later,' my father says automatically as he moves toward the den.

'He was acting like a little king in the wagon, Mom.'

'Who?'

'Ballyhoo!'

'Why do you antagonize Bob that way? Then he crabs at Mari.'

'He crabs at Mari anyway.'

Now she is rising, twisting as she rises, keeping her neck straight, and the meal is over.

'You and Dad sure don't talk much anymore.' I don't usually try a direct attack, but I'm desperate, and it shows in my voice.

Her eyes fall on me, and I'm sorry I mentioned it. It's a look that says more than I wanted to hear. There is anger in her eyes, defensive anger, self-righteous anger, and a promise, a kind of 'you'll see.' It's not a flashing anger. I could accept that. Maybe there would be a fight, or maybe she would start complaining about Dad. That would be better. This looks like a twisted and bitter anger, an old misshapen stone in her mind. Then her eyes lift off me, and she moves stiffly into the kitchen, leaving me chilled.

I can feel the gleeful silence creeping around the house, stretching like a panther.

I don't live in the house. My brother Phil remodels houses. Two years ago, as a favor to my parents, he began to complete the forever-unfinished room above the garage. He must have been in one of his rare good moods to agree to do this – for cost plus half his rate. It was a good deal, but soon the arguments began between Phil and my father. My father was way behind in paying him, even for the materials. So Phil stopped before he put the bathroom in, and said he'd start again when he saw some money. My father is naturally tight, and he's very anxious about his store and his meager profits, but he also treats Phil poorly. I don't understand their war.

Finishing the room above the garage was my mother's idea. She wanted to rent it out. We suspected she wanted the money for her France fund, but without a bathroom, she could not rent it, so I live there. I eat in the main house and use the bathroom there, sometimes watch television in the den with my dad, careful not to speak, even during the commercials – but I do my homework, make my phone calls, read and sleep in my own separate place above the garage, and that's where I have my hobby.

I step outside on our patchy front lawn and watch the last of Saturday bunching in a corner of the sky over the ocean. I see the sky filtered through our two trees which are forever competing, the fir inching above the oak and then, the next time I look, the oak taller by a twig. I still call them the *sapin* and the *chêne* as my mother taught me. They were the first French words I learned.

I can hear the cars humming on Wilshire and a burst of alien laughter from my father's television set and the clatter and chimes of my mother's work in the kitchen. I move toward the garage and the outdoor stairway to my room, but I don't go up yet. I sit on the stair that's exactly halfway, a midpoint between my home and their home and between the obscure, milky sunset and Wilshire Boulevard and between now and later. I freeze time by sitting on this stair, and in the lingering moment think about the ugliness between my parents. I can still feel the wound it made in my chest.

I'm not analyzing this ugliness and its sudden growth this summer; maybe I'm afraid to. I'm just studying the memory of it.

A car turns off Wilshire on to our street and whines toward me with an ever-climbing high note and a slight rattle, and I'm relieved to know that Benko is coming, and that he will break my grip on this dark minute.

I move my butt over on the step as a kind of greeting, and Benko sits beside me and sighs. He's not tall but very thick and wide, his round knees massive and shiny under his baggy shorts.

'Sucks.'

'What?'

'I asked Rema if she wanted to have a burger with us later tonight and to bring Donni Loma for you . . .'

'Loma's for *you*.'

'Bullshit,' Benko says. 'Anyway, she said maybe, and she just called me and said, no, they couldn't.'

'Nice she called you.'

'Well, I called *her*. I mean earlier tonight I called to confirm, and I left a message. So she just called back.'

'At least she bothered.'

'Jesus, Cheevey. Jesus. Don't be so grateful. Who is *she*? Y'know? Christ.'

'She's Rema, and I love and desire every part of her, even the bottom of her feet, even her shins and every bit of clothing that has ever touched her skin, and even the *lint* on the clothing that has touched her skin, and so do you. I love her dandruff. I love the fingerprints she leaves and all the crumbs on the table after she eats.'

'Why don't *you* ask her out?'

'I will.'

'When?'

For an answer, I let the last of Saturday dissolve into the Pacific, meaning 'all in time' or 'someday' or 'you can't rush these things.'

I had a steady girlfriend for almost two years, and that was far too long, because after a year, all the pleasure had run out of the relationship, and yet we carried the empty shell around, like the shell of an egg, speaking softly, moving carefully and predictably so as not to crack it, until, finally, we barely spoke, barely moved at all. I shudder when I remember how numb and quiet we were because it reminds me of the silence growing inside my parents' house, and I wonder if there is a seed of that silence in me.

'Can I see the new figure?'

Benko follows me up the stairs, which creak and tremble and wobble away from the wall. Phil quit before he strengthened the stairway.

I'm proud of how my room looks, especially at night. When I hit the switch, three clamp-on lights highlight the shelves I put in with Phil's advice, and on those shelves are the possessions I care most about – my books on military history and my miniatures. I have 273 lead soldiers. I painted thirty-four of them myself, and I'm working on the thirty-fifth.

The glossy paper of the book jackets and the bright-colored miniatures reflect their light into the dimness of the rest of the room, and it gives me a feeling I can't articulate. It's more than pride. I love my collection of lead soldiers. These figures are stitched through my memory since memory began. (I started with six Scots Greys sent by one of my Chicago uncles when I turned two.) They were not 'part' of my childhood. They 'represent' my childhood to me. They carry the weight of most of my childhood days and nights, and they 'represent' my imagination, too, and then there is the part of this that is difficult to say and probably impossible to understand. I feel like I'm one of them, as if they collected *me*.

'Cool.'

Benko is squatting to be eye-level with my library table. I use half of it for homework and half for painting. I turn on the desk lamp, directly above the new figure so Benko can see the detail. I have finished the face and hat and jacket. I like doing the most intricate work first. I kneel beside Benko to stare at the soldier, and it strikes me that most people would have picked up the miniature to see it, but Benko and I come to *it*, and let it stand there as it was meant to stand, legs apart, rifle cradled in one arm, head cocked to its left. It's not exactly reverence, the two of us squatting and kneeling there, but it *is* a kind of respect.

The man is a sergeant in the British Army, the Royal Green Jackets, they were called. Benko knows.

'Peninsula campaign?'

'Yeah, around 1809. Ninety-fifth regiment.'

His big blunt finger touches the tiny gun, moves it gently. 'Baker rifle?'

'Mm-hm.'

'Eyes look good.'

'Thanks. Mouth didn't turn out, so I gave him a moustache.'

'Works with the sideburns. You *had* to use a magnifier for this sash – and these buttons!'

Benko knows I never use a magnifier, and I smile, proud of myself.

'Nope.'

'God, Cheevey. He'll be your best.'

My nod is slow and important as I stare at my new sergeant. Benko rises and goes to the shelves.

'The Zouaves are still my favorite, though.'

I join him there. On the shelves I have whole lines of charging Zouaves and Highlanders, ranks of marching Gurkhas and Bengal Lancers on parade, also French Legionnaires firing standing, kneeling and prone, and six Arab warriors charging right into the French rifles. I have Napoleon's Old Guard and Wellington's Dutch troops from Waterloo, also his artillery. There is a squad of cavalry from Pulaski's Legion in the American Revolution, plus Dervish and Zulu irregulars, Welsh and Russians, Germans from the

Franco-Prussian War and the Heavy Brigade and what is left of the poor battered Scots Greys from the Crimea. When I was younger I would knock my men across the room with dart guns and rubber bands – before the deep respect set in.

'When I was showering today at Mari's, Dash was there.'

'Dash kicks it,' Benko says with admiration. We are still inspecting my troops.

'She came in – while I was showering.'

'Dash?!' Now he's turned toward me, but I keep my eyes on the soldiers. 'Dash came *in*?'

'Yeah.' I dress a line of Prussians, a one-quarter-of-an-inch move to the left.

'Why?!'

'She said she had to pee.'

'Bullshit! She said that *during*?!'

'Yeah, she came in and sat down.'

'Bullshit! What did you do?!'

'Well, y'know there's no shower curtain, just a glass door.'

'What did you *do*?!'

'I turned around.'

'Which way?!'

'Away from her, you cod. What d'you think, I *flashed* her?!'

'You turned your ass to her.'

'What could I do?'

'What did *she* do?'

'She apologized and peed and said she wasn't looking, and she left.'

'Bullshit. Extraordinary bullshit, man, Christ. You *know* she was looking.'

'So what?'

'Christ. Dash.' He says the name with some awe. He has met Dash many times when we have stopped at Mari's together or given them a ride somewhere or when Benko has been with Ballyhoo and me, and Mari and Dash have come to get him. Dash Markel with her fine face and sexy laugh and showy legs has always been desired and untouchable, five years older, with a look in her bright eyes that makes us children.

'You should've showed her your wand.'

'Oh, sure.'

'God. Dash. Radical *bueno*, you know?'

'Very *issimo*.'

'*Muy issimo*.'

'*Si*.'

'She kicks it. She's great.'

'Everybody kicks it, to you, Benko.'

'Bullshit. I have my standards. *You're* the cod. You even said my *sister* kicks it.'

'She does.'

'She's fifteen, *imbecilico*.'

'She kicks it in a fifteen-year-old way.'

We're moving to the door and I'm reaching for the light switch, but I turn for one more glance at the troops. Even in that one second before my finger erases them, I savor the sight of the uniforms and the bright bayonets and lances and flags, and I know that during my aimless cruising with Benko, and even while I'm eating the burger, I'll be waiting to return here and finish the painting of my new sergeant of the Rifle Brigade.

Benko catches my look. He is an excellent fielder of glances, moods, jokes, nuances. He drops nothing. As we walk down the dark, wobbling stairs, he asks me, 'You still writing the novel?'

'Thinking about it.'

'That's what I mean.'

Benko knows that as I paint and study my troops, I daydream a story, chapter by chapter, using the soldiers as characters. He is the only other person who knows this, and I am slightly uncomfortable about it, even though I know he would never betray me. Benko and I are both characters in this story. I have always called it *Cheever's Legion*. I began it when I was fourteen or so, but I have started over several times. Benko used to ask me what was happening in the book, and I would tell him of our latest adventure. He would sit very still and listen. I was giving him a second life, and he appreciated it. Now, at nineteen, we're both self-conscious about it, and he seldom asks.

'What chapter?'

'I keep redoing chapter eight.'

'Out of how many?'

'I don't know.'

'Am I . . . ?'

'You're still in it.'

'Am I still a sergeant?'

'Yeah. You want a commission?'

'No. I prefer to be the veteran sergeant. I like that. Victor McLaglen. Sean Connery.'

'Bob Hoskins.'

'Hoskins?'

'*Zulu Dawn*.'

'Oh, yeah.'

I don't play music when I paint. There is only the sound of my own breathing. There is the smell of paint and the dipping and careful application of the brush. There is the slow dressing of the soldier, button by button and belt by belt. There is the color of life brushed on to the dead metal until his hands seem capable of moving, and his eyes are ready to blink, and, by now, the sound of the breathing I hear could be my own, or it could be his.

I don't mean that I believe the figure 'lives' in the outer world, but he comes to life in my imagination, and the movement from lead to living soldier is without effort, like the movement of oil.

This moment is fragile, and it is exploding like thin glass now, shattered by the ringing of my telephone. As I reach for the phone, I glance at the clock. It's four minutes after midnight, so I know who my caller is.

'Hi.'

'So what d'you want to do for your birthday?'

Mari is half-whispering. Bob and Ballyhoo are sleeping, and she is in the kitchen. I know all this from all the other phone calls, and I know that she is very upset and trying not to panic, and that is why she is calling, and I know we will take our time getting to the revelation of what is frightening her.

'I was thinking about the beach. You think everybody would come to the beach? Can you see Mom and Dad coming to the beach? I don't know.' I am keeping my tone light and relaxed as if this is truly the subject of this phone call. 'Phil likes the beach. Ballyhoo likes . . .'

'I told you never to go to the beach, Cheevey. I thought I had impressed that upon you. I thought you had promised me you would never ever go, and if you go, for God's sake don't go into the water. There are living things in that water, microscopic clawed things. They imbed in brain tissue and eat the grey matter slowly, steadily. There's proof of this. There's the whole surfer subculture as proof. Your hair lightens. Your taste in clothing deteriorates. Your language changes. You say "dude" over and over again, and you can't help it.'

If I could see my smile now, I know it would be the kind described as sad – if a smile can be sad. I suppose it's just a smile that arrives on your face at the same time as a sad thought, and the two of them exist together. I was smiling at Mari's usual ice-pick wit and feeling sad about the wine that was slurring her words.

'So these ocean bug things crawl into your frontal lobe and eat it?'

'Right,' she says, and I can hear her pouring more wine.

'Like alcohol,' I say, and this brings a whole thirty seconds of dead air.

'You can be such a fuck.'

'That's a definite drunk word. You've already passed through muddy one and muddy two and you've dropped through limbo and you're all the way to drunk. Why didn't you call me an hour ago?'

'You're such a little shit.'

'I'm bigger than *you*.'

More dead air.

'Cheevey, can you meet me in the park? Please!'

I close my eyes and sigh and think of all the reasons not to do this, knowing I *will* do it. 'What if Ballyhoo wakes up and you're gone?'

'What if he wakes up and I'm *here*? Do you want him to see me like this?! Please!'

'I'll meet you in front of your place.'

'No. The park.'

'It's too late for you to be out walking alone.'

'I'll drive.'

'Mari, you can't.'

Her voice drops so she can yell at me in a whisper. 'I *can*. I'm still in muddy one, and all my reflexes are fine-tuned. Be at the park by Wilshire in ten, Cheevey. Please. Please. Please.'

'Stay in the car till I get there.'

'It happened again with Ballyhoo, only worse. You know, when he disappears? He's there, but I can't see him, and my heart almost stops, and I know I've done the worst thing of my life, the worst thing a woman can do. I've lost my child, and I sweat and shake – and then there he is just a few feet away, looking at me, but for a few seconds I couldn't see him. It happened at the library.' Mari sits on a park bench, just on the edge of the first board, but then rises again and continues to pace, shivering a little. I'm wearing my sweats with a hood, and I'm still warm from the run.

'We can talk in the car,' I say.

'No. I have to move.' She steps about absently as she speaks, glancing at her shoes, at the sky beyond the rim of light. We stand near the boulevard under a street lamp for safety.

'It was story day at the library, and he likes that, sitting on the floor with a lot of other kids . . . Anyway, the woman was reading a book, and I drifted. I stopped listening, and when I came back, I felt my heart clutch and the sweat coming, and I knew I had done something terrible, and I looked around, and he wasn't there. I looked, Cheevey. I looked at every kid and then all around the library, and I was screaming inside, not just, "Where is he?!" but "Where am I?!" I didn't know where *I* was, Cheeve. But I knew I had lost the one thing I was never supposed to lose, and I yelled out loud, and guess what I yelled?'

Now she stares up at me, and her lips tremble and I see her shoulders move in a shiver, and I wish I had something warm to put around her besides a damp sweatshirt.

'I yelled, "Coretti!"'

Her eyes fill and trickle over, and she wipes quickly at the corners, never breaking off her stare. 'Coretti!' she repeats with a quiet sob. I hold her, and she rests the side of her face on my shoulder and keeps talking.

'And I knew where I was then. I was lost in Coretti's books. I was lost, Cheeve. And when I yelled, everybody turned to look at me, and one of the faces was Ballyhoo, and I hadn't seen him. He was there, looking at me like I was a stranger, and I was, for a minute. And I learned something.' She is wiping her face with her fingers again. 'I used to say, when this happened, that somehow Ballyhoo gets into my blind spot, like I have a physical and psychological blind spot, but now I know that's not it. *I* go away. *I* disappear.'

Now she just weeps, and I just hold her, not very tightly, enough to give comfort. This has happened before, too many times, and I'm busy thinking about what I should do. What I should say that might break the pattern. The Coretti idea is a new one. John Coretti is a novelist-philosopher who writes dense, obscure books. I can't penetrate them, but Mari loves everything he has written. Coretti is the subject of her doctoral thesis. She says it's her job to decode him for the world. That's her mission. This thesis was approved in outline form almost two years ago. Mari is stuck at the beginning. She works in a bookstore part-time. She takes a high-level Lit. class at UCLA. She takes care of Ballyhoo, and she tries to crack this Coretti paper. And she drinks. Coretti is no help. He used to lecture at UCLA now and then, but he disappeared three years ago. Nobody knows where he is, and this mystery attracted Mari as much as the man's writings. Once she publishes his paper, she says, once she explains him to the world, he'll come back. 'Come Back, Coretti' is the unapproved title of her paper. 'Beneath the Bottom Line: John Coretti's Perspective on a Wasted Century' is another.

Her weeping has ended in long, weary breaths against my shoulder.

'You're not sleeping enough, and you should quit drinking and get help, and why can't you wake up Bob and tell him you're scared? And why can't *he* hold you?'

'Oh, Cheevey, only you can understand my babble.' She says this matter-of-factly as she disengages and walks to her car. I'm wondering if it's all over and realizing I've said nothing new to her.

She opens her car door and hands me a corked bottle of Chardonnay, about one-eighth full.

'Pour it out.'

'So you're quitting again?'

'Don't say "again." Pour it out. I want *you* to do the ceremony.'

I pour the wine into the gutter and leave the bottle there, too.

'No. Give me. I recycle.'

I put the bottle on the floor of the car, and we stare at each other a moment.

'I'll be all right.'

'When?'

'When Ballyhoo grows up and doesn't need me anymore or when I finish my paper – whichever comes first.'

I shake my head, looking off, frowning at the space where the ocean was today and probably will be tomorrow and may be tonight, though I can't see it. There's a little fog. No moon.

'Don't spend time worrying about your sister.'

I face her now, and it strikes me as arrogant that she thinks all my worry centers on *her*.

'What?' She sees me on the edge of a thought.

'Oh, Mom and Dad,' I say. 'It's getting worse.'

'How?'

'They're really pissed at each other. It's open – well, I can see it. I'm not used to it. Something's . . . I don't know.'

Her mind gets busy again. She's had her outburst. She feels better. I can see her gathering her words and ideas and memories. She's preparing to teach. I think she loves teaching me. I want to let her have that tonight.

'Do you remember them openly angry?' I ask her.

'Of course.'

'I don't.'

'You weren't there.' She steps away from the car to look at the void, and when I join her, shoulder to shoulder, she begins: 'Phil caught the brunt of it – whatever the hell that means: the "brunt." Where the hell did that word come from? Whatever it is – he caught it – in the teeth. Mom and Dad hadn't buried all their rage yet and turned into tunnelers.'

I can hear her breath still quivering a little on the intake, leftover from her weeping, and I'm reminded that Ballyhoo wept today. Maybe he's dreaming right now, back in the wagon, being the Emperor Jaka again, or maybe he's dreaming of the library, and his mother's wild eyes that don't see him, and her voice calling out a stranger's name.

'Cheeve, have you seen any of the World War Two prison camp movies – the old ones? British, mostly. I love those old movies. At first the prisoners are very feisty – fighting and yelling, being punished, tortured. Then it all gets very quiet. The prisoners don't fight anymore. They co-operate. They go about their prisoner lives in a very dull, dead fashion. You know why – because now they're tunneling. They put all of their hopes, all of their anger, all of themselves into their secret tunneling. What they leave behind, on the surface, are their dull dead faces and tired, pliant bodies, murky eyes.'

'Murky?'

'Murky eyes that only light up when they're tunneling. Just like Mom and Dad. It used to be torture – when I was a tot and Phil was moving toward the double digits. Before you. Before you, there was terror and torture. Now they tunnel. Mom tunnels toward France. Dad tunnels into the television. That's why they're zombies – no laughing, no crying, no fisticuffs. They co-operate. Because they have their secrets. You, too, right, bro?'

'Me?'

'The soldiers.'

'It's a hobby.'

'I've heard you speak to them, bro. More than once.'

Mari, the teacher, always finds a way to turn her lesson

back to me, and this one makes me nervous. She doesn't know about the novel I daydream, but it's not tunneling, I tell myself. Someday I'll write it out. And the words she heard when I was younger . . . 'I spoke *for* them. I would be their voices on the battlefield when I played, when I actually played with them. I'd say: "Charge! Fire! Fix bayonets! Arrgh, I'm hit! Retreat!"'

She is shaking her head, still staring at the absence of ocean. 'Conversations. I remember heavy conversations. Soldiers talking about home, about *home*, bro. That's tunneling. Don't go off the road like the rest of us.'

'Oh, you're saying kids can't play out loud, and there can't be hobbies, and there's no such thing as married family life and Phil can't just . . . go remodel houses if he wants to? Why is that off the road?'

'You think I'm living married family life? I'm acting. This is theatre, kid, a kind of ritualistic "no" theatre, but not the Japanese kind – with the "H". This is just plain "no". I'm playing the part of a wife and mother. It's very old, very traditional, this "no" stuff. I have all the masks and costumes. All the lines are written. There are probably a lot of us, a large number, maybe a hundred thousand "no" actors in California alone – just in my role, in the young wife and mother role.

'The word comes from a classic question and answer. Are you alive? Are you real? Are you truly *in* your life? Are you in your minutes? The answer: "no". No, I'm tunneling. My particular tunnel is a labyrinth. I tunnel into books, not to come out anywhere. I tunnel to get lost where it's dark and damp and safe to remove the theatrical garb. That's another word for you: "garb." A garb should be a fish or a small mammal or something. And Phil is not just building houses. He's trying to build his own house – every time. He's trying to reconstruct the house he wishes he had grown up in, the happy home. Don't shake your head. Don't doubt your sister. I'm the one cursed with eyes. I'm the seer, the unwilling seer.'

Her stare is dead on and deep, and I can see her insight and her pain, and I never know what to do with them. She lunges at me and kisses my cheek and starts back to the car.

'You're the best, Cheevey. Come on. I'll drive you home.'

'I'll run.'

She stops, then, and turns to me. Her eyes shine – with new tears? I wonder?! 'They're just a mother and a father, that's all they are, Cheeve. Everybody's got them – like birthmarks. Ignore them. Banish them. Walk with pretty girls and see the Nile.'

She waves. I wave. Then I'm jogging again.

It's after 1 a.m., but I'm not ready to sleep. I'm painting the sergeant of the Rifle Brigade, my hands and my eyes keeping busy while a whole company of worries march through my brain. I should have driven with Mari to her apartment and then run home from there. Even though she was talked-out and calm, she still had a lot of alcohol in her. And I'm worried about the empty wine bottle I put on the floor of the car. I should have put it on the passenger seat so she'd be sure not to forget it. Bob takes the car to work in the morning. If the bottle is still in there . . . And I worry about my parents, and the hate I saw today. Hate. That's what it looked like. I imagine them now sleeping together. How can they lie beside each other? Their bed must turn to ice. Or maybe, in the dark, they touch each other. This image is also troubling, even twisted, as if, masked by the dark, they become different people, or not people at all but just warm-blooded mammals needing comfort, and they clutch and cuddle and bring each other ease until the daylight comes and they become people again, with names and histories, and they remember their hate. I just keep painting because I know these thoughts will finally march out of sight and be gone, and I'll be left with my story. I'll be leading Cheever's Legion. If that's tunneling, I really don't care.

Another reason I run everywhere is that my parents never willingly lend their cars. My mother whines and my father frowns and sighs. I saw this same behavior when Mari lived at home and was negotiating for cars, and I couldn't stand it then. So I'd rather not ask. If I asked, they'd say yes. They always say yes eventually, but you have to accept the whining and frowning and sighing along with the car, and that makes the car too heavy to drive.

When it's too far to walk or too complicated to take buses, I try to get rides from Benko or Mari, but this is Sunday morning. I'm supposed to show up at Phil's house in Culver City at nine. I'm helping him remodel a house in Palms. I could buy a car. Not having one is embarrassing at my age, but even a cheap one would take all of my savings, so my only hope this morning is my parents.

At eight my mother is already dressed, sipping a *café au lait* at the kitchen table and working the crossword puzzle from the Sunday *L.A. Times* magazine.

'Mom, how about a one-way trip to Phil's? Just drop me off, and then you've got your car all day and Phil will bring me back tonight – what d'you say – take it . . . *Mom*?'

She stares at the wall. She's thinking this through. I've asked her to decide about capital punishment or whether or not there's an afterlife. She takes in a long breath and it comes out not in a father-like sigh, but a mom-like whine.

'I just started this puzzle.'

'I'll drive, and you can keep working it in the car.'

'I can't write in the car. Ask your father.'

'Still sleeping.'

'No, he's in the bathroom.'

The odds are strong against any request made through the bathroom door, so I wait until he's out and ambling into the kitchen in slacks and slippers and an old Lakers sweatshirt that used to belong to Phil.

'Will you be using your car?' My mother asks this without looking up from her puzzle.

'Why?' The answer of a cautious man.

'Dad, how about a ride to Phil's or *near* Phil's? Just drop me at Sepulveda and Washington, and he'll bring me home tonight. So what'd'you say – take it – *Dad*?'

He fills his chest with a great intake of air and stares at the floor. I've asked him to explain the roots of the Great Depression. He gets the sigh only halfway out when my mother glances up sharply from her puzzle.

'Your car is just going to sit here all day,' she says.

He flings his eyes to meet hers. There is that clash of blades again, but stilettos, quiet and deadly. 'So is yours.'

'I'm shopping today,' she parries and stabs. 'You're watching ten hours of television.'

'You don't know *what* the hell I'm doing.'

'Oh? Then tell me.'

'Jesus Christ, forget it! Fuck it – I'm gone.' I'm walking quickly out of the kitchen, passing my dad as he bellows right into my ear: 'Watch how you talk to us!'

His shout shocks me, but my answer is there without my having to think about it.

'"Us"?! What d'you mean, "us"? You mean you and Mom?! You call that "us"?! You think you're acting like an "us"?!' I'm not sure he knows what the hell I'm saying. His face is angry, but there is also confusion in it. I just want to be out of there, and I'm jogging even the three steps to the back door. The screen door slams behind me as I jump the steps, hitting the ground at a slow run, cursing under my breath and leaving them their cars and their house and each other and the silence, and hoping – while my anger is at its peak – that the silence eats them both.

I'm at Phil's house in less than an hour. I've run most of the way, and I ache all over and my legs are shaking badly. I walk about and then sit on his front steps. Inside I can hear a radio. I can't hear the words, but the broken rhythms of commercials and now and then a song that Phil is singing. Old Beach Boys probably. Phil used to surf. I hear him curse, and I figure maybe he burned or cut himself so I rise up from the steps and knock on the door. His girlfriend, Cindy, moved out almost a year ago, and I'm glad. She was so cold. Benko and I called her the undead.

'It's open, sport.'

I like it when Phil calls me that. It gives him a little class, I think, like Gatsby.

'You hurt yourself?' I'm walking through an incredibly rumpled living room into a cluttered kitchen. Phil is frying eggs standing there in a T-shirt and briefs, bare feet, hair still uncombed. He is very muscular. He has a bit of a beer gut, but the rest of him is hard, his biceps bulging aggressively. I passed him in height years ago, but I'm a bendable birch tree to his unmovable oak.

He looks at me without really focusing. I don't know if his eyes have ever stopped and studied me. I used to try to catch and hold them. When he was still at home, when I was six and he was sixteen, I used to follow him around. I used to make up elaborate stories. I used to practice and then show him how I could bark exactly like our dog. I can still mimic Snowy perfectly, but he's been dead so long no one but me remembers what he sounded like. Nothing helped me capture Phil's attention. He would look at me – while I lied about what happened at school, while I barked – he would look the way he is looking now, a glance, really, with his eyes ready to slide away. I have always wished to be the bringer of important news to Phil. Ever since I can remember I have fantasized telling him something that would make him stare with wonder and study me deeply as he said; 'Really? Wow! Tell me more.'

'What?' he asks, his eyes going back to his pan of eggs.

'Did you hurt yourself? I heard you bitching through the door.'

'It's when I move a certain way.' Now, as he turns the eggs, he pulls up his T-shirt to show me a sprawling, multi-colored bruise on his stomach, just to the side of his navel.

'Jesus,' I say, thinking immediately that if *I* had such a bruise on my face, maybe then his eyes would come to me and linger.

'Cop,' he says.

'What?'

'I'll tell you about it. Why don't you get the truck ready? Both tool boxes and all the sledgehammers. How come you look all strung-out already? Christ.'

I'm surprised he noticed.

'I ran here.'

'You ran?!' he says to the eggs.

'I'll tell you all about it,' I say, and I leave to go to the pick-up truck. If I can't gather and hold Phil's attention, then at least I can *be* like Phil or at least *act* like Phil. Phil seems not to crave or need anyone's rapt attention, and I practice that feeling walking out to the truck.

I'm driving Phil's truck to the job site. Sitting beside me he holds his stomach and curses, and I remind him to tell me the story of the bruise.

'Cop did this.'

'You said that. Why?'

'Henry Bollinger did this. You don't know him. He's a cop. You know why? 'Cause I beat him up in high school. Fucking ten no twelve what-am-I-saying almost fifteen years ago. I fucked him up once. Not bad. One good punch. I mean a high school, a schoolyard punch. Not a really big punch. He went down – got right up, but he was crying, you know? He was finished. Okay, I didn't press it. He walked away cussing me out. I let him walk away. Now he's a cop. He rousts me outside of Malone's. *Outside.* I wasn't breaking up the place. I had stepped outside with a couple of idiots who were talking tough. We were all pissed, I guess. Anyway, he grins. "You slime, Cheever," he says. "I've always wanted to do this." Bam! In the gut with his nightstick. Shit! You ever . . . ?' Phil lets the question fall away, remembering I'm not a fighter. 'Anyway, bam. In the gut. Why didn't you turn there?'

'It's the same from Motor.'

'What?'

'It's equidistant this way.'

'"Equidistant." Jesus. You and Mari. Where was I?'

'Bam.'

'Oh, yeah. So now I'm all doubled up and I can hardly breathe, and he starts *arresting* me. The other cop takes him aside. Anyway, they walk away. Henry Bollinger. Jesus.'

I drive for awhile before I say, 'These are fairly small cities here – Santa Monica, Culver City . . . How can you find so many people to fight with? Don't you all know each other in these bars by now? It must take a lot of organization and scheduling so you don't fight the same guy twice.'

'Through here.'

'I know.'

It's illegal to do major construction on a Sunday – city codes about noise, I guess – but what we're doing today is demolition, and I enjoy that. We're taking down three whole rooms, including a bathroom, which is my territory. It's slow, quiet work, disconnecting all the fixtures and setting them aside, then it's time for the sledgehammer.

I enjoy working alone. I also enjoy the fact that Phil is nearby, that we're on this job together, but I like having my own task and territory, and this demolition is intriguing because it's creation in reverse. Somebody built this house. Many people filled it with their lives. Now it's being erased. Destruction is so much easier than creation, and kind of ruthless when you think about it – some giant demolition ball swung by a crane, blasting through the work of masons and carpenters, electricians, plumbers, tile workers, painters, and crashing through the spaces where people lived and slept and carried on as though the world around them was solid and eternal.

I'm taking out a medicine cabinet, chipping away at three layers of paint, maybe twenty years per layer, maybe more. It's an old house. I break the plaster around it and ease it out of the wood framing and as I pull it out, I notice hundreds of old razor blades, double-edged blades, lying among the insulation and the framing boards. The cabinet is the kind with a slot in the back of it, for the disposal of used blades. I suppose it was considered safer than dropping them in a waste basket – and it was so handy. A man finished shaving, decided the blade was getting dull, took it out, opened the cabinet, and dropped it through the slot, causing it to disappear. That went on for years, maybe a lifetime. What I'm looking at, as I hold the cabinet to my chest and stare at the exposed inner wall, is an intimate detail of some stranger's life. I'm looking at all those morning shaves. I'm looking at all those used-up blades he took out of his heavy old Gillette and dropped like secrets through that slot, trusting that they were gone forever in some dark recess of a solid and permanent house. I'm looking at a way of measuring time, and I'm wondering how much the face in the mirror aged from the first blade to the last. I'm looking at the fact that nothing really disappears. It just goes somewhere else.

'What're you looking at?'

Phil's eyes are already off me as he busies himself in the hall outside the bathroom.

'Nothing. How careful should I be with this tub?'

'We'll junk the tub.' He is dismantling an old light fixture. 'But I want the shower door, the faucets . . .'

'I know.' We work in silence while I search for a way to begin. By now I'm sure he has forgotten that I ran from Santa Monica all the way to his house this morning.

'Remember I said I ran to your place this morning?'

'You ran what?'

'Mom and Dad were so bitchy about their cars . . .'

'What's new, sport?'

'Well, no, it *is* new – to me, anyway. They're changing.'

Phil just keeps working.

'Christ, you remind me of them, Phil, no kidding. I'm talking, and you're on Saturn . . .'

'I'm listening. Mom and Dad – what?'

'They're fighting. It's pretty ugly.'

'Arguing?'

'No. Not arguing. Just . . . I mean, I remember it wasn't *that* long ago, they bought those nerdy jogging suits . . .'

'Matching blues.'

'Yeah, and kind of limped around the neighborhood before dinner. They did a *few* things together. They didn't seem to *hate* each other.'

Phil just keeps working. He hears my frustrated sigh.

'What?'

'What do you mean, "What"? I'm telling you. Our father and mother act like they hate each other. *Hate*. What do you think about that? It scares me. It depresses me. It's really ugly.'

'You should get out of there, sport.'

'Whether I'm there or not is not the point. It's how *they* are. That's what I'm telling you. If I wasn't there it'd be worse. *They'd* probably be worse. Did you ever think they hated each other?'

Phil pulls down the disconnected light fixture and walks away – walks away! I hear him all the way out at the truck. I pick up a long-handled sledgehammer and bare my teeth and swing the heavy tool like an executioner, killing the tub, cracking the porcelain, turning tile and plaster to dust, making rubble out of somebody's past. Then I toss the hammer down and sit on the disconnected toilet, gripping my knees.

Phil comes back and never even glances my way. He starts to work on another hall fixture, and says, 'Save the heavy hammering for later in the day so nobody around here complains.'

I stare at him. We're both sweating. He's wiping around his eyes with a bent wrist, then trying again to get his screwdriver into a small, rusted screw-top.

'Mari says you just keep trying to build the house you wish you'd grown up in. That's why you build houses – or *remodel* houses. You're trying to fix your own past.'

'Mari is a fruitcake.'

'We're all tunneling into something, she said, and now I think Mom and Dad are coming out of their tunnels.'

Phil is making little grunting sounds as he digs in with the screwdriver and turns that screw by millimeters. Then he frees it, and it turns easily and he says, 'Mari talks through her ass.'

'Jesus, Phil.'

'Jesus what?'

'What the hell do *you* think is going on?! What's *your* opinion? If I'm not supposed to get any insight from Mari, then who's going to tell me about Mom and Dad and how it was before? Talking to you is like talking to stucco.'

Phil laughs then, and his laughter is very high-pitched.

Cheevey •

It is such a shock to me and even a little flattering that something I said has struck him as funny, so I laugh, too, even though I'm upset. He lets the screw drop into his hand then hangs his head down and rubs the back of his neck as he continues chuckling, sounding like a sparrow. He sits then and puts his back against the hallway wall and flips the screwdriver and catches it absently. I'm not sure if he's thinking anything. Maybe he's just taking a break, but in a while he begins.

'Mostly they just yelled at *me*. It was something they had in common, being pissed off at Phil. Sometimes they'd hit me.'

'I don't remember any hitting.'

'Maybe you were too young. Yeah. That was when you were a baby. They'd slap. It lasted a few years – but, you know, once Mom slapped me, and I made a fist at her. I was . . . thirteen, pretty strong. It scared her. I can't remember why Dad stopped. Maybe she told him. Anyway, I never heard them yell at each other or hit each other, but I saw them spit once.'

'Spit!'

'Yeah, Dad gave Mom a real *bad* look, kind of a sneer. I don't know what it was all about, but she spit at him.'

'Spit! How? I mean . . .'

'You mean what?'

'Spit?!'

'Yeah. She spit at him as he was going by her, and he spit back. I don't know if any spit came out, you know, not real spit, but just that gesture, that spitting gesture. I guess that's hate. I never thought about it. I just wanted to get out. You should get out, too.'

'Jesus.'

Phil is back on his feet, screwdriver aimed at the fixture again.

'Jesus.' I just keep shaking my head, first trying to create an image of my parents spitting at each other – then trying to get rid of it.

'So . . . you think they *do* hate each other?'

Phil is intent on the screw, then he stops and holds his stomach for a few seconds. I guess he's hurt himself.

'You all right?'

'Hm? Sure. Goddamn' bruise.'

'So, Mom and Dad . . .'

'What? What? Christ, Cheevey, what the fuck about Mom and Dad? I don't try to figure them out.'

'Well, how could they have stay together, if . . .'

'Who cares?'

'Well, I've been living there all this time! *I* care!'

Now he looks at me. It's still one of his glances. He's not studying, but at least he's looking.

'Why?' he says. He's not really asking why. He doesn't care why I care. He's telling me not to care.

'God – they're my parents.'

'Yeah, well . . .' He's talking to the light fixture now, his forearm tightening, muscles popping as he forces the next screw. 'Get back to work on the sink.'

When I said I was hungry, Phil said lunch was coming, but he didn't say from where. Now it's one-thirty and a dirty silver Civic is pulling up next to the house. I watch as a red-haired woman gets out of the car, carrying two bags from Arby's. She's wearing a soft-looking blue shirt and jeans that fit her well. I'm thinking she's attractive, and then she smiles, and she's beautiful.

'You must be Cheevey,' she says.

She's older than Phil, maybe in her middle-thirties by the lines around her eyes and mouth, not deep lines, but she has an outdoor feel about her, a face unafraid of sun and wind. Her hair is short, legs are long, though she's not over five-seven. She takes her time.

'I'm Lauren.'

Even her words are unhurried, and her voice is loose, not stretched thin, loose and a little smoky.

I meet her on the front steps and shout back into the house for Phil. We eat sandwiches right there on the steps, and my shyness doesn't last long with her. There is an ease that spreads from this woman. That's what makes her beautiful. I don't know if other people would call her that. They'd say 'pretty,' but then, if they kept looking, they'd see the peace in her eyes. She is the most comfortable woman I ever met, and she studies me when she asks a question. Her eyes linger on me like friendly hands.

'I'm studying history and lit. at Santa Monica College.' 'I'll be twenty next week.' 'I work in my Dad's TV store.' 'We live over on 23rd in Santa Monica.' I would tell her my social security number if she asked and my weight and all my favorite foods and books and movies. Her attention honors me, and she has a warmth about her that promises tenderness and safety. I would tell secrets to this woman and trust her with dreams. She watches me, smiling, one knee drawn up and rocking as she sits on the steps and chews a sandwich, and her chewing is almost languid.

'Does everybody call you Cheevey?' she wonders.

'I encourage it.'

'Why?'

'My real name is Claude.'

'What's wrong with that?'

'It's pathetic,' Phil says, 'and fruity.'

'Claude,' I say again. 'It just sort of drops out of the mouth and thuds on the ground. Our mother gave us all French names.'

This last comment gets me a quick, dark look from Phil, but it's too late. She turns her eyes, sparkling with fun now, on to Phil, and her eyebrows arch upward.

'Phillipe?'

He stops sucking on his soda straw and gives me a full turn and a look of certain death, and Lauren laughs, and I laugh, and even Phil smiles.

She's only with us twenty minutes, and for hours after that, every time Phil and I pass each other in the house or take a break from our destruction, I ask him about her.

'Are you friends or more than friends or . . . ?'

'Can't have too many friends, sport.'

'So you're not answering?'

He says, 'She's good people,' and vague things like that, focused on his work. I, of course, am picturing them as lovers, and I don't like the picture because I'm envying Phil and because I don't think Phil would appreciate her, and what does she see in this tough, uncommunicative short guy with all those muscles? She should be with somebody much more sensitive. Some guy in his forties who has the same sense of ease, the same smile . . . I'm going stupid over this.

'Where'd you meet her?'

'Hm?'

'Lauren. How did you meet?'

'She's a very together lady.'

'Phil, Jesus . . .'

'Got a kid about . . .'

'A kid?!'

'Yeah.'

'Wow.' I'm staring into space, absorbing this, as Phil's glance hits me like a rubber ball, bouncing off again.

'What d'you mean, "wow"?'

'I just . . . Well, just think of having her for a mother.'

'What about it?'

'Well, she's so *nice*. She's so . . . peaceful. What kind of kid? How old?'

'Girl. Seven, I think. Molly.'

'Wow.' Now I'm not sure who I envy the most – Phil,

her probable lover, or Molly, the daughter who gets to be cradled in all that tender ease.

'Cheeve, get on the program.'

'What?'

'Break up that foundation. Then we'll quit. Shoot some pool.'

Phil walks around the table with the pool cue in his hand, hunting for a shot, doing the physics and geometry in his head, computing the risks, weighing the odds. Then he stops and leans in quickly, as if surprise is a factor, pumps the stick only once before stabbing the cue ball, and then follows the action with that same hunter's focus, dropping his prey in the side pocket with a click. He's off hunting again without any change of expression. I guess he's having a very good time. When Benko and I play here at the dim, smoky House of Billiards, we're always shouting and swearing and talking most of the time – and watching the other people.

Phil never seems to care, and rarely looks up from the table. I like coming here with him, not only because it's the only non-work time we spend together, but because I enjoy watching the people watch Phil.

He gathers their eyes like a TV screen – one with no sound, so that he is not watched steadily, but never quite ignored.

It's tribal or even animal the way the males look at Phil in terms of battle, and the females in terms of sex. He stalks around the table with those powerful arms and that intense focus of his – Phil is very good at doing one thing at a time – and people are drawn to him by his very disinterest in them, by the power of someone who doesn't care how he's doing in your opinion. I've tried to copy that, but I'm always glancing over my shoulder – not because I'm trying to impress anybody, but because I'm just so damn' curious.

'So you know my birthday's coming up.'

'I know, sport. Why don't you try for the three?'

'I'm not hitting the long shots anymore. Angle is off. So, I was thinking . . . I told Mari, maybe we'll have a little party, maybe at the beach. Would you come?'

'When?'

'Well, my birthday's on a Wednesday. Shit. I should've made that shot. But I thought the Saturday before. So, next Saturday. What d'you think?'

'When next Saturday?'

I don't speak for a while because he is lining up a shot. He misses, but his slight frown just flicks on, flicks off, and he's chalking his cue.

'I don't know. Afternoon. Or early-evening.'

'Later the better for me. I'll be working on the house.'

'So you think you can come if it's after work?'

'I think so.'

'Would you care if Dad was there?'

'Dad? On the beach?'

'I'm hoping Mom and Dad will show up for awhile. I haven't asked them yet. Well, it's my twentieth, you know? It's a big deal.'

'It is?'

'Fuck you.' He smiles, picking up his beer, and I press on. 'So I'd like to have the family together for a change. I think it would be good.'

'You do?'

'Come on, Phil. Can't we spend one half-hour together?'

'All right with me.'

'Is it? Good. I know you and Dad . . .'

'I don't care if he's there.'

'Good. Okay. I'll start setting it up. So who do you think you'll bring?'

'Hm?'

'To the party.'

'Aren't you going to shoot?'

'"I'm shooting, fat man, when I miss, *you* can shoot."' It's a line from *The Hustler*, but I don't think Phil knows that. I choose my shot, but before I stroke, I say, 'Could you bring Lauren?'

I just *barely* kiss the seven ball, the closest pass possible. The cue ball doesn't even seem to touch it. There is no sound. Just a few random, jumping molecules from the surface of one ball nudge a few random, jumping molecules from the other, and the seven teeters on the lip of the pocket and drops.

'Good shot, sport.'

'Thanks. Why don't you bring Lauren?'

'Lauren?'

'To the *party*.'

'Mm-hm.' He's scouting the green felt for the most vulnerable prey, hunting again. He finds a shot and bends low over the table, but when he pumps the stick back, it touches one of the guys at the next table who has *also* bent over a shot. This happens often in the House and every other parlor I've been in. The two players usually mumble 'excuse me' and somebody says 'go ahead,' and they take turns. It is unwritten and understood. Public pool has its own sportsmanship that probably goes back to the Renaissance, or maybe this is an older law of the hunter-gatherers. When two men are about to spear their game, and they bump, they turn and grunt some kind of 'go ahead' message and take turns, but Phil has touched a tall, long-haired boy who makes a loud 'tsk' with his tongue and turns to Phil, jerks his head to get the long hair out of his face, and says, 'Ma-an,' drawing out the word and giving it an irritable tone.

Phil looks back along the butt of his stick and sees that his way is clear now, and he shoots, and he *makes* the shot and then reaches for his beer, never even looking at the tall kid's face. So the tall kid puts his frown on *me*. I look away and begin searching for my next shot, but I'm a little tense now. I've never seen a fight over pool-playing manners. I've never even seen a heated confrontation at the House – but I'm with Phil. The rules are different with Phil.

It's not all his fault. The three guys at the next table have their antennae stretched way out, feeling for any wisp of conflict so they can make a show of toughness. The problem with Phil is that if they break through his wall of disinterest, and he takes note of one of their challenging looks or comments, he won't ignore it. He never does. He steps in. He moves *toward* conflict. He doesn't initiate it, but he has no capacity for avoiding it. I've seen him come close to three or four fights, and I don't spend much time with him. I'm an avoider. Most people are. I know the darker side of myself admires Phil's willingness for battle, but I also know that fighting has nearly ruined his life. His hands are slightly misshapen from fighting. Several bones in his face have been broken, and he has an arrest record that goes all the way back to high school. Fighting and drinking have both scarred and somehow weakened his life. When he's had bosses, he has always argued and quit or been fired. When he's had partners, he has always split. His construction business is hit and miss, and his life, I suppose, is mostly lonely.

But I hope he's there when I make that move to twenty. I hope they're all there because there is something to love about each Cheever, and somewhere in some bone or vessel we must all love each other, and I want to see us standing like a family around some cake from Von's next Wednesday while I'm blowing out candles and somebody is taking a picture, and I want to see that picture in a book I'm leafing through when I'm ninety-five, and I want to linger on that page and smile – just for a second. I don't think that's too much to ask.

I walk home the four blocks from the House of Billiards. Phil has stayed to shoot and drink on his own. When I turn off Wilshire on to 23rd, I'm surprised to see Mari's Toyota. It's across the street from our house, and I feel a moment of pleasure, thinking she's visiting with Ballyhoo. She seldom comes to the house, and Phil hasn't visited since his fight with Dad over the spare room. Any sense of family in the home makes me feel expansive, and I walk around with a grin so big it leaves my face sore as I romp with Ballyhoo, the silence dashing ahead of us like a frightened kitten, but my second glance at the car shows me that Mari is sitting *in* it, in the back seat, in the dark.

I walk over with a sense of dread. The window is down on the driver's side, and I put my face there. Mari's eyes are wide on me, but then she smiles her vanishing smile – it's gone almost before I notice it – and puts a finger to her lips. Ballyhoo is asleep, his head in her lap. She whispers: 'I was hoping you'd see us, so I didn't have to yell and wake him up.'

'Why aren't you in the house?'

'I couldn't take Mom and Dad right now. I just wanted to get out and talk to you so we've been waiting here . . .'

'How long?!'

'Just about an hour. It's okay. It's fine. He fell asleep, and I've been able to think.'

'You didn't go in at all? How did you know I wasn't home?'

'I called. Anyway, sitting here was good.'

'Let's go in.'

'No.'

'I mean, we can just go up to *my* room.'

'No, Cheeve, I don't want to wake him. Get in and we'll talk. Come in quietly. Stay in front so I don't have to move him.'

I open the door as quietly as I can. The overhead light

blinks on, and the boy stirs and sighs, but I slide in quickly behind the wheel and shut the door with only a click. He does not wake.

'Thanks.'

'I was with Phil.'

'I know. You're all dirty.'

'Where's Bob?'

'Studying. We had a fight.'

'Great.' We are whispering, and my neck hurts, turning around to see her, so I straighten out and adjust the rear-view mirror until her face is in it.

'It's not all his fault, Cheevey.'

'I don't know why you defend him.'

'Because it's not all his fault. You know I screw up.'

'Everybody screws up.'

'I read him a poem.'

'Why should that start a fight?'

'It was about him. He can't be teased.' Now she is laughing in a whisper.

'Why can't he be teased?'

She keeps laughing and tries to stop. Her laughter is shaking Ballyhoo, and he stirs again.

'Because he's so serious. Because he's so angry. Poor guy.'

'"Poor guy"?!'

She laughs again, straining to stop, hissing through her teeth, a breathy chuckle. I can see her eyes are moist with laughter and maybe with sorrow, too. I can't tell.

'Poor guy. Yes. He's so worried. He's so scared.'

'Bob?'

'Yes! Bob. He's scared of failure. Terrified. He won't play games. He hates Monopoly. He only plays Hearts because he's good at Hearts. He wins at Hearts.'

'You probably *let* him win.'

'Sometimes. Listen to the poem. Listen.' But she whispers another laugh and can't go on.

'Mari . . .'

'No. No. I've got it. Listen. Here . . . "I've been thinking about how bland-you-are. Wondering if your problem could be glandular."' She tightens around another laugh, holding everything in but the hissing.

'Too bad he didn't laugh.'

'I know, I know. Poor guy. He used to laugh.'

'I don't remember.'

'I used to call him "Bland Bob,' and he'd smile and call me "Morose Mari."'

'I don't remember that.'

'He's better in private.'

'I hope so.'

'Cheevey, when he failed the bar, he wept. He sobbed. He made me promise not to tell anybody.'

'I won't tell anybody.'

'I know.'

'I like the poem.'

'Thanks, but that's not what I wanted to tell you. I've had some new thoughts about Coretti.'

I don't really want to discuss her thesis now or her obscure novelist-god. 'I want to talk about my birthday first. Next Saturday. Okay? Evening – but when it's still light.'

'But not the beach. Okay?'

'Why not?'

'It's a mess. The sand. The water. And it scares me.'

'Scares you?'

'You know. Bally.'

'What about him?'

'If he gets away from me. If I don't see him – like I told you. I can't stand that feeling. I never take him anywhere dangerous now. I'm afraid I'll just drop inside myself like I do, drop through some slot in my brain and disappear like

I do, and then I come back and for a minute I don't see him, and it's the worst feeling in the world. I told you, not the beach. Okay? How about the park? We could barbecue at the park.'

'Mari.' I just stop and sigh.

'What?'

'We'll all *be* there. How could he get into any trouble if we're all there? *I'll* keep an eye on him.'

'No. It's your birthday. You should have no responsibilities that day. Let's just do the park. Please. It's cleaner.'

I'm quiet for a while, watching the house. The porch lights are on and some inner lights. I can picture my dad in the den, Mother in the bedroom. 'I wish you'd come over more.'

'Mom says it's bad for her back to have Ballyhoo around. She said that.'

'She doesn't have to pick him up.'

'I know. She just says it's painful – like his *presence* hurts her back, his *voice* hurts her back. I don't know. I'm sorry about her back. It's probably my fault. It's probably all those cracks I stepped on on the sidewalk. Remember?'

'Yeah, I remember. Anyway, I'd like us all together Saturday. The park is fine. Six o'clock, I guess. All right? For once? Can we all be together?'

'Cheevey, don't want it too much, because Dad won't want to come, and Mom'll say her back hurts. Phil won't even . . .'

'Phil is coming. We've established that. He's coming after work. And I'll talk to Mom and Dad. I'll say it's important. Christ. Just for half an hour or so. I'll buy everything. They can come and stay half an hour and go. The rest of the time, you'll be there and Ballyhoo, Benko and maybe Dash. You think Dash wants to come?'

'Yes. She probably will. She liked your buns.'

'She *said* that?'

'Shhh.'

We are still whispering, and when we want eye-contact, we glance at the rear-view mirror.

'What did she say?'

'She said, "Your brother has great buns." I couldn't believe she went in there. Why didn't you lock the door?'

'I don't lock bathroom doors. Public bathrooms, I do, but at home and at your place, if the door is closed, somebody's in there. That's the unwritten rule, the code of the bathroom, it seems to me – now, I'll take care of all the preparations, and I'll make sure Mom and Dad are there . . .'

'Cheeve.' Now *she* sighs a heavy sigh.

'What?'

'They won't come, and you know Phil. He'll *say* he's coming and won't show up. Don't *depend* on us. You know us better. We're the five Cheevers, remember? Five fingers, but there's no hand. There's nothing connecting us, Cheeve – and you're always trying to be the hand. Just invite your friends – lots of friends. I'll come with Ballyhoo and Dash, and that'll be that.'

We're silent awhile. 'Mom and Dad are worse,' I say. 'Do you think they hate each other?'

'No. And they don't hate Phil, and I don't hate *them*. There's no hate. It's just that we're missing something. We're missing the connective tissue.'

'What the hell does that mean? That doesn't mean anything. They raised us, for Christ's sake; they had us and raised us, and we all lived together, and I still live with them – sort of, and I know things were never great, but we *were* a family.'

'No. We were the Cheevers.'

'Come on, Mari.'

'The Cheevers are a different breed. You used to understand that. Way back – when we went to church regularly.

Remember? You couldn't say Episcopalians, so you just said "Palians." "We're Palians," you would say, and that was it. You had uncovered the truth. We were all masquerading as an Earth family, but we were really aliens – that's what you were saying, really, without the "P." Aliens. That's what you knew instinctively in your pure, child's brain, your untrammeled brain. Fresh snow is how I see Ballyhoo's brain and soul. See? I said "soul." I'm still a Palian, I guess. Anyway, fresh snow is how I see his brain, and I hate to step in it. I just hate to.

'So, you knew we were aliens when you were a child, you just forgot. Your snow got all muddied up, like the rest of us – or *almost* as bad as the rest of us – and you forgot, but you had us pegged then. We're not from Earth. Somewhere there's a planet where we fit in perfectly, where everyone is like us, self-absorbed, isolated, undependable – I don't mean you, I mean *us* – the other Cheevers. I mean me and Phil and Mom and Dad. I'm so glad we left that planet. I'd hate to live in a place that was populated with people like us.'

All of this coming in a whisper makes it sound confessional, intimate. I look away from the mirror and I realize I'm stroking my hand, rubbing the palm with a thumb, thinking about Mari's image of five fingers without a hand. 'You're making it worse, Mari.'

'I'm not making it, Cheeve. I'm describing it. I'm defining it for you.'

'I don't want to talk about it anymore. Just don't forget about the party. Bob's invited, too.'

'God, Cheeve. You're so magnanimous. Maybe we adopted you. Maybe you were switched in the hospital with the withdrawn kind of self-involved asshole I was *supposed* to get as a brother.'

'Thanks.' She needs another nudge away from this subject. 'I thought for a minute Phil and I would get into a fight with some guys tonight at . . .'

'Oh God – you mean Phil almost dragged you with him into one of his juvenile sandbox engagements? He's still in nursery school fighting over the shovel. He's . . .'

'Mari!'

'Shhh.'

'It wasn't his *fault*. These guys . . .'

'How can it not be his fault seventy-two times? He's sick. He's as neurotic as I am, except he can't talk, and that's all I *do*. What he really wants to do is punch Dad, but he can't punch his father so he punches everybody else. Don't hang around with him. Just leave after work. God. Phil is why we have wars. Phil *is* war. He's Aries. He's an Aries and Bacchus mix. War and wine – except with him it's beer. Speaking of wine, I'm only drinking at dinner now. Glass and a half. So far I don't miss it too much, but that's why I left tonight after the fight. I didn't want to wait until everybody was asleep and reach for the Chardonnay. See, Cheevey, you're helping me stay on the wagon. I suppose that expression is self-explanatory. I suppose drunken serfs were always falling off their carts and wagons on the road. Anyway, keep away from Phil.'

'Oh, sure. Keep away from my brother.'

'You *should*. You should keep away from *me*, too. You should run like hell. *Away*, not *to* us. You're always running from one of us to the other, like a medic, with bandages.'

'Jesus, Mari. I'm going to go in.'

'No. Wait. Wait.'

'I'm really down about all this, and you keep making it worse.'

'I know, that's my strong suit. Now, is that a card-playing analogy? That phrase – strong suit – as in bridge? Wait, Cheevey, please. Don't run away yet. See how selfish I am? I tell you to run, then I beg you to stay, but please, listen to my new approach to Coretti.'

I lay my head back on the seat and close my eyes. At

least this will keep her off the Cheevers for a few minutes. Sometimes her mind is like a pinpoint light, a laser sight moving across the family landscape on a search-and-destroy mission. There *are* some good things about us. There *are* some good memories. And I can work alongside my brother and shoot pool with him – that's something, that's familial. And now, listening to Mari's rush of whispers, like prayers in the dark, *that's* being close; and even this morning when my father said, 'Watch how you talk to us' – that's *something*. There has to be some shred of feeling in him about the two of them as parents, as husband and wife, as a couple, for him to say 'us'. We're not as separated as Mari believes. The five Cheevers are still some ragged sort of 'us'.

'I mean "actual" codes,' Mari is saying. 'Coded messages *within* his writings.'

I have not been listening. 'Wait a minute. Give me that again. You're saying . . . ?'

'He uses the word "code" three times in his last book, *Waterlife*.'

'The whole thing's a code. Nobody can understand that stuff. How can he write for such a limited audience – himself. How can they publish it?'

'He's a great mind, Cheevey. People said the same thing about *Finnegan's Wake*, and there are riches in there. People are going to revere Coretti the way they revere Joyce, even more because he's a true philosopher. And I'm going to help. I'm going to be the channel, a kind of biographer of the man, and now I'm on to this code thing. It's my idea. I think in *Waterlife* he was really playing a word game, a mind game with us, and he has hidden his message. It's there, but in code. That's what he *says* – practically.' She quotes from memory. '"Torquing through cosmos dust on dust fuel gone all decoders on fritz." We've lost the code, he says, forgotten it, so I'm proposing that he built an actual word code into the book. What do you know about code-breaking?'

'Nothing.'

'Well, I'm checking out books on it. I'm very enthusiastic about this.'

That's *something*, I think. At least she's positive about something. I'm suddenly very tired, legs shot from the morning run, the work and even the pool games.

'I'm beat, Mari.'

'What d'you think about the code thing?'

'You might be on to something.'

'Don't patronize.'

'No, I mean it. I've always wondered why somebody would write such obscure stuff. Maybe it was a game – a kind of test. A secret.'

'And nobody got it, and so he went away. He gave up, dropped out of sight. But I'm going to crack it, Cheeve.'

I reach back toward her with my palm turned up. She slaps it lightly.

'Now I've got to go to bed.'

'It's early.'

'I'm shot.'

'All right.'

'Cover his eyes. I'm going to open the door.'

'It's okay. I have to move him now.'

I get out and bend the seat down, and Mari struggles through the opening, cradling Ballyhoo. We both stand outside the car, and the boy lets out a whimper, burrowing into her neck.

'Let me take him,' I say, no longer whispering.

'Just for a minute. Don't let him get cold.' He murmurs again like a puppy, half awake, annoyed at being passed around, but soon I've got him close against me and he nestles in. He's a little damp with sweat. To soothe him, I sway as I stand there, like a sailor on a slow-rolling sea. Mari and I look up at the night sky and don't speak for a while. It's clearer than usual. No moon. One handful of stars scattered like seed. 'You think there's life up there?' I'm tired and not very serious about this question. It's just talk.

'No. No life. No death.'

'No death?' I never thought about it in those terms. 'Just the universe dying,' I say, 'collapsing in or something? I think I read that. Just a theory.'

'Universes don't die,' she says softly, looking above. 'They have no predators.'

I close my eyes a moment, feeling Ballyhoo's moist softness against me, heavy with sleep. We are breathing together at this moment, his little body rising and falling with my chest as if he is a part of me, and I am a part of him.

I shower in the house, and speak to no one. I am exhausted, climbing the steps to my room, but I sit up and watch my troops glittering in the light. My new sergeant of the Rifle Brigade is finished, but he still stands on the table, apart from the rest of the soldiers. I decide it's time he joined the ranks, but I don't bring him to the shelves. Instead, I begin to pick up the others, lifting them carefully, laying them gently across my palm, bringing them to the table by threes and fours until the new figure is surrounded by a hundred Scots and Welsh, French, Dutch, African and Indian troops. I enjoy carrying them, feeling the familiar weight of them, and by setting them up on the table I seem to give them life. They stare at the new soldier. He stares at them. I put my face at table-top level to gaze into the bright colors, into the tiny faces. My body aches and my eyes ask for sleep, but I keep studying my men from several angles, and when the telephone rings, I realize why I didn't go to bed in the first place. Without being conscious of it, I knew she would call, and I was waiting for it.

'Hi.'

Mari is speaking low-voiced from her kitchen again, her family asleep.

'Cheeve, did the sloth get its name from the sin, or did the name of the sin come first, and then, when they discovered the animal, they named him after the sin because he seemed so lazy?'

'I only know history.'

'That's history.'

'I only know military history.'

'Who won at Gettysburg?'

'Mike Tyson. Third round, TKO.'

'Thanks for tonight, Cheeve.'

'Sure.'

'I love you.'

'See? See, Mari? *Something's* all right.'

'Yeah. Something. Good night.'

''Night.'

I hang up, and leave my army where it stands. I snap off the lights and slide into bed and send myself into sleep like throwing a stone through a window.

'This one we just reduced.'

My father says that about every television set he shows to every customer. He has always said it, at least from the time I started at the store as a sweeper and duster at age fourteen. I watch him now with a man who seems too young for his clothes. He's wearing a bulky, older suit with a white shirt and plain blue tie. Even the neck of the shirt is too big for the guy. He seems no older than I am, just as tall and thinner. His pants are too short. I can see the tops of his scuffed wingtips. Who sent him out in his father's clothes? I'm thinking. Or is he flush with his first paycheck from his first grown-up job, out looking for his first television set? He has the look of those dedicated young men, dressed awkwardly in Sunday clothes, who try to sell you Bibles or give you pamphlets.

'Still too expensive for me,' he says quietly with an embarrassed grin.

'Well, we have these smaller sets.' My dad walks him to another shelf and snaps on a set while the young man stares hard, not at the screen – where the shopping channel appears – but at the prices.

'These are also reduced.'

The man coughs into his hand and mutters something I don't hear. I will bet my dad isn't listening. He's watching the screen and studying a necklace that's for sale. The man coughs again.

'Uuh, still a little high. I guess I'll come back . . .'

My father is staring at the screen. He's the same height as the boy (my height, too) but he has sagged in the last five years. He's not fat, but loose. His face, longish like mine, has softened, too, like overripe fruit, softened and slightly discolored here and there. He brushes his hair in a careful pattern to hid the thinness now, and I notice how much he works his mouth when he's not speaking, a nervous habit, I suppose, pursing and flattening his lips. The young man starts to edge away and I walk over there.

'What did you have in mind,' I ask, 'as far as budget?'

Now my father turns from the screen and stares at me, but I'm focused on the customer.

'Well, uh . . . I need a VCR, too, so I can't spend so much on the set. I don't . . .'

'Why don't we look at these TV-VCR combinations?' I gesture to a table, but the young man is in escape mode. I see the fear in his eyes. He has approached the buying climax, and he has choked. The prices have beaten down his courage. He pictures all that money draining away. It's a kind of shoppers' panic. I've seen cases of this before and suffered from the same disease.

'Thanks anyway,' and he's gone.

My dad turns back to the screen. They're showing a watch now. 'Why'd you come over?' he asks me, and I'm struck by how often he and Phil speak to me without looking at me. It's very presumptuous, really, when I think about it, as if they are always sure I'm standing there to receive their words, waiting, watching them – and I usually am.

'You had zoned into the TV, Dad. He was talking, and you didn't hear him.'

My dad says, 'What?' still looking at the watch with the Roman dial and turquoise inlay band.

This makes me smile. I clap him on the shoulder. 'Let's get lunch, Dad. I'm buying.'

Now he turns to me. His eyes are grey, like mine, and there seems to be some humour shining deep inside them. I can see glimmers. It seldom makes it all the way to the surface – but it's glimmering now, half-submerged.

'That means McDonalds, I suppose.'

'I'll go Arby's. I'll go Fatburger. I'll even go Johnny Rockets.'

'Just bring something back for me,' he says. 'You have money?'

'Yeah, Dad, but I wanted to talk.'

'Oh. How much is *this* going to cost me?'

He's not smiling, and he has just swept all the fun out of my face, too. Every third sentence of his is about money.

'It's not about money. It's about my party. My birthday.'

His face actually seems to darken. I don't know why. He turns back to the set. I turn the set off. He stares at me with a flicker of anger. I step closer to him, breathing in deeply to stay calm and steady.

'Dad, I'm turning twenty. It's important to me. I'm having a party Saturday. I'm paying for everything. It's just a barbecue in Palisades Park, this Saturday, and I'd like you and Mom to come. You don't have to stay long.'

He just stares and sighs, and his eyes go off me again, but he's not drifting. He's thinking a heavy thought.

'What do you say?'

'You'll have to talk to your mother.'

'I will. Sure, I'll talk to her, but I'm talking to you now. Mari'll be there and Ballyhoo and Benko and a few other friends – after you close the store. Just pick up Mom and come over for a while, have a burger. Benko'll make 'em. He's excellent. Okay?'

He slowly lifts his big hands and puts them on my shoulders. He doesn't often touch me. His face has softened. 'Twenty,' he says. I stare at him and nod, wondering. Now we're both nodding, and his hands squeeze my shoulders for one second before letting go, like a very subtle hug.

'Ask your mother.'

His eyes sweep the place for customers. There aren't any. He moves away toward the counter, and I watch him. He walks slowly, glancing to his right at a row of eight sets all showing a soap opera, a close-up now of a nurse with a very intense look, and then glancing to his left at a big screen with the volume on, but low, where a baseball game appears, a pitcher warming up. We get the steady, distant sound of the crowd, like a seashell held to the ear. He pauses in the midst of the sets and slowly glances left, glances right, as though choosing which way to go, as if, when he moves again, he will enter one screen or the other, walk into the soap, disappear in the crowd in the bleachers. I find myself calling out to him, my words thrown to him like a rope, wondering if he'll hold on, if he'll stay.

'So, you want me to bring back a hamburger?'

He seems to have chosen the baseball game, watching the batter now, but he holds up two fingers. 'Chicken sandwich,' he says. 'Two.'

I turn and head out the door, feeling tight in my stomach

and confused. The sun hits me hard, and I reach for my sunglasses, but I must have misplaced them. While I'm checking pockets, I notice that Jack-o-lantern has come early today. He is sitting on the sidewalk, his dirty bags and blankets beside him. His flabby face is turned to our store window, big round eyes full of expression as he speaks to his image in the glass.

I move closer to the man, and he drops his voice but keeps talking. I can smell his unwashed body and clothing. He seems to be sharing an important secret with the man in the glass today, his puffy lips moving rapidly. I get a peek at his gappy mouth, a tooth in place every few inches like the battlement of a castle. His tongue gives him a slight lisp, darting between the gaps. I hear the hurried words, 'Absolutely, absolutely. Swear to God. There's evidence.'

I move closer now and squat down, trying not to breathe through my nose so I don't receive the full force of his odor. His words turn to whispers and then stop. He does not look at me.

'So, Jack. You know where Palisades Park is? The north end? Saturday. Four days from now. Six o'clock or so. It's my birthday party. No gift necessary. Free burgers. Okay? Jack?'

He moves his head about as if confused and turns again to his image in the glass, as if seeking comfort from a familiar and friendly face. I gesture toward the window with my head.

'He's invited, too. Okay?'

'What can I do?'
  'Set the table.'
  'Sharp knives?'
  'Everything.'
  'Cloth napkins?'
  'Don't get fancy.'

My mother's humor, dry and deadpan, may be buried, but it's not dead. Like my dad's, it still glimmers. It was always slight, like a twenty-five watt bulb. Now it's more of a nightlight.

'Bowls?'

'No, but a salad plate.'

'Oh? We're not having a salad *entrée* tonight? What did you make, Mom?'

'Quiche.'

'*Formidable*.' I have piled all the plates, silverware, paper napkins for a one-trip operation into the dining room.

'Don't drop that.'

'Have I ever dropped it?'

'Because I've always told you not to.'

'You're a laugh, Mom.'

'I'm a scream.'

My mother has been thin and small and fragile-seeming as long as I recall, and now her back pain and the awkward, rigid movement it causes have increased the feeling of frailty about her, but in spite of this, she has always done her work – as she is doing it now, moving from counter to cutting board to stove, creating dinner.

'Is your father home?'

'Any minute, I suppose.'

'It'll be ready at six-thirty.'

'Always is. Efficiency is your middle name, Mom.'

'I wish it was. I hate "Emma."'

'What are you doing Saturday at this time?'

'Why?'

'I thought I'd have a birthday party.'

'Here?' I hear fear in the word.

'No. At the park. A barbecue. Benko and I will do it. I would just like you to show up.'

She keeps wiping her hands on a dish towel. They couldn't possibly be wet anymore. She is staring out the window, which is only a view of a large oleander shrub, and wiping and wiping.

'Mom?'

'Your birthday isn't till Wednesday.'

'No kidding.'

'I mean, I thought I'd make a cake for Wednesday. I planned to.'

'That's fine. But this is Saturday. Mari and Ballyhoo will be there, even Phil and Benko and a couple of friends from school, and I'd like you and Dad to show up – just for a little while. I mean, you can stay as long as you like if you *want* to, but you don't *have* to stay long, and you don't have to bake anything.'

She stares and wipes her dry hands.

'Ask your father.'

'What is it with you and Dad? Look, do you *want* to come?'

'Why would you want *us*?'

'Why?! Because it's my birthday. Twenty is a milestone. Goodbye child. Goodbye teenager. Hello early manhood. It's a passage, Mom. I'd go out and kill a lion, but they don't like that in Santa Monica, and I'm not going to do that sun dance with the sticks in my chest, so I've settled on a barbecue in the park with everybody who's close to me.'

She stops wiping, but she is still staring at that bush, and from the side view I have, I can see that her eyes are filling.

'What, Mom?'

'Ask your father.'

'I *did*.'

'What did he say?'

'Guess.'

Now she turns to me. There is a distant threat of tears, but hardness now, too, the old anger.

'Tell me what he said.'

'He said, "Ask your mother."'

'Oh, perfect.'

'Well, that's what *you* said. Jesus, I don't see what's so difficult or complicated or momentous about this decision. It's not like I'm asking to borrow anybody's car.'

Her anger chases away the possibility of weeping. Her lips twist to match the slight, stiff twist of her shoulders.

'Don't get smart.'

'I *am* smart, Mom.'

'I don't know about the party. I don't know. I was thinking next Wednesday . . . next Wednesday we'd have a cake – here – the three of us.'

'We can still do that.'

'I don't know. We'll see about Saturday. We'll probably come. We'll probably come for a little while.'

'Great. The north end – by the barbecues. I'll be there from like four on – with Benko. You'll come, then.'

'We'll probably come. We probably will.'

'You haven't seen Mari and Ballyhoo in a . . .'

'Don't call him that. Will you please call him Billy?'

'What's the matter, Mom?'

'Nothing. My back hurts. Don't set for me. I'll eat in my room.'

'Okay. *D'accord*, Mama. And don't worry about gifts or anything. Don't shop. Just show up.'

'Yes.'

'Yes?!'

'*Oui*.'

'*Merci*, Mama.'

Mari and I have both studied French. At first my mother encouraged this and used the language often around the house, but when her children passed her by and became more proficient, with better pronunciation, she began to hold back – not exactly jealous, Mari says, but afraid that we were taking something that belonged to her. She claims all things French as her particular and peculiar dream. Now I only speak small-talk French with her, and she seldom responds, but she does now.

'*Certainement, mon fils. Excuse-moi.*'

She walks by me and through the hall into her bedroom to sit or lie in there for the ten minutes until dinner. I walk to the window and stare at the oleander, as if the shrub will help me understand what she was thinking when she almost wept. I search the lush white blossoms and long slender leaves for messages.

I am sitting cross-legged on top of a beaten-up picnic table, claiming it with my body, as other families party in the park around me. One group, Armenian or Greek, are grilling skewers of meat and vegetables, and though it's only 4:15, the smell is opening up my stomach. The picnic tables are chained down on a cracked and bulging cement pad under a grove of twisted, shaggy trees. Saturday has blown in cool and gusty, and now and then the trees hiss overhead and sticks fall and dead leaves go airborne. Everyone seems more active with the heat wave cracked, and the air feels lighter, cleaner. Over my left shoulder, the Santa Monica mountains stand sharply defined for once, the haze blown away.

I'm at the northern limit of the long, narrow park, the turning place for the determined joggers and walkers who reach the tables and make a small circle and go back the way they came, like mechanical figures on some great clock.

In front of me is a group of children in clothing so bright, the colors themselves seem to be laughing. One of them is batting at a piñata as the others wait, staring above them like worshippers, praying for rain. There couldn't be a better party day ordered and delivered, and I smile at the revelry around me, glancing to the street now and then, looking for Benko's car.

I have a bag of bread with me, hot dog and hamburger buns, and I have my camera around my neck. I'm wearing jeans and a new blue shirt, and I strolled to the park and did not jog for once so that I wouldn't be sweaty. I'm excited about the party, partly because it's year twenty, but also because everyone I asked said yes – even Rema and Donni Loma – and because of the weather, too, as if the cool wind has blown through me, chasing out dead leaves and dust and smog.

Benko arrives with Chin, a cool, quiet guy we decided to ask at the last minute. He's a big guy, a football star in high school, but now he's more interested in those obscure upper levels of math – like Benko. I hit advanced algebra like a wall and bounced off and never looked back. Chin also has one of the best comic book collections in the city. He buys and sells on his personal fax machine.

Benko and Chin have brought all the food plus Benko's grill from his home. I try and insist on paying the food bill, but they will only take a third from me, their way of saying happy birthday.

'Look at this cruddy table,' Benko says, putting down bags and six-packs of soda.

'Looks like somebody tried to eat it.'

Chin is right. There are gouges and broken-off bits on the ends and so many layers of carved graffiti that nothing is left readable. I hadn't even noticed.

'A table is a table.'

'Yeah, but we should've brought one of those party table cloths,' Benko says. 'There was a pink one there that said "Birthday Big Fella" on it. I almost bought it. This wind will wreak havoc with the paper plates, Cheeve.'

'Not once they've got food on them,' Chin says. 'Leave 'em wrapped. Hey, Cheevey, Benko says Rema is coming, and I say he's a lying scum.'

Benko is chuckling as he sets up the grill. 'Put money on it, man.'

'Everybody's coming,' I say. 'Including not one but *several* beautiful women.'

'Several?' Benko says, working on the grill. 'Rema, Donni . . . Oh, Dash!'

'And Lauren.'

'Who's that?'

'You'll see.'

Chin and Benko look at each other and start to nod.

'Better give it to him.'

'Better give it to him now.'

They have wrapped a coughdrops-sized box in tinfoil for me – my first present of the day. I'm already close to giddy, tearing the foil. It's a box of condoms with a joke label that says: 'Contains 12 "E-ride" tickets. Good at Fantasyland, Knott's Cherry Farm, Orgasmic Mountain, and Sex Flags amusement parks. You must be this tall to enter.' And there's a ruler printed along the edge of the box.

Since we're the party *givers* – Benko, Chin and I – I consider all the others to be *guests*, and the first of these to arrive are Mari, Ballyhoo and Dash, arriving in Dash's car. I'm standing on the low wall, separating the picnic area from Ocean Avenue, waving my arms and grinning like a happy-face, watching Mari bending down to Bally and pointing my way and waiting for the boy's eyes to find me. Even at forty yards I see the pleasure come into his face, the slightly embarrassed joy, and then he starts to run. I jump down from the wall, ready to gather him up, but his face changes, struck by a thought, and he suddenly turns and runs back to Mari and Dash. Mari hands him a sheet of paper and a small package, and he's running at me once more, joyous again without transition.

He's in my arms, held up to my face, his worldly grin twisting.

'Birthday hug,' I say, and he clutches my neck, even though his little hands are full.

'Gotcha present.'

'Great!'

Mari is approaching in her usual flurry of words, like a cloud of gnats that moves with her. '. . . so excited he wouldn't nap or even . . . Look at all the people! Cheeve, you don't look a day over nineteen. Show him, Bally. He's so excited. These are from him.'

I set Bally down, kneeling to be at his level, and he thrusts his little arms out at me, a gift in each hand.

'Happy birthday, Cheevey,' Dash says, and my eyes are pulled away from the boy, flicking upward to where she stands beside Mari, smiling a smile with a little wickedness in it, her pretty face framed in windblown hair. A pair of pink running shorts leaves her bare thighs gleaming at me – eye level. It's a delicious picture, but even this can't hold me now. I'm anxious to return to Bally.

'Hi, Dash! Glad you could come.' Then I look back at the boy who hasn't moved an inch, his presents held out to me.

I take the sheet of paper first. It's a crayon drawing of a soldier.

'Wow!'

He has a blue coat, a stick rifle, and an enormous green hat.

'Bally, this is great!'

'I drew it. It's a soldier.'

'Wow. You sure you didn't cut this out of a book?!'

'Nope. I drew it.'

I can hear Mari moving on toward Benko with, 'I heard you were cooking today, Benko, so I ate already – just kidding. I'm starving,' and Dash continues talking to me.

'How does adulthood feel? Are you ready?'

But I can't dilute Ballyhoo's moment as he proudly pushes his second present toward me. It's wrapped in tissue paper and a rubber band.

'What's this?'

'Open it.'

'Another one?!'

'Yep.'

'I'm still a kid until Wednesday,' I say to Dash as I pull apart the tissue paper. 'Holy Kaboly! Is this for me?!'

It is one-half of a metal cap gun, having come apart at its seam, but this is the half with the trigger and inner springs, and I click it, testing the action. It's a snub-nose police kind of gun. I look from the gun to the boy and see in his eyes that this is a moment he had been imagining and waiting for, and it is weighty for him and full of joy. This is a personal present, not something purchased or suggested by a parent, but picked from his own private treasure, his first personal present to his Uncle Cheevey. I know it's the best present I will receive all day – maybe the best one ever.

'Wow, Bally, thank you! It works, too, and it looks so *real*. Do you have the other half? We could have matching guns.'

'Lost it.'

'This is great. Thank-you hug.' Even though he's one step away, he runs that step and circles my neck. I hear Dash say, 'Awww,' and I lift the boy and carry him to the table.

In the bursts of overlapping conversations, Chin is introduced; the weather is gloried in; I am presented with gifts from Dash and Mari; and Dash silences everyone with one of her very brazen and throaty laughs as she staggers about, holding the condom box. 'Did you *see* this?' she shrieks to Mari.

Mari reads and makes a face. 'Oh God – a male bonding type gift. It's beneath you, Benko.'

'Chin picked it out.'

'Bullshit, man.'

'I love it,' Dash is still chuckling wildly.

Bally is edging toward the group of his peers around the dead piñata, watching with feigned indifference. I receive a sweater from Mari and hug her, during which she never stops talking.

'I knew summer would end eventually. I mean, I had faith when everybody else couldn't stand to *look* at coats and sweaters. Hold it up. See? Great with his eyes. It goes fine with jeans, Cheeve, but not that shirt.'

During the hug, as our faces pass closely, I smell the wine on her breath and feel a catch in my chest, a small shock of fear and disappointment.

'Happy birthday.' She kisses my cheek.

'Thanks.'

'Open mine now.' Dash tosses her small package, and I catch it, tear at the paper and slip out a pair of sunglasses.

'Hey, great!'

'Mari said you lost yours.'

'I *did*. Thank you.'

'I think they'll be right on your face.'

I put them on. 'Benko?'

'Cutting edge, man.'

'Chin, how do I look?'

'Cool.'

Benko is nodding, preparing the briquets now. 'Cutting edge of fashion, Cheeve – and frog-like.'

I shoot Benko with my half-a-cap gun and then shout to Ballyhoo, 'Bally! Come on! Quick!'

I run and dive behind a tree and begin clicking the gun at imaginary enemies, and Ballyhoo joins me and sinks immediately into the action, pointing a finger gun and firing with a sound like 'Pachoo! Pachoo!'

'There's too many, Bally! What'll we do?'

'Get 'em! Pachoo. Pachoo. Pachoo.'

*   *   *

As Benko cooks, I begin using my camera, snapping one of Dash, mugging with the cook, and one of Mari and Chin as she pulls a conversation from him and waves me away with: 'No media. No media.' I hand Bally the half-gun to pose with, and he immediately drops to one knee and points the gun at the camera, making a menacing face, and I want to run and grab him and crunch him in a hug, but I take the picture.

Rema and Donni arrive with John, a Pakistani student we know slightly. He's kind of British proper, tall with the posture of a lance, wearing dress slacks and even a tie. Rema and Donni are in baggy walking shorts and T-shirts with sweatshirts tied at their waists. They are very pretty, and they make me feel proud, waving and smiling as they walk toward the group. I'm showing off a bit, I suppose, hoping to impress Mari and Dash and Chin with the arrival of these girls. John is carrying a large bag, and when they reach the table, he pulls out three bottles of champagne – cold.

'Happy birthday, Cheevey.'

'It's from all of us,' Donni says.

'But John's idea, and he wouldn't take our money,' Rema says in her low-voiced accent. She is Venezuelan with definite pre-Columbian traces in her face bones and perfectly black hair which she slowly draws away from the side of her face like a curtain, smiling and saying, 'Happy birthday.'

'Many returns,' John adds, and his nod to me is just short of a bow. 'I hope you don't mind my barging in, but . . .'

'Not at all. Welcome! This is great.'

'Anyway, we *needed* John,' Donni says, 'since nobody else could buy the champagne.'

'Pop it, man,' Benko says.

'Better watch out for the police, though,' Mari says, reminding me of our mother.

Introductions are made amid the popping of corks; plastic glasses are filled and foaming over. I see Benko give Chin an elbow and a look that says: 'I *told* you the girls were coming,' and within Dash's quick study of Rema, over the lip of her glass, I think I see a glimmer of competition.

The gusts of wind continue to sweep the day clean, and I'm reminded of the windows of my father's store. It is as if some giant squeegee has passed over this scene in the park, leaving it wet and shining, with all the colors crisp. More twigs and leaves rain on us, and the long rows of tall palms drop some of their heavy fronds. I breathe in each gust, and the day fills me and expands me. I am light and joyous and at ease, and soon the champagne goes to work, and I feel afloat, but on a gentle sea.

We are all seated around the table now. Having savaged Benko's burgers and dogs, we've moved on to the carrot cake, careful to leave some food for late-comers like Phil and my parents. I am the focus of the teasing, and glad to be.

'At twenty,' Mari is saying, 'you put away childish things. Without even realizing it, you suddenly mature, Cheeve. It's a special hormone that clicks in. You find yourself buying wing-tips, thinking about things like . . . insurance. You hear yourself saying things like: "Well, the Republicans aren't all *that* bad."'

The laughter is very loud, and gets louder when John admits quietly that he *is* a Republican.

'Tell us what you're going to *do*, Cheevey,' Donni says. 'Something historical, probably.'

'Like a chimney sweep,' Benko offers.

'Tell you what,' Dash says, and *everything* she says has a wicked slant today – or is it me, or the champagne? 'Just tell us your attributes, and *we'll* tell you what you're suited for.'

'He's tall.'

'He's well-meaning,' Mari says, and for some reason we all laugh.

'He can run long distances.'

'Like a horse.'

'So far we have a tall, well-meaning horse.'

'Mr Ed.'

I raise both hands. 'I do have a goal. I know exactly what I want to do. One summer we drove up through the redwood country – remember, Mari? I was ten or so.'

'I remember. Dad wouldn't stop unless there was a Motel Six.'

'Well, we stayed at this private campground one night, and part of it was surrounded by a log stockade. It was built to look like a fort, and it was called . . .'

'Fort McGuire,' Mari says. 'Sooo hokey.'

'They had hayrides and fake Indian dances and square dances, and all the while this one guy was parading around in buckskin, carrying a musket. He was kind of a greeter employed by the campground, and part of the atmosphere. When he wasn't greeting people and posing for pictures, he'd walk along the stockade, looking over the wall like he was some guard, looking for Indians in the forest. He even had a coonskin cap. I followed him all over. Some of the kids laughed at him, but I just kept looking at him and following him. I wanted to dress like that. I wanted to carry the musket. I wanted to *be* that guy – and I still do. And I would do it very well. He didn't even know much about the musket, 'cause I asked him, and I knew more than he did, *and* he wore a goddamn' watch! He wore a modern wristwatch and kept checking it. So *I* would be the perfect greeter at Fort McGuire because I know the era, I know the weapons, and I would *not* wear a watch. So the day after I graduate from Santa Monica College, I'm off to Fort McGuire to take over for this guy – wish me luck.'

I raise my glass, and they are all staring at me, some of

them smiling, some not, and I wonder if I have said too much, or made it sound too serious, but then, one by one, their glasses come up in slow salute.

'To Fort McGuire.'

'To my brother – born too late.'

'To career goals – no matter how weird.'

The laughter has taken over again, and Benko stands and shouts, lifting his glass.

'To the regiment!'

It's 6.45 and I'm happy to see Ballyhoo sitting in Rema's lap as he shows her and Donni the picture he drew for me. Mari is now in an intense conversation with John, but I can't overhear because the rest of us have moved away from the tables to play catch with a Frisbee Benko dug out of his car. Dash is at her best, playing with four men, enjoying the attention, but she's also very athletic and as good at the game as any of us except Chin. I'm not sure if she's aware how showy she is, or if her movements and her bending in those high-cut shorts is purely natural and unselfconscious. The thin pink shorts don't hide but just translucently screen from us her beautiful upper thighs and ass and her wonderful, lacy underpants. The pants are white and each glimpse of them is like a little gift, a bright offering, like her smile and the smile in her eyes, all bright offerings as she plays the game.

'Cheevey?' someone calls, and we all turn to look.

Lauren is standing about thirty feet from me, halfway between the street and our game. I smile and wave, and she returns the smile, but doesn't come over, so I jog to *her*. She is wearing jeans and a bright green flannel shirt that makes her short red hair more fiery and deepens the green in her eyes. She wears no makeup, and standing there in the grass, she looks like a woman on a ranch or a farm, somebody who feels comfortable with the earth.

Any minute, I'm going to imagine birds landing on her shoulders and a little deer coming to nuzzle her hand – but it's true. She radiates an earthy warmth. As I near her, she opens her arms, and I am surprised by the tight embrace she offers, saying with her arms, 'Wait, hold on, these are important, these connections.'

'Happy birthday.'

We part, but I'm embraced again by her smile and touched by her kind eyes.

'I'm so glad you came! Phil isn't here yet. Come on, I'll . . .'

Now her expression changes, the joy moving toward concern, sympathy. I know immediately my brother has decided not to come.

'I'm sorry, but Phil's not going to make it.'

I'm just staring at her. She takes her time, begins the explanation, but I feel punched in the body, and no matter what words come out of her now, I'm going to feel simply that I'm not very important to Phil. I've always felt that.

'He came home early from the job – to get ready, I guess, but he started drinking. He came over – we live next door, did you know that?'

'No, I . . .'

'And I could see he was in no condition to come – so did *he*. I'm really sorry. And *he's* sorry, Cheevey.'

I'm nodding as I absorb all this. 'He said he was sorry?'

'Yes, he did.'

'And he sent you to tell me?'

'Well, I was ready to come with him. Molly and I. We were . . .'

'Molly?'

'My daughter. She's in the car. But he was in no condition . . .'

'Why did he start drinking? I mean, it's early.' I don't really *care* why he started drinking, but I'm angry now, and as we speak my eyes drift to the street. I spot her Civic and see, in the passenger side window, the face of a blonde little girl staring back at me.

'He was talking about your parents, worried about seeing them.'

'Worried?'

'Well, angry. He was bitching about them. I'm really sorry. He wanted me to give you something. It's in the car.' Now she puts a hand on my shoulder, studying me, her eyes very direct. I'm acting a bit tough, pissed, but she can see through that to the hurt, I know she can. 'He *wanted* to come. He planned to. He asked me days ago – and Molly. He just . . .' She shrugs.

'Well, that's too bad. Too bad. Mari is here – our sister. He gets along with her all right – sort of – and some friends of mine. My parents aren't even here yet. It's too bad. I knew he and my dad weren't speaking but . . . I thought this would be good for them – neutral territory.' I'm just babbling now, while I recover from the punch, trying to sound normal and mature about it. After all, it's just a birthday party. It's not like I'm a kid. 'Grow up,' part of me is saying, 'you're twenty, almost, and these things don't matter so much.'

'And Phil is an uncle. He almost never sees his nephew Ballyhoo . . . uh, Billy – a great kid. I want you to meet him, you and Molly.'

'Maybe next time, Cheevey.'

'You're not coming – to the party?'

'Oh, no, thank you. We're just sort of messengers today, you know – without Phil . . .'

'But you could still come. You're *here*.'

'Thank you. You're really sweet, but I just wanted to explain and bring your present. I'll get it.'

I walk with her to her car. 'I bet it was your idea to come and tell me. Phil would've just not shown up. I appreciate it, Lauren. Really. I think you're a very special person.' Part of my brain is trying to stop the other part from talking too much. The first part is afraid of sounding like an idiot, but the second part is made brave by the wine and the glorious day. 'I'd like to get to know you – and your daughter.'

'Well, *thank* you, Cheevey. And here she is.' Lauren opens the door, and Molly, a blue-eyed and tousled blonde, presents a shy smile to her mom and then turns it on me.

'Molly, this is Phil's brother. They call him Cheevey.'

'Hi.' It's a little, breathy 'hi' with a half-raised hand while one foot kicks lightly and repeatedly at the bottom of the seat. She has some freckles and a tiny scar on her chin.

'Hi, Molly, nice to meet you.' I offer a hand, and she puts out hers, and I take it and shake it once. It's limp and cool. 'Do you think I look like Phil?'

'No.' Her smile grows a bit as she searches my face for signs of Phil, and I search hers for signs of Lauren. I see Lauren's mouth and nose, I guess, but mostly I'm looking for the peace – and it's there. This child has a repose about her. I don't know why she reminds me of Victorian children. Maybe I'm thinking of portraits I've seen. There's one in the Country Art Museum – Beaugereau, I think – a child full of ease.

'I know – I'm much better looking than Phil.' I see her smile go all the way to a brief one-note laugh, a piccolo note, her eyes widening, and Lauren is chuckling as she pulls something out of the back seat. It's not wrapped.

'Happy birthday from Phil.'

It's a tool belt, a new leather one, a very good one. It feels good in my hands and I enjoy the leathery smell and the heft of it. It *seems* like a gift from Phil. It evokes him, as if he's just put his strong hand in mine to hold on and say happy birthday. I'm touched by this. It takes most of the hurt away and all of the anger, leaving just a stain of sadness. He couldn't face Dad – didn't want to see him. He's not that comfortable around Mom or Mari either, so he drank too much, and it defeated him. I guess I understand. At least he bought me this tool belt. At least he tried to come and planned to come and asked Lauren and Molly to come.

'It's great.' I keep hefting the belt. 'It's really great.'

'He has so many spare tools. He said he'll fill it for you tomorrow – on the job.'

'He said that?'

'Mm-hm. And this is from us. Molly?'

The little girl pops the glove compartment and hands me an envelope. I open it to find a really pretty birthday card, hand painted it looks like. Lauren has some of the best handwriting I've ever seen, flowing diagonally across the blank inside: 'Cheevey – birthday joys today and many more to follow. Lauren and Molly.' There is a smaller card within it. It's a gift certificate from a restaurant I've never been to, a nice one. 'Dinner for two at Angelini,' it reads.

'Wow. Thank you, this is . . . It's a beautiful card, and this present . . .'

'Have you been there?'

'No, but . . .'

'Do you like Italian food?'

'Sure. Oh, yeah. This is great! Thank you both.'

'Well, I feel I should explain that my store did some work for the restaurant, and they gave me several of these freebies, so I'm passing one on to you at no expense. I confess,' she says, her eyes laughing.

'Well, still! It's a great present. What store?'

'Monica Layman Stationery.'

'Oh, in Westwood?'

'Yes, we did Angelini's menus and flyers – I design, too. Now – do you have a girlfriend to take there?'

'Well . . . no, not a girlfriend – unless Molly is free some evening?'

Molly blushes and Lauren turns a smile on me I swear I can feel, like a hat.

'I'm sure you'll find the right lucky girl.'

'Well, thank you so much. You sure you won't have some food?'

'No, thank you. We'll be going, but you have a great evening. Maybe we'll stop by the job site tomorrow and bring lunch to you and Phil.'

'That'd be great. He'll be in one lousy mood.'

'Won't he, though.' We both grin and wave, and I exchange another wave with Molly and help her close the car door. The Civic starts up and pulls away and I catch two more waves out the windows, like the little car has suddenly grown arms, a woman's arm and a child's. I strap on the tool belt and walk back to my party.

The Frisbee game halts as I walk into the flight pattern, and the players approach me as I model the belt.

'From my brother.'

'Very nice.'

'Are you a carpenter, Cheevey?'

'I help him remodel houses.'

There is a scream now that snaps all our heads around, our eyes searching all the data around the picnic tables at top speed. Mari is standing with her hands covering her mouth, her eyes wild. John is staring at her, mouth open. She rushes now to the stone wall that separates the park from the cliff and the highway and ocean below. Ballyhoo stands at that wall, gripping it, Rema on one side of him, Donni on the other, all of them staring wide-eyed at Mari, who rushes at them and kneels beside her son and brings him to her in a desperate hug.

I walk toward them, setting the pace, saying, 'It's okay. It's all right,' to the others so they don't rush past me and add to the feeling of panic and emergency. They follow me, though. We are all gathering around Mari and the boy, and

I am embarrassed for her and a little scared, too, having witnessed what she's been telling me about, how Ballyhoo disappears or *she* does, and how she thinks she's lost him. It's worse than I thought. Her scream, a kind of brief yelp, was a high, torn note that still rings in my head, a kind of alarm of pain and fear. Most of the people around us are still staring, wondering, and I feel bad for Bally, too. This must scare the hell out of him.

All the frightened eyes – Donni's, Rema's, John's – turn to me now as I near my sister and squat down to be close to her and her son. I hear Bally say, crushed against her, 'I'm all right, Mom.' It sounds like a child speaking to a child, in a soothing tone.

'I know. I know, honey.' Mari speaks very softly, eyes closed, tears in her throat.

Donni and Rema begin: 'He wasn't climbing the wall or anything. He was right here with us. There was no danger. He was just right next to us.'

I turn to them. 'It's okay. I'll take care of them.' I send a look around to all the others so they'll take the hint and leave us alone, but they persist in their wonder and concern.

'She just got scared because she didn't know where he was,' I say.

'We're really sorry,' Donni says. 'We just walked with him a little ways . . .'

'No, it's okay, Donni. Really. Just give us a minute.'

They start to drift off then, moving back towards the tables. Mari is talking very softly again. The tears are still in her voice. 'I'm sorry, Cheeve. I'm so sorry. I'm really . . . so sorry.'

'It's okay. Relax now. Let go.'

Her arms slacken, then drop. She sits on her legs, staring at her son – who is staring at her. Her eyes are full, but she smiles a small, trembling smile.

'I hate to scare you like that, but Mommy gets very excited sometimes when she doesn't know where you are.'

He keeps staring, then says, 'Why don't you just call me?'

Mari laughs a brief, liquid laugh, wiping at the corners of her eyes. 'That would be too sensible. That's what I *should* do. I know that. You're right. I should.'

'Then I'll come.'

'I know you will. I'll try that. I'll try to do that.' Then she turns to me. 'I'm sorry. How stupid. Go back to your friends now.'

'I will. In a minute.' I sit in the grass beside her. Bally sits in her lap, facing me. Mari is touching his hair, smoothing it.

'It's like waking up from a dream, Cheeve, and not knowing where you are, but I don't *care* where *I* am. The thought that strikes me, the one clear thought, is that I've lost my son – and the first thing I thought of is the ocean. We're near the ocean. The water's got him. The sea.'

'Don't scare him all over again.'

'I'm sorry. Don't be scared, Bally.'

'I'm not.'

'It just hits me like a hammer, like pure truth, like a big bell – you've done the worst thing you could ever do. You've lost him. I don't know where that comes from – maybe from feeling like a lousy mother.'

'Bally, would you do me a favor? Would you go over to Donni and Rema and tell them everything's okay?'

The boy stands up, full of his mission, and stares at the group at the picnic table. 'Which ones?'

'The two girls you were with.'

'Okay.' He trots off.

'You're drinking again,' I say when the boy can't hear us. 'Maybe it comes from that.'

'Champagne on your birthday – give me a break.'

'Don't, Mari, I smelled it on your breath when you came.'

She looks at the grass, and begins picking at it and then smoothing it as if it's Ballyhoo's brown hair.

'Bob and I had a fight.'

'You should see someone.'

'Yes, I should have a mad affair.'

'You know what I mean. Therapy.'

'I know what you mean.'

'Will you?'

'Yes. I will. I have to. I know that. I'll find a good psychologist. I'll have a mad affair with *him*.'

'Don't joke.'

'Don't tell me what to do. You're still nineteen until Wednesday.'

'I *am* telling you. Find a very good psychologist and split the bill with Phil. You guys could take turns.'

She looks at me. 'He's not coming, is he? I *told* you.'

'He drank himself stupid so he wouldn't have to come. What is it with you two and alcohol?'

'What do you mean, "what is it"? You know what it is. It's cowardice. We're babies. Who was that woman – what are you *wearing*?!'

'It's a tool belt.'

'Some macho, sadomasochistic . . .'

'It's a *tool* belt!'

'Leather. He *would* give you leather. What an asshole he is.'

'Because he gave me leather?!'

'Was that his newest girlfriend?'

'I don't know. She's his neighbor. She's . . .'

'Phil doesn't relate to women as neighbors. Males, he fights. Women, he fucks. He only has two active areas of his frontal lobe.'

'Mari . . .'

'What? I'm not saying I'm any better – just as bad, but in a much more sophisticated way. I'm *civilized* in my neuroses. Will you go back to your friends now? Come on, help me up. We'll go back, and your crazy sister will apologize. God, those girls are pretty, Cheevey. Rema is *beautiful*. John is very interesting. We were discussing the Himalayas. He's *seen* them. I've only imagined them. So which one of us carries the *true* Himalayas in our mind, the ones closest to classical *truth*?'

'Are you going to see a therapist?'

'Yes! I see them every day. There are *droves* of them in Santa Monica. I bet that's one there, jogging. Let's ask him.'

'I give up.'

'No, you don't, Cheevey. You *should*, but you don't. Hand.'

She reaches out toward me. I frown and rise and take her hand and pull her up.

'You're tho thtrong.'

'Yeah.'

'You are. You're the strongest Cheever. Did you know that? I told you Phil wouldn't come *and* our parents wouldn't come, but you have fine friends, and your sister stands with you, for all *that's* worth, and Ballyhoo adores you, and Dash thinks you're a hunk.'

'Ha!'

'She *said* that.'

We are walking back to the group. They seem more relaxed now that Bally is among them and now that they see Mari and I speaking and smiling.

'She said, "Your brother is a slender hunk."'

'She *said* that?'

'We'll ask her.'

'No!'

'Anyway, I hope you're not too disappointed about the no-shows.'

'Mom and Dad still might come.'

'It's almost seven, Cheeve. Christ, will you let go of that. Don't *let* them disappoint you. I don't give them the chance anymore.'

'I *am* upset about Jack.'

'Who's Jack?'

'Jack-o-lantern. He's the crazy guy who sits outside the store all the time and talks to his reflection in the glass. I invited *both* of them. I thought at least one would come.'

Mari throws her head back slightly in what is for her a hearty laugh, and all the tension is swept away as if by another billowing of the cool, clean wind.

By 7.10 we've eaten every scrap of food and are losing daylight, and everyone is in the early stages of leaving. I'm fielding dozens of compliments about the party and congratulations on my birthday. In the midst of this, Benko catches my attention.

'Your dad, Cheeve.'

I look toward the street and see him approaching across the grass, pausing for a jogger, coming on, and I'm struck by how little I see him out of context anymore. He looks strange to me, not in his store, not in our home, just a man, tall, slightly rumpled, but still with a worn sense of style about him, looking pretty good in a crew-neck sweater and slacks. His thin hair is tweaked up by a gust of wind as if some prankster just ran up behind him. He comes on, vaguely smiling, unaware of this high swirl of hair. He is pale. I hadn't noticed this indoors. And his clothes are too old, not just dated, but slightly unraveled and minutely frayed. I'm embarrassed by this. I glance at Mari to see if she has seen him. She is pointing at him and urging Ballyhoo to go to Grampa, but the boy hesitates. Grampa is only an acquaintance.

'Hi, Dad, glad you came.'

For some reason I offer my hand, and he shakes it and says a few indefinite words, scanning the crowd.

'Well, I . . . Yeah. Sure.'

Now he's waving at Mari and grinning at Ballyhoo who approaches slowly with a shy, twisting grin. I wonder if my father will shake *his* hand, but instead he tousles the boy's hair.

'Hi there, Billy. Hi, Mari.'

'Dad.' Mari gives him a small, suspicious smile. 'You missed the food.'

'Oh well, I . . . yeah.'

'Dad, you know Benko and Dash . . .' I introduce him to the others and he waves a little awkwardly, being polite, but there is a tightness to his grin. When his eyes settle back on me, there is no humor in them.

'Don't let me interrupt anything here. I just . . . your mother isn't up to it. Her back. And we want to have a celebration at home. So, are you coming home after this?'

'I guess so. I thought we were going to celebrate Wednesday.' I'm not really surprised my mother didn't come. I'm more surprised that my dad *is* here, making the gesture.

'Well, we sort of moved it up – as long as you're having a party, might as well have two and, you know, get . . . you know.'

'Get it all over with,' Mari says, the sarcasm barely showing. My dad ignores it.

'So anyway, she baked something. When do you think you'll be home?'

'I don't know. Later.' I want this day in the park to exist by itself. I want time to absorb it. I don't want to go straight home. I don't want a second party. 'Let's do it Wednesday.'

'Can't. Can't, Claudey. She baked.'

'Her back hurts too much for her to come here and *still* she bakes?' Mari shakes her head as if in awe. 'What a trooper.'

Dad looks away and frowns at the ocean. I'm uncomfortable now. 'I'll be home in an hour. About an hour.'

'Okay. Good, good. Go on with your party. I won't interrupt.' He's already stepping backwards and waving, a big wave that takes in everybody.

'This man is your grandfather, Ballyhoo,' Mari is saying. 'Take a quick look before he leaves.'

I turn to Mari to stop her with a look, and I'm surprised to see no anger in her face, only hurt. When I turn back, Dad is walking away across the grass. I realize now why he seems so out of place. He is at least a mile from any of his television sets. His steps pick up speed, and I imagine him rushing home in panic and hurrying into his den to snap on the set so that the screen can soothe him and take him in like a lost child and hold him – and ask nothing from him.

I walk Dash and Mari to Dash's car, carrying Ballyhoo. I get hugs from all and a quick kiss in the ear from Dash, a little lunge with her lips as we're hugging goodbye and a chill when the tip of her tongue touches me in there. She laughs, and I jump a little, grinning, blushing, I guess, and Mari is saying to her, 'What did you *do*?!' as they enter the car. I wave them off and turn to send a final wave to Rema, Donni, and John – but they're all facing away at this moment, walking far down the park. As they walk away, I see Rema put her hand in John's hand – and they walk on that way. I'm finally aware that my mouth is open as I stare at them, and I can feel my heartbeat all through my chest and head. I turn to Benko to see if he has seen this, and Benko, who misses nothing, has caught it. He looks downhearted.

*   *   *

Chin has helped us pack away the grill, and now he plays catch with himself, tossing the Frisbee straight up, sometimes catching it behind his back. I think he's aware that Benko and I need a little time together, so he's keeping busy. Benko and I sit on the cement wall near the tables, watching the ocean darken by degrees.

'So, Cheeve, in a few years you'll be off to Fort McGuire to walk the parapets. Not a bad life.'

'Nah. I'd hate it.' I shake my head awhile, remembering. 'If I were that guy, I'd take my musket and walk away from all the kids and cameras and disappear into the forest – where it would suddenly *be* 1745, and I'd live out my life like Hawkeye, rescuing beautiful women and being a blood brother to the noble Mohicans.'

'Spreading syphilis among the tribes.'

'No, there are no diseases in Cooper.'

'No shitting in the woods, either. Cooper was clean.'

'What about you, Benko?'

He turns from the ocean and gestures with his head into the park. 'Look at the ground – under the palms.'

The ground is littered with stiff, broken fronds.

'Tomorrow – or maybe Monday – some guy is going to come through here driving an electric cart, pulling a big dumpster, and, one by one, he's going to pick up all the palm leaves and throw 'em in and cart them off. That'll be me. Simple, low-stress occupation. Good benefits, and it contributes to the well-being of man and womankind.'

Now we're both looking at the near-empty park, and I'm nodding slightly. 'Looks like a two-man job, Benk.'

'You're hired.'

'Thanks.'

Neither one of us wants to mention Rema, but she's there. The silence is all about Rema.

'Is Mari okay?' Benko asks.

'No.'

Then he turns and studies me.

'How about you?'

I look at him a moment. 'All in all, it was a good day.'

He shakes his head slowly in concern. 'You excuse everybody of everything, Cheeve. You're a priest, a real priest of a guy.'

I shrug, not wanting to examine the day, for the good moments and the bad, pick it apart. 'Ballyhoo kicks it, doesn't he?'

'Kicks it all the way.'

Then we're busy for another minute, watching the sea and not mentioning Rema.

'Ever think about getting back together with Patti?'

Patti Napier was the girl I was steady with for two years. 'No, Benk – that got real sticky. There was nothing there, you know? For a long time. It was habit. That gets real empty. It was depressing.'

I realize I'm not telling him anything he doesn't know because he lived through it with me. He's the only one I confided in – except for Mari. So I wonder why he's asking, and then I figure it out. 'You know, Benk, if you ever wanted to ask Patti out, that would be fine.'

I watch him watch the ocean, his eyes narrowing, almost disappearing in his fleshy face. 'Been thinking about it,' he says.

I hadn't thought of Benko as lonely. Horny, yes, but I guess I thought his family would keep him from sinking all the way to lonely. They're friends to each other, and they laugh a lot. Maybe Rema meant more to him than I thought, or at least, the *possibility* of Rema.

He hops off the wall. We touch shoulders.

'Thanks for everything, Benk. Great grilling. Really. Thanks.'

He holds up two fingers side by side. 'Live long.'

'Do good,' I say, giving him the same salute, and he walks

to his car, gathering up Dan Chin on the way. We borrowed this farewell from Benko's sister. 'Prospering' is out, she says. People have been too concerned about 'doing well' and that's how the world's gone wrong. So now it's 'do good.' That's the only way forward, says Benko's fifteen-year-old sister. She kicks it, too.

I arrive home and move toward the kitchen, but I'm drawn off by the sound of the television in the den. I can tell the sound track of a war film from twenty paces, and it still pulls at me as if I were ten years old. I lean into the den and am surprised when my father turns from the set and stares at me expectantly. I glance at the screen, and I know the film, immediately. Benko and I see all the war films, especially the historical ones. When I look back at Dad, he's still studying me, and it looks like he's holding his breath, waiting. So I tell him what I know.

'It's the Australian Light Horse Brigade attacking Beersheba. World War One. Mesopotamia Campaign – fighting the Turks, Dad.'

But he is still staring, looking to me as though he is on 'pause,' suspended until I release him, but I don't know the command.

'One of the last cavalry charges in history – except they were really mounted infantry. You get the distinction? Dad?'

Now he clears his throat and manages some words.

'Are we ready?'

'For what?'

'At the table.' I suppose he must mean dinner, but there is a look of dread about him.

'I don't know. I'll see.' I walk away, shaking my head, and when I enter the kitchen my mother turns stiffly from the sink, and I see the same expression.

'What's wrong?'

'Hi. Nothing. Was the party . . . How was the party?'

She's busy again, and not waiting for an answer. 'You're probably not hungry, are you? Did you want to eat?' She's almost shaking her head 'no.' It's so obvious by her tone, she wants a negative vote. 'Do we really *need* dinner?'

'No, Mom. I'm not hungry. You and Dad go ahead.'

'We're not hungry either.'

'Oh. So . . .?'

'So I thought we'd just have your cake. I made a cake. We don't really need dinner if nobody's hungry.'

'Correct. Well thought out, Mom. Right to the cake. What can I do?'

'Set.'

She starts to lift three small plates from the cupboard, but they rattle in her hands as if she is shaking.

'I'll get 'em. And cups?'

'Yes. There's fresh coffee.'

'You all right?'

'Go ahead and set and then call your father, all right?'

'Sure.' My parents are behaving as if this is all a trick, as if they are hiding something – and nervous about it. There are probably a dozen people hiding in the house, whispering right now, trying not to laugh, waiting for the right moment, for the cake, I suppose – before they burst into the dining room shouting: 'Surprise.' But I know this is impossible. There's no one to invite. They were all at the park. Unless it's Mack from the store, the other salesman, or the new part-timer, Trevor, whom I hardly know, or my mother's French Club, whom I don't know at all. Strangers, piled into the spare bedroom, waiting to break loose with smiles and shouts. It's a bizarre picture. Maybe Jack-o-lantern is in there, too. That's why he didn't show at the park. He's in there with his two-dimensional twin. They're eager for the free cake. Who else do I know? Bob. I can just see dour Bob who dislikes me, bland Bob in there, ready with a big shining grin, and a gift he will present to me as he slaps my shoulder. And some of my teachers at school. And Phil, too. And Patti, my old girlfriend. Maybe all the people who have populated the last five years of my life are crammed into that room with the exercycle and the sewing machine, standing shoulder to shoulder, giddy with anticipation.

'Dad. We're ready now.'

Immediately, he hits the remote, and the picture disassembles into some kind of electric oblivion as the screen darkens and sizzles briefly. Then he stands, but he doesn't turn, doesn't move. He's still staring at the screen.

'Dad.'

'M-hm.'

I walk into the dining room and now hear him following me. We sit, and my mother enters with a cake on a tray, chocolate frosting, twenty candles ablaze. The firelight on her face is a warm and orangey glow, but the smile it shines upon is forced and thin. She puts the cake down with a soft groan and sits and quickly wipes her eyes. She sees me staring at her.

'What's wrong, Mom?'

'It's chocolate fudge.'

'What's wrong?'

She nods toward the tray. Beside the cake is a small box, wrapped and ribboned. 'Open it,' she says.

I look at my dad. He is also forcing a tight-lipped smile and nodding at the gift. I remove the ribbon and open the box. The present is a painted soldier, a mounted Hussar, man and horse lying in a bed of cotton. 'Oh. Beautiful!' I lift the figure, the weight of it, the sight of it, stirring the magic in some deep well of myself. Why do I love them so, these painted warriors? 'He's terrific. Perfect choice.' I have no Hussars, and they were the most flamboyant of all: bearskin hat with plume, cherry red trousers with yellow stripe, a mass of lacy gold braid on his blue jacket, short cape over one shoulder and a furious black moustache. 'How did you know what to get?!'

'Well . . .' My mother's hands flutter toward the cake, but they are trembling. She places them on the table. 'Benko helped.'

That robs me of some of the wonder and the joy, but it's understandable. They probably sent Benko shopping. At least they thought about it and paid for it and wrapped it.

'British. Eleventh Hussars from the Crimean War – of Balaclava fame . . .'

'Better blow out the candles, Claudey,' my father warns, 'before the frosting melts.'

I stand and smile at each of them, but they have turned to grey stone, eyes averted to the cake. Now *I'm* feeling the dread, too, through them. It tightens my chest. I blow out the candles, forgetting to wish for anything, then I go on about the Hussar, talking too fast now.

'They were part of the Light Brigade, you know, as in the Charge of – which was all a big mistake. The whole brigade charged the wrong Russian guns, charged down the length of this long valley, being murdered from three sides, but they kept going. One of *the* major mistakes of history – like Columbus thinking this was India he had found and calling the native people "Indians," and look at all the confusion *that* caused.'

They are still silent, still grey and motionless, staring at the cake.

'Shall I cut it?' I ask. I pick up the slicer, and now they move. They turn their faces slowly. They look at each other, and I watch the masks fall away. My father's jaw tightens. He is clenching his teeth. He is full of anger. His chin trembles slightly. My mother stares at him with her own rage, but it is deeper, more still, eternal. When she turns to me, her tears come, but she lets them fall, just two.

They expend themselves on her cheeks and disappear. No more follow. She swallows and speaks to me, and her voice is calm.

'Claude, I'm going to France.'

I stare back and begin to breathe again. 'Well, Mom, that's great.' I look at Dad. 'Isn't it?' I search both their faces. 'God, you're finally going. When? For how long?'

Words come from my father now, torn from him slowly as heavy paper is torn. They come through his teeth. 'She's leaving us.'

My mother's hands are palm down on the table, side by side. She stares at them and says, 'I'm not leaving my children. My children are grown. I'm leaving *you*.'

'You hear that?' my father asks me, and his chin trembles mightily, and his hands are fists on each side of his plate.

'I'm not needed here.' My mother is still speaking to her small, lined and veined hands. 'If I was needed here, I wouldn't leave. I didn't leave as long as I was needed.'

'Not needed. Listen to her!'

'By who?!' Now she lifts her eyes, sends them to my dad. 'Needed by who? For what?'

I'm looking from one to the other. If I'm an actor in this scene, I seem to have no lines.

'What *you* want. It's all what *you* want.' My father throws a glance at me like a great hook, trying to stab me and pull me in, pull me to his side. 'It's all what *she* wants.' His whole body is shuddering. 'We have to sell the house!'

'It's time!' She shouts now, and her palms lift and fall on the table. 'It's time to sell this house!'

The candles are still smoking slightly. I'm still holding the Hussar in my hand. My mother is staring at *me* now, brandishing her own hook.

'Claude, you're old enough. You're grown now. He doesn't need this house. He doesn't need me – for what? To cook? He's letting his business fail, *letting* it. He should sell that, too. It's time to sell. I waited. I waited as long as I could. I ruined my health, waiting. Now I'm going. I'm divorcing him. He'll be all right.'

'Sure, I will!'

'He'll be *all right*. There's money in this house. He'll have his half. I'll have . . .'

'Who paid the mortgage on this house?!'

'I worked! I always worked!'

Their rage is meeting halfway across the table and grappling there. Their eyes are terrible weapons. They are both showing their teeth as I stand – and draw their faces to me. I don't know what to say, and my mother leaps into the silence, her throat liquid with tears.

'I'm sorry, Claude. We were going to wait till Wednesday. We were going to tell you then – but you had your party, so . . . It's something we both knew was happening – your father and I, for a long, long time. We've been waiting, and now you're twenty, and I'm not needed, and I can have something for myself.'

'For *years*, she hasn't talked about it. For *years* . . .'

'You always knew!' She throws this at my father quickly, then returns to me. 'I need something for myself now – while I still can. I'm practically ruined – my health. I'm not even sure I can work over there. I'm not sure how I'll feel – and there's red tape, but . . .'

'She's never coming back!'

Her small hands lift again and strike the table again, and her tears come, but she continues: 'I'm not needed. I'm not needed! Whoever wants to can visit me there. I'm finished here. I am finally finished here!'

'Because I'm twenty?' When my words come, they are just above a whisper. 'You're finished now because I'm twenty?'

'You're grown now, Claude. I did all the work I had to do. I did everything, and it almost killed me. It almost finished me, but it didn't. You almost wore me away, all of you. Look at me. But I'm not quite in my grave, and I'm *not* going to give up. That's your father. He gives up. I don't give up.'

'You just "waited," Mom? It was just "waiting"?'

'Don't you do this, Claude. Don't you try to make me feel guilty. That's your father. Look at him. He wants me to feel terrible. He wants me to feel guilty.'

'Just tell me, Mom!' I'm shouting now, too, shaking a bit, like my father, with tears in my throat, like my mother. 'You were waiting? You were counting the years? You were . . . marking a calendar? You were doing your duty?'

'I did everything for you . . .'

'*Why*?!' My hands curl into fists, and I can feel the Hussar and his horse bending in my right palm, the metal pricking my flesh. 'Why did you do it? I mean, why, Mom?! You sound like . . .'

'I'm your mother!'

'You sound like you've been in prison! You make it sound like I've been your prison! Why didn't you ever talk to me?! Why didn't you ever say, "Please let me out"?!'

'I'm your mother . . .!'

'I'm your *son*! I'm not your jail! Why didn't you talk to me – talk to us! Mari! Me! Anybody! I wasn't *keeping* you, Mom. I wasn't *ruining* you! You could've left! You should've left!'

'You were young . . .'

'I was stupid! I was stupid! I was so stupid! I knew your back hurt. I knew you and Dad didn't like each other, and *that* was getting worse. I saw that – but I didn't know you were just waiting, just putting in your time, living out your sentence, Mom. And I was the sentence! *I was the sentence!* That's what I was! Now your twenty years are up! Happy birthday! Happy birthday!'

I throw the bent metal in my right hand as hard as I can against the wall. The figure seems to explode, chipping the plaster. My mother stands, tilted, twisted a bit, pointing at me, screaming at me.

'I won't let you make me feel bad! None of you! I worked my whole . . .'

'I thought you liked me!' My tears are choking me, and I don't know if I can make any more words.

'She only thinks of herself,' my father says, ripping the words like meat from a bone. 'Herself!'

'Shut up!' I realize that my mother and I have screamed those words together, pummeling my father from two sides. My neck is stretched toward him. '*You* don't like anybody! You don't even know we're here!' I turn from the table so quickly, I knock my chair over, and as I hurry out of the room, I see the pieces of the headless Hussar, headless horse, scattered on the rug.

There is a voice inside of me that always argues the other side, that will not put up with my anger, that always tries to blunt whatever guilt or blame I am assigning. I am listening to this voice now as I lie on my bed, clothes, shoes and all, and think about the scene I just exited in the dining room. My breath still comes with a minor shudder, and I can see, in my right palm, the dents left by the Hussar. The voice is explaining to me that every parent parents out of obligation and responsibility, and it doesn't mean they don't also love their children. She was talking about the responsibility part. And many parents get divorced. Sometimes one of them moves away. 'It's not like you're a boy, Cheevey. Grow up,' the voice is saying. But Benko would call this my priest voice. It wants to absolve everybody. The only guilt this voice will allow is my own.

I'm starting to feel bad for yelling at them, for blaming them, for making her cry. Part of me wants to go back down there, into the house, and find her and hold her and say, 'It's all right. I'm sorry.' And it *is* all right. I mean, it's all right about her going to France. It's not that. It's the years of silence that choke me when I think about it. It's her years as a silent sufferer, watching me, measuring me. Is he old enough yet? Is he ready? Part of her must have hated me. Why did she have me? Maybe I was an accident. Maybe all I was to her was an extension on her prison sentence.

If twenty is the magic number in her mind, then six years ago, when Mari turned twenty, she could have fled – except for me. I'm the six-year extension that almost 'ruined' her, almost 'finished' her, but, by God, she completed her term. She served all of her time. What an ugly way to live. Maybe that's what I never really looked at and always denied about our family – hardly even noticed until recently – the ugliness. Look at them. Look at us. All of us. Me, too. Look at the Cheevers. Tunneling, Mari said. All of us tunneling away, away from the center, away from each other. That's ugly. Other families don't do that. Look at it for once. Stare at it.

I don't know how long I stare at it before the phone rings. As I'm reaching for it, I'm hoping it isn't Mari. I don't want to tell this to Mari yet, this news, this ugliness I've seen – and I don't want her to hear it in my voice. But it isn't Mari on the phone.

'Well, hello there. I've called you twice before, but you *never* answer your messages – or you were home and not wanting to be disturbed. Female company, right?'

It is Dash. I quickly organize my thoughts like a drill instructor, lining up the Cheever family and marching them out of my mind.

'Hi, Dash!'

'Am I disturbing anything, I hope?'

'No, I just got up here. I've been in the house. I mean, my parents' house. I live . . .'

'I know, your own little apartment. Mari showed me once. Going to be there awhile?'

'Well, sure . . .'

'Thought I'd come by.'

'Oh. Here?'

I hear that wicked, throaty laugh. 'Cheevey, you can tell me if it's not convenient. Be honest.'

'Well, sure . . .'

'Sure what? Come over. Don't come over. You pick.'

'Well, sure . . .' She laughs, and I laugh into her laugh, feeling stupid, but also cheered by this. 'Come over, Dash. Sure. Please. That'd be great.'

'Good. See you.' She hangs up, and I hang up slowly, still sweeping mightily at the corners of my mind, trying to prepare. Dash.

I'm trying not to wait for Dash, but I've straightened my room and put on a fresh shirt, and there is nothing left to do. I can't get my mind into a book, and I don't want to think about my family coming apart. I don't want to dwell on that, not now, so I ask myself *why* is Dash coming over? Maybe she wants to talk over something with me, something to do with Mari, but if this is true, why didn't she talk about it on the phone? I try not to think about her tongue jabbing into my ear at the park, or about how she called me a 'slender hunk.' I keep pushing that away, because if I let these thoughts in, I'll start fantasizing that Dash is coming here because she's *attracted* to me.

That makes me feel like a fool. I have a serious fear of being a fool, especially where girls are concerned. I've already felt foolish once today, watching Rema put her hand in John's. When I start to expect something or even hope for it, where girls are concerned, I start becoming a fool, and sitting here on my bed, trying *not* to wait for Dash, I can almost feel the giant, floppy shoes growing on my feet and the red, round nose on my face.

I hear a car stop near our house and hold my breath to

listen. A car door closes. I don't move. I count the steps through the yard – slow steps if she's indifferent, hurried steps if . . . I hear her on the stairs already! She must have nearly *run* through the yard. My heart's beating, hard, and I feel fluttery, moving to the door, but not wanting to open it too soon so that she'll *know* I was waiting and listening. I catch myself straightening my hair for the twentieth time and inside I shout, 'Fool! Expect nothing.' I try to compose the right face for greeting – pleased but calm. She knocks. I open the door.

She comes in like leaves in a gust, swirling and clattering with words.

'Hi, birthday boy. Oh, I *like* this place at night. Mood lighting, Cheevey. Very nice. Great party, wasn't it?' Her eyes are racing over my shelves of books, speed-reading titles, I guess. I'm a bit disappointed that she has put sweats on over her shorts. I had been imagining those showy legs gleaming here like lights in this small, intimate space. Expect nothing, I remind myself.

'Yes. Great. Thanks again for the glasses.'

'Oh, sure. Wow. The army. Boys have the greatest toys.' She is bending to stare at my soldiers, and she suddenly bends to the floor, dipping down from the waist to touch the floor with one hand then the other, then rising to twist her upper body, keeping her legs locked, right and left, cracking her back a bit. 'I'm *so* out of shape. That Frisbee game showed me. I *have* to start running again. What are these?'

'Zouaves. French soldiers dressed in a North African style.'

'You painted all these?'

I come close to her, bending, hands on legs, to view my troops with her. 'No. About a third of them.'

'Mari says you talk to them.'

I give one brief, snorting laugh, dismissing that idea.

She turns to me, eyes and mouth smiling mischievously. 'C'mon, you can tell me.'

I've just noticed the scent of wine on her breath. My first reaction is always disappointment. It's from being with Mari or Phil, I guess, and watching the booze take them away from me. I feel cheated, I suppose. *I'm* there, but they're behind an ever-thickening screen of alcohol. I see some of the effects in Dash's eyes. I'm good at detecting it, and I realize now that her words are very slightly slurred. She isn't drunk, but loosened by the wine, and my second reaction is excitement, realizing she's even more unpredictable now than usual. So once again my mind is divided. I'm sorry that alcohol may be part of the reason she is in my room, but I'm willing to take advantage of it.

'When I played with them, I suppose I talked to them – like any kid. Now I collect them. It's different.'

'You don't go with them to Never-Neverland?'

She's teasing me with that great flashy smile of hers, but she's closer to the truth than she thinks.

'I study their histories, Dash. It's my teddy bear that I confide in.'

She laughs wantonly, putting a hand on my arm, but her eyes bounce about the room again as she straightens. She moves to my one soft chair and spins and flops into it, keeping her smile on me, crossing her legs, leaning her head back.

'Now – tell me about Rema. She's beautiful. That olive skin – from a honey jar. She's Mexican?'

'Venezuelan.'

'And you and she are . . . ?' She punctuates with a provocative eyebrow, arched and waiting.

'Friends.'

'Oh, booo. Boring.'

'She's with John.'

'Really? I wouldn't have thought. Too bad. Mari and I

were sure Rema was the next lucky girl. Remember when I met you, you were so tight with that Patti? Nobody since then?'

'Nobody serious.' I sit on my bed. 'So, you and Mari sit around discussing my love life – talk about boring.'

She chuckles deep in her chest. 'We just don't want you to be alone.'

'What about you?'

'Oh, I'm another story.' She hooks the footstool with a heel and drags it toward her and rests her legs on it, the shoes swaying right and left as she stares at me, and her stare is both stimulating and uncomfortable. Flirting seems to be a word defined by Dash's way of being in a room. I don't know what to do with it. It always seems false when I try it, so I become more serious.

'What about Mari? What do you think about the way she was in the park today? I mean, what happened with Ballyhoo.'

Dash's head goes all the way back on the chair and she shakes it slowly, side to side. 'Oh, God, let's not get into Mari. I just got *away* from Mari. God love her, she's *so* neurotic and she seems to play it – like a sport. When she gets going, I feel like she's going to swallow me up. Now she's going through that Coretti, through all his novels with a code book, looking for *messages*.'

'You think it's just a way of not writing?'

'Of course it is.' She sits forward now. 'I've told her to chuck it. Forget Coretti. Get a new topic. She's in love with this guy because he's inaccessible *and* because he's gone without a trace. She *loves* the fact that he's a missing person. Don't get me started on Mari.'

'Sorry.'

'Oh, I'm sorry, too.' She sighs and shoves the footstool away and stands, stretches, twists her neck a bit. She behaves like an athlete, always working her body, aware of it. She's a drama major, but also, like Mari, a Ph.D. candidate doing her doctoral. Hers is on the theatre of the deaf. Dash's sister is deaf, and Dash is a great signer and interpreter and mime. I've seen her do it.

'You're so *neat*, Cheevey, look at this place!' She is moving about, but there isn't anywhere to go so she stretches once more, then comes and sits beside me on the bed. 'Did you do a major clean-up since I called? Tell the truth.'

Here is that smile again – devilish is a good word.

'I straightened. I did not clean.' We're almost touching, side by side on the edge of the bed. She begins to bounce slightly on the mattress.

'My God, your bed's like a stone. Are you a monk, or what?' She suddenly falls back. She's lying across my bed with her feet still on the floor, arms at her sides. 'Well,' she says with a question mark, 'are you going to jump on me – or what?' Then she chuckles and sits up beside me again, her eyes staying on mine for once, but laughing.

I say, 'I never know when you're teasing.'

Her eyes linger, laughing a little less. 'Neither do I, Cheevey.' In another second she's chuckling again. 'You look so serious! What's wrong?'

I shrug. 'You just . . . you seem like you're playing with me.'

The laughter in her look diminishes a bit more, but it's still there. She stands, moves about again, doing a slight, swaying dancer's step, just an absent motion. She spins slowly – and then rests her back against the closed closet door. She folds her arms and sighs and stares at me. 'All right. Here comes the truth. Are you ready for this?'

I feel my chest tightening. I shrug. I try not to predict, not to expect.

'I've been fantasizing about you,' she says. She grins and shrugs.

I'm just staring, waiting, fearing a trap of some kind, realizing I'm in fool territory.

'I do it all the time, Cheevey. I'll see some man around the school or at work or even pass by some guy on the street, and I'll carry his . . . image around, and I'll find myself fantasizing some particular thing, some particular sexual thing with this man, even an old man, strange-looking man, could be any kind of man, but there'll be one thing I imagine him doing to me or doing *with* me, and it stimulates me. It's really kind of fun – but I was surprised to find your image in there. This was only recently. Will you come here, please, instead of sitting way over . . .'

I rise, trying to breathe normally, and I walk close to her as she continues.

'It was just in, I don't know, the last month or two you started coming to mind at odd times, and I was . . . surprised. Mari's little brother. So I started looking at you a little more – and it didn't go away – this particular image, this fantasy. It got stronger. So, I may be being really dumb, but so what. Is this stupid? Maybe. I guess it is, but I thought I'd see if I had the nerve to actually *tell* you what this fantasy is and see if you would *want* to do it, and if you did, then it comes true. That only happens once in a while – where one of these comes true. What are you thinking now?'

I have no words for her. I shrug, and she chuckles that purring laugh and unfolds her arms and puts her hands lightly on my shoulders, studying me in a slightly knowing, even patronizing way – or I guess matronly way. My mind is shouting a series of confused instructions: 'Be careful. Don't expect. Be open to this. Advance. Plunge in. This is real. Repeat. This is real. This is Dash. She is really in your room. She is touching you. She's planning to do something or ask for something sexual. This is true. Stay with this. Concentrate. Don't think too much.'

'You look scared, Cheevey.'

'I'm just . . . wondering.'

'All right. I'll tell you. I've been thinking about kissing your neck.' Even with her hands reaching up to my shoulders, she manages a brief shrug and she blushes slightly. I have never seen Dash blush. Her bright smile is in place, though, lighting her fine features, showing her bright, wet teeth. 'You have this long, strong neck, and my fantasy is me kissing your neck – all over your neck. Does this sound strange to you? Do you fantasize?'

'Well . . . sure.'

'About *me*, Cheevey?'

'Well . . . sure.'

'Like what?'

'Well . . . I mean even today. In the park.'

'In the park what?'

'I liked how . . .'

'What?'

'How your legs looked. I was noticing your legs.' As I say this I am imagining her lips on my neck, figuring I'll have to bend forward for her to reach, thinking details like that.

'My legs. Good. What did you imagine?'

'I don't know. I just . . . They're beautiful.'

'Are they? Thank you. So . . . we'll be equal then. I'm glad.' She lets go of my shoulders, and pulls at the drawstring of her sweatpants. She hooks her thumbs in and pushes down not only the sweats but the pink running shorts underneath. I'm watching her legs revealed and her underwear, the white triangle visible to me at her crotch with errant hairs escaping the lace. She leans a hand on my arm for balance as she bends and steps out of pants and shorts, pulling them over her shoes, and I'm staring at her thighs, and underwear and the glimpse of escaping hair, and then she's standing upright again, and smiling into my face, and reaching for me with her mouth.

Her lips are on my neck. I'm leaning down a bit for her,

and my hands go naturally to her waist, touching cloth at first and then the smooth skin of her hips and back and the elastic band of her underwear. Her mouth is off my neck after just two kisses and moving up quickly to find mine, almost desperately like a breathless person searching for oxygen – and I join our mouths, and she grips my shoulders so hard I can feel her fingernails in my flesh, and suddenly my mouth is full of her tongue, and I flinch, and she pulls back – just a few inches from my face, not smiling now.

'What's wrong?' she asks.

'I'm just . . . surprised.'

Her smile begins to reappear, but it is tighter, and her eyes dance about my face. 'Are you ready now?' Before I even make a sign, she lunges at my mouth again. I smell the wine. I feel her tongue charge in and start shoving, and then it's out, and she's biting my lips and pressing closer, her hands behind my head now, pulling me into the kiss. My lips hurt. I taste blood. My hands are moving up slowly on her back, beneath the cloth, finding immeasurably smooth skin and no bra, and she breaks again for a moment to whisper, in a driven, hurried voice: 'Use your strength, Cheevey.'

I hesitate for an instant, processing this new command, then I begin pressing harder against her lips and pulling her closer, but I'm still off balance, way behind and trying to catch up to her, trying to match her intensity, but it is all so rushed. I feel her remove one hand from the back of my neck, and, as she drives her body harder into mine, she places that free hand between my legs and pushes upward into my crotch, not hard, not clutching, examining.

She suddenly stops and moves back so that her body hits the closet door. She puts her hands to her face, one on each cheek, and shakes her head. 'This is stupid. This is stupid. I'm sorry,' she says. Her eyes find me now and she continues shaking her head. Her hands come back to my shoulders, but gently. Her smile appears quickly as if brushed on with one stroke. 'I'm being so *bad*, Cheevey. My fault. This is stupid. I mean *me*. A bad idea. God. I'm sorry.' She reaches down and snatches up her clothes and thrusts a leg in, and I steady her while she covers the other and ties the drawstring again, smiling at me again now, blushing again. 'Mari's brother. I never should have said a word, Cheevey. I really shouldn't have. I was being very bad. Forgive me, okay?'

Again, I have no words. My mouth is open. I'm shrugging.

'You forgive me?'

'Well . . . for what? I . . .'

'I just should've kept my mouth shut about that dumb fantasy. That isn't something you do with your friend's brother. This is Dash being dumb. So . . . is it okay? We won't tell anybody – and you won't think I'm *completely* crazy. All right?'

There is one second where her eyes lose their humor and focus and penetrate, and it looks as though she's searching for signs of damage.

'Okay, Dash. I . . .' I still have no words in my brain, only a clamor of images and the beginning of an ache. I can't define it yet.

'Good. Thanks. Everything's all right?'

'Well . . . sure.'

'Great.' She kisses me – on the lips, but a quick, friendly goodbye kiss that tries to put everything back in place as it used to be. 'You're great, Cheevey. You really are. 'Bye now. Sorry.' She is chuckling at herself – like the old Dash, I suppose and speaking as she moves to the door. 'You know *me*. I act without thinking. Constantly.' She opens the door, flings her bright smile at me, and leaves. I hear her hurrying down the stairs.

The room is full of her absence. It is not only quiet. For a moment it is dead – and so am I, in a way, not breathing or moving and afraid to begin.

After a few aimless wanderings and the absent touching of things, I retreat to the bed to take stock.

Something has happened. There is that ache growing inside me. I still have not defined it. I was alone in my room. Dash called. She came over. She was here. She just left. All of this happened. She took some of her clothes off. She kissed me with tongue and teeth and great urgency. She stopped suddenly. She left quickly, embarrassed.

Half of my divided mind is busy cataloguing all of these events and explaining them. She was feeling adventurous and high on wine. She was attracted to me. She let it go too far. She realized it was wrong to do this – to become sexually involved with her best friend's younger brother. She broke it off. It's a good thing. It could have been messy – emotionally messy. What would happen between Mari and me? Wouldn't it drive us apart? And where could this go – in reality – this sudden leap toward passion? Nowhere. Dash and I are not alike, and she is five years older than I am, a big gap when the ages are twenty and twenty-five – and I'm not even twenty yet. Just enjoy this as an experience, my mind tells me. Feel good that she was attracted to you. Celebrate having this pretty woman half-dressed in your room, in your arms, kissing and holding you – and be thankful that it ended clean with no one being hurt and all relationships intact.

The other half of my mind isn't saying much – it just *knows*. It knows that I should have made love with Dash Markel tonight, but she was moving too fast, and I wasn't prepared. She asked me to use my strength, but my strength wasn't there. It hadn't come yet. She was way ahead of me. I wasn't ready, and when she put her hand between my legs, I wasn't ready there either. Her hand measured me and found me limp, and that's why she stopped, and that's why she left, and the ache that is filling me now is simple shame.

*   *   *

It's impossible to sleep. Dash left three hours ago, and my two minds are still arguing. I have brought my Zouaves from shelf to table, and I line them up and put my eye at table level and study them. They are red-trousered, blue-jacketed, white-turbaned, bearded men, all at the running charge, rifles leveled at the hip, with bayonets gleaming – warriors. I could never be a warrior, I decide. Warriors need to be of one mind. My warrior mind is shouting at me: 'Why didn't you say, "Slow down, Dash. Slow down"? Why didn't you take over the moment? You had it all in your hands.' My other mind is excusing myself and absolving Dash, too.

Moving and studying the Zouaves, my mind goes back to my years with Patti Napier. We became intimate in our first month together, but our sex was never completely unselfconscious. When it was hurried, it left me more empty than satisfied. When it was slow, too many other thoughts filtered in and diluted the experience. I realized it was because we didn't care enough for each other, didn't really hunger for each other. I came to hate her timidity, and, even more, I hated my own. Often, in the dark, I gave Patti another face, as I'm sure she imagined other faces on me. Sometimes, just before our relationship faded away, I remember giving her Dash's face.

An hour ago, I called Benko, hoping he would drive me to Phil's tomorrow because I don't want to deal with my parents for a ride – not after tonight. The Benkos are going to an early mass tomorrow, so I do get my ride – but straight to the job site where Phil will be already working. This settled, I thanked Benko for picking out the Hussar for my parents to give me. I stopped there, unwilling to share the rest of the events of the night, not the anger, not the shame, not yet, not even with Benko.

The Zouaves are charging straight at me now, uniforms aglow in the lamplight. I can hear their shouts in my mind, all their voices tumbling together into a roar of rage and power, a single animal voice, a warrior voice. I feel the same shout in my hot, torn throat as I lead the Legion over the plains of Shalazed, a sword in my fist and the enemy scattering before me like frightened beasts. I fight without thinking. I use all of my strength. I show no mercy.

I'm still not twenty, but I've aged. I walk down the staircase from my room on Sunday morning, feeling older. Maybe I'm feeling the wounds – from the Dash incident and from my parents' news. I feel like a veteran, a little more like Captain Cheever of the Legion, I suppose, and I wonder if it shows in my walk, in my eyes – or is this all self-pitying dramatics? My two minds are sniping at each other already, and I'm barely awake.

My father must have been planning an ambush. He comes out on the front porch as I descend my stairs. I'm already dressed to go to Phil's. I didn't want to see my parents yet, but he meets me in the middle of the yard. He's dressed, but he hasn't shaved or even looked in a mirror because his hair is having a wild time up there. I remember that moment last night, stretching my neck toward him, shouting, 'Shut up!' and the memory is embarrassing.

'Going to Phil's?' he asks.

'Yes.'

He nods, his eyes leaving me now to look about. Maybe he's hoping to find a television set that's on in someone's window. 'We have to sell the house.'

'Yeah, you said.'

'So we need that bathroom built up there. Sell it for a lot more if your place is a rentable unit – or at least a . . . guest accommodation.'

Now he's staring at my room.

'Dad, what do you want?'

'Ask him, will you?' He glances at me as if checking if I'm

still there, and then he searches the neighborhood again. 'See if he'll build the bathroom now, and I'll pay him out of the sale money.'

I sigh, but that doesn't bring him around. 'Dad.' He looks at me, and before he can look away, I say, 'Why don't *you* talk to Phil?'

'Christ, you're *going* there.'

'Just pick up the phone, Dad. He's probably still home.'

Now I don't *want* his eyes on me because they're angry and hurt. 'You won't even do *that* for me.' He starts to walk away.

I feel a sudden fury, and I shout at his slouching back: 'What d'you mean, "*that*?" I won't even do "that." I do everything you want me to do. Why should I carry messages back and forth?!' The last words I send through the open door as he's entering the house. 'He's your *son*!'

Now I'm jogging, hitting Wilshire and turning east toward Benko's, feeling hot and tight, cursing through my teeth as I go, looking like one of the mentally ill who wander this town like ghosts, the people most others don't look at. I bet if I ran to the store now, cursing aloud to myself, and Jack-o-lantern were there, I bet he'd talk to me, both of them would.

I'm conscious of a car, rolling along parallel to me, but on the other side of the street. It stays in the corner of my vision until I glance and see that it is my mother, driving down Wilshire at about ten miles an hour, cars pulling around her as she stares out her window at me. I nearly stumble when I see this, and I wonder, would she have followed me all the way to Benko's, afraid to hit the horn because it would call attention to herself? My mother is shy in public, not coy or embarrassed but usually silent, avoiding unnecessary contact.

I jog across the street, and she pulls over so I can stand at her open side window, out of the traffic.

'I'll drive you to Phil's,' she says. There is no greeting.

'Benko's driving me.'

'I'll drive you to Benko's, then.'

'I like the jog, Mom. Thanks anyway.'

She looks even smaller than usual behind the wheel of her Volvo. A cushion has her thrust forward a bit. Her neck looks a little kinked the way she's staring up at me. She has her lips tightened so there's no softness showing, only the moisture in her eyes, the distant possibility of tears.

'I hated what you said last night. How could you say that I didn't like you? You know better. You have to know better. That's a terrible thing to say.'

I lean my hands on her door and sigh, hunting for words, finding and discarding them. 'What I meant, Mom . . . what I meant is that it sounded like the only reason you stayed around all these years is because I wasn't twenty. Like I held you back. It makes me feel like shit.'

'That's stupid. I'm your mother. I wouldn't abandon you. I never blamed you.'

'You didn't?'

'No.'

'No? Are you sure?'

'Of course I'm sure!'

'If it wasn't for me, you would have left six years ago, right?'

Her tightened lips tremble slightly as she says, 'But I didn't leave. I didn't. I stayed. And I did *everything*. I ruined my health doing *everything*, and for that I get my gift thrown back in my face.'

She starts to cry, rifling the glove compartment for Kleenex.

I hate to see her cry. I feel like I've done something terrible. I feel like holding her, but she's difficult to hold, sitting in the car like this, and she would only say I was hurting her back. I squat so my face is at the window, and I watch as she bites down on her lower lip, ordering herself to stop crying.

'Mom. Mom, you never looked at me and thought: If it wasn't for him I'd be in Paris? You never looked at me and thought that?'

She sits with her eyes closed, the damp Kleenex balled in her fist. 'Your father,' she says. 'I looked at *him*.'

She opens her eyes then, but doesn't look at me. She's looking through the windshield at her own thoughts, or at Dad. It's that old, rotted anger I've seen before, and it comes over her like a shadow. She seems so absolutely alone at this moment, that I don't speak to her. I just rise up to turn away.

'Anyway . . . I'm not going to Paris.' She says this wearily. 'I'm going to Compiègne.'

I'm nodding, as if this information matters, and I'm raising a hand in a half-hearted wave, about to go. So she hurries her next words.

'I suppose you'll tell Mari.'

This stops me. My wave is still in the air, shoulder high, a spread-out hand. 'You mean . . . *you're* not going to?'

She gives a small, annoyed shrug. 'Well . . . you two talk all the time. I just thought . . .'

'Jesus Christ!' My shout has startled her. '*Jesus Christ*!'

Her eyes are wide with shock, watching me as if I am a stranger, a mad stranger.

'What a family! What a non-family!' I slap the fender of the car and start jogging away, my hand numb, then aching, my eyes hot with tears.

'There are families and there are anti-families,' I say to Benko in the car. 'Families are dense and produce gravity. Anti-families are hollow and therefore without gravity, and mine is exploding outward into the universe.'

He glances at me and keeps driving. 'France is not exactly Pluto, Cheeve.'

'It's not that. It's not the distance, the physical distance. It's not even selling the house and moving. It's that nobody *talks* to anybody.'

'You and Mari talk.'

'Yes. Right. Mari talks more than anybody I know . . .'

'Or ever heard of.'

'Right, and at least she talks to me, and I talk to her, at least that has survived.'

'And Bally. You talk to Bally.'

'Bally is in a separate family, or a separate anti-family, actually. God, this is shit. I'm supposed to tell the world. They sent me out with messages – like Paul Revere.'

'So don't do it. Let *them* tell Phil and Mari.'

'They just won't. They'll just . . . let it go.'

'Where will you move?'

'I don't know. Maybe my dad's got a plan. He didn't say.'

'I wish we could offer you a room, Cheeve. You could crash with me for awhile, you know.'

'Thanks. Really. Thanks.'

He nods, eyes on the road. I haven't even thought about moving. Only so much will fit into my brain. Part of it is still busy with Dash, endlessly rewinding and reviewing the scene and pointing out what I should have said and done, and even when I manage to turn it off, I'm left with that undiminished ache filling my chest, weighing me down. I don't feel like telling Benko about my failure. I don't want to disappoint him. When I told him about Dash coming in while I was in the shower, he was so excited. I'll tell him someday. I'll tell him after enough events have piled up on top of it and it's as dull and yellow as an old newspaper. I collect old headlines – war-related headlines and full front pages, Benko, too. We buy them at swap meets. U.S. LANDS IN ITALY. MARINES TAKE IWO JIMA – that kind of thing. The oldest ones are yellow and fragile, and we keep them in plastic bags, and I am now imagining, as I ride in Benko's car, someday turning the pages of my collection and finding among the headlines: DASH INVADES CHEEVEY'S ROOM. CHEEVEY OFFERS WEAK RESPONSE. RAID LEAVES CHEEVEY IN DISARRAY. This makes me smile slightly, and Benko picks it up, smiling, too, and asking, 'What? What?'

'Someday we'll look back on this, Benko, and laugh our asses off.'

'Yeah,' he says. 'Tomorrow.'

I've been working with Phil for fifteen minutes, and all he has said to me is, 'Hi. Why don't you take a razor and get all the paint off the glass?' I like this job, just a mindless attack on paint spots with a sharp blade and the strength of my hand, breaking each spot's hold on the glass, making it disappear. I am imagining enemy pill boxes. The blade is my artillery. I pound them into white dust. But as I work, I keep glancing at Phil, studying him, as if he is an experiment, the man of no words. I am wearing the new tool belt he gave me, and I saw him notice it. How long will he work before he says anything to me about not showing up at my party? I know the thought is inside of him. He is in a more dark and troubled mood than usual, an apology slowly working its way up through his system like bile, I guess. I don't know why it costs him so much.

I'm watching him for another reason, too, and I'm not proud of it. I find that I'm savoring the bleak news that I bring from Mom and Dad. I'm watching and waiting for the moment, just a little bit glad, finally, to have something important to say to him, something that will capture his attention and cause a strong reaction. It makes me feel ghoulish to be eager to tell him the news of separation and divorce.

'Cheeve?'

'Yeah?'

'There's a hammer by your left foot.'

'Yeah.'

'Bring it here.'

'No.'

He keeps working, thinking I'm kidding, thinking I'll bring it.

'I need it now.'

I stop working and pick up the hammer and then sit on the floor, facing him. He's across the room, fitting shelves. He throws me a black look.

'Come on.'

'No.'

'Goddammit. I'm not kidding around.'

'Me neither.'

'Slide it the fuck over here!'

'No.' Maybe it's the secret I carry that empowers me, or maybe just the feeling that everything is changing, and I must be changing, too.

'I have to hold this in place! Now give me the goddamn' hammer!'

'Not until you say something about my party.'

'Jesus Christ!'

'Say something, Phil.'

'Don't be such a shit! Lauren went there, right? She explained. I'm sorry! I blew it! I got too goddamn' mad thinking about Dad, and I started to drink.'

I stand up and walk over and put the hammer in his hand. He grabs it and hits the shelf as if he's mad at it, just one blow to force it into place, then he lays the hammer down and picks up the next shelf.

'Phil.'

'What?'

'Thanks for the tool belt. It's really a nice one.'

He nods as he works.

'Did that hurt, saying you're sorry?'

'Don't fuck with me, Cheeve.'

'I have to.' He tries to ignore me, working carefully on the shelf. 'I have something to tell you, Phil, and it's going to fuck with you – but I can't help it.'

He is frowning now as he works. 'Yeah? What is it?' I am not yet worthy of the attention of his eyes, but that's okay. Today I hold an ace. Today he can't escape me.

'You have to look at me for me to tell you.'

'Jesus, *fuck*!' He drops the shelf and turns on me, really furious. 'Will you cut this shit?!'

'I can't. I have to do it this way.'

'Do what?! Do what?!'

He's looking right at me. I stare into his wide open anger, unafraid. I play the ace. 'Mom is going away. She and Dad are getting divorced.'

His eyes do not bounce away; for once they screw into me and hold.

'They're selling the house. She's going to France – to live there.'

He's squinting, his brows converging, splitting his forehead with deep lines. It's a look of pain. I didn't expect pain.

'They told me last night. You know why she's leaving – actually, finally leaving?'

He's not ready for a question. He is still working at absorbing the big dark fact.

'Because I'm twenty. She said she stayed until I was twenty.'

I have never held his focus for so long. He seems to have stopped breathing. I'm feeling no triumph, and I'm glad when his stare finally drops to the floor. His mouth slackens a bit. He looks, for a second, like some of the family photos taken of him before I was born – like a small boy.

'Christ,' he says softly to the floor.

'All this time she was just waiting for me to grow up. I hate that. I hate that feeling. She was putting in her time. You know what I mean?'

He looks at me again, still pained, even needy, and still unable to deal with my questions. I don't think he has heard more than my first sentences.

'If I hadn't been born, she would've gone six years ago – when Mari turned twenty. You see what I'm saying?'

His stare is making me uncomfortable now that I have it. It is as though he wants something from me – and I don't know what it is.

'Did you think this would happen? Phil?'

'I don't know.' His voice unnerves me. It is weak and distant. 'What did they say?'

'Just what I told you.'

'Where were they – when they told you? How?'

His questions are surprising. Phil never wants the details. 'Around the table last night. Here's a piece of cake. Here's your birthday gift. I'm going to France. She said Dad knew about it, but he was growling at her, and they fought. It was . . .'

Phil's eyes slide off me and he slips away, ambling quietly to the center of the room, standing there to glance around without looking at anything.

'It was a shitty scene. And the worst part – this morning . . .'

He ambles to a window and stares out. I'm glad it's one of the windows I finished. There are no paint spots. The glass is clean for him. I wonder why that's important to me right now.

'This morning both of them – separately – came and asked me to tell you and Mari. Mom asks me to tell Mari, and Dad . . .'

He raises the hammer with a slow rolling of his wrist and just taps the heavy head on the glass, just taps it again, very lightly, but the taps make me wince.

'Dad wants me to ask you if you'll finish my room now? He said he'll pay you out of the sale of the house.'

He doesn't alter his stance at the window. His eyes seem to be examining the cluttered sky that is cut jaggedly by rooftops and treetops and slashed by phone wires. The small rolling motion of his wrist continues, bringing the hammer head to the glass in a series of light taps, but one of these taps, no stronger, no louder than the others, cracks the window from top to bottom, just two thin lines, one curving into the other, like rivers on a map. He stops, holding the hammer suspended, still scouting the sky.

'Son of a bitch,' he says.

I think he's reacting to the window glass, but then he turns to me.

'He's such a son of a bitch. He's such a goddamn' son of a bitch.' He walks to another window, and I hold my breath, but he doesn't raise the hammer. 'He *never* paid me.'

'I know. He . . .'

'He never paid me for working in the store – and I know he pays *you* shit.'

'Well, he . . .'

'He never paid me for the roof.'

I don't know about the roof. I'm not sure what he means.

'He never paid me for the garage room. He's a shit. He's a real son of a bitch, and *she's* no help. She's no goddamn' help.'

Abruptly, he turns and walks through the doorless passage, out on to the deck and down the stairs, moving toward the truck.

* * *

Phil has been in the cab of the truck for twenty minutes, sipping beer and staring forward as intently as if the truck were moving and he was driving, but he's just sitting there in the driveway of this remodeling site. He always brings a cooler of beer and Cokes to a job. Maybe he's just taking a break to drink and think about the news I've given him, or maybe we're through for the day – though we just began. I tried to ask him, twice. He never answered. He sits now with his anger circling him like barbed wire. Approach at your own risk.

I've cleaned all the window panes and now I sit on the deck, waiting. There is shade here, and I enjoy the scent of sawdust and paint.

I didn't sleep well last night, and now, as I sit on the redwood boards and lean back against the stucco wall, I feel my closed eyes moisten and my breathing even out. The sounds of the neighborhood, the cars and dogs and the faraway voices of children, are being slowly wrapped in cotton. My hands grow limp. My jaw slackens.

I am awakened by the sound of a car pulling into the driveway. I may have been asleep for three minutes or an hour. My mouth tastes of sleep and my body is slow and awkward in rising.

Lauren and her daughter, Molly, have parked beside the truck and are exiting their little car. I suppose they have come from church because they appear in dresses, Molly in blue, Lauren in white. To my sleepy eyes they look like angels.

They stop at the truck, and Lauren says something to Phil about lunch. He answers and gestures toward me. They turn and approach me now, Lauren smiling openly and Molly shyly. The breeze picks up the skirts of their dresses. The sun falls on to their red-brown and blonde hair. Molly's eyes are averted but Lauren's are already touching my face. She brings me her ease in her calm smile and in the unhurried way she moves her body up the steps to the deck and in her voice.

'Cheevey. Hi.'

We embrace, and I am holding bare shoulders, a bare back above the summery dress. 'What's the matter with grouch face?' she says, and Molly chuckles at that.

'Hi, Mol.'

She looks me in the eyes now to say hello, and then I turn to Lauren. 'I guess I brought him some bad news. I mean, no emergency or anything. But . . .' Somehow, I don't want to mention it in front of Molly, protecting her from what?

'What is it, Cheevey?'

'Our parents are getting divorced. I guess it shouldn't be a shock, but . . .'

'Oh, I'm sorry.'

'They told me last night.'

'Ohh.' She makes the sound as if sorry for me – the same sound she makes, I bet, when Molly has fallen and hurt herself, and her face grows sad for me, and she hugs me again. Over her shoulder I see Molly staring at me.

Lauren touches my face. It's a beautiful gesture, intimate, her fingers on my cheek, soft as breath. She doesn't know me very well, but she seems to feel my pain.

'I'm sorry,' she says again, then, 'I'll go talk to him.'

She moves toward the truck, and I turn to Molly, who is still staring, puzzling at something.

'I thought that was just with kids,' she says, finally.

'What?'

'Divorce. You seem . . . sort of old.'

I can't help smiling a little. To Molly, at least, I am no longer a kid. 'Are your parents divorced?' I ask.

'Yes.'

'Sorry,' I say; and she makes a tiny shrug, beginning to twirl slow circles on one foot, moving around the deck.

'Do you see your dad?'

'Sometimes. He's in San Diego. He's a policeman.'

'Oh. What kind?'

'A detective. Sort of.'

'I don't know any policemen.'

'Community relations.'

'What?'

'Sort of what he does. He doesn't use a gun.'

'Uh-huh. Did you go to church?'

'Yep. Will you live with *your* mom?'

'Uh, no. She's going away.'

Now Molly looks at me, poised on one foot for another twirl, surprised.

'She's going to France. You know where that is?'

'Sort of.'

'I guess I'll live with my dad – for awhile. He sells television sets.'

'Didn't *you* go to church?'

'No.'

On her way back to us, from Phil, Lauren casts her eyes down, sorting thoughts, and I study her briefly, looking at her legs beneath the swaying skirt of her dress. She is thin, gracefully thin at the neck and arms, but her legs are shapely and I can see the outline of her hips and thighs through the white cotton, and then I look away.

'He says he just wants to go home, Cheevey.' As she says that, I hear Phil start the engine of the truck, and I hurry past her and jump down from the deck, but he is already pulling out of the driveway, driving too fast. My arms fly up and then fall, and I slap my thighs, angry, frustrated.

'It's all right. I'll drive you home.' She comes beside me. 'I told him I'd drive you home.'

'It's not that. It's just . . . he could *talk* to me. He could say something about it. It's *my* family, too. It's *my* bad news, too. Shit.'

She takes my hand in both of hers and just holds it. God,

how she can disarm me. I wonder if she knows how much I want to dive against her breast and cling there – not sexually. In fact, I find I'm pushing away sexual thoughts of Lauren, and I'm surprised at how hard I have to push. It's the dress, I suppose. It was easier when she was in jeans and shirts. The dress makes her more available, her flesh, her womanliness – but I push at those images and just imagine the comfort, the safety, the deep, palpable tenderness of an hour-long embrace.

She drops Molly off at a friend's house in Venice and we spend the last fifteen minutes of the ride alone together. Next to her in the car, I'm aware of the scent of her. I don't think it's perfume, just soap, I guess, and skin. We are silent a while, and I feel the minutes with her leaking away. I wish we were driving to Argentina.

'Are you and Phil . . . ? Tell me if I'm prying. I'm just curious. Tell me to shut up. I just wonder if . . . Oh, Christ.'

'What?' She is giggling, low-voiced, from her chest and throat.

'I'm pushing it, I know, but, Christ, I can't ask *Phil* about his life. I might as well talk to this glove compartment.' I love her melodic giggle. It drives me forward, or maybe my boldness comes from the changes, from the damage already done. Somehow I have less to lose, or somehow I'm older. I pop the glove compartment and speak to it.

'So, Phil, what about Lauren? Are you seeing her, or what? Tell me about it, Phil. What are your feelings about her?'

Then I move the lid of the compartment up and down like a mouth, and I give it Phil's voice.

'Shut the fuck up.'

She laughs, with lines around her eyes and mouth from strength and from joy. I wish I had a photograph of this moment.

After a while of silent driving, she says, 'We *were* – Phil and I – at first. But we're just friends now. It just couldn't be, Cheevey. God save me from self-destructive men.' She smiles a kind of wry veteran's smile. 'I've been through it before, the drinking, too.'

'Your husband?'

'Ex-husband. Yes. Mm-hm. And others.' She pauses, driving, remembering, and then she adds, 'The wounded.'

'Well, I can see that. I mean, you're very caring. It's great.'

'Well, thank you, but . . .'

'No, really, Lauren. You're such a giving person. It makes me envy Molly – and I was envying Phil, too, because I thought . . . Well . . . Anyway.' I feel like I've said too much, but when I turn to her, she looks pleased.

'That's nice of you to say – about Molly.'

'She's so lucky.'

'Well, I think it's the other way around.'

I knew she would say that. It's part of her gift, this pride in Molly, this treasuring of Molly. It's what she gives her daughter. It's better than diamonds or plutonium.

'You mentioned your stationery store?'

'Yes. Well, I manage it, and . . .'

'Mind if I come in some time?'

'Of course not. Please do. I work Tuesday through Friday. Yes, come in anytime.'

'You look great in that dress.' With her easy smile there comes a subtle blush, and it quickens me. For a moment I allow myself to think of her as a lover, and the thought that comes is from both my minds, speaking together. There is no debate. The thought is this: Lauren would never hurry a man and then measure him and then walk away.

'Claudey?'

My father speaks to me through the bathroom door. It's

not even dark yet, but I'm treating myself to an early bath. I did not eat dinner with my parents. I haven't spoken to them since this morning when my father ambushed me in the yard, and my mother caught me with her Volvo.

'What?'

'Are you all right?'

'What d'you mean?'

'You're in there so long.'

Which means he's waiting to talk to me. 'I'm taking a bath.'

'Oh. Almost done?'

'What d'you want, Dad?'

'It can wait.'

'Dad . . . what d'you want?'

'Did you talk to Phil?'

'I told him what you said.'

'What did he say?'

'He didn't say anything.' Yes, he did. He called you a son of a bitch – two or three times.

'Hm.'

'Why don't you call him?'

I know my father is standing outside the door, but he doesn't make a sound. 'Dad? Call him. I'm sure he's home.'

Now I hear him walk away. I sink to my chin. The water is as hot as I can stand. I don't take baths for cleanliness. I try to boil away all problems, all depression, all confusion. It's a purification, but in order to work, it has to hurt, nearly scalding me as I force myself to place one foot in and keep it there, and then the next, and then to kneel and slowly, slowly sit. Once I gather the courage, I lie back and submerge all but my face. The pain crystalizes at my spine, and then it's gone. I am painless now, afloat in a warm limbo, my worries dissolving like dirt. When I rise, I'll be new, my brain and body clean, my heart and hope restored – at least, that's the plan.

The house is sick with silence. Even my father's television set is more muted than usual, like a voice gagged with cotton, only the lowest sounds throbbing in the walls. The little accents of glass and china and silver are missing from the kitchen. My mother must have retreated early this evening, across the ocean and the English Channel, through her bedroom door into France. I wonder if she's in there counting francs. I wonder if she already has her ticket.

I hear an unusual sound at the front door, a key rattling in the lock, loudly, clumsily. The lock does not give, and the handle is pulled and rattled, and now the key is tried again. The silence is caught off-guard. The television set is quickly turned off. The house holds its breath.

A muffled voice curses the outside door, and the lock clicks open, and a heavy foot treads on the wooden floor of the entrance. The door is slammed so hard that the house shakes, and the windows rattle, and something, somewhere, falls and breaks.

'Lock needs some goddamn' graphite.'

It's Phil, and he's drunk, and I'm already stepping out of the tub, forgetting all about rebirth and renewal and wondering why he's here and what's going to happen. I barely towel off and thrust my arms into my robe, and I hear my father from the living room. 'Christ! Jesus Christ!'

When I step out, Phil's back is to me, and he's facing my parents, who stand in the living room, tilting a bit, like statues not quite in place, their eyes enlarged, mouths open.

'Needs graphite,' Phil says, and he raises an imaginary can and sprays it at them. 'Psst. Psst. In the lock.'

'You slammed it so hard,' my father says, pointing. 'Look!'

We all look at the wall barometer which has fallen

to the wood floor, missing the faded rug and smashing its glass.

Phil looks up from the wreckage and turns to me with a sarcastic smile. His eyes are dull and small. 'Cheeve, how long since that goddamn' thing ever worked?'

I'm still an observer, not ready to take sides. He looks at my father.

'Ten fuckin' years.' He turns. 'Right, Ma?'

'What do you want?' she asks quickly with very little breath.

'What do I *want*!?' His voice seems to shake the house as hard as the door slam. The silence bounds for cover like a frightened tomcat. Phil is back. 'What do I *want*?! What kind of question . . . ? What about, "Hello, Phil. Come on in!"'

My father bends over the broken barometer and my mother moves closer to her eldest, her shock replaced by a disapproving look. 'You've been drinking.'

'Bullshit,' Phil says, bending a bit forward at the waist. 'Bullshit. Now . . . tell me to my face.'

'Tell you what?' my mother asks, but of course she knows. He just stares, waiting. My father stands now, pieces of broken glass stacked carefully in his palm.

'Tell you what?' My mother is weakening.

'Goodbye,' Phil says, and my mother's bottom lip begins to tremble. She catches it in her teeth.

'We have to sell the house,' my father says, but Phil does not move his eyes from his mother.

'I'm not going *today*, for God's sake. You think . . .' Her small hands become misshapen little fists. The tears reach her eyes. Her words are angry. 'You think I wouldn't say goodbye? I'm just letting everyone know what is happening. It's been coming a long time. You knew that. I'm not leaving until next week.'

'Next week!?' I don't mean to shout it, but the words explode from me. 'Next *week*?!'

'Why not next week?! Why not?!' She's weeping now, full of indignation, her little chin thrust at us. 'What's the difference?'

'So everything is planned?' I ask. 'It's all . . . You've got your ticket, your passport, everything? Jesus.'

'What's the difference?!' She practically screams this.

'The secrets, Mom! All the secrets. God. All the . . . You could've told me. I could've helped you! I would've helped you, Mom! You think I would've tried to stop you? You . . .'

'Yes! You're trying now! Everybody is trying to make me feel so bad about this. What about me?!'

'Say, "Goodbye, Phil." Just say it.' Phil's voice is more calm now. 'Say it, Mom.'

But she turns and walks out of the room. Phil and I watch her go, and our father says, 'She only thinks about herself.' In a moment, we turn to him. He holds his palm out toward Phil, the curved pieces of glass layered there. 'You don't have to walk in here breaking things.'

Somehow, I know what Phil is going to do even before he moves, and he moves very suddenly and bats my father's hand so that the pieces of glass fly up and over him, tinkling against walls and lamps and windows, and my father opens his mouth in a wordless shout and steps back and then back again as Phil comes closer. My father is four inches taller than Phil, but Phil is a steady piece of stone, balanced like a boxer, moving even closer to the older, softer, slouching man. I see fear mixed with the anger in my father's eyes, and I'm afraid, too, hurrying toward them.

'Hey, Jesus!' I stand beside them as they face each other, only one foot apart. 'Phil!' I have never seen violence in my home, in my family. Mari says I just don't remember. She says Phil was hit often, slapped by both my father and my mother until he became big enough, strong enough, to hit back – which he never did, but they had seen the warning in his eyes.

'You going to pay me?' Phil asks quietly. 'Are you ever going to pay me?'

'I *said* . . . I *said* I'd pay you! I'll pay you out of the sale! I told Claudey to tell you that!' My father is shouting at Phil, raging at him now, ashamed, I think, of being afraid.

'Are you ever going to pay me?'

'I *told* you!'

'He said he'd pay you from the sale of the house, Phil.' I'm just trying to force words in between them, to pry them apart. 'Phil.' But I might as well be invisible and mute.

'You never paid me.'

'I *told* you . . .'

'You never paid me. Never.'

'Damn it, I *told* you . . .'

'You never paid me for the roof!' Phil moves again, so suddenly there isn't even a blur, but now his left hand is holding my father's shirt and sweater, balling the material in a fist.

My father's eyes go wide and he backs up as far as he can, which is only a few inches, tucking in his chin, expecting a blow.

'Phil! Phil! *Phil*!' I put my hands out, one on my father's shoulder, one on Phil's. Phil is hard and tight with tension.

'*Did* you!' Phil curls his right into a fist and cocks it and I see my father's face distort as if he is already struck, eyes closing, mouth grimacing.

'Wait, *wait*!' I'm shouting, pulling now at Phil's shoulder, and my mother is back in the room, though I haven't seen her enter, and she is shouting, too.

'I'll call the police! I'll call the police!'

'What roof?!' I'm shouting into Phil's ear. 'What roof?! What are you talking about, Phil?!'

'The roof!'

'What roof?'

'*He* knows!'

'Tell me!'

'I'm calling the police!'

'She knows, too!'

'Tell *me*!'

'The roof! He never paid me for the goddamn' roof of the store!'

'What about it?! Tell me!'

He turns to me. He does not let my father go, but he turns to me, and I see that tears have come into his eyes, and his lips tremble a bit like my mother's as he tells me.

'I got my friends to fix his goddamn' roof. It was leaking! I told him I could fix it. I knew how to fix it.'

'Let me go. Let me go!' My father has found his voice, but it is shaking.

'I got my buddies, and we fixed it. We were in high school, but we fixed it. Saved him a lot of money! Thousands. Thousands, Dad!' Now Phil turns back to our father and shakes the man by his shirt and sweater. 'Thousands of dollars! And you said it looked crappy and you wouldn't pay! You wouldn't pay!'

'Let me go!'

'I'm calling! I'm calling now!' my mother shouts, but she's not standing near the phone.

'You wouldn't pay anything! And it didn't leak – you son of a bitch! We fixed it, and you said it wasn't professional, you son of a bitch!' Phil is weeping now. My father is clawing at the hand that holds his shirt and sweater, then pushing at Phil, but Phil is immovable. 'I paid them,' Phil shouts. 'I couldn't tell them what a shit you were, so I paid them! I sold my motorbike! *You* didn't give a shit! *She* didn't give a shit!'

Phil straightens out his left arm which pushes my father into the wall and knocks over the floor lamp, and now my mother screams and hurries to the phone. I move around to catch Phil's right arm as he cocks it back.

'Don't, Phil, *don't*! Jesus, don't hit him!'

My father is making squealing sounds, trying to free himself and to block the blow he knows are coming.

'Phil!' I put all my strength on his arm, trying to turn him away from my father. 'Goddammit, Phil, stop! *Stop*!'

Phil can't move his right arm with me hanging on it. He turns to me, teeth bared, tears of rage leaking from an old wound, and he lets go of my father and sends his fist into my face before I know it's coming. He hits me under the right eye and my head snaps back and I'm suddenly moving backwards, losing my feet and falling, flying, it feels like flying backwards, knowing eventually I'm going to land, but I hardly feel the landing.

I'm suddenly crumpled on the floor in front of the sofa, half-sitting up. My head is numb, and I'm trying to move. My robe is mostly open, and I've landed on it, and it is trapping me. I lie there, naked, stunned, jerking against the robe, then giving up and leaning back against the sofa as the pain sets in. I taste blood, and I see them staring at me. All of them have their mouths open. My mother holds the telephone. My father remains pressed against the wall as if still held there. My brother stands over me, looking more surprised even than the others – as if I have just appeared there naked on the floor at his feet.

Then his body loses its tension. His hands go limp at his sides. He wipes his eyes, covering his face for a moment, and while it is covered I hear a muffled, tearful, 'Shit.' He shakes his head then, a quick movement which seems to clear his eyes, and he says 'Shit' again and turns and walks away, passing close to my mother who moves back a step, out of his way, but he never looks at her. He disappears into the hall, and I hear him leave and close the front door.

It's quiet in the room, then, but there is a loud ringing in my ears. My father sets us into motion by leaving the wall and blustering, outraged, moving toward my mother. 'Do you *have* the police? Are they on the line? Let me talk to them.' My mother gives up the phone as she hurries to me, standing over me, bending over me.

'Claude! Claude!'

I rise enough to pull the robe around me, then I sit with my head in my hands.

'Claude!'

'Hello?' my father is saying into the phone. 'Hello?'

'Do you need a doctor, Claude?'

'Hello?'

'Dad.' My voice sounds far away. It hurts to speak. The words come slowly. 'Dad. Hang up the phone. Hang up the phone.' I don't lift my head to see him hang it up, but at least he stops talking.

'Do you need a doctor?' my mother asks.

I summon words again, feeling some nausea at the effort. 'Just leave me alone. Okay?'

I don't hear them move, but when I finally lift my head from my hands, they are both gone.

The inside of my cheek has stopped bleeding. It's sore to the touch of my tongue. There is no longer a ringing in my ears. The ice I wrapped in a dish towel is almost all melted. I lie on my bed and apply the cold towel to my eye and cheek. The skin there is water-soaked and dead to the touch, but if I press, I can feel the bruising.

I'm still absorbing the incident, going over the actions and the words. It feels like one long, shouted sentence, and the punch I took is the period. I take the sentence apart and listen again. It's mostly Phil's voice I hear, but it's my father's face I see, grimacing, blinking, waiting for the fist.

I keep trying to remember when Phil was in high school,

gathering all the images that I can from that time in order to find the story of the roof, but all I can recall is Phil's motor-bike. I remember him on it in the driveway. I remember the sputtering sound it made. I remember wanting him to take me for a ride. But I never rode on it – and then it was gone. I never knew there was so much happening around me that isn't in my memory. Why doesn't it stick? Was I already buried so deep in my soldiers? I'll ask Mari about the roof.

As I think my sister's name, the telephone rings, and I feel myself tightening inside. I don't want to talk to Mari, not now, not yet. I haven't even told her about our parents splitting up, and I'm sure my mother hasn't called her, and now there is this incident, there is the punch, there is all of Phil's anger and pain gathered in his fist, and my father cringing and then the blow. I am battered, damaged, wrapped in a feeling that I suppose is self-pity, but I want to stay wrapped for a while, like a sick child under a quilt. I want someone to bring me magazines and take my temperature.

My answering machine is set for four rings, then I hear my one-word message: 'Speak.' Then there is the beep, and then a voice surprises me, Lauren's voice. She sounds shaken and very, very sad.

'Oh, Cheevey, I'm so sorry to hear what happened. God, I hope you're all right. Please call . . .'

I throw the wet towel aside and spring for the phone, getting to my feet, wrapping the robe around me because it's chilly now in my room. There is only a space heater, but I haven't used it since last winter.

'Hi.'

She sounds relieved at the sound of my voice. 'Oh, I'm glad you're there. Are you . . . How are you?'

'I'm all right.'

'Are you sure? I mean . . .'

'Just a bruise. Phil told you, I guess.'

'Yes. He cried, Cheevey. I've never seen him so . . . He's destroyed.'

'He's drunk.'

There's a pause. I hear her breathe.

'I don't blame you for being mad at him. There's no excuse. You must feel terrible.'

'Well, it was a terrible night. It was a terrible five minutes, but . . . I'm not as mad at him as I sound. I should be *more* mad at him, I really should. I should come over there and punch *him* in the face. Is he at your house?'

'No. He . . . he just stood on the porch and told me, and he cried, but he went home. Maybe you *should* call him, Cheevey.'

'Let him call me – if he's so sorry.'

'I don't think he can face you.'

'Ah, the hell with him.'

There is another pause. 'Well, don't write him off. Don't hate him, Cheevey.'

'I'm not hating him, I'm just mad. My face hurts, and I'm acting tough, and I'm wallowing in self-pity, but I think I'm entitled to do that at least for about an hour or so.'

I imagine her smiling, and then I *hear* her smile in her voice. 'Now you sound like Cheevey.' The sound of her warms me and her words are bandages.

'You have a really good spirit about you. I knew that right away – and so did Molly. When she met you at the park, you know what she said?'

My face doesn't even hurt anymore. 'What?'

'She said, "He's nice right away." She said, "Some people *get* nice – but he's nice right away." She really said that. And she's right. You put her at ease right away. You know, a single mother gets to know men, gets to figure them out all in one minute – and that's the minute she introduces them to her child. No kidding. I can tell so much about a man by the way he acts when I introduce Molly.'

'How did I score?'

'"A" Plus.'

'I'm not supposed to feel this good, Lauren. You're not letting me wallow at all.' I hear her soft chuckle and then a beat of silence, and I'm suddenly afraid the call will end. 'What did Phil say?'

'Well . . . he just said he had done something terrible. "Rotten" was his word. He said he had gone to the house and there was an argument and he hit you. He knocked you down. I hate even *imagining* that happening to you. I really do.'

I think I hear tears in her voice or at least the possibility.

'He hit me because I didn't let him hit our dad. I grabbed his arm. I was . . . really scared. I don't know; it was like something . . . unthinkable, hitting our father. Even now the thought kind of makes me sick – and it's not because our dad is any great guy. But . . .'

'I can understand that.'

'In fact he's *not* a great guy, the more I think about it, the more I learn – how it was with him and Phil. I don't really blame Phil for *wanting* to hit him, but I couldn't stand to watch that happen.'

'So he hit *you* instead.'

'Yeah. Maybe *I* should hit my father. I can't hit as hard as Phil.'

'You're not the kind to hit.'

'I wish I was sometimes.'

'No, Cheevey, you're better than that.' There is another pause, and I'm not quick enough to fill it because now she says, 'Are you going to be all right?' which is a winding-down kind of thing to say.

'Sure.'

'Really, Cheevey? Can I do anything?'

'You've already done a lot. Really. One thing, maybe. But . . .'

'Sure. Tell me.'

'Well, Lauren, you could kiss it and make it better.'

I hear another breathy chuckle. I'm glad. I'm gambling here, and she could've taken it wrong.

'All right,' she says.

'All right?!'

'Yes, next time I see you. It's a promise. Is it your eye?'

'Not exactly.'

'Where?'

'My tongue.'

Now she laughs aloud, and with that laugh I'm sure of the connection between us, and I feel more free, and I'm afraid I'm beginning to love her, and I know that's dumb and young of me, but since she took away my self-pity, I'll wallow in love for a while until it heals like my bruised face.

'Cheevey,' she scolds, her smile bending the word a bit.

'Just kidding. It's my right cheekbone, but my lip hurts a little, too.'

'Uh-huh,' she says with a joking suspicion. Then she becomes serious again. 'I'm really glad you can bounce back from this, Cheevey. I mean, not let it get you down – or change you. Please don't. You're terrific, and I care a lot about you.' I can't speak after that, and in a minute she says, 'Cheevey?'

'Yeah. Thanks, Lauren. I . . . I just want to say one more time: You really looked beautiful today in that white dress. So . . . goodbye. Thanks.' I feel like a fool, and I feel great, and I just let my two minds battle it out as I hang up the phone. Each mind is shouting, one of them saying, 'Why did you tell her *that*?!' and the other answering, 'So that she knows! So that she knows I love her! So shut up!'

I'm smiling like an idiot, even though it hurts my cheek,

and I'm standing in the middle of the room, energized and not knowing what to do, and not wanting to think about anything. My eyes drift to my soldiers. On the shelves where they stand is a fine layer of dust dulling the polished wood.

I remove all the soldiers from the first shelf, carefully, by twos, and put them on the table, and I use the dish towel soaked with ice water to make the wood shine.

I'm babysitting Ballyhoo. It's Tuesday around four o'clock, and I'm cutting a class to do it, but it sounded like an emergency. When I arrived, both Mari *and* Bob thanked me, and then they hurried off, for an hour, they said. I don't know where they are. Of course, before they left they both asked about my face. There is a trace of black and purple below the eye. I told them what I tell everybody: I was helping Phil, and I fell – which, in a bent sort of way, is true enough. I still have not told Mari anything, and my mother still has not called her. I'm planning to tell her before I leave today, and the idea keeps my stomach tight. I'm not sure how she'll react. Bally helps take my mind off it for a few minutes at a time.

We're playing with a set of plastic spacemen. They are just a bit larger than my soldiers, aliens and earthlings mixed, with helmets and oxygen tanks and breathing tubes and all kinds of weapons in their hands, from crossbows to ray-cannons. I set them up, and Bally rolls a softball at them. We call it death bowling, but it's played cartoon-like. We make the voices of the figures sound like comic characters.

'Eeeyah, here it comes again. The ball! The big ball! Run! Climb a tree! Dig a hole! Call a taxi! Take a nap! Dive under the bed! Jump in the refrigerator!'

Every time I come up with a new way to dodge the ball, Ballyhoo laughs a high-pitched machine-gun kind of laugh, and every time he comes up with one, I pick up on it and reinforce it.

'Jump over it! Here it comes! Pee in your pants!'

He laughs and shouts, 'Jump on the ceiling!' And he rolls the ball.

'Yes, the ceiling, quick! Jump up there! Up! Go up! Ahhhh, too late!'

The ball strikes the figures and scatters them as we make sounds.

'Ow! Ow! Ow! Yahhh! Crashhh! Kaboom!'

Then I roll the ball back to him and set up the figures again.

'My dad says that.' He rolls the ball around, keeping one palm on it. 'Go up.'

'What?'

'My dad yells . . .' He makes a face, eyes closed tightly and arms thrust out. '*Go up*!'

'When does he say that?'

The boy shrugs, rolling the ball under his palm.

'Go up?'

He nods. He speaks again, eyes on the softball as he rolls it in a circle. 'My mom thinks I go away.'

'Mm. Yeah. Like at the park? Like at my birthday?'

He nods again.

'More times? Since then? Today?'

He nods again, now lifting the ball in both hands. 'It's a cannonball,' he says.

'Wow, just think of the size of the cannon, Bal, if these guys are the size of men and that's a cannonball. The cannon is the size of *you*.'

'Just think of a cannon as big as this building,' he says.

'Wow.'

'As big as the world!'

'Wow, Bal. Yeah. What if the *world* is a cannonball? Just think . . .' I look around to find his globe. It's an inflated one, getting a bit soft. I hold it up. 'What if we're living on a cannonball?'

He smiles, his twisty, knowing smile.

I stand up with the globe and move it along. 'What if we're spinning through space on some cannonball and out there somewhere is this giant target?'

But he's looking again at the ball under his palm. 'Dad yells at her.'

'At your mom?' I sit beside him now. He nods, eyes on the ball.

'You mean when she thinks you've gone away?'

He nods. Then he strikes the pose again, eyes squeezed closed, arms spread out. 'Go up!' he says in a mock shout that is more of a whisper, and I stare at him.

'Maybe he's saying *grow* up.'

He shrugs again, but he says, 'Go up.'

'Does that scare you?'

He doesn't answer. He just rolls the ball.

'You want to bowl anymore?'

This he answers by lifting the ball and throwing it. It hits the floor and bounces and lands within the humans and aliens, scattering them, but we make no funny shouts.

Mari and Bob arrive home, both of them unusually quiet. They have brought Bally a toy, a small 'space tractor' of some kind and he gasps with delighted surprise, his eyes and mouth wide, and he throws me that look for a second, sharing his joy with me. Then he takes the present, saying, 'Thanks, guys!' And begins removing it from the box.

'Don't lose any parts, Billy,' Bob says – but gently. 'Careful, there's a few parts to it.'

Bally sits and removes the toy more carefully. Bob watches him, smiling, but soon he's just looking at the floor, deep within some troubled thought. When Mari comes close, I toss her the inflated globe I'm still holding.

She catches it and throws it back. I catch it and glance at Bob, wondering if I should include him in the throwing and catching. I like to give him a chance. But he is walking out of the room. Bally is driving the tractor along with one hand, his face on the floor beside it. He is making the noise of its motor. I toss the globe at Mari. She catches it and walks very close to me, speaks in low tones the boy can't hear.

'We went to a shrink.'

'Oh. Well, that's good.'

She shrugs and then puts the globe back in Bally's toy corner. 'What'd you guys do?'

'We played, and we figured out the big bang theory.'

'Oh, good. Is there any money in it?'

'Sure, once we publish.'

'Bally gets fifty percent of everything.'

'It's a deal.'

'And I get ten percent of your fifty percent since you were in my employ while you two thought it up.'

'Five percent.'

'Seven and a half.'

'Done.'

'Have your lawyer call my lawyer.'

'Don't you want to hear the theory?'

'Lay it on me.'

'The big bang is a cannon, somewhere in the universe. The planets are cannonballs. We are living on a cannonball that is hurtling through space after being fired by the big bang. We haven't figured out exactly what the target is – or the date of impact.'

'Could be tomorrow.'

'It could be right this . . .' I look at my watch. 'No, I guess we're still hurtling.'

'It's not a cannonball, Cheeve.'

'Oh? You have your own theory?'

'Just a slight adjustment. It's a pinball, bouncing around endlessly in this giant game. The stars are the lights going on and off.'

'Who's working the flippers?'

'God.'

She sits heavily in a chair, and I sit on the arm. 'So . . . are you going back,' I ask her, 'to the shrink?'

She stares off and shrugs, reminding me of Bally.

'I have to talk to you about something.' I'm suddenly aware of my heart. It feels like it's growing, filling my entire chest. 'About Mom and Dad.'

Now her eyes are on me. 'What about them?'

'Want to take a walk?'

'Cheevey, don't. Just tell me now.' She is already upset, and I dread this, but once she hears the news she may just shrug and say: 'Of course, what did you expect?' I'm hoping for that.

'They're splitting up.'

She just stares at me.

'Mom's going to France – I mean, to live.'

She hasn't moved.

'I suppose you're thinking "finally," or "of course," but I didn't see it coming. I mean, I saw them getting worse, but, Christ, it knocked me over.'

She is still until her eyes begin to blink rapidly. I can see tears coming, but she is unwilling to accept them. She is blinking them away. The tears are in her voice, too, when she begins to speak, but she clears her throat and says, evenly, 'When did they say this?'

'Saturday night. Mom's leaving next week. Dad's selling the house.'

The blinking continues – with her eyes never leaving me, waiting for more.

I shrug. 'I guess you really had it nailed – about the tunneling, people tunneling away from each other, secretly moving away . . . You're more prepared for this, I guess. Right? Mari?'

'She's not really going,' Mari says calmly – but her eyes are still blinking. 'She always used to threaten that she was going. But she's not.'

'She *is*, Mari.'

Mari shakes her head, very definite. 'It's talk. It's worse than I thought. I haven't heard her talk like that for years, but it's talk, Cheeve. Both of them. It's all victim talk, martyr talk. They're both busy nailing themselves to crosses. I used to see this all the time. Dad's crying about money, right? And she's talking about sacrifice. They're fighting for sainthood. It's an old war coming back.'

'I don't think so . . .'

'Listen to me. I know what I'm talking about. Can you imagine, can you for one second *imagine* her living any other way? Or him? It's just come back to the surface. It's like an old volcano. Here it comes again. Maybe it's healthy.'

'Mari . . .'

'I'll show you.' She stands suddenly, and calls out sharply, 'Bob! Bob, do you have to work now?'

He walks in from the bedroom, staring curiously, wondering at the edge in her tone.

'I need to go with Cheevey for a few minutes. I need to leave Bally here.'

'Go where?'

'Home. I mean, to my mother – for a few minutes.'

'Why?'

'Bob!' She is looking at him in a very steady, even businesslike way, but she is blinking and now she is shaking a bit, her hands mostly, her head slightly.

Bob looks at me. 'What's going on?'

'Our parents,' I say. 'It looks like they're splitting up.'

'They are *not*,' Mari says. 'They're just talking about it again. They're scaring Cheevey. They have him believing it, and it's not right. She just needs to talk it out and yell and cry. I know her. So I'm going over there.'

Both Bob and Bally are standing the same way, very still, heads tilted a bit, looking at her with the same expression, surprised – and a little afraid.

'Just for a little while,' she says, already looking for the car keys, sweeping them off the table. 'Bally, be good. I'll be right back.' She heads out the door and starts down the stairs, saying, 'Come on, Cheevey.'

Bally and Bob have turned to me now.

'Maybe she's right,' I say to them, without any confidence at all. I shrug and follow my sister.

On the way home, I tell Mari about Phil and the incident. She says 'Jesus Christ' several times, shaking her head, angry, but she never takes her eyes off the road.

'Do you remember about the roof?' I ask her. 'How Dad wouldn't pay him for fixing the roof?'

She just keeps driving, keeps blinking. I let go of the subject and just ride along.

When we pull up in front of the house, we see that a realtor's 'For Sale' sign is in the yard, a shingle hanging from a substantial post that has been planted in our weedy grass. It lists phone numbers and says to ask for Wendy or Thia. I have never seen this sign before.

'Must have put that up after I left for school today,' I say.

Mari is staring at the sign, blinking as fast as she can, but she can't blink them away anymore. She leaves the tears on her face and just stares, and then she leaves the car and walks to the house. I follow slowly, stopping to study the sign, absorbing what it means. We have gone public now with our darkness. The brightly painted wood might as well say, 'The family that lives here is coming apart. Ask for Wendy or Thia.'

When I enter the house, I hear the voices moving from the kitchen to the master bedroom, the female voices of our family, striking almost the same notes. The only words I hear are '. . . didn't *call* me.' And '. . . please don't try . . .', and then the bedroom door is closed. Quietly, I walk close to that door, but once inside they have settled into low, almost secretive rhythms.

I don't know why they have closed me out, but I don't touch the door handle. I respect the private, female tones inside, and I walk away. Actually, I feel some relief now. It is as if I have brought the doctor to a sick home, and I can step back. I can surrender my fear and confusion and frustration and just wait. Maybe this change is not as certain as I thought, though the realtor's sign makes it seem that way. Signs can come down, and, anyway, I've seen For Sale signs in front of homes for months in our neighborhood. Plenty of time to change minds and even to heal. What we need, I decide, sitting alone in the little-used living room, is a family meeting, all of us in one room – actually speaking to each other, actually listening. I am going to suggest that.

Mari and my mother have been in the bedroom for almost fifteen minutes. I want to know what's happening, and I want to bring them my suggestion. I go to the door and listen again to the quiet, female hum. This time the voices sound more ragged, maybe cracked by tears, but I'm not sure. I put my hand on the handle and turn softly, open the door slowly.

My mother is seated at her desk-table, but turned around in her swivel chair to face Mari, who is sitting on the foot of the bed. They both turn to look at me as I enter. I see that they *have* been crying. They soon look back at each other and resume talking. After that first glance, I am accepted but invisible, and I drift into the room like a spirit, moving toward the bed in order to sit beside Mari.

Mari wipes at her face and speaks in a broken and

wet voice, slightly whining, like a little girl. The words stop me.

'I could help you get settled,' she says.

'Mari,' my mother says, 'I told you. It's all taken care of.' I am staring at my sister, wondering where her strength has gone, her knife-point wit, her needles of sarcasm. She has dropped all her weapons and her certainty and her anger.

'I could still help. I speak better than you do, Mom, you don't have the ear for it.'

'Don't be silly. Mari, what a thing to say. You know I'm fluent. I'm practically fluent.' My mother's tone is more soothing than harsh.

Mari is unfolding a damp, half-shredded Kleenex. 'You were going to take me after high school.'

'I got sick,' my mother says. 'You know I got sick.'

Now Mari uses the Kleenex to wipe her cheeks and under her nose, turning to me and speaking through trembling lips with sharp intakes of breath like a girl of six or ten. 'Remember, Cheeve? I was going to go to France with Mom as a graduation present.'

'I got sick, Mari. You remember that.'

But Mari goes on, speaking to me.

'We had it all planned. Remember?'

I am just staring, surprised. I don't respond soon enough so she turns back to my mother.

'We could still be together over there for a while, and then I'll come back, but we could have some time like we said – at the cafés and the Louvre and shopping, and I could bring Bally, maybe. It would be very good for him. And you wouldn't have to pay for me.'

'Please, Mari . . .' My mother turns to me now, pleading her case. They are still speaking softly, secretively, though there is no one outside the door now. 'There are people meeting me. It's all arranged through Club Français. It's all arranged. I've been planning this . . .'

'You could've told us,' I say, and my mother touches her forehead with her fingers, looking at the floor.

'Don't you start now, Claude. I knew this would happen. I knew you would try and talk me out of this.'

'She's not talking you out of it, Mom. She wants to go with you.'

'She can't. I can't. It's all arranged.'

'You mean you don't want me,' Mari says. 'You don't *want* to go with me. You never did, Mom. That's why you got sick after high school.'

'Don't say that! I practically went to the hospital.'

But Mari has risen from the bed and is walking out of the room.

'Mari, I had bronchitis!' My mother turns to me again. 'Claude, *you* remember.'

'I don't know,' I say, thinking back about seven years. 'I guess so. I remember her practicing French so much it drove me crazy. Yeah. I remember how excited she was.'

'And you remember I got sick. Seriously ill.'

'I guess so. I guess I do.' I am on my way out of the room.

'I was sick most of the summer,' my mother says, and as I leave the room, she is still talking. 'You don't fool around with bronchitis.'

Mari stands at the window in the living room, still getting some mileage out of that same, shrinking piece of Kleenex. I see her back shudder a bit, and then she blows her nose into about an inch of tissue. I walk into the bathroom and come out with a whole box for her. When I join her at the window, she whispers, 'Thanks,' and pulls out two fresh ones, and then she says, 'I want to see Dad now. Will you come?'

My father is busy with a customer, so Mari and I hang back and wait. He glances at Mari now and then and smiles a nervous little smile. Mari has that weary and vaguely blurred look of someone who has just wept. She is not in the mood for talking, which is rare. She was silent in the car the whole way – yet she thanked me for coming with her. She drifts to the line of floor models, all showing a newscast without sound. I just amble about and notice that Jack-o-lantern is there, outside our window, speaking to his friend in the glass. I stand in his eye-line, but his focus is on his reflection and does not penetrate into the store. I look about and pretend I'm adjusting a stand of brochures, and I squat down so that my face is just a foot or so from the window. I place my face so that it takes up the same space as his reflection, and I stare at him, and, for once, he sees me. He looks *through* his reflection to my face. It is the first time I have ever held his eyes. I am surprised to see a clarity there, an intelligence. There is a brief moment of contact. His fleshy face seems to harden a bit with tension and with a kind of darkness. He is suspicious and somehow sad and somehow lost. Then he refocuses his eyes. It is the most delicate and minute movement, quick and slight as a thought, but in that shift of focus he has escaped, he has leapt into another universe. His mouth moves again. His face grows animated, speaking to the glass man.

I stand and go to Mari.

'Mari, let me show you something.'

She keeps her eyes on a pretty anchor woman on a television screen. 'What?'

'Jack-o-lantern. Remember? The guy who speaks to his reflection in the window. Let me show you.'

'Not now.'

'Just for a second.'

'Not now, Cheeve.'

I look where *she* is looking, at the newscaster whose hair is too perfect and make-up impenetrable, and we wait for Dad.

When he comes back, he keeps his smile in place, though he looks very uncomfortable. I am surprised when Mari hugs him so tightly. So is he. He glances at me briefly as if not knowing what to do. Then he closes his eyes and hugs her, too.

When they separate to arm's length she is crying again, silently.

My father is nodding, and he finally discards the smile. 'I guess Claudey told you?'

'Daddy, will you come over, please? Come and have dinner with us.'

'Oh, well . . . I . . . You know *me*. I just take a quick bite and I like to, you know, watch some TV and just be alone awhile. It's this place. You know. I need to get off away from everybody in the evenings . . .'

'Daddy,' she says, 'I know. I know that. But I'm saying . . . Well, you know what, then? I'll come by at lunchtime and we'll walk somewhere. What time do you have lunch tomorrow?'

'Oh, well . . . It, uh, depends on customers, and . . .'

'One,' I say, and he shoots me a look that is not angry, but helpless. 'Trevor'll be here tomorrow, Dad, and you usually break at one.'

'One o'clock,' Mari says. 'Okay? Tell me how you're doing?'

He is at a loss. He's used to fending off sarcasm from Mari, but she has none today. He sort of folds in, collapsing a little, slouching more than ever.

'Well, it's really shit. I *have* to sell the house, you know. I *have* to. She already has a lawyer. She's just walking away from everything. This is a lousy time to sell the house.' He glances over at the customers who he let wander on their own awhile.

'Tomorrow,' Mari says. 'I'll come by at one and we'll go talk. All right?'

He is still watching the customers. He nods. 'She's just thinking about herself,' he says. 'What am *I* supposed to do?'

The customers glance at him, and he nods and gives them a tight-lipped, efficient grin. Mari takes one of his hands and squeezes it, surprising him again, bringing his eyes to her.

'Tomorrow, Daddy. I'll see you.'

'Okay. All right.' We're leaving. He's waving. 'Say hello to . . .' He lets it trail off and walks toward the customers. I open the door for Mari and she walks out, passing Jack-o-lantern without a look.

We drive to the park without speaking. She pulls up to a meter and leaves the car unlocked and puts no money in the slots. I watch her walk to a bench and sit, facing the sea. I slip a quarter in the meter and crank it, and suddenly there is a limit to our time, a blind eye watching over us and ticking. I push the car's lock buttons down and re-slam the doors and follow Mari.

I don't join her on the bench but stand behind her, staring at the same calm sea, my hands on her shoulders. Slowly, she tilts her head so that her cheek rests on one of my hands. Almost by themselves my fingers begin to work the tendons and muscles near her neck. Her body settles into the bench. We watch the grey-blue mass that just now is as flat as plastic.

I am still tasting disappointment and trying to let go of all anger. Mari was going to set things straight. If she wasn't going to talk them out of this splitting and scattering, she, at least, was going to tell them off, spitting out insights, revealing their list of sins, explaining this family in her own terms. I feel as if she let me down. Phil, too. I can't make sense out of what I've seen.

'I thought you were going to help me understand all this,' I say, and then I'm sorry I said it.

She doesn't answer for several breaths. 'Don't be mad at me,' she says in a small, tired voice.

'I'm not.'

'You should be, Cheeve, but don't be. I couldn't stand that now.'

'I'm not, Mari.'

'I was supposed to help you,' she says.

'Well, you just heard about it. It's hard to swallow. You haven't had any time with it.'

'Yes, I have.' She sighs and continues in her weary way, and I continue a gentle massaging with my fingers and thumbs. 'I've had years. I was supposed to help you when they left. Phil was already beyond help, I guess. I don't know. Poor Phil. But I was supposed to help you.'

'When they left?'

'Years ago. They were slow about it. They eased away from us, and I should've taken their place. My age says so, my gender says so. I was supposed to become a little earth mother. It's why I have breasts and periods. I could've helped you. Maybe even helped Dad. Maybe everybody. Even her. I should've been the glue. The girl child. I should've been the glue, but I don't know how. There's something wrong. It's supposed to be instinct. I don't have it. There's a missing piece in me. It's missing for Bally, too.'

'Mari . . .'

'I should have it for Bally, but I don't. It's supposed to be primal. I'm supposed to have the ability to create the center and soften it, the core, the center around which the family revolves. I'm supposed to be the nexus. If Mom drew back, then I should've stepped forward. She slipped away. He slipped away. I was no help.'

'Will you stop? Mari, please . . .'

'I should have raised you, I should've done it without thinking. I could still have all the learning. I could still have all the study. I'm not talking about choices. I should have done it without thought. There should be a place in me that took over, took over *me*, too. A place that knew. Like now, like with Bally. It never kicked in. The instinct, the knowing, the female, mothering, tribal . . .'

'That's bullshit.'

'No, it's not.'

'You think every woman is a mother or *has* to be a mother?'

'No. No, Cheeve. Of course not. But we're supposed to have a nurturing instinct, some DNA, something that makes us natural care-givers.'

'You do that. I've seen you do that.'

'No. No, with me it's all bluff. It's all stumbling. I don't know anything. I don't know my lines. It's a complete fake.'

'You love Bally and you love me . . .'

'Of course. Of *course* I love, but look at me.' She suddenly moves forward, out from under my hands, and she walks to the stone wall that lines the cliffs. She stands there and keeps her eyes on the water. I see a hand rise quickly to brush at a tear, then drop to her side.

I walk to her and stand with my back to the ocean, lean on the fence and stare at her.

She won't turn from the sea. 'There's a missing piece,' she says again. 'And a missing peace. Both kinds of peace, Cheevey.'

'You're not *supposed* to feel *anything*. I don't think it comes that way, Mari. You're not obliged to *know* – just automatically. You're just beating yourself up, taking blame. Christ. It's not your fault.'

I don't think she has heard me at all. 'I'm like the opposite of a magnet,' she says. 'Like the kind of magnet that repels things, when you see nails and other magnets jump away from a magnet – that's me. Things fly away.'

'I don't fly away from you. Bally doesn't fly . . .'

'Yes, he *does*.' Now she has turned to me.

'Not really. You just imagine . . .'

'So does Bob. So does Dad. So does Mom. Even Dash is flying away. Now she never calls me.'

'Dash is . . .' I hesitate.

'What?'

'Dash is no great friend.'

'What d'you mean?'

'I don't know.' I shrug. 'Shallow, I guess. Not like you.'

'Not like me.' She turns back to the ocean. In a moment she nods toward it. 'There's a secret out there that I'm supposed to know. It's the missing piece. It's the missing peace. Somebody was supposed to tell me. Look at how calm it is.'

I look, and I tell her, 'I just met somebody like that, somebody calm. They're rare, Mari.' But once again, she hasn't heard me. 'Mari, how many people do you know like that? Peaceful.'

She looks at me, then back at the ocean. 'I didn't find any codes in Coretti. I don't know what to do with Coretti now.' She has leaped into another conversation, and I'm trying to follow.

'Dump him.'

'No. At least I can do *that*. I can give that. I can interpret Coretti. I can connect him to the masses or at least to the readers. I can wire him in. I can be that little drop of solder.'

'*He's* got nothing to give,' I tell her.

'The secret,' she says. 'He's got that. It's between his lines. That's what I have to capture – his pauses. "Coretti's silence." That's a new alternate title. I almost wrote a story once, about Snowy. Remember? Our dog?'

'I remember our dog. I *barked* like our dog. I can *still* . . .'

She goes on without hearing me. She is scaring me

now, unable to listen, unable to keep her thoughts strung together.

'"Love Without Paws," remember, Cheeve? We were always saying to the dog, especially when it was muddy, whenever he would jump on us, "No paws!" "No paws!" So I was going to write "Love Without Paws." Without *pause*, you know? It's homophonic. "Love Without Paws." I'm full of homophones today.'

'*I'm* writing a novel.' I'm desperate to break through. I've never told her about *Cheever's Legion*. 'Mari?'

'Hm?'

'I'm writing a novel – kind of in my head. Historical fiction. Remember when Uncle Henry or . . .'

'Harvey,' she says. At least she's listening.

'Harvey sent that box of books to Phil? Old C.S. Forester and F. Van Wyk Mason and all that romantic, historical . . . Mari!'

'What?'

'You're not listening.' I had seen her eyes shift inward, a change of foucs, the same kind of escape Jack-o-lantern made.

'I should go,' she says. 'Bob is with Bally and he needs to study. Shall I drive you home?'

I stare at her awhile, feeling sorrow collect in my throat. I try and swallow it.

'Cheeve?'

'I'll walk.'

'Okay.' She steps into me and hugs, and I hold her tight.

'Please be okay, Mari.'

'Me?' she says against my shoulder. 'Of course.'

'I love you, Mari. Don't kid around.'

As we break, she kisses my chin. 'I love you too, Cheeve. Don't worry.' For a few seconds, she gives me her eyes and her old wry, twisting grin, and then she's walking to her car, walking hurriedly. Her shoulders seem tight.

I wish I had rubbed them more deeply and given her some ease.

I arrive home late from school on Wednesdays, almost five-thirty, and I enter the main house before I go to my room because I need to use the bathroom – but I stop in the hall, as usual, to check the hall table for that rare piece of mail or any notes from my parents, or – as I find today – my clean laundry. My mother has washed and dried and folded it, and there it sits on the table, a neat pile of shirts and jeans and socks and underwear. There is a bright white envelope on top of the pile, a square one, with my name on it – Mother's spelling: 'Claude.'

I open the envelope. It is not glued. I remove a card with a printed greeting on the front: 'To our son on his birthday.' Inside are two twenty-dollar bills and the printed verse:

> To all the love
> And wishes said
> We add our prayer
> For joy ahead

It is signed only, 'Mother'.

I pocket the twenties and put the card in my book bag, and I stare at the pile of laundry. Beyond the cash and the remembering of birthdays, this is something my mother has always given to me. I guess it is symbolizing my mother at this moment as I think about it. Clean clothing has always appeared for me, once a week, neatly folded, as if dropped off by a messenger. I have never thought much about it and probably never thanked her. I am twenty officially today, and it is still appearing. This is probably the last batch. If she is leaving next week, this is the last message I will receive from her in the language of clean cloth. I wonder if the cleaning and the folding represents twenty years of silent duty and obligation, and I hope there was some love in it, in the work, in the hands that spread and snapped and folded all that clothing.

I walk through the silent house and reach her closed bedroom door, and I knock very softly.

'I'm lying down,' she says.

'Are you all right?' I say through the door.

'Just my back.'

'Thanks, Mom.'

'Sure.'

'For the laundry, too.'

She doesn't respond to that, and I walk away quietly.

Up in my room, I am putting away the clean clothes, when I notice there is paper pinned to a pair of jeans. She does this when she finds something in the pocket. It is my birthday present from Lauren, a free dinner for two at Angelini.

This would be perfect, I decide, to raise my spirits and put a cap on this monumental birthday of mine – but who can I invite, especially on short notice? I go to the phone to call Benko, and I notice I have a message on my machine. I press the button and find that in those seconds of rewinding, I'm thinking of Lauren and hoping it's her.

It is Phil's voice, thick and low and hesitant. 'Hey, sport.' Then a long breath. 'I'm sorry. Okay?' Another breath. 'Sorry.'

Maybe this is fate, I think, staring at the machine. Maybe it's dinner with Phil at Angelini, and two brothers putting everything on the table for once – memories, anger, love and pain out there with the pasta and bread and wine. No, no wine – not with Phil. I punch the numbers before I have a chance to think too hard, but after two rings I hear *Phil's* machine click on, and a more animated version of his voice begins asking for the date and time and number. After the beep, I plunge in without planning my words.

'Phil. Yeah. Okay. But I owe you a punch. Like in a duel – when one man saves his pistol shot. When you're least expecting it . . . when you're eighty and I'm seventy, I'm going to clock you, knock your dentures out.' I'm not sure what else I have to say. 'Things are shit here. All mixed up.' I pause again and then blurt out ''Bye' and disconnect. Then I hurriedly dial Benko.

''Lo.'

'Benk.'

''S'up?'

'I've got a free dinner at Angelini, you know, near Barrington?'

'Yeah.'

'Been there?'

'No.'

'I got it from Lauren.'

'Yeah. I remember.'

'What d'you think of her, Benk?'

'Lauren? I don't know. She looked nice.'

'She's great.'

'Great?'

'Yes.'

'Actual greatness?'

'Unequivocal.'

'In what way?'

'Beautiful. Kind. Honest. Calm . . .'

'Gives head?'

'Don't besmirch her, man.'

'Ooh, sorry. No smirch intended. A jest.'

'Forgiven.'

'She's old, right?'

'Old?'

'You said she was Phil's age.'

'Maybe a little more.'

'Too old for *you*, I mean. I mean, this is chaste love from afar I'm hearing. Correct?'

'Negative.'

'Christ.'

'I can't help it. I wasn't even sure until I just admitted it just now.'

'She's a mother of a daughter, Cheeve. She's a definite adult. She pays taxes. She has credit. She's probably a PTA member. Probably remembers the sixties fondly. She has seen Elvis *alive*. Definitely from another dimension.'

'I know all that . . .'

'You're hysterical from all that's coming down around you, bud.'

'She's what I want.'

'A younger version.'

That stops me, and I sigh long and hard. 'I suppose, Benk. You think there are any?'

'We'll look.'

'I wish she was my mother.'

'That makes sense.'

'And I wish she was my lover.'

'You're entering a Freudian zone, Cheeve.'

'Of course. I'll never tell her.'

'Of course. It's perfect that way,' Benko says. 'It's knightly.'

'Chivalric,' I say. 'Are you hungry? Can you come to Angelini?'

'Ooh, not tonight, Cheeve. Got a date.'

'No shit. Great. You didn't say.' He is quiet for a moment. 'Benk?'

'It's with Patti.'

'Hey, that's all right.'

'You said.'

'Sure. That's fine. Where you going? Never mind.'

'I don't know. Shoot pool, maybe – or a movie. I'll say hello from you.'

'No. You don't have to.'

'So she knows it's not behind your back.'

'Christ, Benk, it's been over a year.'

'Yeah.'

'It's okay. You can say hello.'

'Okay. Sorry about the restaurant.'

'S'all right.'

'My *sister* is free.'

'Fuck you.'

'*All* my sisters are free.'

'How's your mother?'

'Free.'

'No, I'll ask Lauren.'

'Land mines, Cheeve. Go with care.'

'I won't embarrass myself. I'll love in secret. I'll write a poem. Remember when you were going to look into the Merchant Marine?'

'Want me to look into it?'

'Yeah.'

'Foreign Legion, too?'

'*Certainement.*'

'*Adieu, Homes.*'

'Later, Benk.' I disconnect and search my table top for Lauren's number, leaving no time for cowardice to seep in. I punch the number. It rings only once.

'Hello.'

'Hi, Molly?'

'Yes.'

'This is Cheevey.'

'Hi.'

'You know what today is?'

'Wednesday.'

'Smarty. Today is my official birthday. You know how old I am?'

'No.'

'Very, very old.'

'You are not.' I can hear her small voice rising toward laughter.

'Yes I am. I'm twenty. Starting today I'm very grown up. Can you hear it in my voice?'

'No.'

'I bet I'm older than your favorite actor. Who's your favorite actor?'

She says, 'Robin Williams,' and then she shouts without covering the phone, 'it's Cheevey, Mom.'

'Forget actors. Who's your favorite singer? I bet I'm much older.'

'Elvis.'

'Elvis!' She has a piccolo laugh, sharp, thin notes, probably the very highest sounds the human ear can hear. She has me smiling now. 'Tell me, Molly, did your mother ever see Elvis in person?'

'Yes. In Las Vegas. Did you?'

'Yes. I saw him yesterday.'

'You did not!' I can hear Lauren chuckling in the background and asking questions, but I can't hear her words.

'He was in Fatburger. He asked about you.'

'You lie like a rug.'

'Where did you get *that* expression?!'

'From my mom.'

'You better put her on. I have to talk to her about expressions.'

'Okay.'

As the phone is passed, I notice my excitement, but I do *not* try to think of what to say.

'*What* are you doing to my daughter?' comes her low, warm voice, her smile showing in the slight bending of the words.

'Lauren. Lauren, this is a question. Would you and Molly, at your earliest convenience, like to be my guests at Angelini for dinner?' I start to wait, but I can't bear the silence. 'This is my official birthday and I'd like to celebrate it with you two . . .'

'You mean tonight?'

'Well, it doesn't have to be. Whenever you two are free. Name a good night. I have the freebie you gave me, and I have birthday bucks, and all I need to make everything perfect is to hear you say yes and name a night in the near future that suits you and Miss Molly, so . . .'

'Yes. Tonight.'

I become a freeze frame. Even my brainwaves lock in place.

'Tonight is great, Cheevey, because I was just thinking, what am I going to cook? The prospects were pretty dreary. What time?'

'Well . . . I . . .'

'Oh, you don't have a car, do you?'

'No . . . I . . .'

'Why don't we pick you up? What time?'

I try to take a deep breath but there already *is* a deep breath in my chest. As the air rushes out, my mind is in motion again. 'I'll . . . I'll bus it.'

'No, we'll pick you up.'

'Not here.' I can't be picked up at my parents' home. I don't want to feel fifteen. 'I need to do a few things, and then I'll meet you there. Is seven okay?' I give myself plenty of time for waiting for buses.

'Fine.'

'Great.'

'What a treat.'

'For me too, Lauren. See you there.'

'All right.'

I hang up and throw my arms wide and laugh like some

fiend in a bad movie. I feel all-powerful, and my woes are temporarily kicked out of sight. I hurry to the closet and rip the plastic bag off my best jacket.

At six-thirty I'm already at the restaurant, so I begin some slow walking around the block to eat up the time. I'm wearing beige slacks and a metallic green sport jacket that fits well. Last Christmas Benko and I found silk shirts at Bullock's for thirty-eight bucks and bought each other one as a gift. Mine is cream-colored and makes me feel rich and Italian. I put one hand in a pocket and adopt an attitude in my walking that is a bit European and aloof or at least self-possessed. I imagine the people in passing cars glancing at me and feeling a sense of mystery. Who is he? Where is he going? He looks foreign. He reminds me of one of Sophia Loren's sons I saw in a magazine – wealthy and worldly, tragically beautiful. He is taking his time, but I'll bet his ultimate destination tonight is a woman, a woman slightly older, experienced, dangerous.

I enter Angelini at ten to seven, tired of walking around. It's a large place, and it's early, and I have my pick of several tables. The hostess is pretty, young, very short-skirted in a kind of checkered suit. She is only slightly aloof and looks like magazine material. I try to hold on to some of my mystery and say very little and smile without showing teeth. I select a table by the wall. She seats me and leaves menus and smiles warmly this time, and as she walks away I allow myself to study the backs of her thighs and her buttocks in that small skirt. As she reaches her hostess station, I notice Lauren and Molly there, too, watching me watch the hostess's ass.

I stand and wave them over with a large gesture, showing teeth, mystery all gone.

I shake Molly's cold little hand, and Lauren I hug briefly, but tightly. She never sloughs a hug. Once seated, Lauren says that we're all here early, and isn't that nice? I agree and wonder if she'll have a drink or some wine. She says no thank you, and isn't that hostess a cute one? I say oh, I didn't notice, and Lauren pretends a frown and slaps my shoulder in a scolding way, and all the ice is broken and melted and gone.

There are meals taken to banish hunger and there are meals eaten as celebrations of the food and of the time spent over the food. There is something spiritual about the second kind of meal, and magical, too. The food turns to laughter. Water dissolves pain. Cups and glasses ring like bells. The meal may be in a palace or a cave. It doesn't matter. The heart is served and the soul is filled, and everyone is drunk with joy.

'This is the best birthday gift I've ever eaten,' I say.

'Do you eat *all* your gifts?' Lauren asks.

'I ate a sweater today,' I say, and Molly laughs into her milk and sprays the table white. Lauren and I are squeezing our laughter so it doesn't become too loud as we clean up. Molly has her napkin over her face from embarrassment, but we see by her shoulders quaking that she is laughing into the cloth.

Lauren looks wonderful when she laughs, her face unmanaged and silly and tinted pink, her eyes and mouth wide as if surprised by her own outburst. She is wearing a black satin shirt, long and oversized, over a black skirt, her hair a mad dash of color with her dark clothing. Molly is in a flowered dress I've seen before with the slimmest gold bracelet on her tiny wrist.

The waiter comes over to help, but he is too late. Lauren is a very efficient cleaner. He leaves us with new napkins.

'That's my daughter's imitation of a hose,' Lauren says.

'No more jokes,' Molly pleads, coming out from behind her napkin.

'I wasn't joking. I *did* eat a sweater. Last night I ate a tie. Once I was given a watch for Christmas.'

'You didn't?' Lauren says.

'Oh, yes. Two years ago, and it's still ticking. You can hear it if you put your ear on my stomach. I swear, Molly.'

Lauren looks at her. 'Want to try it?'

'No! He lies like a rug, Mom.'

'Did you teach your daughter that expression?'

'My mother did.'

I get a sudden image of a line of Laurens, generations of warm and peaceful women who give their offspring their eyes and their hands while they speak to them and while they listen. Time is given like pieces of gold. Attention is handed down like an heirloom.

'So what's your . . . plan, Lauren?' The meal is done, and I'm sitting back, an arm hooked over a corner of my chair, feeling expansive and much older now. 'You want to stay with the store?'

Lauren is stirring honey into her herb tea. She doesn't slouch at all, I notice, no elbows on the table. Molly has the same good posture, though they're not at all rigid, just composed. 'I like the store,' Lauren says. 'And it's good security for Molly and me, but I'm also a calligrapher.'

'Oh?'

'I do some through the store. Freelance, too. I'll give you a card.' She winks. 'Drum up business.'

'Sure!'

'And I'm always taking art classes. Illustration. I like to take my favorite writings and play with them, a combination of calligraphy and illustration. I don't know if I'll ever *sell* anything or publish anything.' She chuckles and shrugs. 'Maybe. Someday. But I enjoy it.'

'I'd love to see your work.' I'd love to see into her brain and her heart, is what I mean. I'm very excited by this, by the fact that she creates something as personal as a drawing. It leaves her so vulnerable. I'll be able to see her dreams.

'Well, I'd enjoy sharing it with you,' she says.

'When?'

I've made her laugh again, and I join her. 'You're just right there, Cheevey. I like that.'

'Not with everybody,' I say, and I see her blush a little as she goes back to stirring her tea. That blush is a beautiful thing. It quickens me. It tells me she has heard me. She knows I care for her. In a soft and subtle way, it is me making love to Lauren, and Lauren responding to me. I spoke. She blushed. I feel we are intimate now. I feel my love for her in every drop of my blood. I am so glad, at this moment, that I am a fool.

'Cheevey, come back close to the table.'

I stare at her, wondering.

'Sit forward, with your elbows on the table, like before.'

Her eyes are so kind and loving, and there is still a trace of that blush left. I would stand *on* the table if she asked me to in that calm, warm way of hers. I sit forward, leaning on the table, watching her.

She reaches out to me. I stop breathing. Molly is watching and wondering, too. Lauren touches my neck and shoulder gently as she reaches to the inside collar of my sport jacket. 'I don't want you to feel embarrassed about this,' she says, and I feel her hand moving, and I hear paper. She pulls her hand back and places on the table a rather large safety pin and a dry cleaner's tag.

I stare at these things. Molly chuckles. My cheeks are warm. 'Oh, God,' I say. 'What an idiot.' Lauren, too, chuckles gently. I keep staring at that pin. It seems enormous. The tag grows in front of me until it obscures the table top. 'Oh, God.' I think about how suave I felt, how collected. I walked through a magazine tonight. I charmed the hostess. I sat here like a Roman, and all the while there was this sign written in the air over my head by some cruel cartoonist. 'Idiot,' I say again, smiling sarcastically at the pin and tag and shaking my head.

'Cheevey,' Lauren says, and I look at her. Her eyes not only touch me. They kiss my forehead. Her look does not diminish me. It honours me. 'It's not because you're an idiot,' she says. 'It's because you're alone.'

Several times during the night I wake after unremembered dreams, and I move to a cooler region of the pillow and burrow in, hoping to crawl back into sleep before my thoughts can catch me. I can hear them like an approaching mob, muttering as they come, angry and scared. I awaken again to lighted windows, and this gives me a kind of electric charge. The day is here – but I don't remember what day it is. Am I excited, or frightened? Is it Christmas morning, and I'm six, or am I twelve or fifteen, and we're leaving on a trip? Then I remember it's the day Mom is going away forever.

I'm completely awake in less than a minute, pulling on a sweatsuit in the chilled room. I have an empty, dry feeling, and I'm jumpy, and I'm rushing. I want to say goodbye. I'm angry, but I want to touch her. I want to look into her face when she says goodbye and see what I see.

I walk down my outside staircase, shivering a little, and am surprised to see my mother standing on our porch with three suitcases beside her. She has on a coat and scarf and looks like a refugee, bewildered and worried. She gives me a wild look, surprised and desperate.

'Mom? What're you . . . ?'

'He won't take me.'

I come close to her, staring, rubbing my arms for warmth.

'I called a cab,' she says. I can see she has been crying, and she looks exhausted. 'But I don't trust them. What if they don't come in time?'

'But your flight's at eleven, Mom. It's not even eight.'

She just stands there, rigid and desperate. 'He was supposed to drive me,' she says, 'but he won't. He won't get
up.' Her eyes are on me like claws. 'He promised.'

'I'll drive you, Mom.'

'Will you, Claude?' She looks so grateful, trying to smile
a little, but still desperate, still wild, a frightened animal, a
small one, a squirrel, a rabbit, a small dog caught and rigid
and tensed for an escape.

'Which company did you call? The cab.'

'It's by the kitchen phone.'

'I'll cancel it and get the keys.'

'Thank you.'

'You know, Mom, we could leave in an hour and still
have plenty . . .'

'No. Please. Now. Please, Claude.'

I make the call and take the Volvo keys from the table,
the keys that are mine, now. I stand still a moment and
listen for sounds of my father, but there are no sounds
in the house except the refrigerator, the heat, and two
clocks. I picture my father lying on his back, wide awake,
staring at the ceiling, grim and angry. Will he think this is
a betrayal? Will he blame me for making it easy for her to
leave? It doesn't matter. She's leaving, and I don't care what
he thinks.

My mother does not relax at all even when we're on our
way. I mention how light the traffic is on Lincoln Boulevard.
I tell her we'll be there in twenty minutes. All she says is,
'Air France.'

'Relax, Mom.'

'I can't.'

'You'll hurt your back. You should lean back and
breathe.'

'My back is killing me, but I don't want to take a pain
pill until I'm on the plane and the plane has taken off. I
want my mind to be very clear for all the . . . for the ticket

and passport and . . .' Her words trail off. She stares ahead. 'Go with him to look for an apartment, Claude. He'll just sit there. He won't do it. I know. He can pay up to a thousand a month, but that will eat into the savings over time. If you can find a rent-controlled . . . Oh, this is all written out for him. Just go with him or he'll never go at all.'

'Mom?'

'What?'

'Why did you and Dad get married?'

She doesn't look at me.

'People get married.'

'People fall in love, Mom.'

She shakes her head slightly, staring hard through the windshield as if already searching for the airport. 'People get married.'

We drive a moment, and I glance at her and then watch the road again. 'You didn't sleep, did you?'

'No,' she says, still staring ahead.

'Look at your hands, Mom. At least unclench your fists.'

'When I'm on the plane.'

'Jesus.'

'You don't know, Claude.'

'You seem like you're escaping from enemy territory, a refugee, for Christ's sake, like I should watch the rearview mirror for signs of the Gestapo.'

'Don't joke about this.'

'Well, look at you.'

'You don't know.'

'What don't I know?!'

'How I feel!' She compresses her lips, fighting off an attack of tears. Her fists get whiter and harder, and she keeps her wild eyes on the road ahead. 'Four times, I tried to go. I was going. Four times. This is the fifth time. I got pregnant. I got sick. And twice I had to put my savings into the store so we didn't declare bankruptcy. We have a second mortgage on the house, you know.'

'How can I know anything, Mom? You never told me. Dad never told me. How is anybody supposed to know?' We're waiting at a light, and I say, quietly, 'I was the pregnancy, right?'

'I never held it against you.' She is speaking out the front window. 'Never.'

We're quiet until the next stop light. I seem to be hitting all the reds. 'Do you know where you'll be living?' I ask her.

'It's all arranged.'

'Is it a secret?'

'Oh, Claude, it's all written down. Ask your father. Everything is written down.'

'You should've given the address to me, too, and to Mari and to Phil. Is there a phone number?'

She is compressing her mouth again, and now her eyes are closed, and she whispers, 'Yes.'

I stare at her, and then a driver behind me lets me know the light is green.

'Thanks for the car, Mom.'

'Drive it safely, *please*.'

'I'm not a teenager anymore.'

'You're a wise old man,' she says. She is still rigid and staring out the windshield, but it is at least a small sign of humor.

'I'm this many,' I say, and open and close my hands twice.

'Don't. Don't take your hands off the wheel. Oh . . .'

I smile at her, and she is shaking her head. 'I'm going to miss teasing you, Mom. Can I call you up and tease you? Do I have to do it in French?'

She closes her eyes, fighting tears again, and one small balled fist leaves her lap and comes toward me and settles on my leg. It just presses there, hard with bone. I'm going to accept this as proof. I've been wondering if she raised me only out of duty and obligation, accepting a twenty-year sentence, serving her time. I've been wondering if there was love in it, and now I have her hard knuckles on my leg as we drive down Lincoln Boulevard to the airport, and I'll accept that.

I help her check her baggage. Her hands are trembling. She can barely speak to the woman who confirms her seat assignment and gives us a gate number. I hold her carry-on bag. It's very heavy. She is close to panic.

'There's plenty of time, Mom.'

'When I'm on the plane,' she says, and her voice is stretched thin.

'You won't board for over an hour.'

We reach a sign that says, 'Only Ticketed Passengers Beyond This Point,' so I can't wait with her at the gate. She doesn't seem to mind.

'Gate A27?' she says, checking her ticket.

'Yes.' I put the bag down. She bends to pick it up. 'Wait. Wait, Mom.' She straightens up and stares at me, hurting, desperate to be gone. 'Just one second.' I open my arms and gather her inside. It is like hugging a statue that somehow trembles. While I hold her to me, she stands rigidly in my embrace. I notice people seated along the wall watching us. One of them is Mari. As I catch her eyes, and my mouth falls open, I see her shake her head at me. 'No,' she is saying with her head and her eyes. 'No, you do not see me.'

I feel my mother move slightly, wanting her freedom, and I relax my arms and take my eyes off Mari.

'I'm sorry,' my mother says in a tight, near-whisper. 'Claude . . . when I'm on the plane.' She is picking up the bag. 'When I'm on the plane, I can start to . . .' She doesn't finish. I am nodding. I kiss her forehead. She touches my shoulder quickly and turns and moves on. I watch her until she is gone. She does not look back. When she is out of sight I turn to Mari and walk toward her.

She is still staring down the corridor where our mother has gone. She looks more like our mother than I have ever seen, and her eyes are just as red this morning and slightly wild. In a moment she turns and looks up at me.

'I just wanted to see her leave,' she says. She is not weeping. She looks a little dazed. 'I just wanted to see her.'

'Dad's got her phone number and address. I'll get it for you.'

She stares at me, and after awhile she nods.

'You want some breakfast?' I ask.

'No thanks.' She stands and touches one of my shoulders briefly like Mom did, and she walks away. I start to follow, to walk with her, but she is moving quickly, and I let her go. I glance again after my mother, knowing I won't see her, and when I turn back the other way, Mari is gone. My wondering glance settles on the strangers in chairs along the wall. Some of them are staring at me, and now they look away. I wonder if they were trying to piece my story together. I don't believe they could ever guess.

By the time I reach home, my father is already up and gone to the store. I shower and change and study a while, but I can't concentrate. I'm not due at the store until two, but I decide to go early. Maybe I can wash the windows early and leave early, and Benko and I can get an early table at the House of Billiards where the game will take me away.

I find my father alone in his store, standing among the screens which are alive with cartoons and movies and a game of golf. Only one set is unmuted, one of the cartoons on very low volume, a distant muttering of screams and shouts, but he's watching the golf game.

He glances at me and then back to the game and tells me, 'There's an open house tomorrow. You know, people tramping through the house. She said she cleaned it. I don't know. It starts at eleven.'

I'm watching the putting now, too. 'I drove Mom. She's airborne by now.'

At the limit of my vision I see him nod.

'Shall we look for apartments tomorrow?' I ask him.

He turns to me, slouched and soft, his face vague at first and then gathering into an answer. 'Might take a long time to sell the house. Why look now?'

I shrug, and then a thought occurs to me. 'Maybe you'll want a one-bedroom. It's cheaper.' He doesn't answer. 'Do you want me with you?' I ask.

'Where would you go?' he asks in return. It isn't the response I wanted.

I shrug again. 'Maybe I'd live with Phil.'

His forehead moves, brows protruding. 'After what *he* did?'

'He didn't mean to hit me. He meant to hit *you*.'

'After that, you'd live with him?'

'I don't know.'

'Probably start drinking, too.'

'Do you think I would?'

'How do I know?'

'Do you think I would, Dad?'

He turns back to the golf game, frowning.

'Why didn't you pay Phil for fixing the roof?'

He asks, 'What?' looking at the screen, then he turns to me sharply. 'For the roof?'

'Years ago – what Phil said. When he and his friends fixed the roof.'

He is staring hard at me.

'So? Why didn't you pay him?'

'The job looked shoddy, and I told him so, and he said, "Fuck you."' I have never heard my father say 'fuck' before. 'You can never tell Phil anything, never could. He just blows

up. "Fuck you," he said, "and keep your goddamn' money."
I was going to pay him. He wouldn't take it. He said, "Keep
your goddamn' money."'

'Well, Dad, Christ, that's no reason not to pay him. Just
because he gets mad and says that.'

'You're taking *his* side. Even after what he did.'

'Dad, he fixed the roof. The roof was fixed – wasn't it? It
didn't leak anymore. He should've been paid. Did you know
he sold his bike to pay his friends?'

'Jesus Christ, that was fifteen years ago.'

'Twelve, Dad. Did you know?'

'He just got mad and that was that. He hardly even talked
to me.'

'Did you talk to *him*?'

'How can anybody talk to *him*? Nobody can. He bites your
head off. You saw he was going to hit me. Jesus. His temper.
Phil's temper is his downfall. He never sticks to anything.
He can't work for anybody. He's always had that rotten
temper.'

'How could you *not* pay him? The roof stopped leaking.
That must've been worth something.'

'I told you. I *told* you.'

'Just because he said that?'

'Just because? Just because! He told his own father "fuck
you," and he said, "keep your money," and he called me
other names, too. You don't understand. You're not old
enough to understand. Don't ask questions if you don't
understand.'

'I think I understand, Dad.'

'No, you don't.' He looks away. He picks a different screen
this time. The cartoon.

'I think I do. I think he gave you an out and you took it.
I think it was the money, Dad. You figured you could save
the money.'

He doesn't turn to me, but I see his eyes retreat from the

cartoon and turn in on his thoughts. His eyes cloud and his mouth slackens, and this is the closest I have ever seen him come to weeping. 'Nobody. Nobody. Nobody understands what I've had to do to keep this store alive. This store fed us and gave us a life and put Mari through college, and it's putting you through college, and nobody, nobody understands or appreciates that.'

We both turn to the door as it opens, but it is only the mailman, who returns our nods and puts the mail on the counter near the register. When he walks out, we both turn back to the cartoon.

'Maybe I'll get my own place to stay,' I say after awhile.

'How could you afford that?'

I shrug. 'I could put in more hours here – for more pay.'

'See? Nobody understands. I couldn't afford that, Claudey.'

'You'd be saving money on the apartment.'

'I can't afford to pay anybody more salary.'

'All right. Fine.' The cartoon ends, and a toy commercial begins, and we look at each other.

'What do you want to do about dinner tonight?' I ask him.

He makes a slouchy shrug. 'I don't care. A can of chili or something.'

'Do you want me to . . .' I almost ask him if he wants me to have it ready for him, his dinner, our dinner, but I stop. Why should I? I don't want to. 'I'll eat out,' I tell him.

'You'll use up all your money that way – eating out with Benko.'

'It's my money, Dad.'

'Is it?'

'What do you mean by that?! It's from working here and babysitting and working with Phil, and I earned it!'

'What about the car?'

'What *about* it?!'

'That car shouldn't have gone to you. She shouldn't

have done that. She should've sold it and split the money with me.'

'*She* bought it.'

'Sure, she bought it, living with me. She bought it, with me paying the mortgage. She didn't care about that. She just gives it to you. It's foolish. You don't need it. You can use my car when you need a car.'

I'm just staring at him wondering how he can let those words leave his mouth, knowing what a battle it is for me *ever* to use his car.

'It's not like you earned *that*,' he says. 'She just gives it – here.' He pantomimes the act of handing over keys. He stands there like that with his hand out toward me, finger pressed against thumb as though dangling a set of keys, but I look past the pretend keys to his face, and I say the words that come up for review in my brain without reviewing them.

'I don't work here anymore,' I say. I say it quietly and a bit thickly. My throat is tight.

He ends the key pantomime and frowns and turns away, and his eyes settle back on the golf game.

I just stand there for a moment, then I walk to the set with the golf game, and I turn it off. While I'm there, I turn off the cartoon, too, on three different sets.

'What are you doing?'

I turn off seven sets in a row that are showing a black-and-white movie that looks like it's taking place in China.

'Claudey!'

I turn off six more cartoons, walking along a row of floor models and tapping the 'power' buttons.

'What the hell are you doing?'

I snap off the two big screens and look around. Only one set is still on, one more cartoon, the one with the low-level volume. As I walk toward it, I hear and feel my father trying to beat me to the set, but I get there first and turn it off. Then

I spin around and look at him. His face is set and angry, but his eyes are on me, and they stay on me. He has nowhere else to put them.

'Did you hear what I said, Dad? Did you listen?'

'You're lucky. You're just goddamn' lucky.'

'Really, Dad? I don't *feel* lucky.'

'You can just walk out of this store. *I* can't walk out of this store.' He is trembling slightly. He sweeps his eyes around, hopelessly, and comes back to me, looking a little lost. 'If *I* walked out of this store, what would we have? Nobody understands that.'

With the sets off, I can hear my breathing and his and the traffic humming by on Wilshire Boulevard and nothing else. I'm trembling slightly, too, and I have no idea how my face looks at this moment, but I bet I look like him.

'What would we have if *I* walked out?' he asks me.

'Dad – what've we got?'

The store is as quiet as a church. A passing truck shakes the floor and rattles the window. We stare at each other like tall, trembling mirror images, and then I turn and walk out the door.

It feels good to be out in the sunlight and the smog and the street sounds. I glance at the dirty window I'm never going to wash, and my eyes are drawn to Jack-o-lantern, who sits at his usual place. He's ruffling through some dirty brown bags. I go to him and touch his shoulder. He stops ruffling and tenses and looks at the sidewalk. I tap his shoulder this time, and now he looks at me, vague and watery and a little afraid.

'Goodbye, Jack.'

An eyebrow slides up a full inch on his putty face, and his mouth opens slightly. I believe I see a hint of intelligence in his eyes, an awareness uncovered like a secret, but it all begins sliding down again, his eyebrow, his gaze, his head bowing toward the sidewalk, his vacant look dropping like a curtain between us.

I touch his shoulder again and walk away, and soon I'm jogging, and I notice I'm on my way to Mari's.

As soon as my shoes strike the stone and metal stairway that leads to Mari's apartment, I see her rush to her screen door and open it and stand above me with a look that stops me in mid-step. Her eyes are wide and she's been crying. 'Oh God,' she says. 'I've been calling you!'

'What? What?!' I hurry toward her, and she retreats inside, leaving me to catch the closing door and swing it open and follow her inside as she puts her hands in her hair.

'Mari, what?!'

'Bally,' she says in a broken voice.

I sweep my eyes through the living room and dining area, and then rush for Bally's bedroom, because I can't wait for her words.

He's there. Bally is kneeling in the middle of his bed, playing quietly with a truck. He looks fine, unhurt but sad. He has only the smallest smile for me. It dissolves in his sorrow, and I feel my heart open and bleed. I start toward him, moving slowly now as Mari comes to the doorway behind me.

'It was terrible, Cheeve,' she says. I sit on the bed and Bally comes beside me. I put an arm around him. He leans into me.

'What happened?'

'I left the screen door open – I mean unlocked!' One hand flutters up to her mouth. Tears come. 'I noticed he was gone, and I knew, I *knew*, Cheeve. I looked up, and he was gone, and somehow I *knew* I had left the door unlocked, and as soon as I knew that, as soon as that thought came, the voices came.'

'The voices?'

'Downstairs. In the street. People yelling. A scream – and I knew he had opened the door and fallen down the stairs, and it was my fault he was dead.'

She covers her face and sobs, and I spring off the bed and rush to her, put my hands on her shoulders and shake her.

'Mari! Jesus! Don't!' I drop my voice so the boy won't hear over her crying, and I say, 'You're scaring him. Don't say that!' Then louder, '*Mari*!' and I shake her again.

Her hands come away from her face. 'But he could have!' she says.

'But he didn't! Jesus! He didn't!'

'But it's just like he *did*!'

'Why?! Why, Mari?!'

'Because he could have. Because I heard screaming! Because I saw it!'

'In your mind – you pictured it, but thank God it didn't happen. So stop it. Christ!' I ease her toward me until I'm hugging her, and when I feel her loosen, I put my arms tight around her. She weeps into my shoulder. I turn us slightly so I can see Bally. He is watching from the bed, sad and worried.

'It happened, Cheeve,' she says into my shirt.

'Only in your mind. You just pictured it.'

'The worst possible thing.'

'You just pictured it happening.'

'A dog died,' Bally says.

'What?'

He turns his sad eyes on me. 'A dog died from a car.'

'You saw it?' I ask.

He nods, then shakes his head. 'Heard it,' he says. 'So I went on the stairs. I didn't fall.'

'A dog got hit?' I ask, and I feel Mari nod against me. 'And that's what the screaming was about.' Bally nods on the bed and Mari once more against my shoulder.

'We'll have to pay for the ambulance,' Mari says, taking a half-step back and wiping her face.

'You called an ambulance for the dog?!'

She pulls some tissues from a box on Bally's dresser and blows her nose, shakes her head. 'For Bally,' she says.

'What? Why?!'

'I saw him there.' She is staring at me. 'At the bottom of the stairs, bleeding.'

'No, *Mom* . . .' Bally says, whining.

'I saw it.'

'I was on the stairs, Mom.'

'That's not what I saw.'

'Jesus, Mari. Let's go sit down.'

We all go into the living room. I sit between them, an arm around each of them. They lean against me. Mari is taking long breaths now. Bally starts waving one shoeless foot back and forth.

'Bob'll kill me about the firemen,' she says and then chuckles weakly.

'Firemen?!'

'Big guys,' Bally says. 'The truck was right here! Really loud.'

'Why firemen?'

'That's who comes,' Mari says, 'when you call 911. Then the ambulance comes after.'

'They came in here?'

'No.' She blows her nose again. 'By then I was sitting on the stairs, holding Bally.'

'What did you say?'

'I said my son fell, but I don't think he's hurt.'

'They checked me,' Bally says.

'But the neighbors said he didn't fall, the people from

downstairs and across the street. The firemen asked Bally if he fell, and he said no.'

'Well, of course he said no.'

'And the firemen looked at me like I was crazy. And they looked at each other like . . . we have a fruitcake here. I told them that I wasn't *sure* my son had fallen. Maybe I imagined it, but I didn't want to take a chance on which was real, the dog or Bally. Would *he*? I said, "Do you have kids?"' Mari chuckles again. 'He was nice. Cute, too. He said he had a daughter and he understood, and then they went to see if they could help the dog. The people across the street – it was *their* dog – wanted to use the ambulance to take the dog, since it was there anyway, but that was against the rules, so they drove away with the dog in their car. The dog was still breathing. We're going to go over there later, Bally, and see how the dog is.'

'I think it's dead, Mom.'

'Well, we'll ask.'

Bally is now waving both white-socked feet back and forth. He says to me, 'I heard the radio on the fire truck.'

'Mm,' I say, and I sit there, touching each of their shoulders, and I remember the reason I came was to tell Mari I quit the store, and I don't want to live with Dad, and I guess I had wanted some sympathy and advice or at least a long talk, and now I don't know if I should even mention it because she's so rattled. While I'm trying to decide, we hear hurried steps on the staircase outside.

'Bob,' Mari says. 'I called *him*, too.'

'Does he think . . . ?'

Bob rushes in and then freezes as he sees us sitting on the sofa. His expressions come one after the other, the old one dissolving away as the new one takes its place – all in an instant – worry followed by relief, followed by anger.

'Bally's fine,' Mari says.

'Hi, Dad.' Bally still sounds sad as he sits there waving

his feet. I don't say anything. Bob's look darkens more and more, his mouth closing tight. He finally speaks through his teeth.

'What the *fuck* is going on here?'

Mari disengages from my arm and sits up straight. She sighs, looking at Bob, but speaking to me. 'Cheeve, will you take Bally on a little walk?'

'Wait a minute,' Bob says to me. 'What are *you* doing here?'

'I just got here, Bob.'

'I called everybody,' Mari says.

'Why?!'

'Hi, Dad.' Bally sounds more nervous now. His feet are waving furiously.

Mari repeats in the same tone, 'Cheeve, will you take Bally for a little walk?' Then, 'Bob, will you say hello to your son?'

'Hi, Billy.'

'Hi, Dad. A dog died.'

'A dog?'

'I'll tell him,' Mari says. 'You go with Cheevey.'

'I want to tell him,' Bally says.

'You can tell him all about the firemen.'

'The *firemen*?!'

'But later, honey. Go with Uncle Cheevey.'

I stand and raise a questioning eyebrow to Bally. He slides off the couch with a frown.

'Shoes,' I say, and we walk to his room.

Bally is sitting on the bed, and I'm lacing his tiny sneakers when we hear Bob's voice rise above the murmuring conversation in the living room.

'Will you *grow up*?!'

I picture Bob just as Bally mimicked him, his eyes closed, aimless hands thrust out into the air, '*Go up*!'

On the stairs, Bally asks me, 'Wanna see something?'

'Yep.'

He takes me to the curb. There is a dark stain there. He points. 'Dog blood.'

'Oh yeah. Too bad. Did you know the dog? Its name?'

He shakes his head, staring at the darkened curb. 'There should be a dog ambulance,' he says.

'Maybe that's what you'll do, Bal, when you grow up.'

He begins nodding a weighty nod, and he turns to me. 'I'll drive 'em to a hospital and I'll fix 'em, and I'll drive 'em home, and they won't bite me.'

'No. They would never bite the dog ambulance man.'

He shakes his head, very serious, very definite. 'They like you,' he says, 'if you're a dog ambulance man.'

When I return with Bally, Bob and Mari are sitting together on the sofa, not touching, but at least they're side by side. Bob isn't scowling. He just looks tired.

'Can I tell Dad about the firemen now?' Bally asks.

'Yes.' Mari stands. 'While we eat lunch. We're going to have lunch now, and Daddy's staying. How about you, Cheeve?'

'No, I . . . I've got to go.'

She hugs me. 'Thanks for coming.' It's a quick hug, coming apart before it fully forms. It's not at all like one of Lauren's hugs, but Mari's eyes brush me with thanks as she moves into the kitchen with Bally.

''Bye, Bal,' I say.

'Bye.'

Then I turn to Bob who sits slackly on the sofa, staring off.

'I don't know if you know it,' I speak softly so my words don't carry into the kitchen, 'but our mom left this morning. So . . . maybe that's why she's so upset.'

Bob's eyes come to me slowly.

'She's taking it hard,' I say. 'She was at the airport.'

Bob is nodding now. 'Yeah. She said they talked it out, had a long talk. She said it was . . .'

'Who?'

He looks at me like I'm very stupid. 'Mari and your mother. She said it was a good talk.'

I stare at Bob and slowly shake my head. He seems to slacken even more.

'It *wasn't* a good talk?'

'They didn't talk, Bob. I was there. Maybe you should know this, so you can see why . . .'

He sighs and leans back against the sofa, begins shaking his head. 'What *is* it with your family?' he says, not looking at me, not really asking, just fed up.

'What a stupid thing to say,' I tell him, and his face snaps toward me. I can feel my whole body tightening. My jaw stiffens so that I bite off my words, shouting in a near whisper.

'My family is falling apart! What am I supposed to do, *apologize*?!' I have stepped close to him, looming over him. My hands are fists at my sides. My throat is full, and I can't say anymore. Bob is looking at me like he doesn't know who I am. I make a sound like a growl and turn away quickly and head for the door, brushing the coffee table with my leg so that a row of Bally's plastic men fall down. In the kitchen, Mari is singing. I pull at the screen door and hurry down the steps.

When I reach the sidewalk, I don't begin to jog. I stop, and I remember that now I own a car. I left it at the store. I jogged away from the store without thinking about it. I start walking now, feeling for the keys in my pocket. I'll walk to the store's parking lot and I'll get in my car, and I'll drive, and I'll turn up the radio as far as it will go without the sound coming apart, and I wonder where I'll end up. But I know, and I'm hoping she'll be home.

*　　*　　*

'Hi, I wonder if you and Molly would like to go out somewhere, shoot pool or see a movie? I could sure use the company.' No, don't plead, Cheevey, that's cheating. 'Hi, I was just driving around . . .' Bullshit. Be honest. 'Hi, this is one of the worst days of my life, and I wonder if I could come in, and we could sit down together, and I could lay my head on your breast and just stay close for a few days?'

I don't even know what Lauren's house looks like, but I know it's next door to Phil's, and there it is, a very well-kept, one-story, Spanish-style home with Lauren's car in the driveway. I have a physical reaction to the sight of that car. I think my heart rate is up, and I know I'm smiling, whether my face has changed or not.

I don't see Phil's truck anywhere, and that's fine. I park down the street so I don't have to pass Phil's house on the way to Lauren's. I've seen all the Cheevers I want to see today. 'Hi, Lauren, it's storming out here. Will you welcome this battered sailor into your home, into your arms?' Careful. I feel like I want to grab her the minute I see her and hold her to me. My heart is drumming as I reach her door and knock too loudly with a shaky hand before I notice the doorbell. I don't hear anything but I *feel* someone come close to the door. Molly's voice comes through the wood.

'Who is it?'

'Robin Williams.'

'It is not! Mom, it's Cheevey!'

I'm in. Molly is stepping back, holding the door, happy and shy, and Lauren is coming in from the kitchen with a smile for me, wiping her hands on a towel. I feel very welcome. The door closes on the storm, and the house swaddles me in the same warmth and peace that comes from Lauren's eyes. She is the source of this home. It has grown out of her, and I want to examine every bit of it because I'll be studying Lauren. I get only one sweeping glimpse of books on shelves, small treasures on antique tables, rich colors and soft furniture, before she gives me one of her dedicated hugs, and I return it, holding on a bit longer, a bit tighter than usual.

'What a nice surprise,' she says. 'What brings you this way? Seeing Phil?'

'No, I . . . Just . . . Well, it's been storming all day.'

'It's sunny out,' Molly says.

'No, I ran into a meteor shower, Mol. It knocked me off course.'

'What a liar.'

'Not a "liar,"' Lauren says, 'a teller of tall tales. So you're lost, then?'

'Looking for a friendly port – but I don't want to intrude. Maybe I could take you and Molly out for lunch.'

'Cheevey, it's too early for lunch.'

'Oh. Well, breakfast, or a game of pool, a matinee, tea party?'

'We're drawing. Why don't you come see?'

'He could draw, too, Mom.'

'Yes. You draw, too.' She is already walking toward the kitchen, Molly following. They stop because I haven't moved.

'Are you sure I'm not intruding?'

'Oh, Cheevey, come on.'

The kitchen is an old but shining kitchen. Everything seems in its place, and every surface is clean, but the breakfast dishes are still in the sink, and I'm glad of that. She's not a fanatic. Beyond the kitchen is a spare room that has become the studio, and it is the one cluttered, disordered space in the house – mad with color, alive with drawings and paintings, shouting with calligraphy both bold and delicate, signs and logos and whole sentences and complete poems penned in every style and tacked and taped to the walls.

'We're working on "The Children's Hour,"' Lauren says and sits at her drawing table. I stand behind her. Molly has a small desk she uses for her own work.

Lauren has written the Longfellow poem in a beautiful script and is working on the illustrations she will use to surround the stanzas. These are pen and ink drawings, very fine, even wispy: a suggested chair, an old man's face, children around him, laughing, made of only a few lines each, but even so, they are very real.

'I can hear them laughing,' I tell her, and I can, and each one has a different laugh. They are that realized. 'It's wonderful.'

'Oh, thank you, Cheevey. I'm not quite happy with any of these.'

She offers me pen and paper, but I would rather watch. I am fascinated by Lauren's images because they reveal her, and I study every one. She points out a portfolio on a shelf, and I leaf carefully through her work. She has chosen the most familiar poems and sayings to write and illustrate, and some of them are a little too familiar – 'Be it ever so humble . . .' – and a little too sweet for me, but her delicate pen-sketches are wonders of economy and suggestion. Her signature theme is an angel or several angels watching the scene, smiling usually, never interacting with the human figures, unseen guardians, I think, caring and wise.

'I love your angels.'

'Thank you.' And I love her intensity as she draws. I love to watch her. I love her. I want to say it out loud, but I don't. I wonder if I ever will. I put aside the portfolio and stand behind her again, unseen and smiling like one of her angels, watching, examining the hand that is making magic on the paper, studying her cheek and ear and hair and neck and her old shirt and paint-marked jeans, and I want to slowly enfold her in my wings and fly off with her to wherever angels lie down and rest and make love.

'Do we really have angels watching us?' I ask.

'Yes,' Molly says, and Lauren smiles slightly as she keeps her focus on her drawing.

I stand behind Molly now. Her work is raw and much more literal, but she, too, is gifted with hand and eye.

'They almost devour me with kisses,' is the line Molly has chosen to illustrate, and she has three girls in the lap of their enormous father.

'Nice, Molly.'

'Thank you.'

'Do you make angels, too?'

'Yes.'

'You draw them last?'

'No. They're already there. Mine are invisible.'

'Very funny.' I hear Lauren chuckle softly at her table.

'So I have an angel, a real one, who's with me right now?' I ask Molly.

'Yes.'

'Male or female?'

'I don't know.'

'Can they *hear* you, too?'

'Sure.'

'Can they lend you money?'

Molly clicks her tongue and shakes her head like I'm hopeless, and Lauren thrusts paper at me. 'Everybody in here draws, Cheevey. That's the law. Sit over there.'

'Yes, ma'am. Do I have to draw "The Children's Hour"?'

'Anything you want.'

'Can I have another pen for my angel?'

'You're supposed to draw quietly,' Molly tells me, never looking up from her paper.

'Cheevey,' Lauren is also drawing as she speaks, 'if you can keep your mouth shut, we'll feed you lunch when we break.'

I'm silent for a moment, wondering what to draw. Then

I say quietly, 'How can I eat lunch with my mouth shut?' and both artists scold me, and I know I've reached my safe harbor and all the watching angels are smiling.

In a while I decide to draw my new car, the Volvo, but a fanciful version with a smiling front grille and giant tail fins and a grinning me at the wheel. It's pretty bad. I can't think of a fitting poem to go with it, so I begin to make one up, going through the alphabet for rhymes. I write it on a separate sheet of paper because I don't think I'll show it to anyone.

> My mother left for France today
> My sister's breaking down
> I quit my father's store and think
> I'll drive right out of town.

It's pathetic, but I find it funny, too. I don't know why. As I'm staring at it, I suddenly feel a presence behind me, and a movement that feels like a breath against my scalp or maybe the soft ripple of air created by a large feathered wing. I begin to glance and then turn sharply because someone *is* there. It's Lauren, and I never noticed her rise from her table and come toward me. I start to ask her how she likes my car, but her eyes are on the poem. She reads it and turns to me, her smile gone. As we stare, wordless for what seems like a long while, I watch the slow gathering of tears, until her look bathes me in sympathy and she leans close and kisses the top of my head. Then she walks away, into the kitchen. I glance over at Molly, who is still drawing. I begin to hear the sounds of glasses and plates and the refrigerator opened and closed, and in a moment Lauren calls us to lunch.

Before lunch, I need to use the bathroom. When I close the door, I notice, hanging there on a hook is a long, pink terrycloth robe and hanging on top of that is something silky. It's in a color they call 'nude.' I've noticed that in the lingerie catalogues Benko gets from his sisters, and I've always thought it was unfair to people of color to call this pinky-beige hue 'nude.' It's like the crayon in the box that's called 'flesh,' but it's only Caucasian flesh, and I hope they don't do that anymore in the new crayon boxes.

I feel guilty and a little perverse, but I pluck at the silky garment on the hook and spread it out to take a look. It has wide, lacy straps and a fairly low neck and the rest of it is like liquid in my hands, and I picture Lauren wearing this, and I judge that the hem, which has a small, delicate lace trim, would touch her upper thighs. I hold her in my mind, standing in front of me, dressed only in this nightgown, and I close my eyes and gently move the silk within my hands, imagining her flesh beneath the fabric, and then I slowly move it closer to me and touch it to my face. I breathe her in and try to keep her scent inside of me, and I realize there in her bathroom with my face in her lingerie and her voice distant through the door and mixed with the sounds of plates and forks and Molly's laughter, that I love Lauren Stater more than I have ever loved any woman or girl in all my twenty years, and that I have never really known what it means to love a woman, never felt it, never even dreamed it, and it is so exquisite and frightening and wonderful that I even love every minute of my life that has led me to this moment in this bathroom. I even love this past horrible week and this terrible morning because all of it was only a path, and every painful moment was only a step on the path, and all the while the path was leading me to my love, and I guess I will never look at life and time in the same way from now on.

During lunch I get a few long looks from Lauren, her eyes going deep and bringing me salve for my wounds, and I know she's thinking about the poem I wrote, and I feel she wants to ask about it, but not with Molly there. When I begin to thank them for the time together and the lunch, Lauren invites me to go with them to the museum.

'We're going to the Getty for some inspiration. Come with us.'

'Yes,' Molly says. 'We're looking for children.'

'In the paintings – to help us with "The Children's Hour." If you have no plans, Cheeve.'

'No. No plans. That'd be fine.' I have come staggering and stumbling into paradise, I feel, sharing this homey, ambling Saturday with the Stater girls. The damp early darkness is receding, now and then actually forgotten, but I do find myself wishing Bally were here. I think Molly would make a great sisterly companion for Bally, a teacher and a pal, and Bally would charm Molly and Lauren with his appreciation and wonder and joy. Someday soon, I'll bring them together.

The J. Paul Getty Museum is built as a replica of a Roman villa, and I am usually more interested in the building and grounds than the contents, but today we are on a special search for the faces of happy children, and we hurry past the fountains and columns and marblework and statuary like children on a field trip, playing our own game.

Molly waves us over to Alma-Tadema's 'Spring.' It's a painting that seems to carry its own soundtrack, a procession of Romans dressed to celebrate spring with wreaths of flowers in everyone's hair and people banging tambourines and playing pipes and flutes, people cheering and dropping more flowers from rooftops. The procession is led by girls about Molly's age, carrying baskets of flowers, their small bare feet so light, like dancers on the marble path.

'That one looks like you, Mol,' I tell her.

'Which one?'

'The prettiest one. In the middle.'

'She does, Molly,' Lauren says. 'If your hair was longer. See?'

Molly is pleased, but she shrugs. 'Maybe. Are these happy enough, Mom? For the poem?'

'We want them laughing,' Lauren says, and Molly hurries off to find another painting.

Lauren and I stay side by side in front of the Alma-Tadema, and in a moment I feel her touch my hand and then take it and hold it. We are looking at the painting and holding hands, and I'm wishing this were the most normal kind of thing, Lauren and I and Molly out on a Saturday, Lauren and I together, holding hands, looking at art. I don't want anyone or any clock to move, and I don't want to hear a voice, but Lauren says, 'How are you doing?'

'Well, it feels so good – being with you.'

'Did you talk to your mother?'

'Yes. I brought her to the airport. It was okay.'

'And Mari?'

'She's . . . in a bad way, but I don't want to talk about it.'

She squeezes my hand a bit. 'When you're ready,' she says.

I squeeze her hand and say, 'I'm really enjoying this. I'm really feeling fine.'

'Cheevey, think of it as an accident. You've had a car accident. It's the same thing. People get right up. They say they're fine, but they're not. They're numb. They're in shock. Then it hits them. I don't want you to be . . . so alone. It's going to hit you. It has to.'

'I'll be okay.'

'Don't try to be tough. What'll you do tonight?'

'See Benko probably. Shoot pool maybe.'

'If it doesn't happen, come back to us. Will you?'

'Back to you?'

'Yes. Don't be alone.'

She is staring at me now with what looks like more than concern. There is love in it, I think. It makes me feel so good I smile, but she frowns.

'Cheevey, I didn't like the way you drew your car.'

'Why?'

'You drew it going fast, and it was snarling.'

'It was supposed to be smiling.'

'I don't want you driving around alone and driving too fast. We're going to visit a friend of Molly's later, but tonight we'll be home watching a video. If you're alone, come watch with us. I mean it.'

'That's really nice, Lauren. Really.'

'Is it all right with your dad? How did you leave it? You said in the poem you quit the store.'

'Oh, it's okay. I don't actually live with him even now. I mean, I have my own little place over the garage. I won't even see him tonight.'

'You have to talk. You have to talk to people.'

'It's okay. I'll talk to Benko. I'll talk to Mari when she's . . . better. I talk.'

'And you can talk to me.'

'I will. Thank you. I just . . . I love being with you. I love this. I want you to know this. It's great.' I'm not saying to her what I want to say, but I'm not sure what I *can* say. I don't want to scare her. I don't want to just come out and say it, here in the museum, and what would I say? Isn't it too soon? I'm starting to worry now. I'm hearing the debate between my two minds. I hate that.

'So come back to us if you don't meet Benki.'

'Benko,' I say, and I laugh, and she smiles at my laughter.

'Okay. I promise. If I end up alone without a plan, I'll show up for video tonight with the Stater women.' I lift our joined hands and I kiss hers. It was an impulse, and I like that, and I like the pleased look she has. This is good. I'm waving now. 'Say goodbye to Molly for me.' I'm backing up. 'Thanks for everything.' This is a good exit. I feel very good. 'Maybe I'll see you tonight.'

'Please, Cheevey. Don't be alone.'

I touch my fingers to my lips and hold up my hand in a final wave. It's a good move, I think. A little bit intimate, but also light, even devil-may-care, in a way, like a pilot heading for his fighter plane. One last mission. Don't worry about me. When I pull the Volvo on to Pacific Coast Highway, I'm in the clouds, watching for enemy aircraft, confident, even a little cocky, ready for a dogfight and already thinking beyond it into the night, when I visit my love. I'll bring chocolates or something. I'm not even calling Benko. I'll just go home, change clothes and kill time. I want no other plan. I'll be back at her door at seven. This is the love of my life.

I could go to a movie and eat up the time until this evening. (I'm figuring that seven-thirty is the right hour to arrive for video watching.) But I know I wouldn't concentrate on the film, and I don't want to blow the money, so I go to the promenade on Third Street and walk and watch people and browse in bookstores. Any large bookstore equals the death of a whole hour for me. I like the photography collections and any large picture book with a historical theme. I work my way into the history section and pull out all the books that concern warfare in the nineteenth century. Sometimes I read whole chapters. This time I also check the poetry section and the children's section to see if I can find examples of illustrated poetry for Lauren, but I don't find any. I am also looking for children's books that combine our talents – the describing and the illustrating of famous battles – but it looks like there is a gap in the marketplace waiting to be filled. I'll mention the idea tonight.

I leave the store at five-thirty and step back into the thick-
ened flow of people moving up and down the promenade.
Third Street is closed to cars, and on Saturday it looks like a
street festival: all ages and types, all accents and languages.
I'm always amazed at the number of people I don't know.

I enjoy being in this ambling river without any immediate
pressure to be somewhere, so I pause and watch some of
the street entertainers, and I even take the time to look
each panhandler in the eye when I say, 'No, I'm sorry.'
One of them, a young man in a dirty army surplus jacket,
is insistent, almost belligerent.

'Aw, come on, man.'

Normally I wouldn't stop or even answer, but I have a
different energy today. 'Try the tourists,' I tell him. 'I live
here and get hit on ten times a day.' My answer doesn't
impress him much, but *I* like it, and I like my peaceful
energy. I know where I'm going. I'll be with her tonight.

I move with the current again, among the couples and
the families and the packs of friends, and I feel no loneliness
at all. Now and then I feel something like a shadow just
over my shoulder, and I know if I turn around I'll see the
whole group of them trailing after me – my mother with
her suitcases, my dad, Mari and Bob and Bally, and even
the ghost of a dog I never met. Even Phil, but I don't allow
my thoughts to turn that way.

I step out of the flow at six-thirty and eat a large frozen
yogurt at an outdoor table, watching the torrent of strangers
and trying to decide what I should bring to Lauren's door.
I don't feel right about flowers, and a box of candy seems
somehow formal. This should seem more spontaneous,
lighter.

I'm lingering over the frozen yogurt, capturing the last
piece of walnut and scraping the cup with the spoon again
and again, when, finally, the right idea strikes me. It's
popcorn. Popcorn is spontaneous and fun and it says that

I've come to watch the video, but it can't be just a bag of popcorn. This is the special part. This is the great idea. It can't be from a store at all. It has to be real movie popcorn, a tub of it, from a real movie concession counter, and it has to be still warm. I love this idea.

Now I have my destination – Lauren's house – and I have my mission – warm movie popcorn – and I rise from the table like a self-assured man who always knows just what to do. There are three multiple-screen movie houses on the promenade, but I know which one to choose because I have a connection. Arnie Golden, a friend from school, has worked at the AMC since it opened, and at other theatres before that. He's been an usher and a counter clerk since junior high, and Benko and I have gotten plenty of free passes from Arnie Golden.

I don't go near the crowded ticket window, but straight to the door, and I take my time. A man with connections doesn't have to hurry.

'Your ticket?'

'Is Arnie working tonight?'

'Who?'

People are crowding by me. The ticket-takers are tearing stubs and saying to your left or upstairs or downstairs or theatre four, and I have to raise my voice a little.

'I'm looking for Arnie Golden.'

'Who's he?'

'He works here.'

'Don't know him.'

'Can I just go in and buy popcorn and come right out again?'

'Only if you have a ticket.'

'I don't want to see a movie. I just want the popcorn.'

'You need a ticket to get in.'

'You can watch me. I'll just go to that counter and buy the popcorn and walk right out.'

'You have to have a ticket.'

'You sure you never heard of Arnie?'

'John.'

Now there's a security guard named John on the way, a plump guy, and when he reaches us, I speak first.

'Hi, can you accompany me to the counter? I'm going to buy some popcorn and leave the theatre.'

'He's trying to get in without a ticket.'

'All I want is the popcorn.'

John shakes his head at me. 'You gotta have a ticket.'

'He's in the way, John.'

I try one last quick shot. My peaceful energy is already gone. 'John, do you know Arnie Golden?'

'Arnie don't work here anymore.'

'Shit. Where does he work?'

'This guy's in the way, John.'

John gives me a shrug, then he points a blunt finger out into the promenade, telling me to go, and I go.

I stand in the river like a rock now, and the flow spreads around me and gathers again behind me. I check my watch. I still have time. Maybe a normal man would go buy a bag of popcorn at this moment, but not a man who's in love. I walk across the promenade and down the block to the next theatre, and I picture it this way. It's Beirut or some other war-torn city. Lauren and Molly are waiting for me. Molly needs medicine. Lauren is counting on me. There is distant artillery fire. There are snipers. There is a curfew. There are armed patrols everywhere. Very few pharmacies are open. For love, a man will do anything.

'Can I explain something to you?'

'Pardon me?'

'I need to explain something to you.'

'What? There are no passes for this showing.'

'No, I don't want to see a movie. My boss sent me for a tub of your popcorn, a special request. I'll just go to the

counter and buy it and leave. I'll leave my watch with you
to make sure – or my jacket. I'll put it right here, and I'll be
right . . .'

'Can't let you in.'

'Please don't get me fired. It'll take five minutes, and I'll
be . . .'

'Can't let you in. Move back, please. Move back, please.'

'Give me a break.'

'Move back, please. Next.'

This girl has a face like a fortress wall. There is no weak
spot, not even one chip out of the stone. I'm worried now
because I don't want to arrive at Lauren's too late. For all I
know, they go to bed very early, and I'm using up valuable
time, but I can picture myself arriving at their door with a
tub of real movie popcorn that is still warm, and this picture
feels so right to me. It's not an ordinary thing to do. It's even
a little dashing.

I hurry to the last theatre on the promenade, imagining
the distant thud of mortar rounds and picturing tracer
bullets in the latening sky. Medicine for Molly. Lauren
will be so grateful. My last chance. I get in line and buy
a ticket.

'One, please.'

'Which movie?'

'Uh . . . any movie.' The woman looks at me suspiciously
as she hits a key and gives me my ticket and change. I hurry
into the theatre and line up at the crowded concession
stand. It is 7.10 by the time I am waited on.

'A large popcorn tub, and please take it from the top, the
warm stuff.'

'Butter flavor?'

'Uhhh . . . no. Wait! Butter on one side, a little.'

I pay for the popcorn and glance around. One of the staff
is in a motorized wheelchair and she looks like she might
be in charge. She is about thirty.

'Excuse me.' I show her my ticket. 'Who can I see about getting my money back? I just bought this, but I can't stay.'

She looks at me, at the popcorn, at me again. 'You can't stay?'

'No, I have to leave, so I need my money back for the ticket. I suddenly have to go. I'm not feeling well.'

'And you just bought that ticket?'

'Yes. Five minutes ago. They'll remember me at the door – or the woman in the window . . .'

'May I see your ticket?' She checks it. 'We'll go to the counter first.'

'The counter?'

'I can get your money back for the popcorn.'

'I don't want my money back for the popcorn. I'll keep the popcorn. That's all right. I'm in a hurry, though. I just need my money back for the ticket.'

'I can't do that.'

'You *can't*?!'

'No. Please wait for the manager.'

'*Wait*?'

'Wait here.'

'But I'm not feeling well.'

'Would you like someone to help you to the bathroom?'

'No! Thank you. No, I just want to get my money and go.'

'Please wait here. Unless you'd like to lie down.'

'No. Thanks. No, but . . . I need to hurry.'

She moves away, and I see her reach a man who carries a small radio. She talks to him. He hands her the radio. She speaks on the radio, glancing at me from time to time. Then she hands the man the radio and comes back to me.

'It won't take long.'

'Good.' But we remain in silence awhile, and I see no sign of anyone who looks like a manager.

'What's the problem?' she asks. 'Are you sure you don't want to lie down?'

'No. No, I just . . . My watch buzzed because it's time to take my medication, but when I reached in my pocket, I realize I left my pills at home, so I have to rush home.'

'I see. Give me the popcorn.'

'Why?'

'While you're waiting for the manager, I'll get your money back for the popcorn.'

'No, that's okay. Really. I *want* the popcorn. It's actually *good* for me to have a little popcorn. It's a blood sugar thing.' I eat some popcorn from the tub. It's not warm anymore. I offer her some, but she declines. She keeps glancing at me, worried for me, I think, while I chew the popcorn. I am surprised by a voice behind me.

'Cheevey. Hey.'

'Arnie!' Arnie Golden is walking across the lobby toward me, smiling.

'What's up?'

'He needs his medication, and he doesn't have it.'

Arnie narrows his eyes at me. 'Medication?'

'Uh, we're waiting for the manager, Arnie.'

'Yeah. I know. *I'm* the manager, Cheeve. What's wrong?'

'Oh. Congratulations, Arn.'

'Thanks.'

'He forgot his pills.'

'Look, Arnie, I just need my money back for the ticket. I have to leave . . .'

Arnie takes the ticket and signs it and hands it back to the woman, telling her that he'll take care of the paperwork, and she goes off to get my seven-fifty.

'Thanks, Arnie.'

'Sure. You okay?'

'Yeah.'

'Come on. I'll get you your money back for the popcorn.'

'No, Arn. I *want* the popcorn. I came *in* for the popcorn. That's all I *wanted* was the popcorn, and I made up the rest so I could get my money back.'

He stares at me, and then laughs. 'Why, Cheeve? Our corn is so overpriced.'

'Yeah, but it's the principle. I'm going to go watch a video with . . . a woman, so . . .'

He nods, smiling, understanding. 'Cool,' he says, and we both take a moment, nodding at the coolness of it.

'Yeah, I'm in love, Arn.'

'Hey, that's great. Here comes your seven-fifty. Give me this.' He takes the popcorn.

'Where you going, Arn?!'

'I'll get you the warm stuff,' he says.

I hurry from my car to Lauren's door, hoping to preserve the warmth of the popcorn. I notice that Phil's truck is in his driveway next door and the lights are on in his house. I feel strange about this, being just fifty feet away from my brother, and I feel a little sneaky. I ring Lauren's doorbell this time.

Molly shouts, 'Who is it?' But it's Lauren who peers through the peephole and opens the door, looking very pleased to see me.

'It's still warm,' I say, holding the popcorn toward her. I am feeling triumphant.

'Oh. Great. Molly, look at this!'

Molly's eyes are on the TV which is showing a movie in the old kind of color, bright and sticky as candy.

'Pause it, Molly.'

Molly stops the tape and turns and smiles and takes a fistful of popcorn. 'Right from the movies,' I tell them. 'I got it in a theatre – just now.'

Lauren has closed the door. 'Oh? What did you see?'

'No, I didn't see a movie. I just barged into the theatre

and said I want some hot popcorn, please – 'cause Molly likes it fresh.'

'Did not,' Molly says, her mouth stuffed with corn.

'Did, too.'

'Did not.'

'Did, too, Mol. And they said, "Nobody walks in here without a ticket, Mister. We're going to have to throw you out."'

'They didn't say that!'

'Did, too, Mol.'

'It *is* warm,' Lauren says, digging a hand in. 'How did you get it?'

'So I said, "You and what army and navy are going to throw me out of here?" I was getting pretty miffed.'

'Mom, he's telling a tall tale.'

'Yes, he is.'

'No, I'm not. So they lined up against me: three big security guards, five ushers and a pit bull.'

'A bull?!'

'That's a dog, Mol.'

'A mean dog,' Lauren says.

'And a janitor with a broom and two ticket-takers and a manager, and I said, "Listen, I came for popcorn, and I'm not leaving without it, 'cause when I knock on Molly's door" . . .'

'You rang the bell. Ha ha.'

'. . . "I'm going to have fresh-popped corn in my hand." And you know what the manager said?'

Both Molly and Lauren say, 'What?' but both words sound like 'Wuff' because their mouths are stuffed.

'Wuff?' I say, and they laugh, Molly losing some of her corn.

'So the manager said, "Did you say Molly?" I said yep. He says, "Molly Stater? That pretty kid? Comes in here with that pretty mom of hers?"' Molly and Lauren are smiling at each other as they chew. Molly is blushing a little. '"The kid who draws real well and has some neat freckles and wears red pajamas?"'

'Cheevey!' Molly throws a piece of corn at me. She is wearing red flannel pajamas and red socks.

'Don't throw it, honey,' Lauren says.

'I said, "Yep, that's the girl. Molly Stater." So the manager said, "Give Molly this popcorn with my blessings, and give her pretty mom" . . .' I reach in my pocket and extract two pieces of paper with a flourish. '. . . "two free passes to our theatre."' I hand the passes to Lauren. She does a little gasp and a smile that shines right through me, honoring me.

'Cheevey, how did you do all this?'

'I got connections.' I flop on the sofa and put my feet up.

'Are they real, Mom?'

'Yes. Free movies.'

'Wow.'

'Thank you, Cheevey. And the popcorn is perfect. What can we get you? Molly, we better be nice to him.'

'Okay.' Molly beats at the couch cushion to soften it under my head. 'Here, Cheevey.'

'Ahh, thank you.'

'We're having ginger ale, want one?' Lauren is heading for the kitchen.

'No, I'll have ginger ale,' I say, and Lauren groans and chuckles at the same time, and I watch her walk into the kitchen in bright red and white socks and her long, pink robe.

'We're watching *Meet Me in St Louis*,' Molly says, and begins to tell me the plot, but I'm only half listening because my mind is caught, hooked by that long, fluffy robe of Lauren's, and I can't let go. I find myself wondering if, under the robe, she is wearing that wonderful, silken short nightgown I saw earlier hanging on the bathroom door. My mind is wrapped around that question, and I can't get it loose. I'm trying to just relax in the midst of this kingly welcome and ease back and not give in to carnal thoughts, but when Lauren walks in with the ginger ale, I'm watching her, and I'm still wondering. She could have almost anything on under the bulky, soft terrycloth, even flannel pajamas, but I can't stop imagining that beige silk against her skin. So after a few minutes, I excuse myself and go into the bathroom, even though I don't need to relieve myself, and I close the door. The hook on the bathroom door is empty. The silken nightgown is gone. It must be under the robe. Now I know. Maybe now I can forget about it. I wait a moment and flush the toilet and run the water and then join Lauren and Molly.

'I saw this movie a long time ago,' I tell them. 'It's good.'

'Do you know the words?' Molly asks.

'The words?'

'I know all the words.'

'To the movie?!'

'To the *songs*, Cheevey.'

Lauren explains that Molly loves to sing, and she knows almost all the lyrics to this film and *The Wizard of Oz* and *The Little Mermaid*.

'She sings along,' Lauren says, 'and we have to sing, too.'

'*We*?! Oh, no.'

'Have to, Cheevey.'

'Have to,' Molly echoes. 'Have to. Have to. Or no ginger ale. No popcorn.'

'It's the rules, Cheevey.'

Lauren gives me a look and a shrug that says, 'That's the way it is.'

'I only know one song all the way through,' I tell them. '"Mr Froggie."'

'Teach it to me,' Molly says.

'After the movie,' Lauren says. 'We better watch or it'll get too late. We're a few minutes into it, Cheevey.'

'That's all right. I hope I missed a song.'

'There's another one coming soon,' Molly says, and when the tape starts again, she settles on a pillow on the floor and watches, completely enrapt.

Lauren and I are on the sofa, the popcorn between us. We watch the film, and now and then glance at each other. She applies smiles to me like poultices. All my darkness is gone. All the poison drained away. I try not to stare at her. She crosses her legs, and the robe falls away, and I pointedly do *not* look at her bare leg as she deftly covers it, eyes on the movie. Our hands meet and touch in the popcorn tub. Now and then we fight a comic duel for a handful of corn, still watching the film. Lauren will take two handfuls from time to time and fill a separate bowl on the floor for Molly.

Molly eats without ever looking away from the screen, but she is not watching the way my father watches television – blindly. Molly is so deep within the story that I feel she might appear any moment on the screen itself, standing there between Judy Garland and Margaret O'Brien, one of the family. When the songs come, Molly does not stand up, does not perform, does not imitate whoever is singing. She just sways back and forth and sings along in a sweet, soft voice. I stare at her, grinning like a fool, and Lauren sees me and enjoys my reaction, the two of us sharing the magic of her little girl.

On the trolley song, Molly is more animated, and shouts for us to join in, and we do. Lauren knows the words, but I'm faking most of them, and too shy to sing out at first, but I'm encouraged by a kick in the shin from Lauren, and by her own clowning. We are doing a semi-opera by the time the song ends, Lauren with her arms spread and her chin tucked down, trying to sing bass. Molly laughs and twirls and sits back down again, locked in the story once more.

When 'Have Yourself a Merry Little Christmas' is sung, Molly eases back against her mother's legs, and Lauren touches her hair. I watch Molly and think she might cry, then I look at Lauren, and she, too, is close to tears. I watch the screen and Judy and Margaret and, in spite of myself, feel my own heart aching, and when I turn back to Lauren, she is wiping her face and looking at me, and she begins to laugh at how sad we all are. It is a moment I want to press and keep like some bright leaf. We are, for a moment, a family, watching the story of another family, feeling their sorrow and bound together by our own unashamed sentimentality. Lauren touches my shoulder and pushes me slightly as she chuckles silently and wipes her face again.

When the film ends, we applaud, and I tell Molly what a fine singer I think she is. She is pleased and proud, and as she does a kind of ballet around the living room, she tells me that next year she starts voice and piano lessons. We discuss her future on Broadway, but Lauren says they are leaving opera open as an option.

'There's a restaurant called Verdi. Do you know it, Cheeve?'

'Yes. But I've never tried it.'

'They sing arias there. It's beautiful. We'll all go soon.'

She sounds so casual and certain. I am proud to be included. 'Yes. I'd like to. Do they sing "Mr Froggie" there?'

'We can request it,' Lauren says.

'Now teach it to me, Cheevey.'

'Okay, but it's a lap song.' I have sung this many times to Bally, bouncing him in my lap to the rhythm of the song. I'm not sure if Molly is too shy to come into my lap. She darts a look to Lauren then comes over and sits, primly, on my knees, sidesaddle, turned toward me and waiting.

'Ready?'

She nods.

'"Mr Froggie took a ride, mm-mm, mm-mm. Mr Froggie took a ride, with sword and pistol by his side, mm-mm, mm-mm."' It's an old folk song from a Burl Ives record Phil played when he was learning the guitar. I hope he still plays that guitar. I sing the six verses I know, and Lauren watches us, and Molly smiles at the words, but she also seems to be studying, memorizing.

'Sing it again.'

'Oh, poor Cheevey. Let him rest. We better start thinking about bed for you. We were up at six,' Lauren tells me.

'Six?! What are you, farmers? Up before light to milk the chickens?!'

I have Molly laughing, but it is partly the forced, slightly manic energy of an over-tired little girl. We talk a bit more about her singing, and the subject of careers comes around to me.

'What do you think you'll do, Cheevey?'

I hesitate a moment, then ask Lauren, 'Have you ever drawn a soldier?'

'Yes. Once. Why?'

'Can I see it?'

'Does this have to do with your career?'

'Yep.'

We follow her into the studio. She searches and pulls out a half-done rendition of Alan Seeger's 'I Have a Rendezvous With Death.' Her drawing shows a soldier of World War I being shot and falling from a barricade. He is falling into the waiting arms of a kneeling angel. It is beautiful, and the soldier is very well drawn, though his dropped rifle is too short. I smile. I feel like I'm holding the future in my hands.

'You're going to be a soldier?' Molly asks.

'No. I'm going to write about soldiers – and if she'll do me the honor, maybe someday your mother will illustrate what I write.' I turn to Lauren and raise an eyebrow. I'm smiling and keeping this light.

'Oh, Cheevey, *I'd* be honored, of course, but I don't know much about armies.'

'I'll teach you.' I'm still staring at her. 'Now you remember this moment. Someday we'll be interviewed on a talk show, and we'll be asked how did you ever get the idea to team up? And we'll say, it all happened one night after *Meet Me in St Louis*.'

Molly draws out her goodnights, and then goes to bed for one half-hour of reading before lights out. Lauren and I settle on the sofa, half turned to face each other. One bare knee is thrust out of her pink robe, and I try not to think about it. I'm trying not to think at all.

'You're a wonder, Cheevey.' She is serious. With Molly out of range, her voice has become more intimate. Her look is deep.

'A wonder?'

'You're in pain, but you're still giving so much – to Molly. You were wonderful with her.'

'Molly kicks it.'

'She what?'

'She's great.'

'Yes. She is. Thank you. Now . . . tell me. How is it – with your family?'

'It's a mess.' She keeps staring, wanting more. I sigh and dig for more, and I shrug. 'I guess I never knew how thin it was.'

'How thin *what* was?'

'I don't know – the crust, the crust of the world that my family was standing on. Maybe I didn't *want* to know it, but it all caved in so fast. It's ahead of me. I can't absorb it all.'

'Are you scared?'

'I don't know. Scared? Not really scared. I'm worried about Mari. I'm scared for Bally. I'm just . . . I guess I feel helpless, and I feel very heavy – when I let myself think about it. And I feel pissed.'

'At who?'

I try to answer everything without checking myself. 'My dad. My mom. Phil. I even found myself getting mad at Mari today, or annoyed, because she's the one that talks to me, and she couldn't even hear me today. She doesn't know I quit the store. That's why . . . well, that's why it's so great having you. Really. When I'm with you . . . you balance everything for me, Lauren. I mean that. You're so good, you balance all the bad.'

'I'm really glad, Cheevey.' She reaches out and touches my knee as she says that. She seems moved by what I'm saying, and I haven't even told her half of what I feel. 'Are you nervous about going home?'

'I'm nervous about this night ending – this time here with you. I don't want to go home and start thinking.'

'Stay here,' she says, and I'm not sure I hear her correctly. Maybe I'm making it up. 'Stay the night. It might be easier for you to face things in the morning. You can stay right here on the couch. It folds out.'

I guess I'm staring at her in some weird way because she asks me what's wrong.

'Nothing's wrong. I just . . . think that's so great that you're inviting me to stay.'

'Of course. Sure you can. Why don't you?'

For some reason, I can't answer. I think I'm afraid that if I open my mouth, all the wrong words will rush out.

'Will you stay?'

'Yes. Thank you.'

'Good. I'll do a quick clean-up in the kitchen and then get some sheets and a blanket. Do you want more tea?'

She is up and heading for the kitchen. I just watch her go. I can hear the tap water running now. I rise and follow the sounds of water and china. I watch her from the doorway. She has pushed up the sleeves of her robe. She is working very efficiently at the sink. She tosses me a quick smile, then goes back to her washing, but she keeps the smile. It lines her face a bit, and I want to trace each line with a fingertip. They are lines of kindness and pleasure. I want to kiss them. I move and stand behind her. Her short hair leaves some of her neck bare. I choose a spot of smooth skin. I may be having a heart attack. I can't control my breathing. I bend down and kiss the skin at the back of her neck. She stops still for a moment. Then she turns, and I back up a bit to allow her to turn, and when she's facing me she hugs me, her head fitting just under my chin and her wet and soapy hands held out straight, but her elbows hug me. I put my arms around her.

'I don't want you to be sad, Cheevey,' she says, her breath on my throat. I release her slightly, and we are staring into each other's faces, and I lean down again and kiss her gently on the lips. My eyes are closed, and my body is quivering slightly. I don't know if she can feel it. She does not move in my arms. When I pull back and open my eyes, I see that she has a look of quiet surprise. She stares through my very bones, looking for something, wondering.

'I really love you, Lauren.' My voice comes in a broken whisper.

She wipes her hands on the sides of her robe and lifts them up. They are moist on my face. She bends my head down slightly and kisses my forehead. Then she slips away.

When I walk out into the living room, she is gone, but she returns from the hall with sheets and a blanket, and a pillow. I meet her and take the stack of linens from her.

'I'll do it,' I say.

She doesn't quite look at me. 'It folds out,' she says. I nod. She looks around the room, stalling, I guess, not sure what to say. Her eyes come back to me, very direct, searching again. I want to drop the bedclothes and hold her again, but she says, suddenly, 'Cheevey, I'm going now. I'm going to bed. Do you have everything here, everything you need?'

I nod again.

'There are clean towels in the bathroom.'

I nod once more.

'You can watch TV. I can't hear it, and Molly sleeps like a stone.'

I don't nod this time. I'm just staring at her, holding the folded bedclothes and the pillow.

'Will you be all right?'

I only stare.

She comes close and puts her hands on mine for a few seconds as I hold the bedding, just flesh on flesh, just a moment's connection, but it fills me so that I have no room for breath or thought or word, and then she walks away in a flutter of pink and turns and disappears into the hallway.

I don't fold out the couch. I just lie on it with the pillow under my head and the blanket thrown over me. Sleep seems like something trivial, useless. I have no plans for sleeping. I lie here and listen to the house quieting, and I live, over and over again, the kiss.

Molly's light went off an hour ago. I heard rustlings from Lauren's bedroom down the hall. The master bedroom has its own bathroom. I heard a flush. I hear the ticking of the heat ducts. Now and then the refrigerator hums. I kissed her on the lips. She could not mistake that kiss. I held her, I kissed her. I told her I loved her, but love can mean friendship, a word can miss the mark, but a kiss . . . There is an electric clock that buzzes a bit, and its second hand moves with a blind, relentless thud. I can hear the wind. There are no lights on. I kissed her full on the lips. I tasted her. I hold the taste in my mouth. Her body was close to mine. I felt only the thick robe, but her body was in the robe, clothed in silk. She looked at me. She was asking me. She was asking herself. I wonder what she answered. I wonder if she is lying awake now, listening to the wind and searching for an answer.

I have no more questions. My way is clear. I don't know what will happen, but as for me, I am a statement. The world will have to react to me. Lauren will have to react to me. I am an action. I am a verb. I am an unwavering arrow. I love this woman, come what may.

The wind grows louder and the traffic subsides. I kiss the back of her neck a hundred times; I kiss her lips a thousand. I press her body to me. She hugs me with her elbows. She looks at me for answers. A dog barks far away. A neighbor somewhere has wind chimes. Not Phil. I write the first book in our series. It is about a drummer boy in the Crimean War, an English boy. Lauren's drawings are perfect. We win an award. A motorcycle goes by. The sprinklers go on.

An idea strikes me, and I don't even question it. I am fearless. I am fearless now because I have no choices to make. I move, and the world reacts, and it is out of my hands. I want to see her. I want to see her sleep. I want to hear her breathe. I rise, as silent as the moon, and walk first to Molly's closed door. There is no sound from her room. I move down the hall. Lauren's door is open. I love my new courage. It is the courage of clarity.

I stand in Lauren's doorway and stare at the wide bed. In the moony dark, I see her head on the pillow, turned away from me, and the tips of her shoulders just above her quilt. I look about the room. Even in the darkness, it welcomes. There is an antique vanity with a curved antique chair. I walk into the room, noiseless on the thick carpet, and I grasp this chair and lift it and place it beside the bed. I am barely breathing. I am smiling, and I am brave. I sit in the chair, and I watch my love sleep.

I'm surprised I don't hear her breathing, and I study the quilt, trying to detect the slow rise and fall of a body asleep. I remember, when babysitting for Bally, when he was very tiny, watching *his* covers, and even putting my face close to his miniature face, holding my own breath and waiting, suspended, for a sign that he was alive.

Lauren's head rises from the pillow and turns toward me. She stares a moment, then lowers her head, her eyes open, watching me.

I speak just above a whisper. 'I'm sorry. I didn't want to wake you.'

She stares a moment more before she says, softly, 'What are you doing?'

'Just watching you sleep.'

Her eyes are studying me. She's calm. 'I wasn't sleeping.'

'You weren't?'

'No. I was thinking about you.'

'Really?' I think she makes a slight nod there on the pillow. I can't quite tell. 'I can't stop thinking about you,' I tell her.

'What do you think about me?' she asks.

'Just that I love you very much. More than that.'

She watches me, and then turns over and lies on her back. I can see only her face and neck and shoulders and the wide lacy straps of her gown above the covers. She looks at the ceiling and then turns to me again, and I think I see the moonlight in the moisture of her eyes, then I'm sure because a hand comes out of the covers and a finger touches her cheek, dissolving a tear into her skin, but her eyes never leave me.

'I love you, too,' she says. 'You're a very special boy.'

Slowly, I feel a rueful grin spreading on my face, and I'm glad I can smile, and I hope she can, too.

'Boy?' I ask, and I see her features slowly realign into a smile that's just a little distorted by tears.

'I'm twenty, Lauren. Turning twenty is very tough, tougher than I thought. I think it's aged me ten years. I'm almost as old as you now.'

'That's pretty old, Cheevey.'

We stare and smile in the near dark. 'I don't love you as a boy,' I say, and our smiles slowly dissolve. 'I love you as a man. Okay. That sounds stupid. Well, I love you as a very old boy.'

She is studying me again. Her words come even more hushed. 'I thought you might come in here tonight.'

'You did?'

She nods slightly. 'It can't be that way, Cheevey.'

'It can be any way you want it to be, Lauren.'

'We can't be lovers.'

'Okay. But don't say "can't." Please. Just say you don't "want" that, but don't say "can't," because we can be whatever we want to be.'

'I'm thirty-four years old.'

'Well . . . I'll make an exception.' I have brought her teary smile back. 'Most of my women are much older.'

'Cheevey.'

'Tell me to go and I'll go. Or I'll sit here all night and watch you sleep. Or, if you want, tell me to come into your bed. I'll sleep beside you and never touch you, if you want that, or we can hold each other and sleep and do nothing else, or we can make love to each other if that's what you want, and I'm not saying I'm very good at it, or that's all I want, because it isn't. That's not what I'm looking for, although, if you would want me, I would love to touch you. I would really love that. But I'm not pushing for that. I'm just saying, I love you in every way possible.'

She keeps staring. 'Cheevey.'

'You keep saying that.'

'I have a daughter. She's down the hall . . .'

'She sleeps like a stone.'

'An eight-year-old daughter, Cheevey.'

'She likes me.'

'I know she does. I know. Very much. And she needs that. A man – a boy – a male here. It's good for her.'

'See?'

'So be our friend, Cheevey.'

'I'll be whatever you let me be.'

'But I know what you want – how you look at me.'

'You can tell?'

'Yes. But you're going through something very tough right now, Cheevey, and you're hurting.'

'Bullshit. I'm sorry. I didn't mean to say that. Cancel that. But you're wrong. This doesn't have to do with hurting. This doesn't have to do with my family. This is separate. This is parallel.'

'You're confused now.'

'Lauren. Lauren. Lauren, I've never been less confused. I am finally not confused. My feelings for you are so clear, and they exist outside of anything else. I know this. I've examined this. I accept all that I'm going through. I even embrace it because, in a way, it led me to you and to these feelings I have for you, and nothing can ever . . . rob me of how I feel. It's momentous, how I feel. It's monumental. It's the finest feeling in the world – to love somebody the way I love you. Even if you don't believe it. Even if you don't accept it. It's still the finest feeling in the world, and no matter what, I will never ever regret feeling so much in love with you that . . . the inside of my face is always smiling. My heart is laughing. And crying, too; having a good cry, weeping with joy. All my limbs are dancing, even right now, sitting here. I'm writing your name on my soul, right now, while we're talking. It will never be erased. No matter what. Your name will always be there.'

She has rolled on her side to better stare at me. Her tears are back, and a slight, sad smile, too. One bare, graceful arm is out of the covers. Her fingers touch her tears away as she studies me and listens to my ravings. When I stop, she keeps staring. We don't move.

When she finally speaks, her voice is more tear-broken than I expected. I can hardly hear the words. 'We can't have a love affair, Cheevey.'

'Don't say "can't." I mean, okay, whatever you want. But don't say "can't." Why can't we?'

'One of us is a responsible mother.'

'Let's see . . . that's *you*, right?'

Her smile is bent by her tears. I want to kiss that smile, sip those tears. 'Look, you're a woman. You're a single woman. You're alone in that bed. Would you like a man in your bed who loves you? Someone to hold and be held by, touch and be touched by? Would you like that in your bed, in your life?'

'Of course.'

'Good. Okay. Fine. We've established that. That's clear. Okay.'

'But a relationship, Cheevey. It has to make sense for me – and for Molly, too.'

'Does it have to make sense . . . tonight?'

We stare awhile more. She moves to her back again, wipes her face with her hands and stares at the ceiling.

'This is just one night,' I tell her, 'out of . . . I think I read that we live about twenty-five thousand nights. Twenty-five thousand. This is one. Just one.'

'Just one,' she asks the ceiling.

'Yes.'

She takes a long, shuddering breath and then turns to me and studies me for another long while.

'Just one,' she says. It's not a question.

'One,' I say, 'out of twenty-five thousand.'

It's such a long, sad stare she gives me. I want to cry. I want to hold her.

'Lock the door, Cheevey.'

There is a long silence, because I'm not moving. I'm not even breathing. I stare at her, and I hold her words to me, her unbelievable words close to me, and I'm afraid that even the next tick of the clock might shatter this moment like glass. Finally, I say, and I'm whispering now, 'You don't have to do this for me.'

She whispers, too. 'I know.'

'It's not . . . just for me?'

She slowly shakes her head on the pillow.

I rise and go to the door and softly close it. There is a lock within the knob. I pinch it and turn it, noticing that my hand is trembling slightly. I walk back toward her. She whispers again.

'Sit on the bed.'

I sit beside her. If she had said jump over the bed or walk on the ceiling I would have done that, too. Her words come after a long, deep stare.

'Promise me, Cheevey.'

'Yes. What?'

'Promise me this is the last time.'

'The last time?'

'The last time you'll ask me for this.'

'For what?'

'To be intimate.'

I swallow. I'm so close now, I could move my hand six inches and touch her, touch the skin of her arm. How I love the sound of that word in her mouth. Intimate. 'All right.'

'Promise me.'

'I promise.'

'One night, you said.'

I nod. 'All right. One night.' I keep nodding. She keeps staring, studying, and now whispering again.

'I want to touch you, Cheevey. I want to hold you. I want to feel you holding me. But . . . we're not going to . . . You won't enter me.'

'All right, Lauren.'

'And you promised me.'

'I promised.'

'You won't ask me again.'

'I promised.'

She stares, then she whispers, 'Hold me, Cheevey,' and she says it as if she needs me, not desperate or even very emotional. She just stares her deep, sad stare and asks me for something she needs.

I move my hands to the tops of her arms and touch the skin with my palms, then grip them gently and lean close to her. I kiss her forehead and then I kiss the moisture beneath each eye and taste the salt, then I kiss her lips, and I begin to lose myself, and I feel my grip tightening on her arms.

She moves slightly, and I pull back from the kiss. We are staring at each other. I am not sure what to do. She moves again, against the grip of my hands, and I release her. She slides away from me, closer to the center of the bed, and she sits up, and in a sudden move she pulls the silken gown up and over her head and off her arms. For a second her upper body is naked in my sight in the near dark, and then she slides under the quilt and sheet again, covered to her shoulders, and turns toward me and waits.

Sitting on the bed, I begin to take off my clothes. It seems to take so long. Shirt, T-shirt, shoes, socks. I glance at her, and she calms me. She looks at me with a faint, loving smile and a look of ease and peace. I slow down. I push my jeans and underwear down and leave them bunched beside the bed, and then I lift the covers and slide under them. I look at Lauren again for courage and calm. We are twelve inches apart in the bed, staring. Her faint smile is still there and her loving look that seems to know and understand everything. She reaches out slowly and touches my bare shoulder. I move to embrace her.

When we meet, skin to skin, when I feel her flesh and muscle and heat and smoothness against me, against every part of me, I am exalted. I am more than I was before. There is an electric fire inside of me, a charge that is both animal and spiritual. I have never felt so much love and so much desire colliding in me. My hands, my legs and my lips engulf her. I have never been so strong and I am trying to be tender. When I am not kissing her, I find myself whispering 'God' and 'Jesus' and 'Lauren,' and then I realize that she is whispering, too.

'Slow,' she says, and she holds my face and kisses my lips softly again and again, but taking her time, and she whispers again, 'Slow.'

I let my body loosen. I try and match her rhythm. The kissing is lush. It becomes its own celebration, instead of a fierce and urgent step toward something else. I feel her fingers giving me shape in the darkness, every part of me, and I do the same, gently this time, slowly. We move together as if we're underwater, too deep for any light to reach us.

She moves on to her back and I lie on top of her. I see that she is looking at me. Between kisses, she is staring, peaceful as before, but her look is slightly blurred by her own passion. Her own. I love that. The sight of her being touched, being moved by me, being taken somewhere by our loving thrills me and chokes me. I want to cry out. I want to devour her. My erection presses on her belly. She stops kissing me to lock eyes with me, and that small loving smile is in place, but softened, blurred, and she whispers: 'It's all right, Cheevey. Let it go. Let it go on my skin.'

I kiss her mouth like a drowning man, and I kiss her

breasts and then I *do* cry out, a cry that sounds like grief, and my body convulses again and again in what seems to be some kind of ecstatic death by electrocution. I become a rigid, petrified man, and then I crumble, and I ease my weight down upon her, wet and weak.

My heart is flailing inside of me, and I'm trying to breathe again. She puts her fingers in my hair, touching my scalp in slow circles. The animal is gone from me. I feel tamed and soft, and I want to curl on her and rest in her warmth, but I become self-conscious about my weight on her small body, and I'm aware of the stickiness that binds us together. Slowly I start to move off her, but she holds me close.

'I'll get you Kleenex,' I whisper. 'Where is it?'

'No. Shhh.'

She moves slightly, and I follow her unspoken directions until I'm on my side pressed close against her, and she lies on her back, full in the moonlight now. The covers are down about our feet. She puts her fingers in the wetness on my stomach and chest and gently rubs it into my skin. Her eyes find mine, and her deep and peaceful stare tells me everything. I touch the wetness on her smooth skin and spread it with my fingertips and paint her with it until it disappears.

'You're so beautiful,' I whisper. 'Your body is so beautiful and what's inside you, what I see in your eyes, Lauren. God, this is . . .'

'Cheevey.' She draws the whispered word out languorously.

'What?'

'Shut up.'

She smiles, and I kiss her smile. I'm up on an elbow. She turns on her side and faces me. We just stare for the longest time, both of us faintly smiling.

'Can I speak now?' I ask.

'No.'

'Lauren.'

She shakes her head slightly and laughs once, a whispered laugh, at my expression. I busy myself with her body then, taking advantage of the moment and the moonlight to travel three fingertips over every part of her I can reach: face and neck and shoulder and arm and breast and flank. As I touch her breast, she closes her eyes. I concentrate on that area. She captures my fingertips and holds them and brings them to her mouth and wets them, and then she replaces them on her breast – and I touch her a long time, wetting my fingers from my own mouth.

She sighs heavily and lies on her back. I think this is a sign to begin on the other breast, which is reachable now, but as I touch it, she captures my fingers again. She releases two and takes only my index finger and brings this to her mouth. Her eyes remain closed. She probes her lips very softly with my finger, moving the fingertip from one side of her mouth very slowly to the other, probing slightly deeper each time, so that my finger moves her lips more and more, separating them and touching the wetness within – and now I feel the tip of her tongue. She has placed it at one side of her mouth, so as my finger draws through her lips and parts them, it feels the bump of her tongue and slides over that bump – then back again through the soft, wet flesh to the bump of her tongue again, back and forth, and her breathing changes, and she sighs and lets go of my finger, and I continue as I have been shown, and I'm good at it now, gentle, and going just deep enough, and touching the tongue and back again, so glad, even honored to be giving her pleasure. I close my eyes, too, and begin to revel in this tender intimacy, until I feel her take my hand and stop it, and I see she is looking at me.

She speaks in the softest whisper. 'Now, Cheevey. Here.' And she takes my hand with the extended finger and she begins to move it down until it touches the hair between her legs. I look at her, and she nods and she eases her legs apart a little. I keep staring at her, wetting my finger on my tongue, and she nods again and then closes her eyes.

I find where the flesh parts, and I move my finger tenderly in this passage, not penetrating, but traveling between these deeper, pulpier lips to reach the wetness and slide along gently, and then I feel it, and as I touch this bump – like the tip of her tongue – Lauren shudders and gasps a small gasp, and I understand what she has given me and what she wants, and I feel like I hold a sacred trust, like I've found the Holy Grail.

I strike a slow rhythm to the touching, and Lauren's body answers that rhythm with deeper shudders and gasps that become small outcries. She is moving to the touch of my hand, and I love her even more for trusting me, for leaving herself so vulnerable to me. I have never known such pleasure as the quaking and whimpering of this woman as she surrenders to my touch, and as I continue, the shocks to her body are even greater and her little cries more desperate and helpless. I hear a word within her whimpering. 'Faster,' she says. I change the rhythm, and almost immediately, she cries out and pulls away, turning on her side and drawing her knees up, curling there and fighting for breath.

I fit myself against her back, curving into her, moving my arms around to hold her. One of my hands rests on her breast and she covers it with her own hand as we lie there a long while and her breathing slows.

'Did you?' I ask, my words whispered into her hair.

'Shhh. You're not supposed to ask.'

'I know. I'm sorry. Did you?'

Her hand presses mine and I can picture her smile. 'No. I might yell.'

'Molly?'

'Yes.'

'She sleeps like a stone, you said.'

'Can't risk it.'

I think about that a while as I hold her. 'It doesn't seem fair,' I say.

'It was wonderful, Cheeve.'

'It was. God, it was.' I'm silent awhile, and then I say, 'Every time I say "I love you," I want it to mean more. I want it to sound different.'

She waits awhile, too, and then says, 'You don't have to say it. I can see it. I can feel it.'

I nod my head against the back of hers. 'I guess I want to talk about everything.'

'No kidding.'

I squeeze her in my arms. She presses my hand again. We lie together another long while in silence. Slowly, I feel myself wanting her again, and I ease my thickening body against her back. I'm not sure she's awake until she speaks. There is no sleepiness in her whisper.

'Cheeve. You have to go now.'

I kiss her head. 'I do?'

'Yes.'

'That's not an easy thing.'

'Talking will make it worse.'

'In other words, "Shut up."'

'Yes.'

She turns in my arms and studies me again. There is love and a little fear in her look. Everything I start to say, I discard. She's right. In some cases silence is better. I kiss her. It's a long kiss, and she returns it, and when it ends I see her eyes have filled. I'm afraid if I kiss her again, I'll never be able to go. I ease away from her, hoping she'll stop me. She doesn't. I move to the side of the bed and begin to dress. Each time I look at her she is studying my face. She has pulled the covers up to her chin.

When I'm dressed, I stand staring at her awhile. The moon is even brighter now. Her eyes are sad and deep, and they don't change. I think of several goodbye gestures and discard them all. I force myself to turn away. I pick up the chair and move it back to the vanity. I go to the door and pinch the small lock in the knob. My hand is steady this time. I softly unlock the door and open it. I look at Lauren one more time, and I whisper, 'I'll just go home now.'

I see her nod.

'I'll call you.'

She nods again slightly, her eyes full and unchanged. I wait just a few seconds, wondering if she'll say anything. She doesn't. I turn and walk through the dark house and quietly let myself out.

I move off her porch and cross the yard, and I say to myself this is not the same moonlight that was on her bed and on her skin. This light is much colder.

My name wakes me. My father's voice. He's knocking. He almost never climbs the stairs to my room and visits me. I can't seem to form any words. It's daylight. I came home from Lauren's and didn't fall asleep for hours. I sit up and draw my legs together and manage a grunt that sounds nothing like 'Yeah?' which was the word I had in mind. My eyes are small and blinking, and sleep is still packed around me, like gauze.

'It's after ten, Cheevey.'

'Hm?'

He enters with a sweep of sunlight that clubs me, and I look away.

'Remember? They're coming at eleven.'

I squint in order to look at him, backlit in my doorway. I see his tall slouching presence, but no features until he ambles inside. He has put on a tie for some reason, and his hair is well combed. He glances about my room, an uncomfortable stranger here, like a party guest who has wandered into an empty den. He scans the books, the soldiers, my homework on the table, touching nothing.

'Open house,' he says.

'Oh yeah.' My words are thick, but recognizable now. 'I got in late.'

'Mm.'

'It's ten?'

'Ten-ten.'

'I'll come down and shower.'

'Just so the bed is made.'

'Sure. I'll straighten up.'

'Oh, it's neat in here. It's very neat. Just so you make the bed. And after your shower – leave the bathroom neat.'

'All right.'

'Wipe it down, kind of.'

''Kay.'

'Hang up the towel.'

'Dad. I always hang up the towel.'

He is nodding, rocking a bit on his heels. His lips press together into a brief, mild smile. 'I guess that was Phil,' he says.

I'm wondering what kind of foggy labyrinth his mind is, mixing decades and transposing sons.

I slide out of my bed and make it and smooth it, and he remains there, rocking slightly. I feel the strain of yesterday's argument between us. I turned off all his sets. I walked out of his store. I quit. None of this shows in his mild, slightly absent eyes.

'I heard from your mother.'

'You did?'

'Mm. She's okay.'

'The trip and everything? She's settled – I mean, she's where she's going to stay?'

'She's with a family, she said. For a few days. It was all arranged, I guess. But she has a place to move into.'

'How did she sound?' I picture my mother transformed somehow, stepping off the plane on to French earth and taking a deep breath and suddenly standing straighter, maybe smiling, maybe even dancing.

'Sounded okay. Tired.'

'She say anything else?'

'No. Said things were very expensive.' He gives a small, bitter, one-note laugh.

'Nothing else?'

'Well, she said to tell everybody she's all right.'

'Did you tell Mari? Why don't you tell Mari Mom said hi? I mean, to her, specifically.'

'You can talk to her, Claudey.'

'Dad.' I say the word as a sigh and then just shake my head. 'All I can say is that it'd be really nice if you called your kids and said hello from their mother. I think it would mean a lot. That's all.'

'Phil'd just take my head off.'

'No he wouldn't.'

'You don't know.'

I stare at him now, wrapping and belting my robe, and I notice that his eyes stay on me, and that he seems ready for a fight. 'So you're not going to call Phil or Mari? What about Mari?'

'You can't even do me that favor?' he asks.

I slump in front of him, both of us tall and slouching now, and I shake my head. 'Jesus, Dad – well, look, it's up to you. Anyway, I'm going to shower, then I've got homework, then I'm going over to a theatre to fill out an application. A friend of mine said they're hiring. Then, tomorrow, I'll start checking on a room, an apartment to share. I'll look at the ads. I'll check at school. Okay?'

He looks at me and nods and his nod carries away his stare as if he's following a bouncing ball. He's looking out the open door when he says, 'Do what you want.' Then he moves to the door and starts down the stairs. I pace in my room, agitated, but it's only a three-step room, and I quiet myself by thinking about last night. What is all this compared to last night?

I call Lauren and Molly, but they're out, probably at church. When their machine beeps, I sing the first measures of 'Meet Me in St Louis, Louis.' 'I had a wonderful time with you two yesterday and last night,' I say. 'Thanks for including me. In fact . . .' I pause just a moment, knowing Lauren will understand '. . . in some ways it was the best night of my life. 'Bye. Talk to you later. Live long. Do good.'

I need to finish this paper on U.S. Imperialism and the Spanish-American War for tomorrow, and I've reached the part I'm very comfortable with, the charge up San Juan Hill, but every ten minutes or so the realtor comes up the stairs and shows my room to prospective buyers. She always says the same thing. First I hear her on the stairs along with the loud creaking of footsteps. She speaks over the creaking, maybe so the shoppers won't notice how wobbly the staircase is.

'This is a great spare room or office and it's "bathroom-ready".'

I'm keeping the door open today, and she always steps in first, and her shoppers always enter and stop, surprised to see me and embarrassed to be invading my room.

'This is Claude, the youngest child,' the realtor says, 'and he doesn't mind if we take a look.'

At this point the shoppers nod and smile at me and then glance about and trade a few hushed words so as not to disturb me. The realtor stands there grinning proudly and says, 'All built-in shelves.'

The shoppers send their eyes around the room, politely avoiding me. I feel invisible. I become a ghost. I imagine these people are on a guided tour. A bus waits for them outside. You see? the guide asks them. This is where Claude Cheever wrote during his early student years. That's his desk. There are his pens. Still undisturbed. Imagine that, someone in the tour group says, he was right here in this room. The others nod, looking about, awed.

For inspiration, I carry several soldiers from my shelf to my desk, an American trooper from the Cuban campaign and a few Mexican infantrymen who will have to do for the Spanish. Instead of taking me deeper into my assignment, they spirit me away toward my story and my Legion. Today we liberate Pashkatt. The enemy will be routed. The women will be grateful.

The ring of the telephone come like a blow inside my chest, and I jump a bit in my chair, wondering why the phone jars me so sometimes, and other times it is hardly more than a mild interruption. I'm wondering if it has to do with the energy of the caller and what it is they have in mind to say. I pick up the phone and say, "'Lo,' and I hear Lauren's voice, and she is upset and talking fast, and I'm thinking my theory is correct, but I'm already forgetting what my theory is because I'm listening to her tell me about Phil.

'He's just standing there with all these broken windows, and then . . .'

'Where?'

'At the construction site. We came with lunch – Molly and I – and the neighbor was out there, wondering if he should call the police.'

'The police?!'

'Well, yes – with somebody breaking windows.'

'Phil is breaking the windows – in the remodel?!'

'Yes. I walked in there.'

'What did he say?'

'He's drunk. He didn't really say anything, but he walked

over and knocked all the glass out of a window he had broken. I tried to talk to him. Maybe you could come and take him home. If I didn't have Molly . . . I'll drop Molly off and . . .'

'Yes. I'll drive over now. I'll get him home. Somehow.' Phil is never drunk on the job, never before this.

'I'll drop Molly off and meet you at his house. If you're not there I'll come back here – to the site. I'm calling from the neighbor's.'

'Did anybody call the police?'

'Not yet.'

'I hope they don't.'

'I'll tell them it's all right – that you're coming to take him home. I'd try to help him, but Molly is scared, and I'm a little scared, too.'

'I'll take care of it, Lauren.' It feels good saying that, even though I don't know if I *can* take care of it. It also feels good that she called me. She called me for help. You call people you trust, people you can count on. I'm thinking that, even though I'm already rushing inside, my mind already on its way to Phil. 'I'll hang up now, Lauren, and I'll see you at Phil's – and I love you.'

'Oh. Thanks, Cheevey. 'Bye.' She sounded awkward. I guess I threw her off. Her mind is full of Phil right now, and maybe the neighbor was standing there beside her.

I stuff my feet into my sneakers without untying them and snatch my keys off the table and then stand still for a few seconds, arms half-raised. Am I forgetting anything?

This pause brings an image of drunken Phil and the windows, and this opens up the sickness I keep covering. It's in my stomach and my throat, a dark, wet feeling of loss and shame, too, over what's happening to my family, this awful unraveling. The Cheevers have just unraveled a bit more, and the worst part, the part of the sickness I can't stand to look at because it's like looking into my own wound is this: Maybe I never had a family around me. Maybe I imagined them there. Maybe I held them to me by pretending. Maybe I never looked at the wound even then – when I was a little boy. Maybe I kept my eyes away.

When I reach the remodel, Phil's truck is still in the driveway, and I don't hear any sound from inside. I can only see framing from here. The newly finished windows are in the back and sides of the house. I pause at the open doorway and speak his name into the house. There is no answer. I step in and walk through the unfinished living room into a dining room that Phil panelled, and here all four windows are broken, not only shattered, but all the glass has been knocked out except some small chips and shards around the frames.

'Jesus, Phil.'

I hear him make a sound, like a brief, high-pitched laugh. I walk into the hall and my foot kicks an empty beer bottle which rolls away and strikes another. I look into one of the remodeled bedrooms, and Phil is there, sitting on the floor. There is a hammer in his lap. He is drinking a beer. All the windows are broken.

'Christ.'

'Christ what?' He finishes the beer. He's drunk, I guess. His eyes are shrinking and looking a little stupid, but he's not slurring his words.

'What're you doing?'

'Nothin'. I'm done.'

'Christ.'

'Stop saying "Christ," Cheevey. It's Sunday. Want a beer? The fuckers are warm.'

He has an empty near him and a full bottle, and he now drains the bottle in his hand and stands it up, carefully, beside him.

'Let's go home,' I say.

He is sitting with his legs straight out and crossed at the

ankles. Now he pulls them up and rests his muscular arms on his knees. He shakes his head 'no,' not looking at me anymore. I sit beside him, hands on my knees also.

'Have the last one,' he says.

'No, thanks.'

'Then hand it to me.'

'Nope. If you pass out, you're too heavy to carry.'

'Don't be a shit, Cheeve. Give me the beer.'

'Nope.'

He sighs and leans his head back on the wall, closes his eyes. We're silent a while as I look around the room again – at the window. 'You call this construction?' I say. That strikes him as very funny. Keeping his eyes closed, he opens his mouth and begins his sparrow-like laughter. It even goes up an octave and rocks him so that he tumbles over on his side and lies there, his knees still drawn up, his body shaking with nearly silent chuckling. He sighs and wails, weary from the laughter, and then he suddenly starts again. In spite of myself I have to smile.

When he's quiet again, I just let him lie there awhile. His breathing becomes deep and regular, and I wonder if he's sleeping. He is facing away from me.

'You asleep?'

'No.'

'Why'd you do it?'

He doesn't answer.

'Phil. Why the windows?'

He takes so long to answer, I'm ready to try again, when he says, 'Fuckin' glass.'

'You don't like glass? You suddenly don't like glass? You know the police were almost here? How do you think your customer is going to feel about this? Don't they drive by and check it out a couple of times a week? Didn't you tell me that? Phil? What about the glass?'

'Didn't like what I saw.'

'In the glass?'

'Mm-hm.'

'What? You mean yourself? Your reflection? Jesus.' I put my head on my knees. The sickness I feel moves down from my throat and up from my stomach and fills me. 'Will somebody explain to me what's going on? Was it always this bad? Will you please tell me that? Was it always this fucked?'

'Her,' he says.

'What?'

'Saw her – in the fucking glass.'

'Who?!'

'Mom.'

I leap to my feet, pointing at him, so scared now I'm shaking. 'What are you saying?! Don't do this! Jesus Christ! Mari and you! Mari and you! You both acted like you didn't give a damn! You couldn't care less! Mari had them all figured out – Mom and Dad. She acted like she had them all figured out, and you just ignored them, like you didn't care, like you both didn't care, and now you're both going crazy!' Phil has turned and is sitting again, staring at me as if I'm a face he can't quite place. 'You're both going nuts. She sees Bally fall, and he doesn't really fall, and you see Mom in the glass!'

He puzzles over my face awhile, and then he says, 'My mouth and my eyes, sport. Just like hers. I never really saw it before. I noticed it last night. I was looking through pictures.'

'What? What, Phil?'

'I looked at the pictures and noticed it a little bit. But now. Shit. Today, looking in the glass. Look at me. Look at my mouth.'

'You've got pictures? You've got family pictures? You actually look at family pictures?'

'Yeah. Sure. I've got some pictures. Look at my mouth.'

'Yeah.'

'Yeah?'

'Yeah. You *do* look like her. You and Mari both look like her. I knew that. You didn't know that?'

'Not this much.'

'Christ.'

'Not this much, sport – since I've gotten older. Wow. Just like her.'

He's got his bulging arms resting on his knees again, squatting now, staring at the wall, at his thoughts. I stare at him a long time, my fear draining away, just a sour sadness left, heavy as oil.

'She said hello . . . to you.'

He looks up at me.

'She called Dad. She told him to say hello to you and to tell you that she's all right.'

'To me – she said?'

'Yeah. Dad told me. I'm supposed to tell you – for her. She called last night, I guess.'

He stares at me a while, then back at the wall.

'I think *I'm* going, too,' he says.

'What? Where? France?!'

He shakes his head dully. 'Alaska.'

Phil has spoken for years about a vague plan to go and live in Alaska and build homes there. He has talked about all the space there and the newness of it, just a few words now and then. At first I used to question him about it. I even read up on it so I could give him information, but he wasn't receptive. He wanted it to be his own vague frontier dream, and so I forgot about it.

'So you think you'll go?'

He nods, still staring at his thoughts.

'Well, let's go home first.' I put out my hand. He looks up. We grab wrists, and I brace myself, but he rises easily, and I hardly feel the pull.

Once in motion, Phil seems much more drunk. We have to stop several times on the way to his truck because he is dizzy. While driving him home, his head rolls loosely on the back of his seat and he moans now and then.

My mind is trying to penetrate the mystery of Phil and the family pictures and the windows, but it keeps bouncing off and running toward Lauren. Maybe I'm pulling it away. Maybe that's what I do. I don't know, but I can't help thinking about her and feeling a buzz of anticipation all through me because I'll be seeing her soon and hearing her voice, and she'll be close to me, and I'll feel her warmth and breathe her scent and watch every gesture she makes and love that gesture. I am so totally in love, I want to dig an elbow into Phil right now and tell him. I imagine it, and I find myself smiling. 'I was in her bed last night, Phil. In her arms. Lauren!' Of course I would never tell him, but the image of his expression, his surprise, makes me smile, and I know it's not appropriate to be smiling as I drive my drunken brother home from a job he has just destroyed while our family is unraveling, but total love feels like a kind of madness, and I feel privileged, even awed, to be one of the insane.

She is waiting on Phil's porch in her white Sunday dress, and she comes to meet us in the driveway with both relief and concern mixing in her look.

'I'm *so* glad you got him out of there,' she says. I come around to Phil's side and open the door. I actually have to force a look of concern on my face and obliterate my mad smile as I look at her and watch the breeze finger her hair and skirt and study each of her gestures.

'We just talked a few minutes, and he came with me. He's half passed out now, though.'

I open the door on Phil's side and start to help him out, but he pushes my arms away and steps to the ground, bracing himself on the fender. He doesn't look at us. He seems angry now, his old self. I start to take an arm, gently, but he swats at me, saying, 'Goddammit.'

'All right then, walk on your own!' I stand back with my hands on my hips. He keeps leaning on that fender, looking mad and miserable. Lauren steps into him, puts an arm around him, bringing his hand to her shoulder. It's all very sudden and graceful. She steps away from the truck, and he leans on her a little, just for guidance, and together they move up the walkway toward the door. I'm watching, angry at him and jealous, too. I admit that.

I follow them inside.

Once in the house, Phil stands still. Lauren slowly disengages, and he makes his way into the bedroom by touching various pieces of furniture and several walls. There are handprints on all the surfaces he touches, dozens of prints, layers of markings from all his drunken passages from the front door to the bed.

We follow him into the bedroom where he crawls then lies on the bed, on his side, knees drawn up, fetal and moaning. Lauren starts pulling off his shoes, and I come around the bed quickly.

'I'll do that.'

But she already has them off. She plucks off his painter's hat, too, and then starts on his belt buckle.

'Lauren.'

'Hm?'

'You don't have to take off his pants.'

'He'll sleep better.'

I sigh and take his feet and pull his legs straight so that he flops on to his back, and she can get at the buckle now. She unbuckles and unzips, and I take fistfuls of his cuffless jeans and pull them off. I glance at his bulging briefs, and I'm uncomfortable. She is folding over the spread, covering him, and it's not that I'm embarrassed, I realize, but jealous again, upset at this reminder of *their* intimacy. I don't want to think about that. I don't want to remember that they were lovers. She practically said so. She said it didn't work and they're friends now – something like that. So that means they tried it out. That means he knows her in that way. His body knows her, remembers her that way. She's fussing over him now, and turning to the window to darken it for him and behaving as if she's done it all before, almost as if they're a couple and I'm – what? I'm the gawky younger brother, barely visible, hardly thought of. I feel closed out of something, something adult and intimate – but it's not true. It was me she held last night. She looked at me with love in her eyes last night. Last night I made her laugh, and I made her tremble. That was me.

'I think he's already asleep,' she says.

Not quite, because he throws an arm across his eyes and moans a little. She watches him for a moment. Her eyes get lost on him. It unnerves me.

'What are you thinking?'

She turns to me then, surprised, and she sighs. 'About my ex-husband.' She leaves the room, and I follow. She is standing in the messy living room, arms folded, following a thread of thoughts again. I send my eyes scouting among the litter of clothing and magazines and mail. I'm looking for the family photos Phil was talking about, and I find them on the coffee table.

There are only three. Two of them are posed family portraits. A copy of one of these is on our mantel at home. This is before I joined the family. My parents are smiling, but the smiles are impenetrable. I don't discover any guilt in the eyes. Mari is two or so and Phil is six and smiling a little in one of them. In the next he's eight or nine and somber. My parents wear the same weak smiles. Mari is biting her cheeks. She is still round with baby fat. In the third photo Phil is twelve or so. I must have been two, but I'm not there – just Phil and our mother, standing on the beach. She could stand straight then. She's almost at attention in a blue one-piece bathing suit, dark and slender. She looks impatient, and Phil wears the same expression. He was already muscular for his age, standing hands on hips in long, baggy shorts and no shirt. They are not touching each other. I try to look at the beach photo with Phil's eyes, studying the resemblance. It is fairly dramatic, all in the eyes and mouth, especially the eyes, and in what the eyes are saying: I don't want to be here.

The most surprising thing about the photos is that Phil has kept them. This fact lends them a poignancy that makes my throat fill, and I'm swallowing, and Lauren is now beside me, studying with me.

I turn to her. She's still staring at the photo in my hand. I want to lean toward her and kiss her cheek. I want to be sudden and forceful and grab her into my arms and feel how thin the cotton dress is that covers her. I want her nakedness and her heat and her love so badly, I wonder if she can hear my heart hammering.

She looks at me then. 'Sad boy,' she says about Phil. 'In a sad family. Do you remember your family being sad?'

'I think I was trying not to notice.'

She nods at me awhile, then starts toward the door. 'Do you want lunch or coffee or something? Why don't you come over?'

It's a physical pleasure entering Lauren's house again, the house of the sacred night. It's a kind of cathedral now. It hushes me. I'm disappointed, though, that there is no sign that I was ever there. The living room is tidy, all the bedding put away, no traces of popcorn.

Even the kitchen, where she leads me, is all in place and shining.

'Are you hungry?' She sounds tired.

'Not right now.'

'Me neither.' She pulls out a chair and sits at the kitchen

table. I do the same. I realize it is the only time I have been alone with her in this house. She stares at me, and I hold my breath.

'Why did he do it?'

'Hm?' I thought she was going to say something about us, about last night. Phil comes rushing back at me now, bringing the darkness, the open wound. 'Oh.' I shrug and study the tabletop, not really wanting to grapple with this, not now. But I say, 'Because he saw his reflection in the windows – and it reminded him of our mother. He looks like her.'

She stares at the tabletop, too, and through it. 'I think it's terrible she went away like that – without . . . I don't know. She could've come and talked to him, spent a few hours with him.'

'Afraid, I guess.'

Her eyes jump to me.

'I think both my parents are afraid of Phil. They're afraid of his temper. It's probably guilt. They're afraid of Mari, too, afraid of her mind, her words. They use me to talk to Phil and Mari. They have for years. It's been getting worse. Everything's been getting worse. And I *did* it. I was their messenger. I was a liar, too. "Mari, Mom says hello, and I'm supposed to give a hug from her to Bally." Bullshit. I made it up. "Dad sends a hello." Dad sent shit. "Boy, did Mom and Dad laugh when I told them how . . . how . . . how Bally rolled his wagon into that store." *Bullshit!*'

'Cheevey . . .'

'They would barely smile! They would barely *listen*! He's their grandchild, for chrissake! Their grandchild! It was so fucked, Lauren, and I was part of it. I *am* part of it . . .'

'You were trying to help.'

'I was lying for them. I was always making excuses for them – and there's Phil with his three family pictures. Three from what? Eighteen years at home – he's got three little pictures, and he stares at them and he looks at her and he picks up a hammer and breaks his own *face*! And Mari . . . Mari . . .'

'Oh, Cheeve . . .'

'Mari is sitting there in the airport just to watch her, just to *watch* her, just sitting there and wanting to go *with* her, even now! And I'm *still* making excuses and *still* lying for them. I told Phil – today! I said, "Mom . . . Mom . . . Mom . . ."'

'Cheevey, please . . .'

I can't help it. I'm starting to weep. I don't want to weep like some kid in front of Lauren, but I can't catch my words. They're out too fast. I can't stop my voice, and the tears are hiding inside my voice, and now they're surprising me and mocking me in front of Lauren.

' "Mom says hello, Phil. Mom told Dad to say hello to you, and tell you she's all right." He liked that. Phil liked that. I could tell. He looked at me like a little boy when I told him that – and I thought, Shit! *Shit*! Why *couldn't* she have said that?! Why *didn't* she?! Christ! And why . . . why . . . why didn't . . .'

My hands are shaking on the table, and I feel like a child as the weeping tortures my words and fills my mouth with spit and makes my nose run, and Lauren stands up, her chair scooting back, and she comes to me and touches me, and I wrap my arms around her waist and bury my wet face in her white cotton dress, pushing into her stomach and trying, trying to stop, but the sobs are coming. I can feel them in my stomach and chest, and I can't stop them, and I know I'm squeezing her too tight and getting her too wet and behaving like a boy, a boy, but I sob against her, and she holds me and kisses the top of my head.

I let go of Lauren, but she stays close to me. I pull my face from her stomach, embarrassed by my childlike weeping and my runny nose, and I turn before she can get a look at me, and I rise and leave the kitchen.

I go into the hallway and into the bathroom and close the door. I don't see Kleenex, so I use toilet paper to blow my nose and wipe my upper lip. I run water on my shaky fingers and wet my face and dry myself on a fancy hand towel. When I feel that my breathing is close to normal, I open the door.

As I step out into the hall, I notice the open door to her bedroom. I walk in, and I stare at the bed. It's made, but spilled in its center is a small pool of silk that is her short gown, and draped across the foot of the bed is her pink robe. I sit on the bed and stare at the gown beside me. I want to touch it but I don't. I just sit and breathe a while, and soon Lauren comes to stand in the doorway, and we look at each other.

'Feel all right?'

I nod. She comes in, bringing sympathy, but not too much. Her eyes don't pity me and make me a child, and I'm glad. 'Sorry,' I say. There are small wet spots on the midriff of her white dress.

'Don't be.' She sits beside me on the bed, not quite touching. In a moment I put an arm around her, cupping her shoulder and gently pulling her toward me. Her other shoulder leans in against my ribs. She lays her head on my chest. I can smell her hair now. The scent thrills me, but so does the touch of my hand on her shoulder and the weight of her leaning into me.

'You know what I'm wondering?' she asks me.

'What?' My breath is caught, I'm hoping she'll speak of us now, now that we're in this room again, on her bed.

'I'm wondering if someday – even though I think I'm doing the best I can – I'm wondering if Molly will ever break any windows.'

'Oh, no, Lauren. No. Not Molly. Not you. Absolutely not.'

I can *feel* her smiling somehow.

'Cheevey, nobody knows.'

'I know. Cheevey knows. I really do. I'm an expert. I know two things well – military history and poor family dynamics. The second one I know firsthand. You are way out of your territory here. No, you cannot join the ranks of lousy parents, and you never will. You're the *reason*, listen, you are the reason I know the difference. I didn't know the difference, not so *completely*. You taught me.'

'Cheevey, what . . . ?'

'You taught me what it could be like. I remember saying to Phil, the day I met you, and he said you had a daughter, I said, "Imagine, just imagine being her kid. Just imagine having that kind of . . ." and then I saw you with her and I witnessed . . . I am a witness. You treasure Molly – and she knows that. She feels it. She absorbs it. Now Bally is a treasured boy, too, but it's mixed with darkness, *our* darkness, Cheever darkness. Yours is pure.'

'Nothing's pure.'

I turn and take both her shoulders and say this into her face. '*You* are. You are the giver, you are the one who knows how to love. You, Lauren. And I love you.'

Her eyes are full and sad and pleased at the same time, and she has never looked so soft, so pliant. I lean forward and tilt my head and kiss her on the lips. It is a wet and pulpy kiss, a promising, intimate kiss and soft, so very soft. When it ends and I pull back, she looks downward, as if shy, as if a young girl. I stare at her and feel older again, manly again, her equal, her lover.

I still hold her shoulders, and her body, turned toward me, has one knee drawn up on the bed – which pulls the hem of her dress and reveals the beginning of her thigh. I kiss her forehead. I cannot see her downcast eyes. I send my fingertips to her bare leg, my flesh brushing the skin of her knee and then upward to where her dress hem lies and then further, slowly pushing the white cotton ahead of my fingers, revealing more of her thigh and tracing the roundness to the inside of her leg and the incredible, hidden softness there, and then she stops me with a whisper.

'Cheevey, please.' It is a very soft, slightly liquid whisper. She still does not look up at me. I close my eyes and allow my fingers to linger on the protected, velvety flesh where thigh touches thigh.

'Please,' she says again, so soft it's as much a breath as a word.

I take my hand from her leg and put it in her hair and gently tilt her head back and kiss her again and again, lips and cheeks and eyes and lips again as other words whisper from her like breath, broken by my kisses. 'Don't. Che . . . Do . . . Don't. Cheev . . . Ple . . .'

She suddenly pulls back and covers her face with her hands. I stare at her, and then take her wrists very gently to pull her hands away, but she stiffens and then wrenches away from me and stands and drops her hands, and I am so surprised to see her anger.

'What are you doing?! What are you doing to me?!' Tears come with her words. I am gaping at her. 'You think it's easy for me?! I'm . . . You're hurting, and I'm trying to help you! I'm feeling so bad for you, and you . . . You promised, Cheevey! We *said*. We *said*. It was *once*.'

'Lauren. Lauren . . .'

'It's not fair.'

'Lauren, I love you so much.'

'We *said*.'

'I know – but forget what we said.'

'No!'

'Yes! Everything can start now. Our lives can start from this minute now, and we can say whatever we want. We can change it.'

'You promised.'

I stand and reach out, and she steps back, but her voice is softer. 'You promised, Cheevey. Please. Please don't make it so hard; don't let it be bad now . . .'

'Bad? How can it be bad if I love you, and you said you loved me?'

'I never should have . . . Last night I should have made you go.'

I feel like she's just hit me – or shot me. I don't move or speak or breathe.

'I should've said no. I was wrong. I'm sorry. It's my . . .'

'How can you regret that?!' I'm shouting now. 'How can you possibly regret that?!'

'Because of this! Because of now! Because you're too young, and I was stupid, and I *do* love you, but not like that, not for that.'

'What are you saying?!'

'Cheevey, don't do this!'

'Don't tell me I'm too young. Nobody is ever going to love you like I love you right now. Nobody! Who? Phil? Men like Phil?!'

'Don't, Cheevey.'

'You think Phil is so old – so grown up? What's the difference?! Years? Time? What? He's a man, and I'm what – a boy?'

'Yes!'

'A boy!?' I'm shaking with anger. I want to make her understand. I want to make her see how wrong she is. 'Was I a boy last night?!'

She is weeping now, her face twisting as she tries to speak. 'You're a wonderful boy and . . .'

'Don't say that! How am I a boy? What's the difference?! What's a man? Lauren?! What?!'

'Cheevey, stop!'

'A man enters you – is that what he does? Is that what it is? That's the difference!?'

One shaky hand covers her mouth, and the other suddenly slaps my shoulder, but I don't stop.

'Is that what a man does to you – so I don't qualify?!'

She keeps the one hand pressed to her mouth as the other hits at me, at my shoulder and my chest, and I hold up my hands to block her blows. 'A man . . .' She releases her mouth and slaps at me with one hand and then the other, slapping my raised hands, not very hard. Her face is twisted with hurt and anger and weeping, and I'm suddenly so sorry. I'm so surprised that I could allow myself to cause her pain, and I'm so terribly, terribly sorry. 'A man . . .' she hits once more and raises her voice '. . . keeps promises!' A sob escapes her and the sound is a blade in my stomach. She gives in to the sobbing and covers her face again, and I stand there more wretched than I have ever been.

'Lauren.'

She turns her back to me and wipes at her face and starts to walk out of the room. I follow her, just a few inches behind her. 'God, I'm sorry. Please stop, please, please, please.'

She does stop – in the middle of the hall. It is a wonderful thing – her stopping. In the midst of her hurt and her anger, she hears me and she stops. She gives that to me – even now. I guess it is the finest thing anyone has ever done for me. If she had walked away, closed a door, I would have broken – like a pane of glass. She stands with her back to me, very still, very stiff. Tentatively, I put my arms around her from behind, and I lean my head on hers. She does not loosen.

I have to swallow several times before I can speak.

'I ruined everything.'

She sighs in my arms. I feel one more sob, like a spasm, and then the loosening begins, very slowly.

'I'm sorry, Lauren.'

I feel her nod slightly. In a moment she is relaxed, even weary now within my arms.

'I'm going to go.'

She nods again.

'I'm sorry I spoiled . . . what was so good.'

She starts to move, and I quickly release her. She turns and moves around me, back into the bedroom. I watch her get a tissue from her dresser. She blows her nose and gets more tissues. 'Your car's at the construction site,' she says without looking at me. 'I'll drive you.'

'No. Lauren, no. I'll walk.'

She looks at me now, and it is as though I have punched her. Her face is blurred. Her eyes battered. I feel the blade turn in my stomach.

'Don't be silly,' she says.

'No. No, I'll jog. I like to jog, and I'd hate for you to drive me. I couldn't stand that because it would make me feel like a kid, like a boy – which is what I am, I know, but I don't want to feel that way now. I want a better exit than that.'

Her face almost musters a slight smile, but not quite.

'How could I do that?' I'm not really asking her. I'm asking me. 'How could I possibly hurt you and make you cry? I don't understand how I could possibly do that, loving you the way I do.'

She shakes her head as if erasing my words, erasing the whole issue. 'My fault, too,' she says.

'No.' I look past her, to the bed. I have a sudden impulse, and then I bury it – and then I release it, deciding to be bold. I walk to the bed and reach out and touch her short, silken gown, and then I pick it up, half of it balled in my hand, and I turn to her. 'Can I keep this?' And then I add, 'Is that too weird?'

Now her smile comes, through the bruising of tears, with a little one-note laugh that is almost a sob, and her eyes say that she loves me still, after all.

I unbutton one button on my shirt and stuff the silk in against my chest and smile some kind of smile at her. I'm not sure how I look, but I walk out of the room then without any further words or mess and make a decent, maybe even manly, kind of exit.

It's Tuesday, and I'm hoping to hear today about the theatre job from Arnie Golden. I've started looking for a place to live, too, and after school I saw a pretty dismal apartment. I'd be sharing it with a couple. They're renting out one of the bedrooms, but I'd have to share that bedroom with the man's eleven-year-old son who comes over every other weekend. I was told he was a nice kid and asthmatic.

The place was dark, even on a sunny day. I only met the woman, and she seems nice enough. She works out of the apartment. Telephone sales. She was still in her robe at three-thirty. I guess when you do telephone sales you can wear anything – or nothing – but I didn't like the way she shuffled in her slippers. She was young, only thirty or so, but she shuffled, and she didn't care about her hair. Now every time I answer a phone and there's someone trying to sell me something, I'll picture the person in a robe and those quilted boot-slippers. They were orange.

I don't know if I can tolerate the proximity of strangers. I've had my own private nest for years. I suppose it's something I'll have to get over. I put the word out to my friends, too, and Danny Chin says he knows of a place that might be opening up in a few weeks. I'd be sharing with three others, but at least they'd all be students. Maybe that's worse. I worry about music. I hate to have to listen to other people's music, inside or outside, anywhere. I can't concentrate. I sit there hating the fact that it is forced on me, and hating the people who blow their music in your face like smoke.

When I get home I'm depressed by the thoughts that are waiting for me. They overpopulate the place like heavy, slouching bodies: Phil, Mari, Lauren, Mom, Dad, filling all the chairs and spilling on to the table, the bed, all of them scowling or weeping. Well – it's Lauren who is weeping. I try very hard to imagine her any other way, but I can't. Even when I go to her nightgown hanging in my closet, and I touch it, even then the memory of the night with her is only a grey, faded thing compared with the crisp, glossy memory of her in tears, slapping at me.

Last night I took the nightgown to bed with me and laid my face on it and concentrated, and I was in bed with her again, but every time we embraced, the other Lauren would burst in, the hurt and crying Lauren, slapping at my arm.

I suppose this is what I'll think of someday when I'm old and close to death and someone asks me – some reporter or talk show host or some priest asks me – 'Any regrets?'

I'm also depressed and a little frightened by the thought of moving. That apartment worries me. It is so gloomy, and pieces of it are missing, deep gouges out of the plaster, jagged bits of Formica broken or bitten off the counter, and some of the cabinet doors are gone – as if something is feeding on the place.

I'm happy to see I have a message on my machine. Maybe Danny Chin has news, or I got the theatre job. Underneath all of this, I'm hoping it might be Lauren.

But it's Phil. Sober. His words are few and clipped and interrupted by long, weary sighs.

'So. Cheeve. I talked to Ben Black. Remember? I used to work with him. He's taking over the remodel. I already talked to the owner. So. Call 'im. Told him about you. Says he can use you. So. 'Bye.'

I play it again, and then I just stand there, letting it sink in. Phil told him about me. Phil has found me a job. This is a really good thing. Even if the job doesn't work out. In the midst of all the unraveling, Phil has thought of me and tried to secure me a job. This is a surprising thing.

I call Phil and get his machine and say only, 'Hey, thanks,

bro. Really. I'll call Ben now. Call you back later. Hey. Thanks. You all right?'

I find Ben Black Construction and call, and somebody tells me they'll beep Ben, and he'll call me. I hang up and sit and drum on my knees. This is good. I want to tell Lauren about this. Maybe she already knows. Maybe she even reminded Phil so he *would* ask about me. It's still a good thing.

Ben Black calls me, and he remembers me from when I helped him as an extra man when he and Phil were partners. He's busy. He can give me all the time I can handle. We figure it out. It's twenty hours a week – Saturdays and after school. I'll take home about a hundred and thirty. I'll be painting and doing lath and plaster and a little framing and a lot of scud work – the demolition and the clean-up – but that's fine. This is a very good thing.

I want very much to share this with Mari, and I call her, and she's home.

'Can I come over? You going to be there awhile?' I ask her.

'Yes. Good. Come over. You can spell me.'

'Spell you from what?'

'Watching Bally.'

'Oh. Sure. But you'll stay awhile. I mean, I want to talk. Okay?'

'Talk? *Me*? Have you ever known me to shut up? Bob says I even talk in my sleep. Bob loves to snorkel, but I said I don't want to try it because you can't talk when you're doing it. It makes bubbles. I have to get back to Bally. Come over now.'

I haven't had good news for anybody in a long time, it seems. It makes me lighter as I lope down my staircase, and I feel so good I don't want to drive, so I jog.

'Mari, can I tell you what I came over to tell you?'

'Wait, let me finish.'

We're in Bally's room, sitting on his bed, watching him. He's busy in the middle of the floor, building a fortress out of plastic beams and walls, and he's talking to himself just under his breath. I think he's supposed to be the man operating the crane which he moves now and then, making a pretty good crane sound. I don't know why we're sitting in here at all since he's so deep into his play, but Mari hasn't stopped talking since I arrived.

'So I just stopped. I put the pen down,' she is saying, 'and I knew that it was different from all the other times I had put the pen down. I knew this time I was never going to pick up the pen again.'

'What d'you mean?'

'Let me finish.'

'You mean you finally dumped Coretti?'

'Not yet. Not *literally*. But I think I will dump him, and "dump him" is exactly right, but what I did is I put all my papers – all my false starts, all my millions of notes, all the research – into a cardboard box, and I even *sealed* it – with tape.'

'So you've stopped?'

'Listen. Yes. All my thinking on Coretti, all my theories and research, is in this box, and I'm through with it. So listen to what I'm going to do. You know what they do with leftover books they can't sell? At least they used to. First they "remainder" them. They sell the remainder of their stock at discount. It's called "remaindering" – doesn't that sound like cannibalism or organ harvesting? Anyway, if they still have stacks and stacks of unsold books, what they do, or what they *did*, maybe now it's against some ecological law or something, is they would dump them in the ocean, in the Caribbean Sea, actually, or the "Caribbean." So think of it. There are these mounds of waterlogged books down there, rotting down there. All the characters from all these books are bloating down there

– you know, like five thousand Oliver Twists are sitting around on the floor of the Caribbean or the "Caribbean" with ten thousand Scarlett O'Haras, except that the books on the floor of the sea are full of characters we never heard of and never *will* hear of because that's who gets remaindered and then dropped overboard – the obscure, the unknown, the unread.

'So what I'm going to do is take this box and throw it in the ocean, thereby passing over all the steps of trying to write my dissertation and trying to get it published only to see nobody buy it and watch it get remaindered and then drowned like an unwanted puppy. I'm skipping all that. Splash. It's gone. All my notes will be down there joining all the other unread reading matter on the floor of the sea with the squids and sharks and starfish.'

'Well, good, Mari – I mean I'm glad you're off Coretti. I always thought he was a dead end.'

'*He's* not a dead end, Cheeve. He's brilliant. I just can't communicate his brilliance, so I'm not going to try. It's *me*. It's not him. I was going to bring him back, remember? He's in some kind of hiding, a self-imposed exile from the world that won't recognize him, and I was going to change that, but now I see I can't, so if he ever comes back on his own, I'll just write him a letter. *That* I could do – just a typical kind of fan letter. "Thank you for writing. Your pen touched my soul." No. Not that drippy. Just, "Thanks – loved your books." Something like that. No, he's great. He's the best. It's *me*.'

'He's too dense. It's not you. Anyway, who will you pick now?'

'Nobody. I'm retired. I quit the bookstore, too. I'm a full-time mom. I have to be. I need to be. Watch him while I go pee, all right?'

'Watch him?'

'Bally.'

She is up and moving to the door which is closed.

'What d'you mean, "watch him"?'

She opens the door and leaves and closes it behind her, and I hear the knob rattle a bit as she tests the lock. She has locked us in. I keep staring at the door, absorbing this – and then I look at Bally. He is still building and half-whispering and making the sounds of construction.

'Bal?'

He doesn't look up. He is intense and seems to be rushing, his little hands working quickly at the plastic beams and walls and gates.

'Bally?'

Now he looks at me.

'You're building fast, huh?'

'Before they attack.'

'Who?'

'Tee guys.'

I notice his army of golf tees bunched in the corner. They are usually from Jupiter.

'Jupitarians,' I say.

'Mm-hm.' He is building again, but more slowly. I've thrown him off a bit, pulled him up to the surface of his play. He had been in so deep.

'Why'd she lock the door, Bal?'

'She always does.' He keeps building.

'Then she . . . comes in.'

'Mm-hm.'

'And she watches you?'

'Mm-hm.'

I wait, and Mari comes in and closes the door and sits beside me on the bed again.

'Why don't we go into the living room?' I ask. 'And let Bally play.'

'Can't.'

'What d'you mean?'

'I don't want to leave him alone.'

'Why?'

'Remember the fall?'

This chills me. 'The fall that didn't happen?'

'Happened to *me*, Cheeve.'

'You mean you imagined it.'

'Saw it.'

'In your mind – God, we've been through this. Your son never fell down the stairs.'

'Good. Now he never will.'

'Can we please go in the living room? I want to talk to you about Phil.'

'What about Phil?'

'Come on.'

I rise and go to the door and open it. She looks at Bally. Bally is almost finished with the fort – and just in time. He is starting to bring the Jupitarians out of the corner.

'Mari?'

She looks at me, then she rises from the bed and comes to the doorway, but she looks back at Bally. I slowly close the door. We're in the hall outside his room now. She is staring at the doorknob.

'It's open,' I say. 'I mean unlocked.'

'You unlocked it?'

I nod.

She touches it, turns it slowly. 'Unlocked.'

I nod again. 'You're freaking out, you know.'

'I'm just being careful.' She stares hard at me. 'I'm just – for the time being – being very careful so I can get rid of this feeling. I'm trying to feel safe, Cheeve. I haven't felt safe since it happened, and I'm trying to give myself some peace of mind.'

'You talk to the shrink about it?'

'Yes. Well, Bob did. Bob saw fit to.'

'"Saw fit"?'

'Yes. "Saw fit." That's a carpentry term, I believe.'

We both smile. It is a relief to me, but just on the surface. 'What did the shrink tell you?'

'She said to work on it. I'm working on it.'

'We'll work on it now. We'll go into the living room and we'll sit there, and you'll forget about Bally because you'll be listening to me. I actually have something good to tell you, something about Phil. It's good.'

She stares, then leads the way to the living room and sits on the sofa. I sit beside her and angle toward her. Her look flashes to the hallway, but then back at me. She spreads her hands as if to say: I'm ready, see?

'Phil quit the remodel. He thinks he might be going away.'

'Alaska,' she says.

'He *told* you?'

'Sure. When he was in high school, and about once a year since.'

'But maybe he'll really go now. He gave up the remodel.'

'Why?'

Well, he was drinking a lot. So he gave it up, and I think he might make some changes.'

'Like go to Alaska.'

'Yes. You don't think he'll go?'

'I *used* to think that. Now I don't. Now I think that maybe Phil *will* go to Alaska. See, Cheeve, I always thought Alaska was Phil's place never to go to like France was Mom's. They both had favorite places never to go to. But I was wrong. Obviously. She's there right now, saying, *"Garçon, plus de beurre, s'îl vous plait."* So I'm wrong. I was wrong all along. So I know that as soon as I say Phil will never go to Alaska, there he'll be, in Nome, ordering butter in Eskimo, and I'll be wrong. So, good. I hope he goes and loves it there.'

'But that's not what's good. What's good – surprisingly good – is that he called his old partner, who is taking over the remodel, and he asked the guy if he would hire *me*. He thought of *me*. He found me a job. I already talked to the guy. I've got about six months of work I can count on. Phil did that – which is great. 'Cause I quit at Dad's store.'

'You quit?'

'Yeah.'

'No kidding. Why?'

'Well . . . I want to be more independent now.'

'Really. Well . . . all these changes. I feel out of touch. You didn't tell me.'

'I'm telling you. But mostly I wanted to tell you about Phil. Isn't that nice – what he did?'

'You could probably work at the bookstore, you know, since I'm leaving.'

'Mari, I'm talking about Phil. While everything's coming apart, he does this. Finally, something good. Isn't it?'

'Sure it is. It's good. For Phil it's more than good. For Phil it's extraordinary, and I think we should notify the Nobel committee in Sweden and put him in the running. I mean it.'

'Mari . . .'

'I mean it, Cheeve. Okay. I don't mean it. Forget it. I was exaggerating. Maybe a local citizen's award is more appropriate. I'm sorry. I'm not making fun. I really think it's nice that he did that. I just wish you weren't so goddamn' surprised by one nice thing happening in this family. I find that very sad. Don't you?'

'No. I've *been* very sad. This actually makes me a little happier, and I wish it did *you*, too. I mean – make you happy. Not sad.'

'Okay. Sorry.'

I sigh and my eyes trail about the place. I can hear Bally through the wall making big explosion sounds. The attack is on. I'm not happy anymore. I try to get back to the feeling I had when I first heard Phil's message.

'Maybe he's changing,' I say. 'Maybe this crap we're going through will change us for the better.'

She touches my hair, then leans in and kisses my cheek. 'Cheeve, you're the best we've got.'

I look into her eyes, which have filled, and I like her softness and I liked her kiss, but I say, 'I don't feel so "best" right now.' I sigh heavily again. 'I fell in love with a woman, and I screwed it up – all in about two days.'

'What?! Who?!'

I rise from the couch and stretch. 'I'll tell you more some time.'

'Oh, you shit. You scoundrel. No. Really. Are you serious? Who!?'

'I need some distance from it first. I need to see that she can at least be my friend. It's still . . . raw . . . and unsettled. But I botched it.'

'Ohh, Cheeve, I'm sorry. It's bad to botch.'

'Yes, I hate botching.'

'Isn't that an Italian game old men play with their balls?'

I smile, and she rises and hugs me, being big sister again, comforting. 'I'm really sorry,' she says softly against my shoulder. 'I don't see how any girl could let you get away.'

I hug her, too. 'Thanks. And please, Mari, ease up. Can you ease up – with Bally?'

'It's getting better.'

'Is it? Really?'

We break, still holding hands on arms, and she nods, a little teary. 'It's definitely better.'

I kiss her forehead. 'I'll babysit. Call me a day ahead. I'll give you and Bob a night out.'

'Oh good. Thanks. We'll go dancing. I'll rent a tux. He'll buy a gown.'

'Mari, I'm serious – take yourselves out.'

She smiles, and the teary eyes shine. She kisses my chin. 'I'll call you,' she says.

I pause at the door for a dashing wave that starts with a kiss at my fingertips and ends with my hand flung wide. I hear her chuckling as I descend the stairs, and I can still hear, faintly, the attack of the Jupitarians on the fortress of Earth.

Danny Chin had called by the time I jogged home from Mari's and showered and came up to my room. I'm going to see this place Friday, the one I would share with three other students. They're all Asian-Americans, Chin said. The first thing I thought of when he said that was the quiet. I picture most Asian-Americans as quiet and polite. It's probably stereotyping. I don't know. They seem that way in school, and Danny is *usually* that way, though I've seen him cut loose. But I like the idea of the quiet. The thing that strikes me now, as I look around my room, is the amount of packing I have to do – mostly books and, of course, the soldiers. I wonder how I'm going to live with the absence of shelves.

I realize I should trim my books and my collection down to a minimum for travel. I don't think I want my soldiers on display in a place I'm sharing. Maybe I can store most of them with Dad until I get a place of my own someday. Mari has no storage space.

I stare at my troops for a long while before deciding to pack them. They've never been out of my sight except for the few vacations I've taken or overnight trips. It's a strange feeling – as if I'm saying goodbye. In fact I find myself explaining to them, in my mind, that it's *not* goodbye. I'm letting them know that storage is temporary, like sleep. We'll be together again – in a year or two, I suppose.

I keep a box of tissues on my table, and this I bring to the shelves. I kneel before my army, and I lift the figures one by one, carefully, touching them as gently as if they were encrusted with gems. I wrap each one in a tissue, making sure the fragile bayonets or swords are especially protected. The larger mounted figures need two tissues each to swathe them. Once wrapped in white, I place them in a shoebox. I realize I'll need about three shoeboxes. As I cover them and nestle them into the box, making sure no metal is touching metal, I note how hushed and heavy I feel, as if this isn't packing but burial.

Triggered by the weight of the warriors in my hands, my mind slips without effort into my story, and I am Captain Cheever, and my Legion is camped below the cliffs of Balkeshar. The enemy holds the heights. This will not be easy.

My father interrupts me. I hear his slow steps on the creaking staircase and then the soft rapping of one knuckle on my door.

'Come in.'

I go on packing as he enters. 'Hi, Dad.' I glance at him, and then go back to my troops. He's standing there at a slouch, watching me.

'Why are you packing now?'

'Well, I'm going to look at a place Friday. Rent's good.'

'Mm. So you're moving out.'

'I don't know. I'll check it out Friday.'

'But you've decided to move out.'

I turn to him now and get up off my knees. 'Well, you're selling this place, right?'

'Yes, but you know what I mean.'

'No, Dad.' I really don't know what he means.

'I mean you've decided not to live with me in the next place I go.'

'Well . . . we talked about that. You can get a one-bedroom, and I can be . . . more on my own.'

He starts nodding and then looking around my room. 'Is it because you're mad at me?'

I'm surprised by his question. 'I don't feel mad,' I say. 'Why?'

He shrugs, frowning-in-general as he looks around. 'Everybody usually is – in this family.'

'I'm not mad at you. Not now. Mari isn't mad at you. Bally's *never* mad at you.'

His frown deepens. He's looking at my half-filled shoebox now.

'How do *you* feel about it, Dad – about my not living with you?'

He shrugs at the shoebox. 'You're old enough to do what you want now – if you can afford it.'

'That doesn't tell me how you feel about it.'

Now his eyes come off the box and settle on me. The frown is still there. I can't read the eyes.

'You can always talk, Claudey. You always could talk. And Mari can talk.' He shrugs, just a quick spasm of his slouching shoulders. 'Some people can't.'

'You can't talk?'

'You know what I mean.'

'No I don't, Dad.'

The frown spreads like it's a crack line on his face and I lose his eyes.

'Dad, I'm not being sarcastic or mad or . . . What do you mean? You can't talk about how you feel?'

The quick, jumpy shrug comes again. 'Some people can't.'

Now I start nodding as I study him, a steady wordless nodding. Maybe I got that from him. 'Well, Dad, people need to hear it – about how you feel. They need to hear it *sometimes,* or they think you don't.'

I get his eyes back now, challenging. 'You think I don't?'

I find that I give him back the same exact shrug. Except for his age and his slouching, I could be having this conversation in a mirror. 'I don't know, Dad, I really don't. It's a mystery to me. You're pretty much a mystery to me.'

He looks a little angry, and I notice he's breathing rapidly. His eyes begin to trail away, but then jump back to me.

'What's so mysterious about going to work every day? What's so mysterious about that – working every day, so there's a house and food and insurance? Phil didn't want college, but you and Mari did, and you got it. Is that some mystery?'

'Supporting us?'

'Support.' Now he's shaking his head steadily in an endless 'no.' 'You think support is automatic? What about getting out of bed and going to that store every day?'

'I thought you liked the store. I thought you loved it, Dad. I thought you went there for *you*.'

'How can I love it when I'm worried about it? I was always worried about it. It's still a big worry. It's in the red. I like the store and I hate the worry. I hate it.'

I stare at him a long time, and when I speak I notice that my voice is soft and fragile. 'Now you're talking, Dad. You said "hate". You're telling me what you hate.'

He turns halfway around. I'm losing him.

'I'm not being sarcastic, Dad. I *want* you to tell me. Tell me more.'

'I told you.'

'You worked at the store every day, and you think we didn't appreciate it?'

'Still don't. Nobody understands that.'

He starts to leave.

'Wait, Dad.'

He stops and half-turns. 'I have a broken radio in my car. I used to listen to the news every morning on the way to the store. It went out years ago, maybe . . . two years ago. I never fixed it, Claudey. Do you know what I'm saying? Anybody understand that?'

'I'm trying to, Dad.'

'But you need money for books, and Mari, I still pay her health insurance. Christ.' This time he makes it to the door, and he opens it, and doesn't turn as he says, 'We got an offer on the house. I'm taking it.' And he softly closes the door and starts down the stairs.

I just stand there awhile, and then I go back to my shelves and kneel in front of my army, but I don't keep packing. I sit and stare at the glossy soldiers, and I think about everything my father said, trying to understand a man who loves you by not fixing his radio.

'Did you check out the Merchant Marine?' I ask Benko.

'Forget the Merchant Marine, Cheeve. My uncle told me stories. Drugs. Fights. People disappearing overboard in the night.'

We're in the House of Billiards on our third game. I feel good. Calm. It's the lighting, I think, one light per table. It creates a separate world. And it's the game, the expanse of green felt, the sound of the balls on the table, humming quietly when they roll and then clicking like worry beads, taking my tension.

'Yeah, but your uncle – that was what, twenty years ago?'

'It's still a two-fisted world, pilgrim.' Benko misses an easy shot and looks at the ceiling and does a silent scream, his arms spread out and wiggling like a baby's.

'*I* have two fists,' I say, and I sink the four ball on a long shot. He pretends to try to break his stick over his thigh. I now have a difficult shot in the corner.

'Well, then, it's a three-fisted world. Christ. Leave me a shot, will you? Leave me a crumb. Don't play so mercilessly. It's not who wins, you know, Cheeve. Don't be so goddamn' competitive. What are you, a law student? Jesus.'

'Shut up. I'm trying to concentrate.'

'Somebody just opened the door, so there's a wind factor of ten knots you should figure in . . . Wow, look at that babe. Now *that's* a short skirt. Oh my God, she's not *wearing* a skirt!'

He has me grinning, but I still make the shot.

'I've always hated you, Cheeve.'

'Did you check out the Foreign Legion?'

'Forget the Foreign Legion.' I *have* left him a good shot if he can use some backspin on the cue ball, and he does, and he makes it and performs a little twirl, very light on his feet for all his bulk.

'Why should we forget the Foreign Legion?' I ask. 'My heart's set on the Foreign Legion. We'd have great adventures in exotic places. We'd come back and be those two mysterious guys with scars who speak French and smoke Gauloise, and the women, the women, Benko . . .'

'I'm tryin' to shoot here.'

'Is that an earthquake? Feel that?'

'Shut up.'

'Benko, I think we should go stand in a doorway.'

'"I don't rattle, kid."' That's a line from *The Hustler*. We always invoke *The Hustler* when we play. It's like a sacred text. He misses the shot and bites his cue stick.

'You didn't even check it out, did you?' I say. 'The Foreign Legion.'

'I did. I did. Forget it. You have to join for five years. You have to get up at dawn and run fifteen miles which includes running through icy water up to your armpits. Couldn't we just learn French and smoke those cigarettes and buy those hats?'

'I love those hats,' I say, and I sink my last ball and then turn to the eight ball and pop that in, and the night stands at two-to-one in my favor as we rack up for the next game.

'I finished the novel,' I say. 'While I was packing.'

'You did?!' He is very surprised. He stops filling the rack.

The story of the Legion has been part of our lives for five years. 'No kidding. You finished?'

'Yes. Finished it today.'

'Jesus, Cheeve.' He goes back to gathering the balls, but his mind is on the story. He looks up at me, and he's back a few years. He looks to be fifteen or so – in his expression. 'Do I live?'

'Yes. But Captain Cheever dies.'

He is awed by the information, as if these are people he has known very well. 'Wow. You going to write it now?'

I shrug, filling the rest of the rack.

'Aren't you going to write it?'

I look up at him and shrug again. 'It feels finished.'

'Well, yeah, but . . .' He is rolling the cue ball under his palm on the table, rolling it in a small circle. He looks at me again. 'Aren't you going to miss it?'

'Yes,' I say. 'I packed all the soldiers.'

'You did?'

'They're in Kleenex, in shoeboxes. I don't want to take them to where I'll be living. Maybe just a few.'

'Wow. The Legion – in shoeboxes.'

'I was going to ask my dad – but maybe I could store them with you?'

'Sure. Sure, Cheeve. Put 'em in my closet. I'll even put 'em out on my shelves if you want.'

'No. No, we'll let them rest. Until I get a place all to myself someday – or maybe you and I . . .'

'Yeah. We should get a place.' He has said this before, and is a little shamefaced as he says it, because we both know he likes living at home.

'When you're ready,' I say.

'Yeah, when I get a job and . . . I should move out but . . .'

'Benko, it's fine.'

'Well, I'm twenty . . .'

'You're still in school – and you *like* it with your family. So would I if I were you. Your family kicks it.'

'But you'll be on your own,' he says, and we both feel that he's looking at me now across some gap. I've crossed. He hasn't.

'It was kind of forced on me,' I say.

He nods and goes back to rolling the ball under his palm. 'How did he die – Captain Cheever?'

'Attacking the heights. A hail of bullets from above. Shot in the chest. He went pretty quick. There was no pain.'

Benko nods, watching his hand roll the ball in small circles.

It's only 10.30 when I get home, but I'm tired. I notice I have two messages, and I hit the button and close my eyes, hoping, maybe even praying, that the next voice I hear is Lauren's, but it's not. It's Bob. Bob never calls me.

'Cheevey,' he says, and his voice is low and tight. 'Shit. I wish you were there. Maybe you're with her. Call me. As soon as you get this. Or if you see Mari. Call me right away.'

This first message leaves my breath all in my chest as I wait for the second. It's Bob again, and his voice is worse, weak and rattled.

'God, I was . . . hoping your machine wasn't . . . or you hadn't listened to it. You really have to call here . . .'

I finally move, jumping for the phone and dialing, while he's still talking on the machine.

'It's about Mari. So . . . call me.'

The voice on my machine ends and the same voice is suddenly in my ear, very urgent and a little hopeful.

'Mari?!'

'It's Cheevey.'

'Do you know where she is?!'

'No.'

'Shit. Jesus Christ.'

Now my heart is quickening, and my throat is dry. He sounds close to crying.

'Bob . . . what . . . ?'

'Can you come here?'

'Sure. What's going on?'

'She's gone. I got home, and she was gone. It's been hours. Christ.'

'Where's Bally?'

'She locked him in his room! Jesus.'

'Is he okay?'

'Yes. He's okay. But he won't sleep. Can you come over?'

'Sure. She's probably just . . . She's walking or she's at the park. I'll go by the park.'

'The cops are looking,' he says.

'The cops?!'

'Yes, but go ahead. Look in the park, then come here – but fast, okay.'

I can still hear the tears in his voice, and I'm surprised. I would have thought he'd be more angry.

'Okay. Listen, she's just walking, I bet.'

'God. God, I hope so. She left a note.'

'A note?! What'd she . . . what'd she say, Bob?'

'Will you just come here?' he is saying and the tears have come.

'What'd she say?!'

He lowers his wet, torn voice. 'Goodbye. She's saying goodbye.'

I speed to the park, and no one is there where Mari and I usually stand and talk, and no one is on any of the benches. I think I see a body on the grass, and I park and run to the body, but it's a sleeping, homeless man rolled in a dirty flowered quilt. I look around and see no one else nearby.

I holler, 'Mari!' as loud as I can. The man scrambles to his feet, blinking at me, terrified. I shout again, but see no one and hear no answer.

I drive to the apartment and hurry up the stairs, telling myself I have to be calm for Bally. Bob opens the door before I get to it. He looks ill. He barely meets my eyes. 'Bally wants to see you,' he says.

'Any word?' I ask foolishly. He would have told me.

'No.'

'Can I see the note?'

He sighs and sits on the sofa. I hear Bally calling through the walls. 'Cheevey?'

'Be right there,' I call back.

Bob has pulled a piece of paper from his pocket and unfolded it. It is half a sheet of computer paper. He hands it to me. I'm hoping that it doesn't really say anything like goodbye. I'm hoping, and I'm praying, as I bring the paper close to me, that *I'll* understand what Bob couldn't, some message from Mari that I'll be able to read that no one else might, a clue.

Bob is rubbing his face and mumbling. 'Police wouldn't help except for the note. I told them . . . I showed them the note. They . . .'

The note is handwritten in Mari's small, precise style. It reads:

Bally, I'm so sorry for letting you fall.
If I end, you can begin, and you won't fall anymore.
Cheevey, you are very worthy. Remember, help yourself

The paper ends just below the last line, clipping off the stems of all the Y's. I read it again and again. *If I end. If I end. If I end.* That sounds bad. That sounds very bad. Feeling suddenly hollow, I sit on the sofa next to Bob. I keep reading the note. *If I end.* The last part I don't understand. *Cheevey, help yourself.* I don't understand that. Help myself to what? Or help *myself* and not anyone else? And why is it cut off? It doesn't seem to close. Why didn't she sign it? There is no period after the last word.

'She didn't sign it, Bob.'

'No.'

'Where did you find it?'

'Kitchen. Standing up against the toaster. We always . . . we leave messages there.'

'But it looks like she didn't finish. Maybe she changed her mind.'

'But she stood it up – by the toaster.'

'Right. Right. When did you find it?'

'About six.'

'How long was Bally alone, before . . . ?'

'He doesn't know.'

'So it's been at least . . .'

'Five hours,' Bob says. He rubs his face again.

'Jesus.' I can't sit still. I rise and pace. I don't want to accept this. She changed her mind – or by 'end' she means disappear. 'She could just be running away,' I say.

'Yes,' he says behind his hands.

'Did she take any money?'

'No.'

'Shit. Christ.'

'Cheevey!' Bally's shout, muffled by the walls, is an urgent plea now. I hand the note back to Bob and walk toward the hall, but I stop. 'Did you call Dash?'

'Everybody,' he says behind his hands.

I walk into Bally's room. It's dark, but the light in the hall spills in. Bally is in bed in a blue knit pajama suit. There used to be a red 'S' stitched on the chest, but only the outline is left. His eyes are huge, deep wells, pulling me toward him. I sit on the bed, and he sits up, and we hug.

Against my chest he asks, 'Where's Mom?'

'Probably out walking,' I say.

'Why?'

'Maybe she needs to think. Sometimes people need to be alone, and they walk for hours, just thinking.'

'About what?'

'Different things. Maybe they're mad about something or scared or sad.' I feel him nod against my chest. I am only partly here with him. Most of me is busy pushing thoughts away, pushing away the dark possibility, swatting at it, like I might flail at a bat that is coming too close. Too close. *If I end. If I end.* End. Mari. I am speaking to her inside, as I sit with Bally and answer questions, I am sending Mari my thoughts. I see my thoughts reach her, catch her coat like a hand and stop her and turn her. I see her face. I say, come back. Mari, come back. Come back now.

'You should sleep, Bal.'

He nods again. 'Sleep with me, okay?'

He lies down and I cover him and lie on the covers beside him.

'Close your eyes,' I whisper.

But he keeps staring at me, and I don't want to look at his sadness and fear because there seems to be such wisdom there, such knowing, as if he has accepted what I am fighting and flailing at with all my strength. 'Close your eyes and sleep.'

He closes his eyes. We lie there a long time. I think of all the places Mari could be. She has a credit card. I become excited by the possibility that she is at the airport, catching a flight to France, but my excitement is dissipated by the bat which reappears, fluttering near my face. *If I end. If I end.*

I cannot lie still anymore. I force myself to wait another minute. I move off the bed by inches, watching Bally's face. He does not open his eyes. His face seems looser, more peaceful. I pad out of the room into the hall.

I don't go back into the living room. I wander into the

master bedroom. Mari works in here. All her books are here. Maybe there's a clue. Did Bob search? Maybe there are other notes.

The bed is wrinkled, but made. There is some clothing here and there. Maybe she packed. I open the closet. It looks like all the clothing is there, but I don't know. I see all her shoes lined up in pairs, side by side and touching, small shoes waiting for a small woman to stand in them like that, the shoes touching, the woman standing straight – at attention – like our mother is standing in so many photographs.

I move to her desk. It's neat, nearly empty. Above it on the first shelf are her Coretti books, hard copies and paperbacks. They are spread out like a fan, the bookends gone. I remember her bookends. They were elephants from a garage sale, but they're gone, and the books have toppled at the edges of the shelf. I have never seen the Coretti hardbacks. One of them has papers marking certain pages. I pull it off the shelf and look at the marked pages. It's dense and meaningless prose to me. In the margin I see a very precise question mark in the faintest shade of pencil. I try the passage again, but learn nothing and find myself angry at the book.

When I close it, I see Coretti for the first time. He is on the back cover, standing against a Cyclone fence, staring squarely into the camera – and I realize I know him. I have seen him. I hold the book very still in my hands. I doubt if I'm breathing. I stare into his face a long time, but I cannot place it. He seems to be about fifty, heavy, balding. I grab for another book and turn to the back cover, and there he is again, smiling slightly this time, older, and I know him immediately. I know the round saggy eyes and ragged teeth. It is Jack-o-lantern, I would swear to this. John Coretti is alive and speaking to his reflections in store windows and living on the streets of Santa Monica, and his name is

Jack-o-lantern. I would bet all my money and my Volvo. Wait until I tell Mari. I have to tell Mari.

I bring the book into the living room. Bob has not moved from the sofa.

'Maybe she means "disappear,"' I say, 'when she says "end."'

'Disappear?'

'Coretti disappeared, remember? She's obsessed with the guy. He just disappeared. She talks about it all the time. She says he's in self-imposed exile. So *she's* doing it. She's trying to just lose herself, exile herself.'

Bob is staring intently, and with a little hope. 'Maybe,' he says.

'Yes! She's just coming to an end like Coretti did. Let me see the note again.'

I read it several more times. *If I end*. It could be. It could mean disappear. But why didn't she finish it? 'It isn't finished, Bob.'

'It's finished. You and Bally. She was thinking of you two.' He moves behind his hands again.

'It's not finished – but listen, I know where Coretti is. I really have a good feeling about this. I mean, I really feel I'll find her, because she has to know this. She'll want to know this.'

He drops his hands and stares at me, wondering, 'Know what?'

'I know Coretti! He's here – in Santa Monica. I've seen him.'

He just lets that go by, but he's still holding on to what I've said before. 'So you think . . . she might mean "disappear."'

'Yes! I'm going to go drive around.'

'I'd like you to stay,' Bob says.

'Bally's asleep now . . .'

'He could wake up.'

'I'll come back every so often but I want to be driving around, Bob, and looking.'

He sits back on the sofa, staring off. 'I'd rather not be alone,' he says, and that surprises me.

'I'd call my family, but . . . they're an hour away, and I don't want to . . . They'd get all . . .' He just lets it trail off, but he reaches a hand out – for the note. I give it back to him. He looks at it and starts to fold it. The phone rings, and we both jump a bit, him sitting up straight on the sofa, and me tightening into stone.

He gets up and catches it before the second ring. I stare at him as he speaks, hoping and praying and trying to pull the right words out of him, the words of relief.

'Hello. Yes. Yes. They what? Oh, Jesus.'

I close my eyes. I'm repeating her name over and over inside. 'Mari. Mari, listen to me, I'm saying, listen to me. Mari. Please.'

'Oh, my God,' Bob says, and the words are all wrong to me. They are words of surrender. Death words. I don't want to hear this, but I'm straining to hear every word, every tone within his words.

'When? Jesus. Yes. Yes. I know. Yes.'

His last 'Yes' breaks in half, and one hand comes to his face as his other gropes for the phone and hangs up the receiver.

I refuse. I refuse this. She is out there walking along a dark sidewalk, trying to disappear like Coretti. She's alive. I make her alive so strongly in my mind that she cannot be cannot be cannot be . . .

'They found . . .' Bob is saying. I feel strangled. Paralyzed. His words are moving toward me. They are the bats. I cannot touch them. I cannot protect myself. '. . . a woman at the pier . . . drowned.'

'It's not her! It's not! She wouldn't *do* that! She hates

the water!' I start for the door, trembling so much I cannot unlatch the screen.

'Please!' Bob stops me with the pain on his twisted face. 'Please stay with Bally. I have to go. I have to go there now.'

I watch him stand in the middle of the room like a lost child, looking about. I see his resemblance to Bally more than I ever have before. He finds his car keys and comes toward me. 'Please,' he says again. I step out of his way. I cannot quiet my trembling. He, too, fumbles with the screen latch, and then he is gone.

The silence rushes me, and I dodge, moving to Bally's room. The boy is still asleep. I leave the light off, and I sit on the floor with my back leaning against the side of the bed. I can hear his breathing. Now and then he whimpers, very slightly, in his sleep.

I close my eyes and concentrate. The bats dive at me, but I avoid them, and I begin to manufacture what will happen – the next scene of my life – I build it by small moments. I will hear Bob's car return. He will climb the stairs and enter the apartment. He will call out my name. I won't answer, not wanting to wake Bally. Bob will come to the doorway of this room. He will see his sleeping child and see me sitting here, and he will draw in a big breath and let it out and say, 'Thank God, it wasn't her.'

I play the scene very slowly, in real time, creating each sight, each sound very carefully. I watch Bob in the doorway saying those words. I hear those words in his voice. They quiet me. They drive away the bats, but the bats are not far, I know. They're circling. But, meanwhile, I am free to think and create another scene.

I create Mari. She's in Westwood. She's walking through the dark, nearly deserted campus of UCLA. Coretti taught at UCLA briefly. She has gone there to begin her journey into oblivion. The campus is the beginning of her end.

She is following Coretti's steps toward disappearance and invisibility. She is wondering which street *he* took when he walked away from his life, and she is making up her mind. She walks to Sunset Boulevard at the campus's northern limit and walks east. Cars rush by her. A late-night jogger runs past. Sunset will take her all the way downtown. Downtown holds a thousand lost people. She will drop her name along the way on the shoulder of Sunset Boulevard and let her past leak out of her as if through a hole in her pocket. By the time she reaches downtown, she will already be one of the invisible.

But I have her now, so clear in my mind's eye, and I send words to her like hooks. 'Mari. Mari, listen. It's Cheevey. Cheevey. Listen to me. You have to stop. Stop now. Stop walking. You have to remember. Remember me. Remember Bally. We're both calling you. These are *our* hooks you feel. Yes. Stop. Good. Now listen, we love you so much that we can't let you go. We are connected so tightly, Mari, that our bond cannot be broken. If you turn around now and start walking west, toward us, you will end up in our arms and we will hold you so tight, so tight – that no matter what your pain is, we will beat it, and no matter what your fear is, we will beat it. We can do that. We can. And listen. It's no good anyway – following Coretti – because Coretti has been discovered. You see? It's all a circle anyway. He's back. He's back in plain sight. I have seen him. He is invisible no more. So turn now. Good. Yes. Walk this way. Walk west. It's over. It's over. Coretti is on the streets of Santa Monica, and you're walking home, and it's over.'

I see her very clearly, walking west on the shoulder of Sunset, squinting into passing headlights, making her way home.

I hear a voice outside, and it startles me. The voice is on a radio. I cannot make out the words. Then there is static. It sounds as though there is a police car outside. I rise and move into the living room and go to the door. There are two police cars in the street. Most of their doors are opening now. One of the people exiting the cars is Bob. Bob's car is being parked in front of the building by a police officer. Bob's face looks white, and his eyes are sunken, and his lips are twisted into an expression I have never seen him wear. He starts up the stairs followed by a man in a down jacket and then four officers, one of them a woman. I open the screen door as they troop up the staircase, and Bob looks up at me, and he gives me this terrible nod. It is the worst gesture I have ever seen. It falls on me like murder – that nod. My stomach turns. There is something hot in my throat. I am suddenly on the stairs, moving down, passing them all. They have to squeeze against the railing as I pass them sideways.

'Cheevey.'

'Who is . . . ?'

'Her brother.'

'Wait.'

'I have to *see*!' I am shouting. 'I don't think it's her!'

'Cheevey!'

I hurry to my car and try and steady my hands, searching for the Volvo key on my key ring. Two officers catch up with me.

'I have to *see*,' I tell them.

'Yes,' the man says.

'We'll take you there,' the woman says.

On the sand, in among the pilings of the pier, there are lights shining and a wide, ragged rectangle of police tape, but there is no body.

'They've already got her,' the woman officer says as we walk closer. She gestures toward a crowd of cars farther up the beach. One of them is an ambulance, but we don't walk toward the ambulance. We continue toward the water, to the edge of the police tape. There are half a dozen people conferring and standing about within the tape. Lying on the wet sand is a coat, Mari's winter coat. I step over the tape and walk to the coat and stare down at it. On top of the coat are two objects, side by side. They are bookends, heavy brass ones in the shape of elephants. All my hope leaves me, to be replaced by something else. I don't know what to call it. It is a nest of bats. They are dark and heavy and hanging upside-down, and they fill my mind, and I have to look at them now because they are real, after all, and they are not going to go away.

I realize that the two officers who brought me here have been talking to me. I have missed a couple of sentences, staring at Mari's wet and sandy coat. It is ruined, I guess.

'. . . go off the pier,' the man is saying. He is speaking softly. They are both speaking softly, and I hear the sympathy in their voices. 'A couple saw her jump.'

'Jump?'

'From the pier.'

'Oh.'

'With a box. They said she had a box in her arms. Divers didn't find the box. You know what might have been in the box?'

I am staring at the coat and the bookends. They lie so neatly in the sand it is as if Mari has placed them there herself. I nod for the officers, but then I have to speak because they ask me, 'What? What was in the box?'

'Papers,' I say, and that's when the tears come. It's an awkward sobbing that bends my body strangely and blinds me, and then the two cops are walking me away, guiding me as I step over the tape. A flashing light forces me to open my eyes, and I see the ambulance leaving the beach. I try to imagine Mari in the ambulance, on the ambulance bed, but I can't. She is still walking west on Sunset Boulevard. By now she must be ready to turn south, probably on Bundy, and come through Brentwood to Santa Monica. I put her at about forty-five minutes from home.

They guide me into the police car, seat me in back, and they get into the front. They wait, respectfully, until my wet and clumsy sobbing has stopped.

'I'm sorry to ask you this now, uh . . . I don't know your name?'

I don't answer the man. He continues anyway. 'You said papers were in the box?'

'Yes.' My voice sounds like a woman's or a little boy's. I press my lips closed. In a moment I try again. 'Her notes . . .' I can't say anymore, and I shake my head, and they stop talking to me. In a moment, they start the car and roll off the sand and back on to Ocean Avenue.

'Her notes from school,' I say, and my voice is weak, but it's mine again. 'She said she was going to throw them in the ocean. She said this . . . earlier today.'

'You talked to her?' the woman asks me. I nod. 'In person?' I nod again. 'At her apartment?' I nod again. 'What time did you leave?' This time I shrug.

'What about . . . ?' I start to ask a question, but the weeping clutches me suddenly. I remember her kissing my chin. I remember leaving. What if I hadn't left? What if, when she kissed my chin, I had held her very, very close and said, 'Tell me about this fear. Tell me exactly how you feel.' I wish I had done that. I want to go back and do that.

When we reach the apartment, and the woman opens the door, I don't get out right away. I take some breaths and try to ask my question.

'What about the bookends?'

The cops glance at each other. 'Had 'em in her coat, in the pockets,' the man says. He looks sheepish saying this, as if he is ashamed to know it and to have to tell me, but I had already thought of it. I thought of all the planning she did. I thought about her choosing her heaviest coat, even though the evening was mild. She wanted to make sure. And now I watch her in my mind, with the box in her arms and her heavy coat on, looking so small in that heavy coat, and she is staring at the bookends on her shelf, and she puts the box down, and she picks up the bookends, and the books on each end fall, and the whole row spreads on the shelf like a fan, and she drops one heavy elephant into each pocket of the coat and picks up the box and walks out of the room. I can see all that. I cannot see her writing the note. The note doesn't make sense. It isn't finished.

I am surprised by how crowded the small living room is. Bob is on the sofa with the cop who is in plain-clothes. There are three more officers standing there – and my escorts make five. I sit in a chair. They all eye me, except for the plain-clothes cop who is talking to Bob.

The woman interrupts the plain-clothes cop and tells him in a low voice what she has learned from me. They both glance at me while she tells him. Then he stares at me.

'Your name is . . . ?'

'Claude. Cheever. Her brother.'

'You left here when?'

'About . . . three-forty-five.'

'What about this box?'

'She was giving up on a . . . dissertation, throwing all her notes away. She said she was going to throw them in the ocean.'

'Was she depressed about this?'

'She made a joke out of it. But she . . .'

Bob steps in here. He sort of moans his words, wincing now and then, as if his pain is physical. 'She was depressed, deeply depressed. I told you about . . . the psychiatrist. She . . . ever since our son took that fall.'

'He didn't fall,' I say quietly. 'He never fell. She only *thought* he fell. But he didn't.'

Everybody looks at me. Bob is frowning at me. 'She was extremely depressed,' he says.

'And the last time you spoke to her was the phone call at . . .'

'About five,' Bob says.

'She called you?' I ask. 'What did she say?'

'She wanted me to come home.'

'Why didn't you?' I ask him, and he shouts at me.

'I was working!'

'Jesus, Bob.'

'How could I come home?'

'I just asked. What else did she say?'

'I've told them everything,' Bob says.

I lean forward in my chair. 'I'd just like to know . . .' I stop because everybody is looking at the doorway to the hall. I turn and see Bally there, blinking at us, half awake. He looks at all the police officers, and then he hurries back to his room. We can hear his feet, in the knit pajamas, running down the hall.

The living room is silent awhile. The officers are not looking at me or each other now, just looking away. Bally has reminded them that a mother has died, that a child is a victim here, too. I sit back in the chair and close my eyes. My jaw is starting to tremble but I don't want to cry anymore. I should go to Bally. I should get up and go in there, or Bob should – and what should we say?

'She called you "Cheevey"?'

I open my eyes. The plain-clothes cop has Mari's note in his hand.

'Yes.'

'"Help yourself"?' He reads it and looks up at me.

'It's not finished,' I say, and Bob erupts.

'It's finished! That's all there was!'

I stare at him, surprised and wondering. I don't know

why he should be so angry about it, and then I *do* know, and as I think it, I'm saying it.

'Oh, my God, Bob. My God. *You* cut it. You cut something off.'

'You're crazy!'

I stand. 'It isn't all there. It's cut. Look at it. All the bottoms of the Y's are cut.'

'That's how it was!' Bob shouts, tears wetting his words. 'That's what I found! Jesus!'

The plain-clothes cop is staring at the note, studying it. Bob covers his eyes. He is weeping and speaking through the weeping.

'It's exactly what I found. Please. Please. I can't do this. I need to go. I want to go to my family. Somebody needs to help me.'

'We'll call them,' the woman offers.

Bob is shaking his head, his eyes still covered. 'I just want to go there. Somebody needs to get a coat for my son and . . .'

'I'll get Bally ready,' I say, and Bob takes his hands from his eyes and shouts again, red-faced and tearing.

'Don't call him that! Ever!'

We stare a moment, and then I say to Bob, 'Do you want me to tell him?'

Everyone is staring at me now. 'Shall I tell Bally about his mom?'

Now the others all turn to Bob. Bob puts his hands on his eyes again, lowers his head, elbows on knees. 'No,' he says. 'Later. When I'm with my family. I'll tell him.'

'Why are all the policemen here?'

I'm putting his sneakers right over his footed pajamas. His jacket is beside us on the bed. I haven't found his hat.

'Everybody's looking for your mom,' I say. I feel the secret inside of me, throbbing like a disease.

'Isn't she coming?'

'No. You're going with your dad to his parents' house. You know, City of Orange.'

'Yeah. Is she coming there?'

'I don't know.'

It seems that Bally is only half interested in my information. His eyes are full of his own thoughts, and I see again in him what looks to be a secret knowing, a deep place where he keeps his own counsel.

'What did she say, Bal, when she left today?'

He shrugs.

'Can you remember?'

'Kissed me,' he says and his finger goes to his chin, dimpling the flesh there.

'Kissed your chin?'

He nods.

'And . . . ?'

'She was cryin'.'

I swallow the tears in my throat. She kissed his chin. She wept.

''Cause they yelled.'

'Who?'

'Mom and Dad.'

'He was here?!'

'On the telephone.'

'Oh. Oh. On the phone. She was crying on the phone before she left.'

He nods, looking at his sneakers. I stare at the shoes. I have put them on the wrong feet. We look at each other and share a very small, beleaguered smile.

I take the shoes off, and we start again. When he is ready, we stand and I take his hand, but he doesn't move. He looks up at me and says, 'I don't want to see them.'

'Oh. The cops?'

He nods.

'They're nice, Bal.'

He shakes his head.

'Okay. You wait here. I'll tell your dad you're ready.'

He nods and sits on his bed again.

I go into the living room. Everyone is standing now. They turn to me.

'He's ready, but I can't find his hat.'

One of the cops hands me Bally's Dodgers cap. I nod a thanks, and I turn back to Bob.

'Bally says she was crying on the phone, Bob.'

'Christ,' he says, shaking his head at the floor. 'So it's my fault, right?'

'I just want to know what was said. I want to know Mari's words.' My voice is breaking up but I keep pushing it. 'I want to know, Bob.'

'Her last words are the note,' he says.

'The note doesn't make sense. I think you . . .'

'Make sense?!' he shouts again. I can picture Bally listening from his room. 'Make sense? She *wasn't* making sense. God. God, I would have come home if she was making sense. If she told me why or what she was thinking . . . I never . . . Jesus, how can anybody understand?! Your whole fucking family, Cheevey! Jesus! How can anybody understand?!'

All the police seem embarrassed. Bob and I are staring at each other. His face is red and wet. I break off the stare and go back into Bally's room. I walk to the bed and pick him up.

'I'll take you,' I say.

'I don't wanna see 'em.'

'Close your eyes, Bal.'

He closes his eyes and puts his head on my shoulder. I walk him into the living room. Everyone stares.

'I have to get my jacket and stuff,' Bob says. 'Are we done?' he asks the cops.

'You shouldn't be driving,' the plain-clothes cop says.

'Let us call your family,' the woman offers again.

Bob starts explaining that he's all right, and I move to the door. A cop opens it for me.

'Car's in front,' Bob says.

I start down the stairs. 'You can look now,' I say to Bally, but he doesn't lift his head from my shoulder. Upstairs, Bob is arguing with the cops. Mostly I can hear *his* voice and only a murmur of theirs, but I can't make out his words. I'm on the sidewalk and turning. I hear the screen door open above me.

A cop says, 'Where's he going?'

I pass the police cars and Bob's car and keep walking.

A cop shouts, 'Hey!'

'Hold on, Bal,' I say.

'What?'

'Hold on.' I begin to run.

Sometimes, when I run, I can just set my body like a clock and let it go. I have a long stride, as steady as the movement of a second hand. It feels automatic. The energy, from my waist down through my hips and legs, feels separate from the rest of me. It feels like a machine, and I am riding this machine, watching the city slide past me. My running steps are not loud because my feet are light, not slapping the pavement but only brushing it. It feels like flight, I think, human flight.

I know they are chasing me. I no longer hear their shouts, but I am sure they are there. The ones on foot will never catch me. I have a half-block start, and I have run through these streets and alleys hundreds of times, and even carrying Bally, I know I am too fast for them and too untiring. I have run all my life. I never knew why before.

If they come in cars, they might cut me off, but my path is not straight. I run through the dark parking lots of closed stores and through alleys, and I avoid the street lights.

When I stop to rest, there is no one behind me, no one nearby. My body is pumping hard for air and is covered with sweat. Only my left shoulder aches a bit – from Bally.

'Where are we *going*, Cheevey?'

'Away.'

'From who?!'

'Shh. Don't be scared.'

'I want Mom.'

'Me too. Me too.'

I switch Bally to my right side and run two more blocks, and then I set him on my shoulders, his little legs around my neck, and we walk another block. This time, when we stop in the shadows, a police car prowls by, half a block away.

By now I know where I am going – only because I see it there just a few hundred feet ahead. I see the back of my father's store. I have not planned this, but I feel that I am somehow *inside* a plan, and that it is unfolding around me.

In order to reach the store we have to move through a lighted area, so I wait to calm my breathing and my heart and prepare my arms again for Bally's weight.

'Cheevey?'

'Shhh.'

He whispers, 'Cheevey.'

And I whisper, 'What?'

'Are we going to the store?'

'Sort of.'

'Why?'

'I'm not sure. We'll find out.'

'Is Grampa there?'

'No. He's sleeping.'

'Why are we hiding?'

I just look at him, and then I kneel down to be closer. I kiss his cheek and pat his back. 'Don't be scared.'

'I'm not. You're all sweaty.'

'That's 'cause you're so heavy. You're getting so big. Someday, you know, you'll be running around carrying *me*.'

'You don't have to carry me. I can run.'

'I know. But it's just a little farther, and you're sleepy, and I don't want you to fall. Here we go.'

I lift him again, and I run toward the store. We have almost made it through the lighted area when I hear the siren of a police car, not a wail, but just a short blast, and then an amplified voice. I think I hear my name – Cheever – but mostly I hear my own breath, my own body racing around to the side of the store, to the staircase there.

There is an outdoor wooden stairway that leads to the upstairs, which is all storage. I am pounding up the wooden stairs as I hear a car roaring close beneath me, and this time my name clearly spoken, 'Claude Cheever,' and the word, 'Stop.'

I know that the door at the top of the stairs is locked and barred and alarmed, but I don't care about the door. Where the stairway ends, a ladder begins, metal rungs bolted into the side of the building and painted over a hundred times, leading to the roof.

'Hold on,' I say to Bally, and I feel him cling more closely, embracing my neck as I nestle him in my left arm and free my right hand for climbing.

More cars are arriving, and I hear Bob's voice from below screaming, 'Cheevey!' But I keep climbing.

I'm not sure why I'm trying to make it to the roof, but I have an idea. As I climb, my left arm grows numb from the weight of the boy, and the metal hurts my right hand, and the shouts are thrown at me like rifle shots. 'Cheevey!' 'Cheever.' 'Stop.' 'Stop and come down.' A spotlight hits me and then another, but I know I will keep climbing no matter what. 'Cheever!' Keep climbing, I tell myself, there are only about eight more rungs. I can hear people rushing up the stairs beneath me. Keep climbing.

Maybe, if I make it to the roof, Phil will be up there. I will see Phil and my father up there. They will be younger. They won't see me. They will be looking at the surface of the roof. They will be smiling. My dad will be nodding and nodding, the way he does, and he will finally speak and say, 'All right. Good. Good job, Phil.' And Phil will grin and say, 'Thanks.' My dad will pull a check out of his shirt pocket and hand it to Phil and say, 'And thank your friends for me, too.' And Phil will say, 'Okay, Dad.' Then Phil will leave and come down from the roof and drive away on his motorbike. My father will stay on the roof awhile, smiling over the repairs and over the amount of money he has saved, and then he will come down from the roof and drive home for dinner with his family, and over dinner he will say to my mother, 'Well, I saved some money on the roof, why don't you go ahead and take that trip?' My mother will smile and she'll say to Mari, 'Well, when do you think? Two girls in Paris?' And Mari will become so excited, and they will talk about all their plans, and Mari will ask me, 'What can I bring you from France?' and I'll tell her, 'Bring me a hat like they wear in the Foreign Legion.' And Mom and Mari will go to France and come home, and Mari will grow up and marry a good man and they'll have Bally, and she'll live to be eighty-nine, and that's why I'm climbing to the roof.

'Cheever! Stop!'

'Cheevey!'

The surface of the roof is dark and empty. When I step away from the ladder, I walk to the far edge, overlooking Wilshire Boulevard, and I sit on the four-foot wall there. It is almost two feet wide, and I feel secure, sitting there.

Bally lifted his head as we crossed the roof, and now, sitting here on the edge, he looks over the city.

'Don't be scared. I've got you.'

'I'm not,' he says, looking at the rooftops and lights and streets. There is a babble of voices near the ladder and my name is shouted again, but I pay no attention.

'Maybe we'll see Mom,' Bally says, searching the city.

'Maybe, Bal.'

I turn now to the others. There is a group by the ladder that includes Bob and the policeman in the down jacket. Two of the officers are approaching me, walking slowly. They carry flashlights. It is the woman and a young man, a boy, really, a young-faced cop who looks frightened. The woman is speaking to me. I haven't been listening. Her voice is gentle, but it is too gentle, as if she is speaking to a child or a madman.

'. . . All right? Cheever? Just tell us what you want.'

I stare at them. Bob screams again from the group at the ladder. 'Cheevey!'

She picks up on the name now. 'Cheevey,' she says. 'You're not going to hurt the boy, are you?'

'Bal, am I going to hurt you?'

'No.' The boy drags out the word. He is not really listening. He's looking out over Santa Monica, searching, I guess.

'I didn't hear you, Cheevey,' the woman is saying. 'You're not going to hurt the boy?'

I stare at her and at the young-faced cop.

'What do you want, Cheevey?'

'Please come away from the edge,' the younger cop says. He sounds frightened.

'Just tell us what . . .'

'I want to know,' I begin, and they stop, listening hard, 'what my sister's last words were. I think I have a right to know that. I want to know what she decided to say, when she said she was leaving.'

Bally has turned to me now, listening also. He wants to know, too.

'Tell Bob, I want to see the note. I want to see the whole note. I'm entitled to that. He can't destroy that. It isn't his. It's mine and it's Bally's, too. I want to see it, and nobody better come close to me unless they have it – the whole note.'

'All right, just sit still,' the woman says. 'I'll be right back.' She hurries to the group on the ladder. I sit on the roof edge, holding Bally. The young cop keeps his flashlight on us. He finally speaks in his tight, worried voice.

'I'd feel better if you came off that wall, please, and sat on the roof, on the floor of the roof. Okay?'

I just look at him awhile. 'Lower the flashlight, will you?' I say, and he does, taking the beam off my face.

'Will you come off the wall?' he asks again.

'Let's just . . . wait.'

We wait while they confer by the ladder. More police are coming on to the roof, and more cars parking below. I hear a helicopter in the distance and I wonder if it's coming here, with a light to throw on me. I don't really care. I feel peaceful here on the roof. I wish we could see more stars, but the city lights and the smog dwindle them to a handful.

I hear footsteps on the roof and turn and several cops are walking toward me, a new plain-clothes cop who is frowning, a big guy, and the down-jacket man and the woman. She has her flashlight beam in my face.

'Will you stop, please?' I say, and they do. 'Will you get the light out of my eyes?' She does.

'We have the note,' the down-jacket man says. 'Can we bring it to you? Why don't you let the child go – and we'll bring it to you.'

'I'd like *him* to bring it.' I gesture with my head to the young-faced cop.

'Will you let the child go?'

'If it's really the note,' I say. 'I'll read it and let him go.'

They all seem to frown, and they talk among themselves, and then the down-jacket man hands the note to the young-faced cop.

'Shall I . . . come now?' The young cop is staring at me, and I nod, and he comes toward us.

'What's the note?' Bally asks. He sounds so tired.

'It's from your mom.'

'To me?'

'To you and me. Yes.'

The cop comes close. He's very nervous. I want to tell him, it's all right, it's okay, but I just wait, holding on to Bally.

'It's in two pieces,' the cop says, and he hands two wrinkled half-sheets of paper toward me.

'Why don't you give me your flashlight?' I say. 'And you hold it together, and I'll shine the light.'

He looks at me, wondering. He glances back as if to say something to his superiors, but then he turns and hands over the long, heavy flashlight.

I put the beam on his hands. They are shaking a bit as he tries to line up the halves of the note. He seems to get it right, and he turns it to me.

All I see is glare, and then I adjust the beam, and I read:

Bally, I'm so sorry for letting you fall.
If I end, you can begin, and you won't fall anymore.
Cheevey, you are very worthy. Remember, help yourself first, like in the airplanes. Bob, this is not
your fault, but you could have been kinder.

Mari

I read it several times, and I feel a liquid sorrow seeping into my mouth and throat, my eyes, even my chest.

'Read it, Cheevey,' Bally says in a small, tired voice.

'She says, Bally, I love you, and Cheevey, I love you, and . . .' I have to swallow. I have to steady myself. 'She talks about airplanes, Bal. You know, if you're sitting in an airplane, and some emergency happens, some trouble, the first thing you notice is that oxygen masks drop right out of the ceiling.'

He looks up at me. I nod. 'And what you're supposed to do, if you're a grown-up who's with a child, you're supposed to . . . you're supposed to pull down your mask first and put it on you and make sure . . . make sure you're breathing okay, then you help the child. That's what you're supposed to do.'

He looks at me, and I know he is studying my tears and my trembling jaw, and he is not upset. He seems to know – not what I'm telling him or even what I'm *not* telling him – but all the things unknowable to me.

'Can I take him now?' The young cop has whispered his question. We both turn to him. Then Bally and I look at each other.

'It's okay,' I say. 'He'll take you to your dad.'

Bally nods. The young-faced cop reaches out and begins to ease Bally away from me. I turn to make it easier, and I study the cop's young frightened face, and I try to say, it's okay, it's all right, but I'm silently weeping and I don't trust my voice. I try to smile. The cop takes Bally as if he is made of glass and then, slowly, cradles the boy against him. He starts slowly walking away, and I rise from the wall and follow him.

Once the down-jacket man takes Bally from the young cop, the other two rush me.

'Down. Down!' the big guy says, pinning my arms behind me, hurting me, holding me down, my face pressed into the gritty roof, while the woman cop cuffs me.

Then the big guy jerks me around and lifts me so that I am sitting on the roof now, my hands cuffed behind me.

The woman stands back a few paces, watching me and glancing at the big guy. She looks a little tense, but the big guy is clearly angry at me. I stare at the knot of others near the ladder. I see the down-jacket man hand Bally over to Bob and Bob holds him tight, putting their heads together. I think Bob is weeping.

The big guy bends at the waist so his face is close to mine. 'This could be very bad, very bad for you – do you realize that? This could be kidnapping, do you realize that? Hm?'

'Do you have a sister?' I ask him. My voice is calm.

'What? Yes.'

I stare at him. 'So tell me if I give a shit,' I say.

His frown deepens. The down-jacket man is coming back to us, but he doesn't look at me. He looks at the woman and the big guy and says, 'No charges.'

The big guy seems disappointed. The woman uncuffs me. By the time I'm brought down off the roof, Bob and Bally are gone. The big guy and the down-jacket man drive me away. We say very little. They ask my address. They ask about my car. I tell them it's at Bob's, and we go there. They tell me they will follow me home. When I'm getting into my car, I stare at the apartment. It's dark. I don't see Bob's car anywhere, but it could be in the garage.

Once I park in front of my house and get out of my car, the police drive away, and I'm relieved. I don't want to talk to my father with the cops standing there. This will be bad enough. This will be terrible.

It's almost one o'clock in the morning, but my father is still up – or he forgot to turn out the light in the den. I walk into the room, and he is sitting there in a robe and sweatpants, staring at the TV set which is off. He looks sick, and he looks much older, and I realize that he knows.

He looks up at me, and his face doesn't change. He looks like the photos I've seen of hostages, people who have been imprisoned and tortured. He looks back at the dead TV, and

I hear a sound from his chest, half whimper, half sob, almost a click.

I want to hold him and be held by him, but it is difficult to hug someone who is in a chair. I sit on the hassock in front of him and pick up one of his long, bony hands and hold it. I feel his grip tighten, but he keeps his eyes on the dead set.

I put our clasped hands to my face and sit there a long time before I speak.

'Did the police call?'

He shakes his head.

'Bob?'

He nods. He starts to speak, but only rasps. He clears his throat and tries again, still looking at the TV.

'Called from a police car.' He looks at me now. 'Said you had Billy?'

I shake my head. 'No. Billy's with his dad now.'

He nods and puts his eyes back on the dark picture tube.

'You call Phil?'

He shakes his head.

'Mom?'

'I got the number, but . . .' With his free hand he gestures weakly at the floor. I see that he has brought the phone close to the chair. It is on the floor and beside it is a piece of paper with the word 'France' on it and a number. He is shaking his head. Tears come without changing his face, and he doesn't touch them.

'I think I should tell Phil – not on the phone,' I say.

He nods without looking at me. 'I never thought this would happen,' he says. 'Other things . . . You think of other things.'

'I know, Dad.'

'She seemed all right.'

'Yes. Well . . .' There is no more to say about it. Not now.

I hold his hand in both of mine. I am gripping hard, but his hand is limp now.

'Claudey . . .' I stare at him, but his wet, red eyes are on the set. 'Call your mother . . . will you?'

After awhile, I slowly untangle our hands. I reach down for the phone. It's the kind you can grab from behind and lift the entire telephone, and I hold it, suspended in space. He's not looking at me or the phone. He's looking at the set. I turn to the set, and what I see on the dark screen is the reflection of my father, staring at himself.

I look at this for a moment, and then, as hard as I can, I smash the telephone into the screen of the television set. There is a crash of glass and a dull boom, and my father's reflection disappears. I turn to the man, and his mouth is open and his eyes are wide and unbelieving and he's pushed back into his chair, cringing there. I put the telephone in his lap. Then I reach down for the paper with the phone number on it, and I see that the back of my hand is bleeding. I'm careful not to get the blood on the paper. I place the paper beside the phone in his lap, and I stand up.

His wide eyes are focused on my hand now. I'm dripping blood on the rug.

'I'll go tell Phil,' I say.

His eyes drift up to me, and then I turn and leave.

First I go into the bathroom, and I run cold water on my hand. The sink turns red. I can see two lacerations across the back of my hand where the veins are. I'm not sure how deep I am cut. The blood is thinned by the water, and I don't think I am badly hurt. I wrap a towel around my hand and step out of the bathroom. As I move toward the front door, I can hear my father's voice coming from the den. I can't make out the words. The voice has a wailing quality to it, almost like singing.

My hand is throbbing when I arrive at Phil's, and the hand

towel I used to wrap it is partly soaked through. During the day, I know, Phil's front door is usually unlocked, but I try it now, and the deadbolt must be thrown. That's too bad. I'd rather go in there and wake him with a whisper and a touch. I hate the thought of a doorbell jarring him. I try knocking, just a soft, steady knocking. The house remains dark and silent. I glance to my left, to Lauren's home, next door. It is also dark. Looking at it, I feel an ache, but it is mild and far away. I turn back to Phil's door and knock steadily again, a little louder.

Somewhere, a light goes on. The hall, I think. I feel someone approaching the door, and then Phil's voice comes, sounding dull and raspy.

'Who the fuck is it?'

'Cheevey.'

The bolt is snapped open. I turn the knob, and the door swings in. He stands there in the near dark, dressed only in briefs, his hair askew. He holds a heavy gun in his right hand, pointed at the floor now.

'God, is that loaded?' I ask.

'What the hell you doing here *now*, sport?' He runs his free hand through his hair. His face is puffy, and I can smell whiskey on his breath. I'm disappointed. Somehow, I thought he might stop after the incident with the windows. At least he doesn't seem drunk.

'I cut my hand,' I say.

He turns on a lamp. 'Shit. Let's go in the bathroom.' He leads the way, still carrying the gun.

He puts the gun on the toilet lid and rifles the cupboard beneath the sink. 'How'd you do it?'

'I'll explain.' I unwrap the towel. He bathes the wound in hydrogen peroxide. 'Think I need stitches?'

'I don't think so.' He puts a pad over the cuts and tapes the pad tightly to my hand. His movements are certain and comforting, and I am glad for the contact. He catches me staring at him.

'What?' he wonders.

'Have to talk to you.'

'Yeah. Go sit down,' he says, gesturing to the living room. He picks up the gun and goes toward his bedroom.

I sit in the living room which is even more littered than when I last saw it. Those three family photos are still on the coffee table, and I realize that all that – the broken windows and my fight with Lauren – was just two days ago.

Phil comes into the living room in an old terrycloth robe.

'Wanna beer or anything?'

'No.'

He gets a bottle of beer from the refrigerator and comes in and sits on the sofa. I am in a chair, facing him across the coffee table. My insides feel like they're shrinking, and my chest feels the blows of my heart.

Phil does a mighty yawn, then he sips his beer and waits.

'Thanks for fixing my hand, bro.'

He nods. He doesn't seem worried or upset that I've come so late and just barely surprised.

'Thanks for the job with Ben Black, too.'

'Sure. Sure.' He yawns again. 'How'd you do in your hand?'

'I'll explain.'

'You said that, sport.'

'It isn't good.'

'Never is.'

'This is bad, Phil.' My throat clutched as I said that. My tears are gathering again, and he sees this, and I see him wondering now, staring at me, his hands in his lap and the beer forgotten there.

'Mari is . . . Fuck.' I have to wait for the tears and try and get a long breath to steady myself.

He leans forward, puts the beer on the table. 'Jesus, Cheeve.'

I don't want to be sitting here, across from him, a table in the way. I stand, and I'm very shaky and suddenly exhausted. I want to drop to the floor. I get some words out in a weak voice, higher than my own.

'Gotta hold me, Phil.'

'Jesus.' He stares for just a moment, then he rises and comes around the table, and he holds me. I embrace him, too tall to fit against him, but I lay my head on the top of his shoulder, and I say the awful words. They drop from me like stones.

'Mari is dead.'

I feel him go still. There is no breath in the man. He seems to have emptied out.

'Wait. Wait,' he says, and I begin to nod there on his shoulder.

'She's . . .'

I keep nodding. He is without strength and soon his arms drop away from me. I let go, too. He stares at the floor.

'Cheeve,' he says weakly.

'She killed herself,' I say in my strange woman's voice.

Now his eyes slowly lift to me and stare and just keep staring. He's not wide-eyed or disbelieving. I just see a hurting that is miles deep, bottomless, I suppose, like mine.

He walks away then, not hurrying. He goes into the bathroom and closes the door. In a moment I hear him retching. I suppose I should go in there, maybe hold his head – but he closed the door, and, somehow, I don't want to cross that barrier.

When he comes out, pale·and small-looking, he walks toward his bedroom. I wait awhile, then I follow him.

He is lying on his bed, on his side. I enter the dark room and sit on the bed. We don't speak for awhile.

'Were you . . . there?' he asks.

'No. But I saw her today.' Our voices are soft, just above whispers. 'I saw her a few hours before. She was . . . making jokes, but . . . She's been acting really scared. I mean . . . imagining things. She was seeing a psychiatrist. But . . .' I just let it go and the silence seeps in and stays another minute.

'How?' he asks.

'She went off the pier, Phil. A couple saw her jump.'

'Jesus.'

'She locked Bally in his room and left a note and she went down there . . . Christ.'

I hear him breathing in the dark, then he asks, 'What'd the note say?'

'She said to Bally . . . "If I end, then you can begin." And she mentioned me and Bob.'

'What'd she say about you?'

I wait a while, thinking over the word before I say it. 'She said I was "worthy." Then she said . . .'

'Worthy?'

'Yeah, worthy.'

We are quiet another long while, and I notice him move his hand to his face, and I am surprised to see him wiping at tears because I haven't heard them in his voice, and because I have never seen my brother cry.

'We're both so screwed up,' he says, and now I hear the tears.

'You and me?' I ask.

'No. No. Me and Mari. So screwed up. Shit.' Then in awhile he says, 'You're the normal one, Cheeve. I'm glad. I'm glad. You're okay. How'd you get to be okay?'

I make sure my throat is empty of tears, and then I say, 'I had Mari.'

In a moment I see him wipe his face again.

'I left Dad alone, calling Mom. Why don't we go there?'

He doesn't answer right away. Then he asks, 'Why?'

I shrug in the darkness. 'He's alone.'

'Fuck him.'

'Phil . . .'

'Fuck her, too.'

'Well . . . I think I'm going to go, and I'd really like you to come.'

'Why?'

'So we could all be together.'

'I don't want to see him.'

We have one more long silence together, then I reach over. My hand touches him on his side and I press there and rock my hand there awhile. His hand comes to mine. We grip each other's hands and hold on awhile. I whisper this time.

'I wish you'd come.'

He answers in a moment. 'I'd rather be alone, sport. Need some time.'

Our hands separate slowly, and I rise. 'I need to sleep,' I tell him. 'I'm going to go there and see him and collapse for awhile.'

'Okay.'

'You'll be all right?'

'Yeah.'

I sigh and walk around the bed, heading for the door. I stop near the door and turn to look at his back there in the bed, and I whisper, 'So long.'

'Yeah.'

But I don't leave. My eyes are used to the gloom now, and I can see on the night stand closest to me the automatic Phil was carrying. I walk softly to the night stand. He is facing away from me. Noiselessly, I pick up the gun, and I walk out.

In the living room, I search about, and I choose a tall, glass-doored cabinet with small wooden legs. There is a space between the floor and the bottom of the cabinet, and I slide the gun under there, out of sight.

I leave the house and close the door softly, and I turn again to look at Lauren's home. I go there, on an impulse, cutting across the lawns and stepping over a row of low shrubs.

I ring Lauren's doorbell and wait, hoping Molly can sleep through the sound. In a moment, I hear hurried steps toward the door and then Lauren's low and frightened voice.

'Who is it?'

'Lauren, it's Cheevey.'

There is a pause, then the door is unlocked and opened. She is mussed and soft and bundled in her pink robe; her face is pinched with concern and with a hint of anger.

'Cheevey! Why now?!'

'I'm sorry.'

'It's after two!'

'Yes. I'm sorry, Lauren. Something's happened.'

The hint of anger disappears, and she holds her breath, then she quickly steps back to let me in. 'What? What happened?'

I shake my head a bit and stay outside the doorway. 'If I come in, I'll just collapse, and I can't collapse yet. I have to go home.'

She's waiting to hear, her mouth slightly open. Then an idea moves across her face. 'Phil?' she says.

I shake my head again. 'No. He's . . . Well, listen, it's Mari.' My sister's name is like a trigger now, and my lips are trembling, and I marvel at the amount of tears a body can hold.

'Oh, Cheevey.'

'She died.'

She gasps and steps toward me. I'm embracing Lauren, but fighting very hard against the flood of tears that wants to push through. I could dissolve into her soft, mothering arms. I know I could. I could spread out all my pain before her, but my last bit of strength would go with it, and I want to go home.

'I need to go home,' I whisper, holding her tightly. 'I just told Phil. I wanted him to come with me, but . . . So, he's alone, Lauren. I'm going to be with my dad, so I thought . . . If you could check on him?'

She is rocking me gently as we hold on. I am so much bigger than she is, and she's rocking me, and she's nodding, too, and she whispers, 'Yes. Sure I will. I will.'

I can hear the tears invading *her* now and as we pull back slowly from the embrace it is as though my sorrow is a sickness I have passed on, leaving her eyes wet and hurting. We still hold each other's arms.

'Can you drive?' she asks me.

'Yes.'

'I love you, you know.' She squeezes my arms as she says this.

'Jesus. I'm glad.' I say this with relief, and I take both of her hands and kiss them one by one. We hold hands for an instant, and then I turn and walk down the steps, and she remains in the doorway and then steps out on her porch to wave as I drive away.

I feel more weak than sleepy. I check to see if I'm still losing blood as I walk back into my house, but the bandage shows only one red dot in its center.

My father is still in his chair, his feet up and the telephone back on the floor. I see the shattered television and the drops of my blood on the carpet and then I meet his eyes. He looks as gaunt and tortured as before, but more bewildered somehow. I think he's surprised I came back.

'I told Phil.'

He nods slightly.

'Can I get you anything?'

He shakes his head. I step in and sit on the edge of the hassock beside his crossed feet. 'How did Mom . . . ?'

He looks at his lap as if searching for the phone and then sees it on the floor. 'She just . . . cried and cried.' His voice sounds distant, somehow.

I touch his crossed feet and he looks at me again, bewildered again.

'I feel weak,' I tell him, and I rise and move to the other chair, but it isn't comfortable enough, so I stretch out on the floor and close my eyes.

'What are we going to do?' I hear my father say, but he doesn't seem to be asking for an answer. 'What are we going to do?'

I don't try to speak. I have no answers anyway, just an exhaustion that has invaded me like a drug, and I feel I am dissolving into the floor, and I am glad to be going somewhere else.

I sleep, and when I wake up, the windows are pale with first light and both chairs are full. I see the tops of two heads, leaning back in the chairs. I start to rise, and I feel nearly powerless. It takes forever to gain my feet. I am still sleepy and muddled as I walk around the chairs and stare at my father and Phil. My father seems to be sleeping. Phil is staring at his thoughts, then turning to me.

'What happened to the TV, sport?'

Bob's family is 'handling everything.' We had one clipped message from Bob on my parents' machine, and then later his brother called to give the details on the service. They selected cremation. My father didn't like that. I didn't either, for different reasons. I called them back and got someone else, Bob's sister or sister-in-law. I asked them to reconsider. I said I thought she should be buried at sea or at least have her ashes dropped in the sea since she herself had chosen the ocean for her death.

The woman was polite and said she would bring it up, and she said neither Bob nor 'Billy' was available.

Somebody called from France to say that my mother isn't well enough to make the trip. This angered Phil, but I don't really care. I just wish she had called herself. My father got very sarcastic about it and said, 'She only cares about herself,' and I told him to 'Stop singing that old song – you're no one to talk.' I really said that. He looked at me, but not with much anger. We don't seem to be father and son anymore. I'm not sure what we are. He has no dominion over me.

The funeral is tomorrow, Saturday. I called Ben Black, and he said he'd save the job for me. I haven't been going to school. I have been hanging around my father's store, not working, just waiting. I'm there now, behind the counter with a magazine, looking up every few minutes – at the window.

The day is almost over by the time I see him. I don't really see him arrive, but there he is, already seated on the sidewalk, already babbling to the man in the glass. I stare at him a moment, and then I go outside.

I don't stand too near him. I want to study him awhile. I'm not as sure as I was a few days ago when I stood in Mari's bedroom and looked at his picture on the back of the book, but I would still bet a couple of hundred dollars that Jack-o-lantern is the self-exiled John Coretti.

I go closer now, and feel even more certain. He stops talking and turns away from the glass before I can overhear any of his words.

'Mr Coretti,' I say. He looks at the sidewalk. 'This is for you.'

I slip a five-dollar bill into the pocket of his dirty white shirt. He looks at his pocket but doesn't touch it.

'Goodbye,' I say, and I walk away.

Folded inside the five is a note that says, 'You were the favorite novelist of Mari Cheever Horton. Thank you for the pleasure you gave her.' I signed it: 'Her brother, Cheevey.' I was going to put my phone number on the note just in case, but then I didn't. I'm not really interested in what Coretti has to say – or Jack-o-lantern either.

On Saturday, we caravan down to Orange County for the service. I'm driving my father and Benko and a girl named Clo from the bookstore where Mari worked. Lauren is driving Phil and Molly.

I'm sorry I won't get to see Mari. Bob's family isn't doing it that way. It's a service at the chapel of the cemetery, and the chapel is within the building where the vaults are or whatever they call them – where the ashes will go. Maybe she has already been cremated. I don't like to think about that. In fact, I feel a bit distant from it, like it's not really happening to her, anyway. I think of her in the sea, where her spirit left her body. I don't mean I think of her there physically, but that's where my memories of Mari collect and focus, finally, in the sea.

I have dreamed of Mari every night since she died. This morning I awoke from a dream of her. We were standing and talking as we often did in the park, except where we stood was flooded. It was a shallow puddle. As she spoke, she looked at her shoes, just like she used to, and made little splashes in the puddle. I can only remember part of what she said, the very last part.

'People think being alive is so great,' she said, 'and everything else sucks. They think being alive is the very best way to be, but just because everybody thinks something is great, doesn't mean it *is* great. Remember disco?'

I woke up laughing, and I lay there smiling a long time, and I couldn't wait to tell the dream, so I made sure I memorized it – but then I realized that the only person I wanted to tell it to was Mari.

The chapel is in a beautiful setting in a grove of eucalyptus trees. They are one of the few trees I can recognize and name. There are a few pines around, too. I know pines and weeping willows, but I don't see any willows. Mari didn't seem to care much about nature.

Lauren gives me a smile of support as we near the chapel and I feel Benko's hand land on my shoulder and stay there. Phil and my dad walk on doggedly. There is a crowd of well-dressed people filtering into the building, but I don't recognize anyone. I'm eager to see Bally.

Bob comes to the door as we're about to go in. He nods, and we nod. He looks very subdued, like everyone else, and very serious. As I start to file past him, he says, 'Can I see you?'

I stop, and he walks by me and steps outside. I join him outside the chapel. There are more people converging on the door so he walks off a few more steps and I join him. Nobody can hear us now. There is a slight wind moving the eucalyptus trees and a few rounded leaves flutter down.

Bob looks at me awhile.

'Is Bally inside?' I ask.

The air seems to go out of him and he looks down and shakes his head. 'Are you always going to call him that?'

'No. He'll get too old for it at some point. Why do you take it so hard?'

He finally finds his way back to me. 'He says you told him what the note says – but he didn't say anything about me – about what she said about me. Did you tell him that?'

'No.'

He looks down again and nods. 'Thanks.' When he stares at me, he looks almost vulnerable. 'You tell your family?'

'They didn't ask. They didn't ask me about the specific words. If they ask, I'll tell them.'

He nods. 'But you won't tell Billy?'

'No.'

He looks away again before saying, 'Thanks.' Then he nods to someone who is passing us. When they're gone, he says, 'I'll be living down here. Moving.'

'What about Bally?'

'What about him?' he says, ready for a fight now.

'Well . . . God, I want to see him. I want to spend time with him.'

'You can come down once in a while,' he says without enthusiasm.

'It's far,' I say.

'My family'll take good care of him. Don't worry about him. I'll have plenty of help with him.'

I stare at him now, and wait awhile. 'You don't *want* me to see him, do you?'

He looks down and shakes his head. 'I'd rather not,' he says. When his gaze rises again, someone else catches his eye, and he nods, and this time I turn around. It is Dash. She wears a short black dress and has that same hushed and careful way about her that all the non-family seem to have today. She doesn't know whether to approach us or not. I give her a wave and a slight smile, and she smiles back, a weak and sad smile, and she decides to go on into the chapel. I watch her walk away in her short black dress, and I hear a voice in my mind, scolding and teasing. Cheevey! It is Mari's voice. I'm still half-smiling when I turn back to Bob.

'We better go in,' he says.

'You're not going to try to stop me from seeing Bally, are you, Bob?'

His chin comes out toward me a bit. 'If I do stop you, you'll tell him about the note, right, him and everybody else. Right? Is that what you're saying?'

I stare at him and shake my head. 'Jesus, Bob. You don't understand anything.'

He starts to walk away and I hold his arm. I know if he tries to pull away, I will do something gross and stupid. I will knock him down. 'Listen, Bob, I'm not going to tell Bally about the note. *You're* going to tell him about the note. *You* will. Someday you will tell him – because you can't be a total, total waste, because Mari married you and stayed with you and she even defended you to me – did you know that?' His chin is still pushed out at me, but the vulnerability is there again, softening his eyes. 'She loved you – so that means you'll tell Bally, and that means you'll let me see Bally because Bally loves me and I love *him*, and *you* love him, and there's hope for you, Bob. I always thought there was a little hope for you. I believe that.'

He stares at me, not relenting at all, but I let him go and he walks to the chapel door. The big wide arching door is open, and in the archway I see Dash, and in her arms is Bally. She is speaking to him. She is showing him his father and his uncle Cheevey. The boy looks at Bob as Bob passes him, and Bob touches the boy's face with one finger, and then goes on into the chapel, and then the boy turns to me and sees me, and he gets that small, twisty, knowing grin that tells me that the world is a hard world, but there is heaven here, and I should not be afraid.

William Hugh Horton, 1993

He will not remember this long walk. He is only four years old, and the actions of this day, and its sights and sounds, will settle below the line of active memory and rest in a realm just beyond his grasp. There will be only unexplained feelings and shadowy half-glimpses, impressions that will seem to be made more of dream than remembrance.

His face and his hands are cold, and he carries something dangerous. He enjoys the feel of the wooden boards beneath his shoes.

He passes booths where games are played, and the hundreds of colorful dolls catch his breath and stop him. The man he is with asks him to move on. His hand is taken. Promises are made to return. He walks on.

Now he sees the poles like great wands waving and lines of string dancing from the ends of the poles like the thinnest loops and scribbles in the sky. Men and women and even children are holding the poles, and one woman dangles a shimmering fish from her straightened line.

The sight of the fish and its sudden, shining bursts of desperate motion make the boy forget the dangerous thing he carries, and it pierces his hand and makes him shout with pain and then weep from the shock and the fear and the shame of crying among so many strangers.

The man he is with picks him up and comforts him and walks him away. They stand against a blue metal rail, and the man, who is his friend and his uncle, shows him the vast grey-blue water beneath and around them. The uncle examines the boy's hand, and both of them stare at the perfectly round dot of blood in his palm.

The man is now holding the dangerous thing, which is a flower with a thorned stem. The boy watches as the man dips the soft part of the red flower into the dot of blood. The petal of the flower swallows the blood and grows darker.

The boy has stopped crying. He watches, awed, as his uncle touches a thorn to his own palm and creates his own dot of blood. The boy asks if this hurt his uncle, and the man says, yes, but now this flower is like no other in the world.

His uncle stains the flower once more – with his own blood, and then he smiles at the boy and asks if the boy is ready.

The boy isn't sure what it is he is supposed to do, but he answers, yes, he is ready.

His uncle tells him to hold the flower.

The boy holds it very carefully.

His uncle tells him to drop the flower in the water, but not yet. He must say two words as he lets go of the flower.

They practice.

The boy drops the flower into the water and says, 'Goodbye, Mom.'

They watch the flower splash on the grey-blue waves that seem to be reaching and falling and reaching again. It floats among the reaching waves, and they watch it for a long while. It moves as though guided one way and then another. It turns and turns again. Slowly, it floats out of sight beneath the pier.

The boy walks away with his uncle, and this time they stop at the booths. In the playing of the games, the boy forgets about the wound on his hand and about the flower and the words that he spoke.

Years later he will admit to no real memory of his mother, only a shadow of remembrance, like a dream, and he will wonder why this dream of her is evoked by the sight and the scent of roses.

Exclusive CDs to enhance your reading pleasure

There is nothing better than a relaxing read and nothing quite like your favourite music to compliment your mood.

Each of the CD compilations are performed by the world's top artists. The choice is yours, all you need to do is send £1.98*per CD to cover postage and handling and indicate which CDs you would like. Please allow up to 28 days for delivery.

HOW TO GET YOUR CDS:
Simply complete the coupon below with the quantity of each CD you wish to purchase and send with your cheque to Hodder Headline CD offer, P.O. Box 2000, Romford, RM3 8GP.

Hodder Headline CD offer
Please send me:
Qty........HH01 Essential Opera @ £1.98 p&h each
Qty........HH02 Classical Masterpieces @ £1.98 p&h each
Qty........HH03 Rockin' n' Reading' Hits of the 60's @ £1.98 p&h each
Qty........HH04 Unmistakably Jazz @ £1.98 p&h each
Qty........HH05 Movie Sensations @ £1.98 p&h each
Qty........HH06 Gregorian Chants @ £1.98 p&h each
*Please note these prices apply to the UK addresses only. Please see below for other areas.

Enclose a cheque/postal order payable to FM LTD. Please write your name and address on the back of your cheque/postal order.

Name & Address..

....

....Postcode ☐ ☐ ☐ ☐ ☐ ☐ ☐

POSTAGE AND HANDLING PAYMENT METHOD
UK & Ireland – Cheques or Postal Orders ONLY £1.98 per CD
Europe including Eire – Eurocheque in £Sterling ONLY or Visa/Mastercard Credit Cards £3.25 per CD
Rest of the World including USA and Canada – Eurocheque in £Sterling ONLY or Visa/Mastercard Credit Cards £4.25 per CD

Please debit £................ from my ☐ Visa ☐ Access

Card No ☐ ☐ ☐ ☐ ☐ ☐ ☐ ☐ ☐ ☐ ☐ ☐ ☐ ☐ ☐ ☐

Expiry Date ☐ ☐   Signature...

ENQUIRY HOTLINE: 01708 336888
If you do not wish to receive further mailings for products within the Hodder Headline Group or carefully selected companies please tick here. ☐ Offer subject to availability. Please allow up to 28 days for delivery.

Offer closes 31st December 1996   *you may photocopy this form*